The Books of Great Alta

JANE YOLEN

The Books of Great Alta

Sister Light, **Sister Dark**
White Jenna

Published by arrangement with Tom Doherty Associates, Inc., 49 West 24th Street, New York, New York 10010

Printed in the United States of America

Quality Printing and Binding by:
Orange Graphics
P. O. Box 791
Orange, VA 22960 U.S.A.

CONTENTS

SISTER LIGHT, **SISTER DARK**

For Jessica
who mothered the book
and for
Patty, Ann, Shulamith, Zane, and Kara
who nursed it along the way

Special thanks to Joyce Rankin, who
helped me write down the music of the Dales

PROPHECY & EXEGESIS

And the prophet says a white babe with black eyes shall be born unto a virgin in the winter of the year. The ox in the field, the hound at the hearth, the bear in the cave, the cat in the tree, all, all shall bow before her, singing, "Holy, holy, holiest of sisters, who is both black and white, both dark and light, your coming is the beginning and it is the end." Three times shall her mother die and three times shall she be orphaned and she shall be set apart that all shall know her. So begins the Garunian prophecy about the magical birth of the White Babe, layering in all kinds of folkloric absurdities and gnomic utterings to explain away the rise of a female warrior queen. These "hero birth" tales emerge long after the fact, and it is no coincidence that one tale resembles another. (Cf., the birth of Alta's *Anna*, or *the white one*, motif #275f in Hyatt's *Folklore Motif Index of the Dales*.) This one points to the birth of White Jenna, the Amazonian queen of the Dark Riding, a figure of some staying power in the myth sequences out of the early Garunian period during and after the infamous Gender Wars.

BOOK ONE

The White Babe

THE MYTH

Then Great Alta plaited the left side of her hair, the golden side, and let it fall into the sinkhole of night. And there she drew up the queen of shadows and set her upon the earth. Next she plaited the right side of her hair, the dark side, and with it she caught the queen of light. And she set her next to the black queen.

"And you two shall be sisters," quoth Great Alta. "You shall be as images in a glass, the one reflecting the other. As I have bound you in my hair, so it shall be."

Then she twined her living braids around and about them and they were as one.

THE LEGEND

It happened in the town of Slipskin on a day far into the winter's rind that a strange and wonderful child was born. As her mother, who was but a girl herself, knelt between the piles of skins, straddling the shallow hole in the earth floor, the birth cord descended between her legs like a rope. The child emerged, feet first, climbing down the cord. When her tiny toes touched the ground, she bent down and cut the cord with her teeth, saluted the astonished midwife, and walked out the door.

The midwife fainted dead away, but when she came to and discovered the child gone and the mother dead of blood-loss, she told her eldest daughter what had happened. At first they thought to hide what had occurred. But miracles have a way of announcing themselves. The daughter told a sister who told a friend and, in that way, the story was uncovered.

The tale of that rare birthing is still recounted in Slipskin—now called New Moulting—to this very day. They say the child was the White Babe, Jenna, Sister Light of the Dark Riding, the Anna.

THE STORY

It was an ordinary birth until the very end and then the child hurtled screaming from the womb, the cord wrapped around her tiny hands. The village midwife echoed the baby's scream. Although she had attended many births, and some near miraculous with babes born covered with cauls or twins bound together with a mantling of skin, the midwife had never heard anything like this. Quickly she made the sign of the Goddess with her right hand, thumb and forefinger curved and touching, and cried out, "Great Alta, save us."

At the name, the babe was quiet.

The midwife sighed and picked up the child from the birth hide stretched over the hole scraped in the floor. "She is a girl," the midwife said, "the Goddess' own. Blessed be." She turned to the new mother and only then realized that she spoke to a corpse.

Well, what was the midwife to do then but cut the cord and tend the living first. The dead mother would wait for her washing and the mourning her man would make over her, with the patience of eternity. But so as not to have the haunt follow her down the rest of her days, the midwife spoke a quick prayer as she went about the first lessons of the newborn:

> In the name of the cave,
> The dark grave,
> And all who swing twixt
> Light and light,
> Great Alta,
> Take this woman
> Into your sight.
> Wrap her in your hair
> And, cradled there,
> Let her be a babe again,
> Forever.

"And that should satisfy her," the midwife mumbled to herself, knowing that to be a babe again, to be cradled against the breast of the eternal Alta, was the goal of all life. She had faith the quick prayer would shrive the poor dead woman at least until the candles could be lit, one for each year of her life and an extra for her shadow-soul, at the bedfoot. Meanwhile, there was the child, blessedly a girl, and blessedly alive. In these past years of hard living it was not always so. But the man was lucky. He had only to grieve for one.

Once cleansed of the birthblood, the midwife saw the babe was fair-skinned with a fine covering of white hair on her head and tiny arms. Her body was unblemished and her dark eyes looked as if they could already see, following the midwife's finger left and right, up and down. And if that were not miracle enough, the child's little hand locked upon the midwife's finger with a hold that could not be broken, not even when a suck was made for her using a linen cloth twisted about and dipped in goat's milk. Even then she hung on, though she pulled on the makeshift teat with long, rhythmic sighs.

When the child's father came back from the fields and could be torn from his dead wife's side long enough to touch the babe, she was still holding the midwife's finger.

"She's a fighter," said the midwife, offering the bundle to his arms.

He would not take her. It was all he could do to care. The white babe was a poor, mewling exchange for his lusty redheaded wife. He touched the child's head gently, where beneath the fragile shield of skin the pulse beat, and said, "Then if you think her a fighter, give her to the warrior women in the mountains to foster. I cannot bide her while I grieve for her mother. She is the sole cause of my loss. I cannot love where loss is so great." He said it quietly and without apparent anger, for he was ever a quiet, gentle man, but the midwife heard the rock beneath the quiet tone. It was the kind of rock against which a child would bruise herself again and again to no avail.

She said then what she thought right. "The mountain tribes will take her and love her as you cannot. They are known for their mothering. And I swear they will bring her to a stranger destiny than her tiny gripping hand and her early sight have already foretold."

If he remarked her words, the man did not respond, his shoulders already set in the grief he would carry with him to his own grave, and that—though he knew it not—soon enough, for as they said often in Slipskin, *The heart is not a knee that can bend.*

So the midwife took the child and left. She paused only long enough to cry out the village diggers and two women to bathe and shroud the corpse before it set badly in the rigor of death. She told them of the child's miraculous birth, the wonder of it still imprinted on her face.

Because she was known to be a stubborn woman with a mind set in a single direction—like a needle in water pointing north—none of them gainsaid her going to the mountain clans. They did not know she was more frightened than even she herself knew, frightened of both the child and the trip. One part of her hoped the villagers would stop her. But the other part, the stubborn part, would have gone whatever they said, and perhaps they guessed it and saved their breath for telling her story afterward. For as it was said in Slipskin, *Telling a tale is better than living it.*

And so the midwife turned toward the mountains where she had never been before, trusting Great Alta's guardians to track her before she was gone too far, and clutching the child to her breast like an amulet.

It was luck that an early spring melt had cleared most of the paths to the mountain foot or the midwife would never have gotten even that far. She was a woman of the towns, her duties bringing her from house to house like a scavenger. She knew nothing of the forest perils or the great tan-colored cats that roamed the rockslides. With the babe swaddled and wrapped to her breast, she had started out bravely enough and managed surprisingly well, getting to the mountain foot without a scratch or slip. Many a strong hunting man had not done as well that year. And perhaps it was true, as the villagers said, that *Fish are not the best authority on water.*

She sheltered the first night among the twisted roots of a blasted tree, giving the child suck from a milk crock with a linen teat dipped in. Herself, she ate cheese and brown bread and stayed warm with half a skin of sweet wine she carried. She ate unsparingly, for she thought she had but a single overnight to go before she reached the holds of the mountain clans. And she was sure the women of the mountains—whom she had long desired to visit, that longing compounded of envy and fear—would give her plenty of food and drink and gold to sustain her when they saw what it was she carried to them. She was a townswoman in her thinking, always trade for trade. She did not understand the mountains or the people who lived there; she did not know that they would feed her independent of all else but her need and that they had little use for gold so never kept it.

The second day was bright and pearly. Clouds lined only the horizon. She chose to walk along the bank of a swift-flowing stream because it seemed easier than breaking a new trail. If she had noticed the scat and could have read it, she would have known this was a favorite run of mountain cats, for trout were plentiful in the stream, and foolish, especially in the evening in the presence of bugs. But she was a woman of the town and she could read print only, a minor learning, and so she never heard the cat on her trail or noticed its scratchy warnings on the trees.

That second night she stashed the babe in a high crotch of a tree, believing it quite safe there, and walked down to the stream to bathe in the moonlight. Being a townswoman and a midwife, she valued cleanliness above all other things.

It was while she was bent over, dipping her hair in the cold water of the stream and muttering aloud about how long the trip was taking, that the cat struck. Swiftly, silently, surely. She never felt more than a moment of pain. But at her death the child cried out, a high, thin wailing. The cat, startled, dropped its prey and looked about uneasily.

An arrow took it in the eye, its death more painful than the midwife's. It whimpered and trembled for several moments before one of the hunters cut its throat in pity.

The babe in the tree cried out again and the entire wood seemed to still at the sound.

"What was that?" asked the heavier of the two hunters, the one who had cut the cat's throat. They were both kneeling over the dead woman, seeking in vain for a pulse.

"Perhaps the lion had cubs and they are hungry?"

"Do not be foolish, Marjo; this early in spring?"

The thinner hunter shrugged her shoulders.

The child, uncomfortable in its makeshift cradle, cried out again.

The hunters stood.

"That is no lion cub," said Marjo.

"But cub nonetheless," said her companion.

They went to the tree as unerringly as woodsense could lead them and found the babe.

"Alta's Hairs!" said the first hunter. She took the child from the tree, unwrapped it, and gazed at its smooth, fair-skinned body.

Marjo nodded. "A girl, Selna."

"Bless you," whispered Selna, but whether she spoke to Marjo or to the dead midwife or to the ears of Alta, high and far away, was not clear.

They buried the midwife and it was a long and arduous task, for the ground was still part frozen. Then they skinned the cat and wrapped the babe in its warm skin. The child settled into her new wrapping and fell asleep at once.

"She was meant for us," said Selna. "She does not even wrinkle her nose at the cat smell."

"She is too young to wrinkle her nose."

Selna ignored the remark and gazed at the child. "It is true, then, what the villagers say: *When a dead tree falls, it carries with it a live one.*"

"You speak too often with another's mouth," said Marjo. "And a village mouth at that."

"And you speak with mine."

They were silent after that, neither saying a word as they trotted along the familiar paths toward the mountains and home.

They expected no grand reception at their return and got none, though their coming had been remarked by many hidden watchers. They signaled their secret names with careful hand signs at every appointed place, and the guardians of each of those turnings melted back into the forest or the seemingly impenetrable rock face without a sound.

What messages, what bits of news were passed to them as they traveled through the night, came to them in the form of birdsong or the howling fall of a wolf's call, where bird and wolf were not. It told them they were welcome and recognized and one particular cry told them to bring their bundle at once to the Great Hall. They understood, though no words, no human words, were exchanged.

But before they reached the hall, the moon slipped down behind the western mountains and Marjo bade farewell to her companion and disappeared.

Hefting the child in its cat cloak, Selna whispered, "Till evening, then." But she said it so softly, the child in her arms did not even stir.

THE SONG

Lullaby to the Cat's Babe

Hush little mountain cat,
Sleep in your den,
I'll sing of your mother
Who cradled Fair Jen.

I'll sing of your mother
Who covered Jen's skin.
Flesh of your flesh
Did sweet Jenna lay in.

Sleep, little catkin,
Perchance you shall dream
Of rabbit and pheasant
And trout in the stream.

But Jenna will dream
Of the dark and the light.
Your mother will shelter her
From the cold night.

THE STORY

There were cradles scattered around the Great Hall, some of oak with the grain running like rivers to the sea, and some of white pine, so soft the marks of a baby's nails could be seen, like runes, on the headboards. But for some reason Selna did not put the child in any of them. She kept it on her breast when she showed it in the Great Hall and all the rest of the day, hoping the steady beat of her heart would comfort it.

It was not unusual for a new fosterling to be kept, swaddled, at one breast or another. The women of Alta's-hame shared the care of them, though Selna had never before shown any interest in fostering. The stink of the babes and their high, cranky crying had always put her off. But this one was different. She smelled not of sour milk and spittle but of mountain cat, moonshine, and blackthorn, that being the tree she had been wedged in when the cat had struck her mother. She had cried only twice, each time at a death, which Selna thought an omen. Surely the child must be hungry or fearful or cold. Selna was ready to put her away at the first sign of fretting. But the babe had stared at her with eyes the color of a spring night, as if reading her very soul. And so Selna had kept her heart to heart far into the morning. By then everyone had noticed and commented, so that she could not—for fear of being shamed—let her small burden go. Physical abuse had never bothered Selna. Indeed she was proud of her ability to withstand the worst punishments. She was always in the forefront of any battle line, she was the last to the fire, the first into a cold stream. But she never could stand the tauntings of the women in her Hame.

By midmorning, though, the child was hungry and let her know with small pipings, like a chick in the henyard. She fed the babe as best she could with one of the Eastern bottles so prized by the kitcheners. Both she and the babe were thoroughly splattered in the process, and so Selna took the child down to the baths, heated the water well below her usual steaming, and holding the naked child against her own bare shoulder, plunged in.

At the water's touch, the child cooed contentedly and fell asleep. Selna sat on the third step of the bath, so that only their heads showed above the water. She stayed until her fingers had wrinkled and the water began to grow chill and her hand around the child cramped. Then she got out reluctantly, dried the sleeping babe, and wrapped toweling around herself for the long walk back to her room. This time there were no comments, even though she passed many of her holdmates. Whether she willed it or not, the child was hers.

THE HISTORY

The women of the mountain warrior clans did not take fostering lightly. Once a child was chosen by her foster mother, the woman had full charge of the child's care. A kitchener's child grew up amongst the great pots; took her first steps on the tiled kitchen floor; ate, napped, and slept out her childhood sicknesses in a special children's nook in the kitchen.

So, too, a child chosen for rearing by one of the warrior/huntresses was carried about in a special pack wherever her foster mother went. Lowentrout finds evidence of this in the famous Baryard Tapestries (his essay "Pack-Children of the Western Holds," Nature and History, Vol. 39, is especially interesting). There is a leathern pack unearthed from the famous gravemound at Arrundale, and preliminary examination leads to speculation that it may be one of the Amazonian child-carriers. (For more about this dig, see Sigel and Salmon's video "Graverobbing Among the Dales.") Such burdens did not hamper the women warriors either in battle or on the hunt, according to Lowentrout, and textual evidence supports his claim. The three scrolls ascribed to the Great Archive of G'run Far Shooter graphically depict the battles in which the mountain clans took part. One in particular speaks of "the double heads of the Amazons" and, in another place, "the precious burden carried by (them)." And most striking, "She fought, all the ways her breast to the foe for as not to expose the one at her back." Vargo argues that the word "at" simply refers to another fighter, since fighting back-to-back was a familiar style in sword-battle. She further states that if a pack-child had been meant, the word "on" rather than "at" would have been used. However, Doyle, whose seminal work on Alta-linguistics has just been published, points out that in the old tongue on/at/upon and by were used interchangeably.

THE STORY

"You will have to name her, you know," Marjo said that night, lying on the far side of the bed. The lantern hanging above them cast shadows on the wall and floor.

Selna looked at the child sleeping between them. She touched the soft cheek with a tentative finger. "If I name her, she really is mine forever."

"Forever is longer than either one of us shall last," said Marjo, her finger stroking the child's other cheek.

"A child is a kind of immortality," Selna murmured. "A link forged. A bond. Even if she is not of my blood."

"She will be," Marjo said. "If you claim her."

"How can I not—now?" Selna sat up and Marjo followed suit. "She looks to me first, whoever holds her. She trusts me. When I brought her into the kitchen at dinner and everyone wanted to touch her, all the while her tiny head swiveled around to see me."

"You are being sentimental," said Marjo with a laugh. "Newborns cannot swivel their heads. They cannot even see."

"She can. Jenna can."

"So—you have already named her," Marjo said. "And without waiting for my approval."

"You are my sister, not my keeper," Selna answered testily. At the sharpness in her voice, the child stirred between them. Selna smiled a lopsided apology. "Besides," she said, "Jenna is just her baby name. I want to name her Jo-an-enna in full."

"*Jo* for lover, *an* for white, *enna* for tree. That makes sense, for she was found in a tree and her hair—what there is of it—is white. I presume that *Jo* is because you love her, though I wonder at how quickly such a thing came about. You usually do not *love* so quickly. It is usually your hatred that is quickly aroused."

"Do not be an idiot. *Jo* is for you, Marjo," Selna said, "and well you know it." She reached out to touch her companion across the child.

Marjo's hand met hers halfway and they both smiled.

The child between them cooed.

In the morning Selna took Jenna to the infirmarer, Kadreen, who checked the babe from the crown of her head to the soles of her feet.

"A strong one," said Kadreen. She did not smile, but then she rarely did. It was said she had stitched too many wounds and set too many bones to find life amusing enough for a smile. But Selna knew that even as a young woman, before she was long in her calling, Kadreen had not found much to smile at. Perhaps, Selna thought, the calling had found her *because* of that.

"Her fingers grip surprisingly well for a newborn. And she can follow the movement of my hand. That is rare. I clapped my hands to test her hearing and she startled at once. She will be a good companion for you in the woods."

Selna nodded.

"Make sure you feed her at the same time and she will sleep through the night within the first moon's change."

"She slept through the night last night," Selna said.

"She will not again."

But despite the infirmarer's warning, Jenna did sleep soundly through that night and the next. And though Selna tried to feed her on the schedule dictated by Kadreen's long experience with infants, she was always too busy to do so. Yet the babe seemed to thrive on the erratic meals and, in the woods, strapped to Selna's breast or back, she was as quiet as any seasoned hunter.

Selna boasted of her fosterling at every opportunity until everyone but Marjo grew weary of it.

"You are in danger of becoming a bore," said Donya, the head kitchener, when Selna dropped off a fine roebuck and seven rabbits after a two-day hunt. "She is a fine babe, no doubt. Strong and quite pleasant to look upon. But she is not Great Alta. She does not walk across the Lake of Sighs or ride the summer rainbow or leap between the drops of falling rain."

"I did not say she was the Goddess," mumbled Selna. The child at her breast laughed delightedly as she tickled it under the chin with one of the rabbit's feet. Then she looked at the kitchener squarely and roared. "And I am *not* a bore."

"I did not say you were. I said you were in danger of becoming one," said Donya calmly. "Ask anyone."

Selna glared around the kitchen, but the girls all dropped their eyes and suddenly the room was quiet of voices. All that could be heard was the *snick-snack* of kitchen knives at work. Donya's young ones knew better than to tangle with one of the warriors. Selna, especially, was known for her hot temper, though she, unlike some of them, seldom bore a lasting grudge. Still, not a one of them envied her fosterling that temper when it roared.

Selna shook her head, still angry, and turned back to Donya. "I shall want the rabbit skins," she said. "They will make a soft lining for the pack. Jenna has fine skin."

"Jenna has a baby's skin," said Donya evenly, ignoring Selna's scowl. "And of course you shall have the fur. I will also save you the deerskin. It should make a fine pair of leggings and many mocs."

Selna smiled suddenly. "She will need many mocs."

"But not right away," Donya said, with a laugh.

There was a titter around the room as her own fosterlings enjoyed the joke.

"What do you mean?" The anger was back in Selna's voice.

Donya set down the heavy crockery bowl and wooden spoon, wiped her hands on her apron, and held out her arms. Reluctantly Selna recognized the signal and unstrapped the babe, handing her over to Donya.

Donya smiled and rocked the babe in her arms. "This is an infant, Selna. A babe. Look around at my own maids. Seven of them. And once they were each this size. They walked at a year, only one sooner. Do not expect too much from your child and she will grow in your love. When her moon time comes, she will not turn from you. When she reads from the *Book of Light* and calls her own sister into this world, she will not forsake you. But if you push her too much, you will push her away. A child is not yours to own but yours to raise. She may not be what you will have her be, but she will be what she has to be. Remember what they say, that *Wood may remain twenty years in the water, but it is still not a fish.*"

"Who is becoming the bore now?" asked Selna in a weary voice. She took Jenna, who was still smiling, back from the kitchener and went from the room.

* * *

That night there was a full moon and all the dark sisters were called forth. In the great open amphitheater the circle of women and their children was complete.

Selna stood in the circle's center below the altar, which was flanked by three rowan trees. Marjo was by her side. For the first time in almost a year there was a new fosterling to celebrate, though two of the gardeners and one warrior had each borne a babe. But those infants had already had their consecration to the Goddess. It was Jenna's turn now.

The priestess sat silently on the backless throne atop the rock altar, her own dark sister throned beside her. Black hair braided with tiny white flowers, lips stained red with the juice of berries, they waited until the crowd of worshippers quieted. Then they leaned forward, hands on knees, and stared down at Selna and Marjo, but only the priestess herself spoke.

"Who bears the child?"

"Mother, I do," said Selna, raising Jenna to eye level. For her the word "mother" had a double meaning, for the priestess had been her own foster mother, who had grieved sorely when Selna had chosen to follow the warrior way.

"And I," said Marjo.

They stepped together up onto the first altar rise.

"And who bore the child?" the priestess asked.

"Mother, a woman of the town," said Selna.

"She died in the woods," Marjo added.

They mounted the second step.

"And who now bleeds for the child?" the priestess asked.

"She shall have my blood," said Selna.

"And mine." Marjo's voice was a quiet echo.

They reached the third step and the priestess and her dark sister rose. The priestess took the silent babe from Selna's hands, turned, and placed the child upon the throne. Marjo and Selna were beside her in one fluid movement.

Then the priestess dropped to her knees before the child. She took her long black braid, and wound it about the child's waist. Her sister, on the other side of the throne, did the same. As soon as they were done, Selna and Marjo knelt and offered their hands, wrists up.

Taking a silver pin from a box mounted in the arm of the throne, the priestess pierced Selna's wrist where the blue vein branched. At the same time, her sister with an identical pin did the same for Marjo. They held the warriors' wrists together so that the blood flowed each to each.

Next the priestess turned and pricked Jenna lightly, above the navel, signaling to Selna and Marjo silently with her free hand. They bent over and placed their wrists side by side on the baby's belly so that their blood mingled.

Then the priestess and her sister drew their twined braids over the steady hands.

"Blood to blood," the priestess intoned. "Life to life."

The entire congregation of Alta's-hame repeated the words, a rolling echo in the clearing.

"What is the child's name?"

Selna could not keep from smiling. "Jo-an-enna," she said.

The priestess spelled out the name and then, in the old tongue, gave the child her secret name that only the four of them—and Jenna in her time—would know. "Annuanna," she said. "The white birch, the goddess tree, the tree of everlasting light."

"Annuanna," they whispered to one another and the child.

Then the priestess and her sister unwrapped their hair and stood. Holding their hands over the two kneelers and the babe, both priestess and sister spoke the final prayer.

> She who holds us
>   in her hand,
> She who molds us
>   in this land,
> She who drives
>   away the night,
> She who wrote
>   the Book of Light,
> *In her name,*
>   *Blessed be.*

The assembled women came in perfectly on the responses.

When they were done, Selna and Marjo stood together, Selna holding out the infant so that all could see. At the great cheer that arose below them, Jenna woke up, startled, and began to cry. Selna did not comfort her, though the priestess looked sharply at her. A warrior had to learn young that crying brought no comfort.

*   *   *

Back inside, after the magnificent feast that followed, the baby was handed around the table for all to see. She began in the priestess' arms and was handed over to the plump arms of Donya, who dandled her expertly but "as routinely as a bit of mutton just off the spit," Selna commented testily to Marjo. Donya handed the child to the leaner arms of the warriors. They chucked and clucked at Jenna's chin, and one dark sister threw her up into the air. She screamed with delight, but Selna pushed aside the circle of companions angrily to catch the child on her downward flight.

"What kind of a misbegotten son-of-a-son are you?" she cried out. "What if the light had failed? Whose arms would have caught her then?"

The dark sister Sammor shrugged her shoulders and laughed. "This late mothering has made mush of your brains, Selna. We are *inside*. There are no clouds to hide the moon. The lights of Alta's-hame never fail."

Selna tucked Jenna under one arm and raised the other to strike Sammor, but her hand was caught from behind.

"Selna, she is right and you are wrong in this. The babe is safe," Marjo said. "Come. Drink a toast with us all to forget and forgive, and then we will play at the Wands." They brought their arms down together.

But Selna's anger did not abate, which was unusual, and she sat outside the circle of sisters when they threw the wands around the ring in the complicated patterns that trained them for sword-handling.

With Selna out, Marjo could not play either, and she sat across from her sister and sulked as the game went on. It became more and more complex as a second, then a third, and finally a fourth set of wands was introduced into the circle. The flexible willows flipped end over end in the air, passing from woman to woman, from hand to hand, and soon the dining hall was quiet except for the *slip-slap* of the wands as they hit palm after palm after palm.

"The lights!" someone shouted, and a cheer went up from the watchers around the ring. Sammor's sister Amalda nodded and two of the kitcheners, new enough to the sisterhood that they stuck together as close as shadows, rose to stand by the torches that illuminated the circle.

The game went on without stopping, the wands slipping even more quickly through the air. Not a hand had missed since the throws began. The whizzing of the wands as they passed one another was punctuated by the slapping of palms.

Then without warning both torches were doused in the water buckets and the dark sisters in the circle disappeared. The circle was halved and there was a clatter of wands hitting the floor. Only Marjo, who sat beyond the range of the two doused torches, and the dark sisters of the watchers, who stood far from the game, remained, for the lights from the kitchen shone upon them.

Amalda's voice counted out those who had lost their wands. "Domina, Catrona, Marna." Then she turned and nodded for two new torches to be brought.

The relighted circle arranged itself as dark sisters appeared again. The losers—Domina, Catrona, and Marna and their dark halves—went into the kitchen for something to drink. Playing at the wands was thirsty work. But Selna stood, the child at her breast, and spoke so loudly no one could miss it.

"It has been a tiring day, sweet Jenna, and time we were both in bed. I will put out the light tonight."

There was a gasp heard around the circle. To put out the light was to send your sister back into the darkness. To announce it so was an affront.

Marjo's mouth grew tighter, but she said nothing as she stood with Selna and followed her out of the room. But Sammor spoke to their departing backs.

"Remember, Selna, that it is said, *If your mouth turns into a knife, it will cut off your lips.*" She did not expect an answer and, indeed, got none.

"You shamed me," Marjo said softly when they reached their room. "You have never done such a thing before. Selna, what is wrong?"

"Nothing is wrong," Selna answered, arranging the baby in her cot, smoothing the blanket and touching the child's white hair with a finger. She began to hum an old cradle song. "Look! She is already asleep."

"I mean, what is wrong between *us?*" Marjo bent over the cot and stared at the sleeping child. "She *is* a sweetling."

"There, you see? Nothing is wrong between *us*. We both love her."

"How can you love her after so short a time? She is nothing but a bit of flesh and coos. Later she shall be someone to love—strong or weak, bright-eyed or sad, handy with her hands or her mouth. But now she is only—" Marjo's voice stopped abruptly in mid-sentence, for Selna had blown out the large candle over the bed.

"There is nothing wrong between us now, sister" Selna whispered into the black room.

She lay down on the bed, conscious of Marjo's empty half, for her sister could always be counted on to talk and laugh and come up with a quick answer before they slept. Then she turned over and, holding her breath, listened a moment for the baby's breathing. When she was sure the child was safe, she let out the air with a loud percussive sigh and fell asleep.

THE HISTORY

The "game of wands" has come down to us in a highly suspect form. It is played today only by girl children in the Upper Dales, where the chorus, sung in modal tuning by watchers (usually boys) standing outside the circle, goes:

> Round and round and round the ring
> The willow sword we now do fling.

The concentric circles of players sit on the ground facing one another, wands in hand. Once made of willow (which no longer grows in the Upper Dales, though evidence of a different flora-culture proves willows may have been plentiful a thousand years ago), the wands today are manufactured of a plastine that is both flexible and strong. At a drum signal, the wands are passed from hand to hand in a clockwise manner for seven beats, then returned for seven beats. Next the wands are flipped between the circles in preset partnerships for seven more beats. Finally, to the accompaniment of the choral singing of the watchers, and an ever-rapidly increasing pattern beat out on the drum, the wands are flipped across the circle, first to the partner and back, then to the person directly to the partner's right. The wands must be caught in the sword hand, which gives left-handed players a decided disadvantage in the game. As soon as a player drops a wand, she is "out."

Lowentrout points to the famous "insert piece" of the Baryard Tapestries, which had been found in the vault of the Eastern potentate Achmed Mubarek thirty years ago, as proof positive that the "game of wands" played by warriors in the mountain clans and the nursery circle game are one and the same. While it is true that the "insert piece" (which has been repaired inexpertly by many Eastern hands—some say as many as thirty times, as evidenced by the different colored threads) shows concentric circles of women warriors, they are holding swords, not wands. One of the so-called players is lying on her back, sword in her breast, obviously dead. She is ignored by the other players. Cowan argues forcibly that the "insert piece" has been too mangled over the years to be plain in its correspondences, but that it is more likely a picture of a specific form of execution, as the "insert piece" occurs occurred in that section of the tapestry which deals with traitors and spies. Perhaps the true meaning of the "insert piece" will never be known, but Magon's shrill argument that the inner circle consisted of the "dark sisters" or "shadow sisters," who could be seen by the light of the moon or the heavy tallow candles (still popular in the Upper and Lower Dales) and that the outer circle was that of the "light sisters" harkens back to the last century, when the Luxophists sought to resurrect the Book of Light practices. Those practices had been banned for at least seven generations and the Book of Light has been so thoroughly discredited by Duane's brilliant "Das Volk lichtet nicht" I need not reiterate her arguments here.

Some confusion over the intricately engraved silver rings found in the Arrundale gravemound still exists. Sigel and Salmon call them "wand holders," giving credence to Magon's shaky thesis, but there is even more evidence that these artifacts are napkin rings or possibly pack cups for long trips, and that is convincingly argued in Cowan's "Rings of the Clans" in Nature and History, Vol. 51.

THE STORY

Selna's shameful behavior became the talk of the Hame. Though sisters had quarreled before, little fiery arguments that sent a moment of heat and light and then died down without even embers of memory, what Selna did was unheard of. Even the priestess' records mentioned nothing like it, and the Hame had seventeen generations listed and eight great tapestries as well.

Selna stayed in the bright sunlight with her child during the day and night, babe bound fast to her breast or back, avoided the well-lighted rooms of the Hame. Once or twice, when it was absolutely unavoidable and Selna had to come into a torchlit room, Marjo crept behind her, a thin, attenuated figure. Gone was the dark sister's robust laughter, her hearty ringing tones.

"Selna," she would cry to her sister's back with a voice like a single strand of sigh, "what is wrong between us?" It was a ghost's voice, hollow and dying. "Selna . . ."

Once, in the kitchen begging some milk for the babe, Selna turned for a moment when Marjo called. She put her hands over the child's ears as if to block out the sound of her sister's voice, though it was so low by now it could scarcely be heard. Behind her, Donya and her own sister Doey and two of the older girls watched in horror. They saw in Marjo's wasting figure their own slow death.

Marjo's eyes, the color of bruises, wept black tears. "Sister, why do you do this? I would share the child with you. I have no wish to stand between."

But Selna turned slowly and deliberately away from the pleading figure, back toward the kitchen's light. When she noticed Donya and Doey and the two girls standing there, stricken, she bowed her head and hunched her shoulders up as if expecting a blow. Then she turned and went back without the milk into the darkest part of the hall.

On the thirteenth day of her shame, the priestess banished her from the Hame.

"My daughter," the priestess said, her voice heavy, "you have brought this upon yourself. We cannot stop what you do to your own dark sister. Once you accepted the teachings of the *Book of Light,* we could instruct you no more. What falls between the two of you is your own concern. But the Hame is shattered. We cannot continue to watch what you do. So you must leave us and finish out what you have so ill begun alone."

"Alone?" Selna asked. For the first time her voice quivered. She had not been alone for as long as she could remember. She clutched baby Jenna to her.

"You have thrust your own dark sister from you," said the priestess. "You have shamed us all. The child stays here."

"No!" Selna cried, turning. By her side, the gray shadow that was Marjo turned, too. But they ran into six sturdy warriors who pinned them against the wall and took the babe, despite Selna's screams and pleading.

They took Selna out into the bright day, which meant she would be truly alone at the start of her journey, with only the clothes she wore. Her bow, sword, and gutting knife they threw after her, tied in a heavy bag that took her near an hour to unknot. They said nothing to her, not even a word of farewell, for so the priestess had instructed them.

She left the Hame by day, but she returned that night, a shadow among shadows, and stole away the child.

There were no guards by the infant's cot. Selna knew there would be none. The women of the Hame would be sure she would never return, so shamed and low had they left her. They would trust in the guards of the outer gates. But Selna was a warrior, the best of them, and often she and

Marjo had played among the secret passageways. So silently, Selna stole back in, more quietly even than a shadow. She doused three lights along the hallways before Marjo's pale voice could alert the sleepers.

Jenna awoke and recognized her foster mother's smell. Giving a satisfied sound, she fell asleep again. It was that small wisp of sound that confirmed Selna's determination. She raced down the secret ways and was at the forest's edge again before it was dawn.

As she slipped along the old paths where the rocks were worn smooth by the passage of so many feet, the birds heralded her arrival. She found the large boulder off to the side of the path where she had left her weapons. Shamed as she was, she would still not have raised her sword or bow against her Hame mates. Leaning back against the rock, into a niche that seemed to exactly fit her body, she slipped her tunic down to her waist. Now that she was truly the child's mother, she could nurse it as well. She gave the baby her breast. For a few moments Jenna sucked eagerly, but when no milk came, she turned her head to the side and wailed.

"Hush!" Selna said sharply, taking the child's face between her fingers and squeezing. "A warrior must be silent."

But the baby, hungry and frightened, cried even more.

Selna shook the infant roughly, unaware that tears were coursing down her own cheeks. Startled, the child stopped crying. Then Selna stood up and looked around, making sure no one had been alerted by the child's cries. When she heard nothing, she sat back down, leaned against the rock, and slept, the baby in her arms.

But Jenna did not sleep. Restless and hungry, she caught at dust motes in the rays of the sun that filtered through the canopy of aspen and birch. At last she put her tiny hand into her mouth and sucked noisily.

It was hours before Selna awoke, and when she did the sun was already high overhead and a fox was puzzling on the edge of the small clearing, its sharp little muzzle poking into the undergrowth. At Selna's waking, it looked up, ears stiff with warning, then turned abruptly and disappeared into the shadows.

Selna stretched and looked at the babe sleeping on her lap. She smiled, touching Jenna's white hair. In the sunlight she could see the infant's pink scalp under the fine hair and the beating of the pulse beneath the shield of skin.

"You are mine," she whispered fiercely. "I shall care for you. I shall protect you. I shall feed you. I—and no others."

At her voice, Jenna awoke and her cry was cranky and thin.

"You are hungry. So am I," Selna said quietly. "I shall find us both something to eat."

She pulled up her tunic and bound the child to her back, slipping the ribbands under her own arms, tight enough so that the child was safe, loose enough so that they both could move. Holding her bow and sword in her left hand, she slipped the gutting knife into its sheath over her right shoulder where she could reach it for a fast throw. Then she began loping down the forest paths.

She was lucky. She found tracks of a small rabbit, stalked it easily, and brought it down with a light arrow at the first try. Fearing to make a large fire still so close to the Hame, she nevertheless knew better than to eat a rabbit raw. So she dug a deep hole and made a small fire there, enough to at least sear the meat. She chewed it, then spit the juices into Jenna's mouth. After the second try, the babe did not refuse the offering and sucked it up eagerly, mouth to mouth.

"As soon as I can, I will find you milk," Selna promised, wiping the baby's mouth and then tickling her under her chin. "I will hire out to guard one of the small border towns. Or I will find the High King's army. They like Alta's warriors. They will not refuse me."

Jenna smiled her response, her little hands waving about in the air. Selna kissed her on the brow, feeling the brush of the child's white hair under her nose, as soft as the wing of a butterfly. Then she bound the baby on her back again.

"We have many more miles to go tonight before I will feel safe," Selna said. She did not add that she wanted to stay the night in the forest because the full moon was due and she could not bear to speak to her pale shadow and explain all that she had done.

THE LEGEND

In the dark forest near forest near Altashame there is a clearing. Under a stand of white birch grows a red-tipped iris. The people who live in Selkirk, on the west side of the forest, say that three ghosts may be seen on the second moon of each year. One is a warrior woman, a dark necklace at her throat. The second is her shadowy twin. And the third is a snow-white bird that flies above them crying with a child's voice. At dawn the two women strike each other with their swords. Where their blood falls the iris springs up, as white as the bird, as red as the blood. "Snow-iris," the folk of the East call the flower. "Cold Heart," say the folk from the South. But "Sister's Blood" is the Selkirk name, and the people of that town leave the flowers alone. Though the juice from the iris heart binds up a woman in her time of troubles and gives her relief from flashes of heat, the Selkirk folk will not touch so much as a leaf of the flower, and they will not go into the clearing after dark.

THE STORY

At the edge of a small clearing, a short run to the outskirts of the town of Seldenkirk, Selna rested. Leaning against a small oak which protected her from the bright full moon, she caught her breath and dropped both bow and sword. Her breathing was so labored at first, she did not hear the noise and then, when she heard it, it was already too late. Strong, callused hands grabbed her from behind and twisted a knife point into the hollow below her chin.

She stopped herself from crying out in pain, and then the knife slipped down and carved a circle of blood like a necklace around her throat.

"These be the only jewels an Alta-slut should own," came the gruff voice behind her. "You be mighty far from your own, my girl."

She fell to her knees, trying to twist and protect the child at her back, and the movement frightened the man, who jammed the knife deep in her throat. She tried to scream but no sound came out.

The man laughed raggedly and ripped her tunic down the front, exposing her breasts and belly. "Built like a boy," he said disgustedly. "Your kind be good only dying or dead." He grabbed her by one leg and pulled her out from the forest onto the softer grass of the moonlit clearing. Then he tried to turn her from her side onto her back.

She could not scream, though she could still fight him. But another woman screamed from behind, a strange gurgling.

Startled, he looked over his shoulder, saw a twin of the first woman, her own throat banded by a black line of blood. Turning back, he realized his mistake, for Selna had managed to get her hand on her knife. With the last remaining strength in her arm, she threw the knife at his face. It hit him cleanly between the eyes. But Selna did not see it, for she had already rolled over on her stomach and died, her fingertips touching Marjo's.

The man tried to get to his feet, managed only to his knees, then fell on top of Selna, the handle of the knife between his eyes coming to rest in baby Jenna's hand. She held on to it and cried.

They were found in the morning by a shepherd who always took his flock to that clearing, where the spring grass was sweetest. He arrived just before sunrise and thought he saw three dead folk by the clearing's edge. When he got to them, pushing his way through his reluctant sheep, he saw that there were only two: a woman, her throat cut, and a man, a gutting knife between his eyes. A silent infant was holding on to the bloody knife handle as if she herself had set it on its deadly path.

The shepherd ran all the way back to Seldenkirk, forgetting his sheep, who bleated around the ghastly remains. When he returned, with six strong ploughboys and the portly high sheriff, only the man lay there, on his back, in a circle of sheep. The dead woman, the babe, the knife, and one of the shepherd's nursing ewes were gone.

THE BALLAD

The Ballad of the Selden Babe

Do not go down, ye maidens all,
    Who wear the golden gown,
Do not go to the clearing
    At the edge of Seldentown,
For wicked are the men who wait
    To bring young maidens down.

A maiden went to Seldentown,
    A maid no more was she,
Her hair hung loose about her neck,
    Her gown about her knee,
A babe was slung upon her back,
    A bonny babe was he.

She went into the clearing wild,
    She went too far from town,
A man came up behind her
    And he cut her neck aroun',
A man came up behind her
    And he pushed that fair maid down.

"And will ye have your way wi' me,
    Or will ye cut me dead,
Or do ye hope to take from me
    My long-lost maidenhead?
Why have ye brought me far from town
    Upon this grass-green bed?"

He never spoke a single word,
    Nor gave to her his name,
Nor whence and where his parentage,
    Nor from which town he came,
He only thought to bring her low
    And heap her high wi' shame.

But as he set about his plan
    And went about his work,
The babe upon the maiden's back
    Had touched her hidden dirk,
And from its sheath had taken it
    All in the clearing's mirk.

And one and two, the tiny hands
    Did fell the evil man,
Who all upon his mother had
    Commenced the wicked plan.
God grant us all such bonny babes
    And a good and long life span.

THE STORY

The priestess called off the banishment, for four of the hunters had found Selna's s body hand in hand with Marjo. The hunters had melted quickly back into the forest when the shepherd had appeared, waited out his discovery, then taken Selna, the babe, and the ewe back to the Hame.

"Our sisters are once more with us," the priestess said, and she made Alta's mark—the circle and the crux—on Selna's forehead when she met the hunters with their sad burden at the great gate. "Bring her in. The child also. She now belongs to us all. No one of us shall mother her alone."

"The prophecy, Mother," Amalda cried out, and many echoed her. "Is this the child spoke of?"

The priestess shook her head. "The *Book* speaks of a thrice-orphaned babe and this sweetling has lost but two mothers, her first mother and Selna."

"But, Mother," Amalda continued, "was not Marjo her mother as well?"

The priestess' mouth grew tight. "We may not help a prophecy along, sister. Remember that it is written that *Miracles come to the unsuspecting.* I have spoken. The child will not have one mother here at Alta's-hame hereafter but a multitude." She twisted her long braid through her fingers.

The women murmured amongst themselves, but at last they agreed she was right. So they set Selna's corpse into the withy burial basket and brought her into the infirmarer's room. There they washed and dressed her body, brushed her hair until it shone, then twined the top withes of the basket closed.

It took six of them, one at each corner of the basket and two at head and foot, to carry the burden up Holy Hill to the great mazed cave, Alta's Rock, where the bodies of generations of sisters lay wrapped and preserved, under blazing torches.

Though they went up to Alta's Rock at noon, they waited until night for the ceremony, eating sparingly of the fruits they had brought with them. They spoke quietly of Selna's life, of her hunting skills and her fearlessness, her quick temper and her quicker smile. And they spoke as often of Marjo, not the pale shadow, but the hearty, laughing companion.

Kadreen remarked that it was Alta's luck that had led them to find Selna's body.

"No, sister, it was the skill of my sisters and me. We trailed her through several nights, and if she had not been out of her mind, we would never have picked up her trail, for she was the best of us," said Amalda.

Kadreen shook her head and placed her hand on Amalda's shoulder. "I mean, sister, that it was Alta's gracious gift that we have her body with us at Holy Hill, for how many of our own lie far away in unmarked graves?"

When the moon rose, the group on the Hill was almost doubled, the children alone without dark sisters.

Marjo's body appeared in its own basket by Selna's side, the withy lattice-work as finely done as her sister's.

Then the priestess, her voice ragged with sorrow, began. "For our sisters who are united even in death," she said, then breaking a moment out of the ritual whispered to the two corpses, "There is nothing wrong between you now."

Donya drew a loud, groaning breath, and the two kitchen maids burst into tears.

The priestess sang the first of the seven praises, with the others quickly joining in, singing the parts they had known from childhood.

> *In the name of Alta's cave,*
> *The dark and lonely grave . . .*

When the seventh was done, and only the last lovely echo lingered in the air, they picked up the baskets and carried Selna and Marjo into the cave.

Donya and her dark sister were the last, Donya carrying the white-haired babe, who was so full of ewe's milk she slept peacefully on the kitchener's ample breast.

THE MYTH

Then Great Alta said, "There shall be one of you, my only daughter, who shall be thrice born and thrice orphaned. She shall lie by a dead mother's side three times yet shall herself live. She shall be queen above all things yet queen she will not be. She shall carry a babe for each mother, yet mother them not. The three shall be as one and begin the world anew. So I say and so shall it be."

And then Great Alta picked out of the light a weeping child as white as snow, as red as blood, as black as night, and suckled her until the child was still.

BOOK TWO

The Book of Light

THE MYTH

And when Great Alta spoke, her words were slivers of glass. Where the sun struck them, then were her words like shafts for the purest light. Where fell the tears of her daughters, then were the words rainbows. But each time Great Alta's words were spoken, they reflected back the mind of the listener, shape for shape, shadow for shadow, light for light.

THE LEGEND

There was once a great teacher who came into the Dales from the East with the rising sun. The teacher's words were so fine, those who heard them said they were like the purest crystal, giving off a high, sweet ringing when touched.

The teacher lived among the people of the Dales for a year and a day, and then disappeared into the West with the setting sun. No one could say for certain afterward whether the teacher had been a man or a woman, short or tall, fair-skinned or dark. But all the words that the teacher had spoken at moonrise—for the teacher was mute except at the full moon—were gathered up by disciples in the Dales and set down in a book. The Dalites were surprised how small the book was when it was done, and how light, and so it was called the Book of Light.

THE STORY

Jenna was seven years old when she first touched the *Book of Light*. She stood with the three girls her age in a straight line, or at least as straight as

Marna, the teacher, and Zo, her dark sister, could make them. Selinda always fidgeted. And Alna, who had trouble breathing in the spring, wheezed her way through the ceremony. Only Marga—called Pynt after the small measure—and Jenna were still.

The priestess gave the line of girls a smile, but there was no warmth in that smile, only a formal lifting of the lips. It looked to Jenna like one of the wolves in the forest near Seldenkirk when frightened off its prey. She had seen a pack once. The priestess' dark sister gave the same smile, though it seemed infinitely more welcoming.

Jenna turned slightly so that she could look only straight upon that second smile, but she watched the priestess out of the side of her eye, the way she looked at things in the woods. Alta knew she had tried to please the Mother. But there seemed to be no pleasing her.

Overhead, the full spring moon illumined the stone altar. From the rowans came a rustling of new leaves as a small wind puzzled through the treetops. For a moment a rag of cloud covered the moon, and the priestess' dark sister disappeared from her altar-top throne. No one moved until the cloud passed by and the moon called them out again, all the dark ones. Then there was a quiet, contented sigh from the eighty mouths in the amphitheater.

The priestess lifted her head slightly to check out the skies. There were no other clouds in sight, and so she began. opening the great leather-bound book on her lap, her pointing finger with its sharpened nail underlining each syllable on the page, she read aloud.

Jenna could not take her eyes off that nail. No one else was allowed such a hand, nor would want one. Nails such as a priestess had would crack and break in the kitchen or at the forge, would get in the way of a bowstring or knife. Jenna surreptitiously flexed her own hand, wondering what it would feel like to have fingernails like that. She decided against it.

The priestess' voice, clear and low, filled the spaces between the girls.

"And the child of seven summers, and the child of seven autumns, and the child of seven winters, and the child of seven springs shall come to the altar and choose her own way. And when she has chosen, she shall follow that path for seven more years, never wavering in her mind or heart. And thus shall the Chosen Way become the True Way."

The priestess looked up from the book where the letters seemed to take the moonlight and fling it back at her, causing little sparks to dance across the bib of her robe

"Do you, my children, choose your own way?" she asked.

Her dark sister looked up at the same time, waiting for their answers.

"We do," the four girls answered as they had practiced, only Selinda came in late, for, as usual, she was dreaming about something else and had to be nudged from behind by Marna and Zo.

Then one by one the girls walked up the stairs to touch the book on the priestess' lap, Selinda first, for she was the oldest by nine months, and Jenna last. Touch the book, make the vow, name the choice. It was so simple and not so simple. Jenna shuddered.

She knew that Selinda would go with her own mother and work the gardens. There she could stare off into space without harm, going into what Marna and Zo called her "green dreams."

Alna, also born to a gardener, would choose the kitchen, where she wheezed less and where she would—it was thought—put a bit of weight on her thin bones. She was not happy about the choice, Jenna knew, for she really wanted to stay with her, mother and her mother's dark sister, who babied and spoiled her, holding her through the rough nights when she labored between breath and breath. But every one of the sisters agreed that Alna needed to be as far from the bursting seeds and floating autumn weed silks as possible. The infirmarer, Kadreen, had warned again and again that one day the space between breaths would grow too long and Alna could die out in the garden. It was that warning that had, at last, decided them all. All except Alna, who had cried every night the past month, thinking about her coming exile, so she had told Jenna. But being an obedient child, she would say what had to be said at the Choosing.

Black-haired Pynt, a warrior's womb child, choose the hunter/warrior path despite being so small and fine-boned, her father's legacy. If they tried to change Pynt's mind, Jenna knew she would fight them. Pynt would never waver, not for a moment. Loyalty coursed like blood through her veins.

And what of herself? Mothered by all but fostered by none, Jenna had already tried out many different paths. The gardens made her restless with their even rows. The kitchen was worse—everything in its place. She had even spent months by thee priestess' side, which caused her to bite her nails to the quick, sure evidence that it would be the wrong choice. The fact was, she was happiest out in the forest or when playing warriors' games such as the wands, though only a few times did the women let a child into their circle. And then she and Pynt had been matched as light sister and dark. It was as if Jenna could see better in the woods than in the confines of the Hame. And next year, once she had chosen, she would be taught the bow and knife.

Jenna watched as first mousy Selinda, then wheezy Alna, and then strong-minded Pynt mounted the three steps to the altar where the priestess and her dark twin sat on their backless thrones. One by one, the girls placed their right hand on the *Book,* their left touching the four places that were Alta's own: head, left breast, navel, groin. Then they recited the words of the oath after the priestess, speaking to her of their choices. What was said became so, so powerful were the words now: Selinda to the garden, Alna to the kitchen, Pynt to the hunt.

When Pynt came down the stairs, with a big grin on her face, she patted Jenna's hand. "Her breath is sour," she whispered.

After that Jenna found it difficult to take the first step seriously. Her mouth would not say set in the thin line she had practiced. But once she set foot on the second step, it was different. It brought her closer to her choice. By the time she reached the third step, she found she was trembling. Not with fear of the priestess or awe of the *Book,* but with a kind of eagerness, like the young kit fox Amalda had rescued and trained, when it was in the presence of the hens. Even when he was not hungry, he trembled with anticipation. *That* was how Jenna felt.

Putting her hand on the *Book of Light,* she was surprised at how cold it was. The letters were raised up and she could feel them impress themselves on her palm. She touched her forehead with her left hand and it felt cool and dry. Then she put her hand over her heart, comforted to feel it beating steadily beneath her fingertips. Quickly she completed the rest of the ritual.

The priestess spoke, and her breath was not so much sour as alien, smelling of age and dignity and the trappings of state.

"You must say the words after me, Jo-an-enna, daughter of us all."

"I will, Mother Alta," Jenna whispered, her voice cracking suddenly.

"I am a child of seven springs . . ." began the priestess.

"I am a child of seven springs," Jenna repeated.

"I choose and I am chosen."

Jenna drew in a deep breath. "I choose and I am chosen."

The priestess smiled. Jenna saw it was not such a distant smile after all, but a sad smile and not much practiced.

"The path I choose is . . ."

"The path I choose is . . ." Jenna said.

The priestess nodded, her face oddly expectant.

Jenna took another breath, deeper than the first. So many ways lay open to her at this moment. She closed her eyes to savor it, then opened them and was surprised by the predatory look in the priestess' face. Jenna turned slightly and spoke to the dark sister, more loudly than she had meant. "A warrior. A huntress. A keeper of the wood." She sighed, glad to be done with it.

The priestess did not speak for a moment. She looked almost angry. Then she and her dark sister leaned forward and embraced Jenna, whispering in Jenna's ears, "Well chosen, warrior." There was no warmth in it.

As Jenna walked back down the steps, she heard again the echo of the second thing the priestess alone had whispered in her ear. She wondered if the others had been told the same. Somehow she doubted they had, for the priestess had added, trembling strangely, "Alta's own chosen child."

The lessons began in earnest the next morning. It was not that the woods-days had been a time of play before, but the formal teaching—question and answer, memory tests, and the Game—could begin only after the Choosing.

"This is thimbleflower," said Pynt's mother Amalda, kneeling beside a dull green plant. "Soon it will have flowers that look like little purple bells."

"Why is it not called bellflower?" murmured Jenna, but Amalda only smiled.

"Pretty!" said Pynt, putting out her hand to stroke a leaf.

Amalda slapped it away, and when Pynt looked offended, said, "Remember, child, *Spilled water is better than a broken jar.* Do not touch something unless you know what it can do to you. There are thistles that prick, briars that snag, nettles that sting at the touch. Then there are the subtler plants whose poisons reveal themselves only long after."

Pynt put her smarting hand to her mouth.

At Amalda's signal, both girls knelt down next to her, Jenna close and Pynt, still offended, a little way off. Then her own sunny nature overcame her resentment, and she crowded next to Jenna.

"Smell these first," Amalda said, pointing to the leaf of the thimbleflower.

They leaned over and sniffed. There was a slight, sharp odor.

"If I let you taste the leaves," Pynt's mother said, "you would spit them out quickly." She shuddered deliberately, and the girls imitated her, Pynt with a broad smile on her face. "But should you swell up with water that will not release itself, should your heart beat too quickly and loudly and Kadreen fears for it, then she would make a tea of the leaves and you would soon be relieved. Only . . ." And she held a hand up in warning. The girls knew that sign well. It meant they must be silent and listen. "Only beware of this *pretty* plant. In small doses it is a help to one in distress, but too strong a brew, made with a wicked intent, and the drinker dies."

Jenna shivered and Pynt nodded.

"Mark this place well," said Amalda. "For we do not pick the leaves until the flower is full out. But Kadreen will be pleased that we have found her a dell full of thimbleflower."

The girls looked around.

"Jenna, how have you marked it?"

Jenna thought. "By the big white tree with the two branches in the trunk."

"Good. Pynt?"

"It was the third turning, A-ma. And to the right." In her excitement, Pynt had reverted to her baby name for her mother.

Amalda smiled. "Fine! You both have good eyes. But that is not all that is necessary in the woods. Come." She stood up and strode down the path.

The girls followed after, skipping hand in hand.

The second lesson came close upon the first, for not another turn further and Amalda held up her hand. Immediately the girls were silent, stopped in their tracks. Amalda's chin went up and the girls imitated her. She touched her right ear with her hand and they listened intently. At first they heard nothing but the wind through the trees. Then there came a strange, loud creaking, followed by a high chittering.

Amalda pointed to a fallen tree. They went over to it silently and stared.

"What beast?" Amalda asked at last.

Pynt shrugged.

"Hare?" Jenna guessed.

"Look, child. Listen. Your ears are as important as your eyes. Did you hear that squeaky scolding? It sounded like this." Lifting her head, she made a high noise with her tongue against the roof of her mouth.

The girls laughed in delighted admiration and then Amalda showed them how to make the sound. They each tried and Pynt got it right first.

"That is the sound squirrel makes," said Amalda.

"I know that!" said Jenna, surprised, for now that the name was spoken, she found that she had, indeed, know it.

"Me, too!" said Pynt.

"So we know squirrel watches us and scolds us for entering her domain." Amalda nodded and looked around.

The girls did the same.

"Therefore we look for signs to tell us where squirrel especially likes to come, her favorite places." She pointed again to the fallen tree. "Stumps are often such a spot."

They looked carefully at the stump. Around the base was a small midden heap of cone scales and nut shellings.

"Squirrel eats here," said Amalda. "She has left these signs for us but she does not know it. See now if you can find her little digging places, for she loves to bury things."

They scattered, as silently as two seven-year-olds can, and soon each came upon the small dead-end diggings. Jenna's held a buried acorn but Pynt's only the acorn caps. Amalda praised them for their finds. Afterward she showed them the slight scratches on the trees where the squirrels had chased one another up and over their favorite routes, leaving a few tiny patches of squirrel hair caught in the trunk. Deftly Amalda picked out the hair and tucked it into her leather pouch.

"Sada and Lina will find a use for these with their weavers," she said.

The girls scrambled over several more trees, each coming up with handfuls of more hair. Jenna found a tree marked with larger scratches.

"Squirrel?" she asked.

Amalda patted her on the head. "Sharp-eyed girl," she said, "but that is no squirrel."

Pynt shook her head, her dark curls bouncing. "Too big," she said wisely. "Too deep."

Together Pynt and Jenna whispered, "Fox?" and Jenna added by herself, "Coon?"

Amalda smiled. "Mountain cat," she said.

With that the lesson ended, for they all knew the danger, and though Amalda had seen no recent scat and doubted the cat was even in the area, she thought *caution* a fine moral to teach the girls, and led them back home.

At the noon table, piled high with fresh, twisted loaves of bread and steaming mugs of squirrel stew, Amalda could not help but show the girls off.

"Tell the sisters what you learned today," she said.

"That thimbleflowers can be good," said Pynt.

"Or bad," Jenna added.

"For your heart or . . ." Pynt stopped, unable to remember more.

"Or your water," Jenna said, and then wondered at the chuckle that ran around the table.

"And squirrels sound like this." Pynt made the sound and was rewarded with applause. She smiled, delighted, for she and Jenna had practiced the squirrel call all the way home.

Jenna clapped, too, and then, when the noise had died down, she spoke out, eager to win her share of the praise. "We found the mark of a mountain cat." When there was no applause, she added, "A mountain cat killed my first mother."

There was a sudden silence at the table. The priestess looked over at Amalda from her place at the head. "Who has told the child this . . . this tale?"

"Mother, not I," Amalda said quickly.

"Nor I."

"Nor I."

Swiftly the denials ran around the table.

The priestess stood, her voice deep with anger and authority. "This child belongs to all of us. There is no first mother. There is no second mother. Am I understood?" She waited for their complete silence, took it for approval, spun on her heel, and left.

No one spoke for many minutes after, though the children continued to eat noisily, their spoons loud against the mugs.

"What does all that mean?" asked Donya, peering in from the kitchen doorway.

"It means age is wearing away her senses," muttered Catrona, wiping wine from her mouth with the back of her hand. "She feels heat even on the coldest days. She looks into mirrors and sees her mother's face."

Domina added, "She cannot get a child to choose *her* way, even after so many springtimes of trying. We will have to send to another Hame when *she* dies."

Jenna was the only child not eating, staring at her plate and feeling first hot, then cold on her cheeks. She had wanted attention when she said what she said, but not this kind. She scuffed her sandal against the chair leg. The slight sound, which only she heard, comforted her.

"Hush!" said Amalda, her hand on Domina's arm for emphasis.

"She is right, Domina, Catrona," said Kadreen in her flat, unsmiling way. She nodded her head toward the table where the gardeners sat, meaning—they all knew—that what was spoken here would find its way soon enough into the ears of the priestess herself. The workers of the field always served the one who blessed their crops; they were hers unquestioningly. Not that Kadreen cared. She took no sides in any disputes, just set the bones and stitched the wounds, but she was not above a warning now and again. "And you, Catrona, remember that when the villagers say *There is no medicine to cure hatred,* they are right. I have warned you about these passions. Just a month past and your stomach was bad again and you were abed with the bloody flux. Drink goat's milk as I told you, instead of that rough grape swill, and practice your *latani* breathing for calm. I do not want you back soon."

Catrona snorted through her nose and turned her attention back to her food, pointedly pushing the soup and wine aside and attacking the bread with gusto, smearing it liberally with honey from the pot.

Jenna gulped in a deep breath. "I did not mean anything," she said in a piercing child's voice. "What did I say? Why is everyone so mad?"

Amalda struck her on top of the head lightly with a pair of foodsticks. "Not your fault, child," she said. "Sometimes grown sisters speak before they think."

"Speak for yourself, Amalda," muttered Catrona. She pushed the bread aside, shoved her chair back, and stood up. "I meant exactly what I said. Besides, the child has a right to know . . ."

"There is nothing to know," said Kadreen.

Catrona snorted again and left.

"Know what?" asked Pynt. She was answered with a sharper tapping on the head than Jenna had received.

Jenna said nothing but stood up. Without even asking to be excused, she walked to the door. Then, turning, she spoke. "I *will* know. And if none of you will tell me, I will ask Mother Alta myself."

"That one . . ." Donya said later to her maids in the kitchen, "she will one day tackle the Goddess Great Alta herself, mark my words." But they did not mark them, for Donya tended to ramble and make such pronouncements all the time.

Jenna went directly to the priestess' rooms, though as she came closer, she could feel her heart pounding madly. She wondered if Kadreen would have to give her a draught of thimbleflower potion for it. She worried that if the potion were too strong, she would die. To die just as she had chosen her way. It would be terribly sad. All the wondering and worrying disguised how quickly she was walking, and she came to the priestess' room rather faster than she had planned.

The door was open and Mother Alta was sitting behind a great loom at which she was working on a tapestry of the Hame, one of those endless priestess tasks that Jenna had found so boring. *Snip-snap* went her fingernails against the shuttle; *click-clack* went the shuttle across the threads from side to side. Mother Alta must have seen movement from the corner of her eye. She looked up. "Come in, Jo-an-enna," she said.

There was no help for it. Jenna went in.

"Have you come to ask my forgiveness?" She smiled but the smile did not reach her eyes.

"I have come to ask why you say my first mother was *not* killed by a cat when all the others say it." Jenna could not help fiddling with her right braid and the leather thong binding it. "They say she was killed trying to save me."

"Who are *they?*" the priestess asked, her voice low and carefully uninflected. Her right hand moved over the left, turning and turning her great agate ring. Jenna could not take her eyes off the ring.

"Which others, Jo-an-enna?" Mother Alta asked again.

Jenna looked up and tried to smile. "I have heard that story ever since I can remember," she said. "But is it not peculiar, Mother, I do not remember exactly *who* told me first." She caught her breath because that was not really a lie. She could remember Amalda saying it. And Domina. Even Catrona. And the girls repeating it. But she did not want them to be in trouble. Especially not Amalda, whom she often pretended was her mother as much as Pynt's. She secretly called her "A-ma" at night, into her pillow. "And there is a song about it, too."

"Do not believe songs," said the priestess, her hands having left the ring to play with the great chain of metal half-moons and moonstones around her neck. "Next you will believe the ravings of village priests and the puns of itinerant rhymesters."

"Then what should I believe?" Jenna asked. "*Who* should I believe?"

"Believe me. Believe the *Book of Light.* Soon enough you shall know it. And believe that Great Alta hears all." Her finger with its long, glittering nail pointed to the ceiling for emphasis.

"Did she hear that I had a mother killed by a cat?" Jenna asked, appalled that her tongue spoke what her mind had made up, without waiting for her to judge it.

"Be gone, child, you tire me." The priestess waved the back of her hand at Jenna.

Relieved, Jenna left.

No sooner had the child gone out the door than Mother Alta rose, pushing aside the heavy loom. She went over to the great polished mirror standing in its ornate wooden frame. Often she spoke to it as she would to her own dark sister, when she needed counsel in the day, for indeed the two images were near the same, the only difference being in the color and the fact that the mirror did not talk back. *Sometimes,* Mother Alta thought wearily, *I prefer the glass's silence to the answers I receive from my dark twin.*

"Do you remember the man in the town," she whispered, "the Slipskin farmer? He had rough hands and a rougher tongue. We were younger then by seven years, but older by far than he. He did not know it, though. How could he, used as he was to the coarse women of his coarse town." She smiled wryly at the memory and the image smiled back.

"We surprised him, sister, when we took off our cloaks. And we surprised him with our silken skins. And we surprised him out of the story of his only child, the one who had, all unknowing, killed her mother and the midwife who took her into the mountains and never returned. He will remember our passion as a dream, for we came to him secretly at midnight. And all the others we questioned knew but one of us, disguised in the day, and she an old, old crone." This time she did not smile, and the image stared back at her in silence.

"His story—it had to be true. No man cries in the arms of a woman lest the story he tell be true. We were the first who had come to warm his bed since his wife's death. His wounds though nine months old were fresh. And so there *were* three: mother, midwife, fosterer. Three in one. And dead, all dead."

She bit her lower lip. The eyes in the mirror, as green as her own, stared back at her.

"Oh, Great Alta, speak to me. It is one of thy priestesses begging." She held up her hands and the mark of Alta, incised in blue, stood out vividly on her palms. "Here am I, Mother to thy children, ruling them in this small Hame in thy name. I have neither helper nor child but my dark sister, no one to speak to but thee. Oh, Great Alta, who is sower and reaper, who is in the beginning and in the end, hear me." She touched herself: head, left breast, navel, and groin. "Have I done right, Great One? Have I done wrong? This child is thrice orphaned, as it says in the prophecy. But there have been rumors of others before her. One came from the Hame near Calla's Ford, and one so long ago fostered in the Hame near Nill. But they proved themselves just girls after all.

"Then what is this child, this Annuanna? She is marked with hair the color of new snow, and of such the prophecy speaks. But she laughs and cries like any child. She is quick-tongued and quick-footed, but no better at the games than her foster sister Marga. Many times have I given her the choice of following me as thine own, a priestess to lead thy children. But she chose instead the woods and the hunt and other such follies. How can this be the child we seek?

"Oh, Great Alta, I know thou speakest to me in the sun that rises and in the moon that shapes itself anew each month. I know thy voice echoes in the pattering of rain and the rising up of the dew. So it is written, and so I believe. But I need a clearer sign before I unfold this wonder to all of them. But just the piqued mouthings of jealous women, not just the guilty, tearful confidences of an unhappy man. And not just my own trembling heart. A true sign.

"The burden, Great One, is so hard to bear. I am so very lonely. I grow old before my time with this secret. Look here. And here." She pulled aside her gown to show how flaccid her breasts had become. She touched the loosening skin under her chin. Tears began to well up in her eyes and she knelt before the mirror, sighing.

"And one thing more, Great Alta, though thou knowest it already. Yet still I must confess it aloud to thee. The greatest fear of all. If I am not thy priestess, I am nothing. It is all my life. I need a promise, Great One, a promise if she—Annuanna, Jo-an-enna, Jenna—is the one of whom it is written, the light sister thrice born and thrice orphaned, the one who will be queen over all and change what we know. And the promise I beg is that if it is she, then I will still serve thee as I have. That the place at the head of the table will still be mine. That I shall still sit on the throne under the moon and call thy name that the sisters might hear me and pray. Promise me that, Great Alta, and I shall reveal her."

The mirror image's face flushed suddenly and the priestess put her hand up to her cheeks, which burned fiercely beneath her fingers. Other than the fire in her face, there was no sign.

She stood up heavily. "I must think upon this more." Turning, she went out the other door, the hidden door, behind the heavy patched tapestry upon which the forms of sisters light and dark played at wands.

THE HISTORY

There is, of course, no extant copy of the Book of Light, *the great text of the moon-centered Mother Goddess worshippers. Though presumably each Hame or community of Altites had a hand-lettered and illuminated copy of the Book. Such volumes disappeared during the Gender Wars, either—if the Sigel and Salmon dig logs are accurate—into underground chambers especially constructed against such eventualities or—if one is to trust Vargo's reconstruction of the priestess codes—into ritual fires.*

However, the meat of the Book's *history and its gnomic teachings can be plucked from the rich stew of folk life in the towns that still flourish near the ancient Hame sites. Buss and Bee's monumental work,* So Speak the Folk, *gives strong support to the idea that the Alta Hames (or Alta's Shames, as the priests of the Lower Dales still call them) were in fact merely extensions of the towns and cities which bordered their lands, in effect suburban satellites, at least as far as their speech patterns and folk beliefs are concerned.*

Of course, the story of Alta worship is intelligible only in the light of early Garunian history. The G'runs, an ancient, well-connected noble family from the Continent, had come to the Isles in the invasions of the 800s. Worshippers of a male trinity of gods—Hargo, god of fire, Vendre, god of water, and Lord Cres, the brutal god of the dead—they settled along the seacoasts. Slowly they infiltrated into the upper councils of the semimatriarchal civilization they found there. Trying at first to undermine it, they in fact later compromised and accepted a matrilineal succession only after the devastating Gender Wars wrecked both the ancient Hame sites and the famous palace of G'run Far Shooter.

The religion the Garunians were trying to supplant was anathema to the first invaders because of its emphasis on a white-haired goddess who seeded herself without the aid of a male consort. It was a religion that had grown up in part because of the overflow of women following much earlier, devastating wars of succession which had been fought some four hundred years before. Because of the created imbalance between the sexes that followed the civil strife, it had become the custom to expose unwanted, superfluous girl babies on the hillsides. However, in the late 600s, a female reputedly of great height and with long, flowing white hair (possibly an albino, though more probably an old woman) named Alta wandered the countryside speaking out against the brutal custom and gathering what live children she could find. She fashioned carts linked together to trundle the rescued babes behind her. Slowly this Alta was joined by like-minded women who were either unmarried (there were many spinsters, the so-called unclaimed treasures, because of the ratio of men to women), widows, or multiple wives in polygamous marriages. (Especially in the Lower Dales such radical couplings had been tolerated, though only the children of the first wife might inherit.) Thus was the first of seventeen Hames established, as havens for the discarded children and extra women. This reconstruction, first set forth by the late Professor Davis Temple of Hofbreeder University in his now-classic Alta-Natives, *is so thoroughly accepted that I need not comment further.*

The communities of foster mothers, needing some religious underpinnings, developed the worship of a White Goddess called Great Alta. The genius and genuine goodness of the original Alta was rewarded in this fashion. Over the years, the real Alta and a subsequent itinerant preacher whose name has been given variously as Gennra, Hendra, Hanna, Anna, and The Dark One have merged into the figure of a goddess whose hair is both light and dark, a strange hermaphroditic creature who has babies without recourse to a male consort. The religion borrowed many aspects of the surrounding patriarchal tribes and, later, even took on some of the Garunian worship. (For example, the custom of cave burials, a later addition, was patterned after the G'runs, who came originally from a small valley between cave-riddled mountains where land for cultivation was too prime to be turned over to the dead. Earlier Altite burials were in great mounds.)

Just as the white-haired Alta had been a savior for many a girl child left to die upon a hillside, rumors of a second savior arose. The rumors became belief, set down—if we are again to believe Vargo—in the Book of Light itself. This savior was to be the child of a dead mother; the easy psychological substitution—dead child to dead mother—is the most basic of folk shifts. Not one dead mother, in fact, but three, that magical number. It is a belief still encapsulated in some of the folk songs and sayings in the Upper Dales.

THE SONG

Alta's Song

I am a babe, an only babe,
Fire and water and all,
Who in my mother's womb was made,
Great Alta take my soul.

But from that mother I was torn,
Fire and water and all,
And to a hillside I was borne,
Great Alta take my soul.

And on that hillside was I laid,
Fire and water and all,
And taken up all by a maid,
Great Alta take my soul.

And one and two and three we rode,
Fire and water and all,
Till others took the heavy load,
Great Alta take my soul.

Let all good women hark to me,
Fire and water and all,
For fostering shall set thee free,
Great Alta take my soul.

THE STORY

"What did she say? What did you say?" Pynt asked breathlessly, twisting her fingers in her dark curls. She was sitting on the floor of their shared room by the window. The room tended toward darkness, as did all the rooms in the Hame, so the girls always played close to the narrow slits of windows, winter and summer. "Did she hit you?"

Jenna thought about what to say. She almost wished Mother Alta *had* hit her. Amalda had a quick hand and both girls had had recent willow whippings, Pynt for her quick mouth and Jenna for supporting her. But they were not long or hard whippings and besides, such punishment was always followed swiftly by hugs and tears and kisses. If the priestess had acted so, Jenna might not have stayed beyond the door, quiet as a wood mouse, listening. Was she the babe who had, all unknowing, killed her mother not once but three times? The thought had so frightened her, she had not stayed to hear more but run away to hide, down in the cellar, where the great casks of dark red wine were kept. In the dark she had breathed first very fast, with the sobs threatening to burst out of her chest, because if she were that child, then all her hoping for A-ma to be her mother, all her pretending, was just that: a game. And then she had slowed her breathing down and forced herself to stand dry-eyed. She would find Pynt and ask her.

Only now, standing over Pynt, she knew this was too heavy a burden to share. "She asked who had told me such a thing and I said that I could not remember who had told me first." She slumped to the floor next to Pynt.

"A-ma was first," said Pynt. "I remember. It was like a story. We were both sleeping in the big bed, a special treat, between A-ma and Sammor, and . . ."

"Maybe not," said Jenna, relieved to be past the hardest part. "Maybe I heard it first from Catrona. Or Donya. She talks too much, she probably . . ."

". . . said it three times over." Pynt laughed. It was a common joke at the Hame, even among the children.

"I heard Domina say something about it. And something about my second mother, too. They were friends." Was this treading too close to the treacherous ground? Jenna felt her fingers start to twitch, but Pynt seemed not to notice.

Pynt put her elbows on her knees and rested her chin in her hands. "Not Kadreen, though. You would not have heard it from her."

They both shook their heads wisely. Kadreen never gossiped or gave information freely.

"I *like* Kadreen," said Jenna, "even though she is a Solitary. Even though she never smiles." Solitaries, women without dark sisters, were rare at the Hames, and Jenna felt very much as she suspected a Solitary felt, alone and without the comfort of a companion who knew your every thought.

"I saw her smile once. It was when Alna stopped breathing and then started again with those funny coughs and the bubbles coming out of her mouth. When we were in the garden hunting down the rabbit. Well, the pretend rabbit. Children's games! And you ran to get Kadreen because you are the fastest, and she put her ear down on Alna's chest and thumped it."

"And Alna had a black mark as big as a fist for seven days."

"Eight—and she loved to show it off."

"Kadreen did not smile then."

"Did."

"Did not."

"Did. And anyway, A-ma gave me these." Pynt reached behind her back and brought up two new corn dolls in one hand and a pair of reed backpacks in the other. "She and Sammor made them for us to celebrate the Choosing."

"Ooh, they are nicer than Alna's."

"Much nicer," agreed Pynt.

"And the packs have the Hame sign on them." Jenna pointed to the sign in the circle.

"Now," Pynt said, "we can be truly truly sisters, just the way you like to play it, sharing everything. You take the light pack and the light doll and I will take the dark."

Jenna took the pack guiltily, remembering how little she had actually shared with Pynt, remembering how Mother Alta had looked, standing in front of the great framed mirror, and speaking the words which had so frightened her. She remembered and wondered if she and Pynt could ever be *truly truly* sisters again.

Then the dolls proved much more interesting than her own black thoughts and she put the babe in the pack, the pack on her back, and played at light sister and dark with Pynt for an hour or more, until the ringing bell recalled them to their lessons.

"This afternoon," Catrona informed them, "I shall instruct you in the Game of the Eye-Mind."

The girls grinned and Pynt elbowed Jenna playfully. They had both heard of the Game. The older girls talked of it secretly at the table sometimes. But none of them had ever really explained it, for it was one of the Mysteries reserved for *after* the Choosing.

Pynt looked around quickly as if to see if anyone was noticing them. There were three older girls in the warrior yard, but they were busy with their own things: red-headed Mina aiming at the narrow target and hitting it regularly with comfortable *thumps,* and Varsa and Little Domina having at each other with wicker swords to the accompaniment of Big Domina's shouted corrections.

"Pynt, watch me!" Catrona said, her voice not at all sharp, but laughing. "I know there is much to see here, but you must learn to focus."

"What of the *eye's corner?* Amalda said . . ." Jenna hesitated.

"You get ahead of me, child," said Catrona. She pulled lightly on one of Jenna's braids, not enough to hurt but enough to get Jenna's full attention. "First you learn to focus and then diffuse."

"What is *diffuse?*" asked Pynt.

Catrona laughed again. "It means to be able to see many things at once. But first you must *listen,* Marga." She stopped laughing abruptly.

They listened.

Catrona turned to the table by her side, a small wooden table, much scarred around the legs. It was covered by an old cloth which disguised a number of strange lumps and bumps on the top.

"First, what do you see here?" Catrona asked, gesturing them to the tabletop.

"A table with an old cloth," said Pynt, quickly adding, "And a ragged old cloth."

"A cloth covering many things," said Jenna.

"You are both correct. But remember this—caution in the woods and in battle is the greatest virtue. Often what *seems* is not what *is.*" She whisked away the cloth and they saw that the table was a solid carved representation of a mountaintop with peaks and valleys. "This we use to teach the way through the mountain range in which our Hame is nestled. *And* to plan our stratagems."

Pynt clapped her hands together, delightedly, while Jenna bent over closer to run her finger thoughtfully over the ridges and trails.

"Now what do you see here?" Catrona asked, guiding them over to the alcove where a second table covered with a similar cloth stood. There were even more ridges and peaks under this cloth.

"Another mountain," said Pynt, eager as always to be first with the answer.

"Caution, with caution," reminded Catrona.

Jenna shook her head. "It does not look like a mountain to me. The peaks are not as high. There are round places, as round as . . . as an . . ."

"An apple!" Pynt interjected.

"Let us see," said Catrona. She took the cloth away by lifting it up from the middle. On the table was a strange assortment of objects.

"Oh!" said Pynt. "You fooled me!" She looked up at Catrona, grinning.

"Look back, child. *Focus.*"

Pynt looked back just as Catrona dropped the cloth back onto the table-top, covering it completely.

"Now comes the Game," said Catrona. "We will start with Marga. Since you so love being first, you shall name an object on the table. Then Jenna. Then Marga again. On and on until you can remember no more. The one who remembers the most gets a sweet."

Pynt clapped her hands, for she loved sweets. "A spoon. There was a spoon," she said.

Jenna nodded. "And it *was* an apple, the round thing."

"And a pair of foodsticks," Pynt said.

"One only," said Jenna.

"One," agreed Catrona.

"A card of some kind," said Pynt.

"A buckle, like A-ma—Amalda's," said Jenna.

"I did not see that," Pynt said, turning to look at Jenna, who shrugged.

"It was there," Catrona said. "Go on, Marga."

Pynt's forehead made wavy lines as she concentrated. She put her fist into her cheek and thought. Then she smiled. "There were *two* apples!"

"Good girl!" Catrona smiled.

"On a plate," said Jenna.

"Two plates?" Pynt asked uncertainly.

"You are lucky," Catrona answered.

"A knife," said Jenna.

Pynt thought for a good long while and at last shrugged. "There was nothing else," she said.

"Jenna?" Catrona turned and looked directly at Jenna, who was pulling on her braids. Jenna knew there had been more objects and could name them, but she also knew how much Pynt wanted to win the sweet. How much Pynt *needed* to win the sweet. Then she sighed. "A bowl of water. A pin. Some thread."

"Thread?" Catrona shook her head. "No thread, Jenna."

"Yes, thread," Jenna said. "And two or maybe three pebbles or berries. And . . . and that is all I can remember."

Catrona smiled. "Five berries, two of them black and three red. And you both neglected to mention the piece of tapestry with the wand players or the ribband or the writing stick, tapestry needle and—the sweet! But for all that you forgot, you remembered quite a good bit. I am very proud of the two of you for your first time at the Game." She pulled away the cloth. "Now look closely again."

It was Pynt who pointed first. "Look, Catrona, there is Jenna's thread!"

Lying next to the tapestry piece, but far enough away from it to be read as a single item, was a long dark thread.

Catrona laughed out loud. "Sharp eyes indeed, Jo-an-enna! And I am getting foolish and careless in my old age. Fine teacher I am. Such a miss might mean my doom in the woods or in the midst of battle."

The girls nodded sagely back at her as she picked up the sweet and solemnly handed it to Jenna.

"We will play again and again until you remember *all* that you see. Tomorrow we will play with different objects under the cloth. By the time this Game is done, you will be able to name everything the first time and there will be more than thirty things to name. But it is not just a Game, my children. The point of it is this—you must look at everything twice—once with your outer eye and once with the eye of your mind. That is why it is called the Eye-Mind Game. You must learn to resee everything, to recall it as clearly the second time as the first."

"Do we do the same thing in the woods?" asked Pynt.

Jenna had not asked the question because she already knew the answer. Of course they must do the same thing in the woods. And in the Hame and in the towns. Everywhere. What a foolish thing to ask. She was surprised at Pynt.

But Catrona did not seem surprised. "The same," she said calmly. "What *good* girls!" She put a hand on the shoulders of each and pushed them closer to the table. "Now look again."

They crowded close and stared intently at the tabletop, Pynt's mouth moving in a strange litany as she reminded herself the names of each object there. Jenna stared with such intensity she trembled.

In the evening, the four new Choosers met in their room and sat on Jenna's bed. They each had much to share.

Pynt bubbled through a recitation of the Game and how Jenna had shared the sweet with her.

"Though she really won it," Pynt finished. "But tomorrow I will win. I think I have found the secret." She rocked her new doll in her arms as she spoke.

"You always have a secret way, Pynt," said Selinda. "And it almost never works."

"Does."

"Does not."

"Does."

"Tell us about the kitchen, Alna," said Jenna. Suddenly she could not stand the argument. What did it matter if Pynt sometimes tried to find secret ways or that they seldom worked?

Alna said in her whispery voice, "I never knew there was so much to learn in a *kitchen.* I got to help cut up things. In the garden they never let me use a knife. And I did not hurt myself once. It smells good in there, too, but . . ." She sighed and did not finish.

"You would not have liked the gardens today anyway," Selinda said quickly. "All we did was weed. Weed! I have done that ever since I can remember. How was it different to have chosen? I should have gone to the kitchen. Or the woods. Or to the weavers. Or . . ."

"I like weeding," Alna whispered.

"You do *not,*" said Pynt. "You used to complain about it all the time."

"Did not."

"Did."

"Did not."

Amalda came into the room. "It is time to get into bed, little ones," she said. "You must be like the birds. As high as they fly, they always return to earth." She gave them each a hug before leaving, and Jenna squeezed back extra hard.

Minutes later Selinda's womb mother came in and stayed only a moment, tucking in Selinda and giving each of the other girls a nod. And then, because it was past dark, and Jenna had gotten out of bed again and lit all the lanterns, Alna's mother and dark sister both came in. They gave each girl a touch but they fussed nervously and—to Jenna's mind—endlessly over Alna despite her reassurances to them that she felt fine.

At last Marna and Zo came in and, to everyone's delight, they carried their tembalas with them. Marna's instrument had a sweet sound. Zo's was lower and complementary, just like their voices.

"Sing 'Come, Ye Women,'" begged Pynt.

"And the 'Ballad of Ringer's Forge,'" Alna whispered.

"'Derry Down.' Sing 'Derry Down,'" Selinda said, bouncing on her bed.

Jenna alone was silent as she unbraided her white hair, which was crinkled from its long plaiting.

"And do you not have a favorite also, Jo-an-enna?" asked Marna softly, watching Jenna's swift hands.

Jenna was slow in answering, but at last very seriously said, "Is there a new song we can hear? One just for this first day after the Choosing?" She wanted this day to be as special as it was supposed to be, not just a strange, hollow feeling under her breastbone where all the little squabbles with Pynt and the odd sense of distance from the other girls were growing. She wanted to be close to them, and ordinary again; she wanted to wash away the memory of Mother Alta before her great mirror. "Something we have never heard before."

"Of course, Jenna. I will sing something I learned last year when we had that mission visit from the singer from Calla's Ford Hame. Theirs is such a large Hame, some seven hundred members, one can be *just* a singer there."

"Would you want to be *just* a singer, dear Marna?" asked Pynt

It was Zo who answered. "In a large Hame, our small talent would scarcely be recognized," she said.

"Besides, this is our Hame," said Marna. "We would be no place else."

"But you were someplace else once," said Jenna thoughtfully. She wondered if she would feel different, more ordinary, scarcely recognized someplace else.

"Of course I was, Jenna. When I went on my year mission before the final Choosing, before calling my sister from the dark, just as you shall. But for all the Hames I visited and all the sisters there who would have had me stay, I came back here, to Selden Hame, though it is the smallest of them all."

"Why?" asked Pynt.

"Yes—why?" the other three echoed.

"Because it is *our* Hame," Marna and Zo said together.

"Now, enough questions," Marna said, "or there will be no time for even one song."

They snuggled down in their beds.

"First I will sing the new song. It is called 'Alta's Song.' And then I will sing the others. Afterward, you must all go right to sleep. You are no longer my little ones, you know, and there will be much for you to do come morning."

She began the first song. By the end of the third, the girls were all asleep except for Jenna, but Marna and Zo did not notice and they tiptoed out of the room.

The fire in the Great Hall's hearth crackled merrily and two hounds dozing nearby scrabbled on the stones with their claws as they chased after rabbits in their dreams. The room smelled comfortably of rushes and wood-smoke and of the bowls of dried rose petals and verbena.

When Marna and Zo entered, they saw that all the big chairs near the fire were taken already and the three older girls lay on their stomachs on the rug by the hearth.

"Over here," called Amalda.

They turned and saw that two places at the large round table off to the side of the hearth had been reserved for them.

"How are the Choosers?" asked Amalda intently.

"Are they still excited?" Her dark sister Sammor seemed more relaxed.

"They are quiet for now. We sang them four songs—well, three, actually. They fell asleep before the fourth. Poor little mites, the day had quite exhausted them and I promised them more work for the morrow." Marna sat down heavily in the chair.

"We miss those little imps already," said Zo as soon as she, too, was seated.

Catrona smiled. "This is not such a great Hame that you will not see them every day."

"But they have been our special charges for the last seven years," Marna said. "And I feel them growing away from us already."

Domina sniffed. "You say that every spring at Choosing."

"Not *every* spring. We have not had a Choosing since Varsa, and that three years ago. And now four at once. It is very hard."

Alna's mother looked across the table at her. "It is harder on Glon and me. They have taken our baby from the gardens. To be a kitchener. Under Donya. Feh."

"What do you mean by *they?*" Catrona flared. "You were as worried as we were that she might someday stop breathing out in that weedy trap of yours."

"Weedy? What do you mean? Our garden is as clean of weeds as any you will find in a larger Hame. Weeds indeed!" Alinda started to stand and Glon, next to her, reached out to steady her. They sat down together, but Alinda still trembled with anger.

"She just meant it was hard," said Glon to Catrona. "Forgive her. We are both out of sorts today."

Catrona snorted and looked away.

"The first day after a Choosing is always difficult," said Kadreen, coming to sit at the table's head. "And we say the same thing every time. Are we children to have such short memories? Come, sisters, look at one another and smile. This feeling will pass." She looked around the table and though she herself did not smile, soon the rest were returned to their normal happy moods. "Now are we all here?"

"Donya and Doey are late, as usual," said Domina.

"We must wait, then. This concerns the new Choosers and so everyone who is involved with them must be here." Kadreen folded her hands on top of the table, lacing the blunt, squared-off fingers loosely. "Marna, Zo, why not give us a song while we wait? Something—something bright."

They needed no more prompting, but picked up the tembalas and with an almost imperceptible nod between them to establish the beat, started plucking a quick-step dance that involved a melody which seemed to leap from one instrument to the other. It lightened the mood around the table considerably. They were just reaching the finale, with four strums alternating on the drone strings, when Donya and her dark sister Doey bustled in, wiping their hands on their stained aprons, eager to offer full excuses for being late.

Kadreen signaled them to sit with a wave of her hands, so that the dying strum of the tembalas was accompanied by the scraping of chair legs against the wooden floor.

"As you all know, we must talk now of the future for our new Choosers. These girls *are* our future. First, though, we must know from Marna what to expect. What do they know and how fast do they learn?"

Marna and Zo nodded. "What I say now is not new to you. Over the years I have consulted with the mothers and with you, Kadreen, when there was illness. But telling it again to all may bring out some other truths, hidden even from Zo and me.

"All four are bright, quick learners and have their first letters already. Jenna can read sentences and will soon begin on the first of the *Little Books,* though it is Alna who loves the tales the best."

Alinda nodded complacently. "We always told her stories to calm her when her breath would not come easily."

Marna smiled and continued. "Selinda is a dreamy sort and she needs much recalling to her tasks."

Selinda's womb mother laughed. "Takes after her father. Three boys I had after but a week with their fathers. But Selinda's needed so much recalling to his work, I was with him three months."

They all laughed with her.

Marna waited out their laughter. "Pynt—Marga, as I suppose she should be called now, though I shall always think of her as Pynt—is the very quickest at most things—"

Zo interrupted. "But she forgets caution much of the time. We fear that very quickness will lead her into trouble."

Nodding, Marna added, "We do."

"It has already." Catrona shifted in her chair and leaned forward, over the table. "She did not get the sweet she wanted at her first try at the Game."

Marna laughed at that and Zo explained. "She got the sweet anyway. And the larger half at that. Jenna shared it with her."

Kadreen unlaced her fingers, speaking slowly. "They are like shadow sisters, Jenna and Pynt. It will go harder on them when they have their own dark twins, will it not?" She asked it carefully, aware that as a Solitary she had little right to speak of such things. She had come to the Hame as a full adult, choosing to live apart from the busy towns where she had learned her craft, arriving much too late in life to be introduced to the Hame Mysteries or to learn to call up a sister from Alta's eternal dark. "I mean, they shall have to wrench themselves when . . ."

"That is almost seven years from now, Kadreen. And you know what childhood friendships are," said Marna.

"No," Kadreen muttered under her breath.

"We could consider it if they still hold fast together when it is time for the mission," suggested Domina.

"The *Book* speaks of loyalties," reminded Kadreen. "This much I know.

And Mother Alta has asked me to warn all of you about encouraging their special friendship overmuch. Jenna's needs cannot be met by one friend alone. She must be loyal equally to all in the Hame. Not just one teacher, not just one mother, not just one friend. Mother Alta has made that quite clear." She said the words as if they left a sour taste in her mouth.

"She is a *child*, Kadreen," Amalda said. "I would have taken her long ago as my own, had the Mother allowed it."

The others nodded.

"Perhaps she is more than that," Kadreen muttered, but she did not say more.

THE HISTORY

Another game that has a tangled ancient history is the popular "I-Mine" of the Lower Dales, which Lowentrout, in one of his brilliant but eccentric leaps of scholarship, has dubbed "a classic Alta warrior training pattern game." (See his Letter to the Editor, Games Magazine, *Vol. 544.) His evidence, which is extremely shaky, rests on Vargo's highly suspect linguistic shift thesis and interpretations of the priestess codes, rather than the more laborious but detailed archaeological work such as Cowan's and Temple's.*

The game as it is played today is a board-and-counter game, the board consisting of 64 contiguous squares of 32 light and 32 dark. There are an equal number of counters with inscribed faces, 32 with light backs and 32 dark.

The inscriptions are paired, so that there are 32 of each color. They include: a knife, crossed sticks, ribbons tied in a bow, a flower, a circle (presumably representing a stone, since it is called so), an apple, a bowl, a spoon, a threaded pin, grapes (or berries; both names are given), a triangle, a square, a crescent moon, a sun, a crown, a bow, an arrow, a dog, a cow, a bird, a hand, a foot, a rainbow, a wavy line which is called "river" by the players, a tree, a cat, a cart, a house, a fish, a mask, a chair, and a sign which is designated "Alta" and is, in fact, the sign for female that is as ancient as any in the Dales.

The point of the game is to capture the opponent's counters. The play begins with all the counters turned inscription-side down and shuffled, then set onto the squares in a haphazard manner called "scuffling," though light-

backed counters go on the light squares, dark on dark. Play begins with each player turning over two counters. (They may be two of his own or one of each player's.) Then those counters are returned to their face-down positions.

Now the memory part of the game begins, for each player, in turn, turns over two counters, one of each color. If the inscriptions match, he keeps or "captures" them both. As the player turns over the counters, he says—on turning over his own—"I," and if he suspects a pair, as he turns over his opponent's, "Mine." If he suspects (or remembers) they are not paired, he says "Thine." If he should say "I-Mine" to an unmatched pair, he loses a turn. If he says "I-Thine" to a matched pair, he does not win or keep the pair (which are called "suites") and his opponent then has a free opportunity to turn up the two. That's the game at its simplest. But in tournament and adult play, certain inscriptions are also paired. If those paired signs—hand/foot, fish/river, bow/arrow, flower/grapes—are uncovered by the player right after one another, they count as two "suites," rather than one. If the moon suite is uncovered on the very first play, the player gets an extra turn. If the Alta pair is uncovered last, it counts as three. So the game is both a game of memory and of strategy.

If Lowentrout is correct, then another piece of the puzzle of the Dales has been found. But if—as is likelier—this is a later game phenomenon with no early antecedents among the Altites but rather (as A. Baum writes) "a Continental import" (see his naive but striking piece "Point, Counter, Point in the Dales," Games, Vol. 543), then we must search even further for evidence of Altism in the Isles.

THE STORY

Jenna marked the years after her Choosing by certain accomplishments. By the rind of the first year, she had read all the children's books, the *Books of Little Lights*, at least once through and had learned the Game completely. She played at the Game out-of-doors with Pynt and at night before they went to sleep, until the two of them could remember everything set before them and the colors and counts and placements besides.

The second year Jenna mastered the bow and the throwing knife and was allowed to camp out overnight with just Pynt and Little Domina, who was that year to call out her dark sister, having come home from her mission.

Little Domina taught them a new game, one she had learned in another Hame, that of telling frightening stories of girls who had called out demons and ogres from the dark instead of their sisters. The first time she had terrified both Jenna and Pynt, especially as they thought they heard a cat scratching nearby. The second time only Pynt was frightened, and then but a little. The third time Jenna figured out a trick they could play on Little Domina, which had to do with a rope and a blanket and an old tembala with only its top three strings. It so frightened the older girl that she refused to camp with them again, saying that she had much studying to do before her Night of Sisterhood. But Jenna and Pynt knew better. They had to settle for Varsa, who was not as much fun, being stolid, unimaginative, and —so Pynt said—"slightly dim."

Jenna called the third year the year of the Sword and the Ford. She had learned to handle both the short broadsword and the double-edged blade, using the smaller versions made for a child's hand. When she complained that she was almost as tall as Varsa, Catrona, laughing, had put a large sword in her hand. Jenna was able to lift it, but that was all. Catrona had thought she would be content with just the knowledge that an adult sword was as yet beyond her. But Jenna had sworn to herself that she would handle one easily by the year's last turning. She practiced with pieces of wood, heavier and heavier, not even realizing herself that she was growing at a pace far faster than Pynt or Alna or Selinda could maintain. When Catrona had solemnly placed a big sword in her hand on the very last day of the year, Jenna was surprised how light it felt, lighter than any of the pieces of wood she had used and smaller to grip. It sang through the air as she paced it through the seven positions of thrust and the eight of parry.

That was the same day the Selden River overflowed its banks, something that happened only once every hundred years, and a runner from the town came to beg the Hame's assistance in digging a channel to contain the angry waters. All the warriors and the girls went with him; plus Kadreen, for the town of Selden had but an herbwife and she near eighty-five. Mother Alta sent as many of the others as might be spared, though she had been firm about sending too many. They had done what they could, but seven farmers died anyway, out in the fields trying to save their flocks. The town itself was water up to the rooftrees of the houses. When the Altites tried to return up the mountain, the one bridge had been washed away and they had to ford the still-furious river, going across by holding on to a line which Catrona had begun with a well-placed arrow fired across the flood. Jenna and Pynt admired the strength of her arm and aim. Neither of them was fond of the icy water, but they were among the first across. The Sword and the Ford.

The fourth year they began their instruction in the *Book*.

Jenna could feel an itch between her toes. She ignored it. She could see Selinda settling herself more comfortably and hear Alna's rough breathing and feel Pynt's knee touching her own. But she drew herself in and away from them, focusing only on Mother Alta.

The priestess sat whey-faced and stony-eyed in her high-backed chair. She looked small, even shrunken with age. Yet when she opened the *Book* on her lap, she seemed to swell visibly, as if the very act of turning the *Book*'s pages filled her with an awesome power.

Jenna and the others sat cross-legged on the floor before her. They no longer wore their work clothes. Gone were the rough warrior skins, the smudged smocks of the kitchen, the gardener's dirty-kneed pants. Now they dressed alike in their worship clothes: the white and green of young Choosers, with the full sleeves, the belled pants tied at the ankle, their heads covered with scarves as was the custom of girls in the presence of the open *Book*. They were all shining with recent scrubbings and even Selinda's fingernails were clean for once. Jenna noticed them out of the corner of her eye.

Mother Alta cleared her throat, which brought complete attention to her. Then she began with a series of hand signs, mysterious in their meanings but clearly potent. She spoke in a high, nasal voice.

"In the beginning of your lives is the *Book of Light*," she said. "And in the end." Her fingers continued to weave a descant to her words.

The girls nodded, Selinda a half beat behind.

Tap-tap-tap went Mother Alta's great pointing nail on the page. "It is here that all knowledge can be found." *Tap-tap*. The fingers began to dance in the air again. "And here all wisdom set out." *Tap-tap-tap*. "And so we begin, my children. And so we begin."

The girls nodded in rhythm to her words.

"Now you must close your eyes. Yes, that is it. Selinda, you, too. Good. Good. Bring in the dark that I may teach you to breathe. For it is breath that is behind words. And words that are the shapers of knowledge. And knowledge that is the base of understanding. And understanding, the link between sister and sister."

And love? thought Jenna, closing her eyes tightly. *What about love?* But she did not say it aloud.

"This is how you must breathe when you hear the *Book* and . . ."

Mother Alta paused as if to gather them in more thoroughly. "And when you call your sister from the dark."

It was as if, instead of breathing, at her words they all stopped, for the room was completely silent now except for the faint echo of her voice.

So. *We are here,* Jenna thought. *At last.*

Into the silence Mother Alta's nasal voice began again, a voice of instruction that had little warmth or inflection in it. "The body's breath comes and goes without conscious thought, yet there is an art to breathing that will make your every thought larger, your every gift greater, your every moment longer. Without this breath—which I will teach you—your dark sister cannot breathe. She will be condemned to a life of eternal darkness, eternal ignorance, eternal loneliness. Yet no one but the followers of Great Alta knows these things. And if you should ever speak of them to others, you shall die the Death of a Thousand Arrows." Her voice sharpened at the last.

Jenna had heard of that death and could easily imagine the pain, though whether it was a real death or a story death, she could not guess.

Mother Alta stopped speaking and, as if on a signal, all four girls caught their breath and opened their eyes. Alna gave three quick little involuntary coughs.

THE PARABLE

Once five beasts quarreled over what was most important to life: the eyes, the ears, the teeth, the mind, or the breath.

"Let us test this ourselves," said Cat. And as he was the strongest, they all agreed.

So Tortoise took out his eyes and without them he was blind. He could not see sunrise or sunset. He could not see the seven layers of color in his pond. But still he could hear and he could eat and he could think. So the beasts decided that eyes were of little importance.

Next Hare gave away his ears. And without them he could not hear the breaking of twigs near his home or the wind through the briars. He looked very strange. But still he could see and think and was not without the ability to eat well. So there was that for ears.

Then Wolf pulled out all his teeth. It certainly made eating difficult, but he managed. He was a great deal thinner, but he could see and hear and with his sharp mind he devised other ways of eating. So much for teeth.

So Spider gave away his mind. It was such a little mind, anyway, said Cat, and besides, he was no stupider than he had been before. Flies, being even more stupid, still came to his webs, though the webs themselves were very strange, and no longer very beautiful.

And so Cat laughed. "We have proved, dear friends, that the eye, the ear, the teeth, and the mind are of but little importance, as I always suspected. The important one is breath."

"That is yet to be proved," the other beasts said together.

So Cat himself had to give away his breath.

After a while, when it was clear to the others that he was quite dead, they buried him. And that is how five beasts proved completely that it is breath that is the most important thing in life, for, indeed, without it there is no life.

THE STORY

"It is said in the *Book* that we breathe over twenty thousand times in a single day. Half the time we breathe in and half the time out. Imagine, my children, doing something that many times a day and not ever giving it thought." Mother Alta smiled at them, her serpent smile, all lips and no teeth.

The girls smiled back, except for Jenna, who wondered if she would ever be able to breathe again so comfortably unaware. Twenty thousand. The number was beyond her calculations.

"So—say with me:

> *The breath of life,*
> *The power of life,*
> *The wind of life*
> *It flows from me to thee,*
> *Always the breath."*

Dutifully they repeated her words, one phrase at a time, until they could say the entire thing without stumbling. Then she had them repeat it over and over until it was a chant filling the entire room. Ten times, twenty times, a hundred times they repeated it, until at last she silenced them with a wave of her right hand.

"Each morning when you come to me, we will recite that together one hundred times. And then we will breathe—yes, my children, *breathe*—together. We will make my breath yours, and your breath mine. We will do this for a whole year's turning, for the *Book* says, 'And the light sister and the dark sister they shall have one breath.' We will do this over and over until it is as natural to you as life itself."

Jenna thought about the sisters she had seen quarreling and the sisters whom she had seen laughing and crying at different times. But before she could wonder further, Mother Alta's voice recalled her to her task.

"Repeat with me again," said Mother Alta.

And the breathing began.

That night in their room, before the mothers came in, Selinda began talking excitedly. Jenna had never seen her so enthusiastic about anything before.

"I have seen it!" she said, her hands moving in a dreamy, rhythmic accompaniment to her words. "I watched at dinner. Amalda and Sammor, breath for breath they were, though neither of them was watching the other. *Breath for breath.*"

"I saw, too," Pynt said, running her fingers through her dark curls. "But I was watching Marna and Zo."

"I sat between Alinda and Glon by the fire," said Alna. "And I could feel them. Like one bellows, in and out together. Funny not to have noticed it before. I made myself breathe with them and I felt such power. *Well, I did!*" she added in case anyone dared question her.

Jenna said nothing. She, too, had found herself watching the sisters at dinner, though she had observed each pair in turn. But she had also kept an eye on Kadreen as well. It had seemed to her that the Solitary's breathing shifted from one pair of sisters to another whenever she sat close, as if, without thinking, she were drawn into their twinned breath. When Jenna had tried to observe her own patterns, she found that the very act of observation changed the way she breathed. It was simply not possible to be both observer and observed.

Tired by the excitement of the day, the other girls fell asleep quickly. Alna drifted off first, then Pynt, then Selinda, shifting and turning in her bed. Long after, Jenna lay awake, testing her own breathing and matching it to the sleepers' until she could slip easily from one to the next with scarcely any effort at all.

The rest of the year, far into the winter's rind, they learned about breath from Mother Alta. Every morning began with their hundred chantings and the breathing exercises. They learned the difference between nose breathing *(altai)* and mouth breathing *(alani)*, between chest breathing *(lanai)* and the breath that comes from lower down *(latani)*. They learned how to overcome the faintness that came with rapid breath. They learned how to breathe standing, sitting, lying down, walking, and even running. They learned how the proper breathing could send them into a strange dream state even while awake. Jenna practiced the different breaths whenever she could—Cat breath, which gave great running power for short distances; Wolf breath, which gave the runner the ability to go over many miles; Spider breath for climbing; Tortoise breath for deep sleep; and Hare breath to help in leaping. She found that she could outlast Pynt in every contest of strength and running.

"You are getting better and I am getting worse," Pynt said after they had run several miles, stopping to rest by a cross-path. Her chest heaved.

"I am bigger than you," Jenna answered. Unlike Pynt, she was scarcely out of breath.

"You are a giant, but that is not what I mean," Pynt said. The sweat at her brow and neck had turned her curls into damp tendrils.

"I use *altai* and you use *alani* when running, and you have never practiced Wolf breath," said Jenna. "And that is why you are puffing like one of Donya's kettles on boil and I am not." She crossed her arms in front of her, letting the careful, long breaths out through her nose until her head hummed. She had come to love the feeling.

"I do use *altai*," said Pynt, "but not after the first mile. And Wolf does not help. It is all just words anyway. Besides, *altai* is really for calling up a dark sister, and we have years more to go before we do that. The only dark sister you can call up now is me." She fanned herself with her hands.

"Why would I want to call you up?" teased Jenna. "You just pop up whenever you want to. Usually behind me. You are not a dark sister, you are a shadow. That is what they call you, you know! *Jenna's little shadow."*

"Little, maybe," said Pynt, "but that is because my father was small and yours—whoever he was—was a monster. But I am not your shadow."

"No?"

"No! I cannot keep up with you. What kind of shadow is that?"

"What is it they say in the Dales? *Does the rabbit keep up with the cat?"*

"I do not know if they say it in the Dales. I have never been in the Dales, except for the flood, and then all that was being said there was *Hold this. Bail that. Hurry up.*"

"And *Help!!!*"

They laughed together.

"But Donya says it . . ." Pynt hesitated.

"All the time!" They spoke the three words together and began laughing in earnest, so uncontrollably that Pynt stumbled back against a tree and a small rabbit was startled out of the tangled underbrush and leaped away down the path.

"There, cat, see if you can catch up to that one," said Pynt.

At Pynt's dare, Jenna bounded away into the brush after the rabbit and Pynt heard her noisy trampling for many minutes. When Jenna returned, her white braid was peppered with tiny briars, there was a fresh, triangular tear in her leggings, and a long scratch on the back of her right hand. But she held the quivering rabbit in her arms.

"I do not believe it," said Pynt. "How did you get her? She is not shot?"

"My hand is quick where breath is long," Jenna said, speaking in a high, nasal voice and waggling her fingers in imitation of the priestess. "She is yours, little shadow." She handed the trembling rabbit to Pynt.

"But she is only a baby," said Pynt, taking the rabbit from Jenna and stroking its velvety ears. "Did you hurt her?"

"Hurt *her?* Look at me," said Jenna, thrusting her right hand in Pynt's face. "That scratch is from her hind nails."

"Poor, frightened rabbit," said Pynt, pointedly ignoring Jenna.

"Put her down now."

"I am keeping her."

"Let her go," said Jenna. "If you bring her home, Donya will want her for the stew tonight."

"She is mine," said Pynt.

"She is yours," agreed Jenna, "but that is not an argument to convince Donya. Or Doey."

Pynt nodded. "You know, Alna is beginning to sound just like them. Chattering and pompous."

"I know," Jenna said. "I think I liked her better before, full of coughs and fears."

Pynt let the rabbit go and they trotted back up the path to the Hame.

In the heat of the baths, the scratch on Jenna's hand looked inflamed and Pynt examined it worriedly.

"Should you show that to Kadreen?" she asked.

"And what would I say of it? That it is a scar gotten on my shadow's behalf? It is nothing. We have both had worse." She splashed water at Pynt, who ducked under and pulled Jenna by the legs until her head went under as well. Spluttering, they both emerged from the steaming bath and let the cooler air dry them.

"We will have time before dinner . . ." Pynt began, letting the sentence trail off.

"And you would like to help with the babes," said Jenna. *"Again."* But she nodded her head and followed after Pynt to the Great Hall, where there were three infants in the cradles, all fast asleep, and two younglings, the latest a two-year-old just newly fostered at the Hame.

At dinner Jenna sat with Amalda and Sammor, leaving Pynt to play with the little ones and help feed them. Jenna's patience with the younglings lasted only until the first bit of food was flung. She preferred the company of adults.

"Mother Alta says that the dark sisters dwelt in ignorance and loneliness until we called them forth," Jenna said. "Is that true, Sammor?"

Sammor's black eyes grew wary. "That is what the *Book* says," she said carefully, looking at Amalda.

"I did not ask what the *Book* says," Jenna was quick to point out. "We hear the *Book* every day." She imitated Mother Alta's high, nasal tones. *"The dark sisters dwelt in ig-no-rance."* She elongated each syllable.

Sammor looked down at her food.

Jenna persisted. "But when I ask questions of Mother Alta, she reads me another passage in the *Book*. I think it tells only some of the truth. I want to know more."

"Jenna!" exclaimed Amalda, slapping her hand quickly on Jenna's wrist.

Sammor's hand touched her other wrist, but lightly, more as a prelude to speech.

"Wait, let me explain," said Jenna. "Some things Mother Alta teaches us I can see and feel and make true. Like the breathing. When I do it right, I *am* the better for it. But when I talk to the dark sisters, they do not seem to be ignorant. And I have heard Catrona weep with loneliness, though she has a dark sister. And Kadreen seems to savor being a Solitary. So the *Book* does not explain everything. Mother Alta answers no questions beyond what is written."

Sammor breathed deeply. "The *Book* tells all the truth, Jo-an-enna, but it is how we hear it that makes the difference."

"So . . ." Jenna waited.

Sammor and Amalda breathed together several times, slowly, before Sammor continued. "If darkness is ignorance, then I dwelt in ignorance before I saw the light. If to lack knowledge is ignorance, then indeed I was a fool. If to be sisterless is to be lonely, then I was truly alone. But I did not know I was ignorant or lonely before I came here at A-ma's behest. I simply *was.*"

"Was what?" asked Jenna.

"I was myself in the dark but without any understanding of my condition."

Jenna thought a minute. "But Kadreen is solitary and she is not lonely."

Sammor smiled. "There are many kinds of knowledge, child, and Kadreen has but one. There are many ways to be alone and not all are lonely."

"There are also many ways of being together, and for some that is as bad as being alone," Amalda said.

"You talk in riddles," Jenna said. "Riddles are for children. I am not a child anymore." She looked across the table, past the sisters sitting there, to the little table where Pynt was spooning food into two-year-old Kara, Donya's latest fosterling. The child was laughing as she tried to eat, and both she and Pynt were covered with porridge. "Do all loneliness and all jealousy and all anger end when your sister is called forth?"

"So it tells us in the *Book,*" Amalda said.

Behind Jenna, Sammor snorted. "Do not try to fool this one, A-ma, this child who is not a child. She heard Donya curse out Doey this evening for a sauce slightly burned. She sees Nevara still mooning after Marna. She has heard of Selna . . ."

"Sammor, shut up!" Amalda's voice was hard.

"What about Selna?" Jenna turned to Sammor, whose mouth was in a thin line. When she turned back to Amalda, her mouth was the same. "And why does everyone always shut up when I ask about Selna? She was *my* mother, after all. My *second* mother. My fosterer. And no one will talk to me about her." Her voice was low so that it reached only the two of them.

They were silent.

"Never mind, then. I shall ask Mother Alta in the morning."

Amalda and Sammor stood as one, and each held out a hand to Jenna.

"Come, Jenna, come outside," whispered Amalda. "The moon is full and we can walk the paths, all three of us together. Do not ask Mother Alta anything. She will just hurt you with her silence. She will try to break you with obedience to the *Book*. We will tell you what you want to know.

Outside there was a small breeze puzzling through the far trees. The Hame walkways were of a dark stone flecked with something shiny that reflected the moonlight. As the three of them paced by the great walls, the moon was occasionally hidden by thready clouds. Each time Sammor would disappear for a moment, reappearing with the cleared moon.

"There is a story, Jo-an-enna, of the thrice-orphaned child," said Amalda.

"I have heard that tale ever since I was little," Jenna spoke impatiently. "What does my life have to do with stories?"

"There are some who think *you* could be that child," said Sammor a moment before the moon was once again cloud-hidden. Her voice trailed off. One minute her hand held firmly to Jenna's, the next it was gone.

Jenna waited until Sammor reappeared. "That is not I. I have had but two mothers. One dead in the forest and one—I do not know where or how. No one will tell me."

Amalda said softly, "If I had had my way, you *would* have had three mothers, for I would have fostered you."

"Whether you have the name, I always called you that in my mind, A-ma," Jenna said.

"You have called her that in your sleep as well," said Sammor. "And the one time you were sick with the Little Pox. But it was the fever speaking or the dream."

"You see, I have no third mother and besides, you are alive and shall remain so for some time, Alta willing." She held her hand up in the goddess sign, thumb and forefinger touching in a circle. "So, you see, I can *not* be the One spoken of."

They placed their arms around her and spoke as one. "But Mother Alta fears you are and has ordered that no one foster you in truth."

"And my mother Selna?"

"Dead," said Sammor.

"Dead saving you," said Amalda, and she told Jenna all of the tale save the last, about the knife in the babe's hand, though why she left it out she could not have said, but Sammor, too, was careful not to add it.

Jenna listened intently, pacing her breath to theirs. When they were done with the story, she shook her head. "None of that makes me the One, the Anna. Why, then, did she force this orphaning on me? It is not fair. I shall hate Mother Alta forever. She was afraid of a nursery tale. But for me it is my life."

"She did what she thought was right for you and for the Hame," Sammor said, stroking Jenna's white hair on one side while Amalda stroked it on the other.

"She did what she wanted to and for her own reasons," Jenna said, remembering the time she had watched the priestess speak to her mirror. "And a priestess who cares more for words than for her children is . . ." She could not finish, her anger hot and hard.

"That is not true, child, and I forbid you to say it again," said Amalda.

"I will not say it again because *you* forbid it, A-ma. But I cannot promise I will not think it. And I am glad my mission year comes soon, for I want to be away from her stale breath and bleak eyes."

"Jenna!" Amalda and Sammor said together, their shock evident.

Sammor added quickly, "There will be other Mother Altas in the Hames you visit."

"Other Mother Altas?" It was Jenna's turn to be shocked.

"Child, you really are very young," said Amalda, holding her hand. "We may be a small Hame, but in shape we are like them all. There are warriors and kitcheners and gardeners and teachers. And each Hame is headed by a priestess with the blue Goddess sign burned into her palms. Surely you understood that."

"But not like ours," said Jenna, a pleading in her voice. "Not a hard, uncaring woman with a serpent's smile. Please." She turned to Sammor, but the moon had gone suddenly behind a great cloud and Sammor was no longer there.

"*We* may be different—each hunter, each gardener," said Amalda, chuckling. "But, my darling Jenna, I have found that priestesses tend to be the same." She stroked Jenna's cheek. "Though I have never been able to figure out if they start out that way or simply grow into it. However, sweetling, it is time for bed, and besides . . ." She looked up at the sky. ". . . with the moon so well hidden, we will not be able to include Sammor in our conversation out here. Inside, where the lanterns bring her forth, we can say our good-nights. She will be furious with me if we stay out here. She hates to miss anything."

They turned and walked quickly up the stone stairs and into the hall. At the first trembling lantern light, Sammor returned.

Jenna stopped and held out a hand to each of them. "I shall miss you both with all my heart when I am off on mission. But I shall have Pynt with me. And Selinda, who, for all her dreaming, is a good friend. And Alna."

"That you will, child," said Sammor. "Not all are that lucky."

"We will visit as many of the other Hames as we can. A year is a long time. And when we return there will be other young ones for Mother Alta to trouble. I will be old enough then to call my dark sister out, and there is nothing in the tale that says the thrice-orphaned child has a twin! Besides, look at me—do I look like a queen?" She laughed.

"A queen and not a queen," reminded Sammor.

But Jenna's laugh was so infectious that both Amalda and Sammor joined her and, still laughing, they walked toward the girls' room.

Standing in front of Mother Alta's great mirror, each girl in turn raised her hands and stared into her own face intently.

"Lock eyes. Then breathe," Mother Alta instructed. "*Altai* first. Good, good. *Alani*. Breathe. Slower, slower."

Her voice became the only sound, the silvered twin the only sight. In those moments, Jenna could almost feel her own dark sister calling in a far-off voice, low, musical, with a hint of hidden laughter. Only she could not quite make it out. The words were like water over stone. She concentrated so hard trying to hear, it took a hand on her shoulder to recall her to the room.

"Enough, child, you are trembling. It is Marga's turn."

Reluctantly Jenna moved away and the movement of her mirrored self was what finally broke the spell. Pynt stepped in front of her with a broad grin that was reflected back.

So the pattern of the fifth year was set. Breathing exercises, mirror exercises, and then a reading from the *Book* with long, weighty explications from Mother Alta. Selinda mostly dozed through the history lessons, with her eyes wide open. But Jenna could tell from the glossy blue of her eyes that she was fast asleep. Alna and Pynt often had trouble sitting through the endless lectures, poking each other and occasionally breaking out into fits of giggles, for which they were rewarded with a bleak stare by the priestess. But Jenna was fascinated by it all, though why she could not say. She took it in and argued it out, though when she spoke out loud, she was silenced by Mother Alta's short responses that were not, after all, answers but merely simple restatements of the things she had just said. So Jenna's arguments soon became silent ones, the more unanswerable because of it.

THE HISTORY

In the Museum of the Lower Dales is the remainder of a large standing mirror whose antiquity is without question. The ornate, carved wood frame has been dated at two thousand years, and is in fact of a type of laburnum not seen in those parts for centuries. Riddled with wormholes and fire-scorched, it is the one whole wood piece discovered in the Arrundale dig. It was not directly in the gravemound but buried separately some hundred meters distant. Wrapped in a waxy shroud and contained in a large iron casket, the mirror is notably unmarred from its long interment.

We know this was a mirror because large fragments of coated glass were found embedded in the shroud. Obviously of sophisticated make, the shards had beveled edges and a backing of an amalgam of mercury and tin, which indicates a glass-making craftsmanship unknown in the Dales but popular in the major cities of the Isles as early as the G'runian period.

What, then, was such a mirror used for and why its elaborate burial? There have been two likely theses put forth by Cowan and Temple, and a third, rather shaky mystical suggestion by the indefatigable mytho-culturist, Magon. Cowan, reminding us that artwork was practically unknown in the Hames save for the great tapestries and the carvings on the mirror, argues the provocative idea that handsomely framed mirrors in which living figures were artfully framed were—in fact—the artwork of the Alta sororities. Lacking the skill to draw or sculpt, they saw the human figure as reflected in the mirror as the highest from of art. The burial, Cowan further asserts, suggests that this particular piece was the property of the ruler of the Hame; perhaps only her image was allowed to be reflected in the glass. It is a fascinating theory set down with wit and style in Cowan's essay "Orbis Pictus: The Mirrored World of the Hames," Art 99. What is especially intriguing about Cowan's thesis is that it flies in the face of all other anthropological work with primitive artless cultures, none of which feature mirrors, great or small, in their tribal homes.

Professor Temple, on the other hand, stakes out the more conventional ground in the chapter "Vanities" in his book Alta-Natives . He suggests that the Hames, being places of women, would naturally be filled with mirrors. He offers no explanation, however, for the peculiar burial of the piece.

Though his later work has been pilloried by feminist dialecticians, it is the very sensibleness of his thesis that recommends it.

Off in the stratosphere once again is Magon, who tries to prove (in "The Twinned Universe," monograph, Pasden University Press, #417) that the great mirror found in the Arrundale dig was part of a ritual or patterning device in which young girls learned to call up their dark sisters. Leaving aside the flimsiness of the dark-sister thesis for the moment; we find the monograph offers no real proof that the mirror had any but the most mundane of uses. Magon cites the odd carvings on the frame, but except for the fact that each carving has a mirror image on the opposite side—a perfect symmetry that reflects its use as a mirror frame and nothing more (if I may be forgiven the little joke)—there is little else to back up his wild thesis.

THE STORY

Mother Alta touched the Goddess sign at the right side of the mirror frame and sighed. Now that the four girls were gone, the room was quiet again. She had come to treasure more and more the quiet aftermath, the echoing silence of her rooms when no one else was there. Yet this very evening the rooms would be filled again—with Varsa, her foster mother, and the rest of the adult sisters. Varsa would be saying her final vows, calling her sister from the dark. That is, if she could remember all the words and could concentrate long enough. It was always hardest on the slower girls, and Varsa was none too bright. And if, as had happened before, the dark sister did not emerge on the Night of Sisterhood, despite Varsa's years of training and the vocal encouragement of the others, there would be tears and recriminations and the great sobbing gasps of a disappointed child. Even with the assurance that the dark sister would eventually appear (and Mother Alta knew of no instances when one did *not*), the girl's hopes were so entwined with the ceremony it was always a terrible blow.

She sighed again. She was definitely not looking forward to the evening. Putting a hand on each side of the mirror, she drew herself so close to it, her breath fogged the glass. For a moment her image looked younger. She closed her eyes and spoke aloud as if the mirror twin could hear her.

"Is she the One? Is it Annuanna, Jo-an-enna who is the White Goddess returned? How can she not be?" Mother Alta opened her eyes and wiped the fog away with the long, loose sleeve of her robe. The mirror's green eyes stared back at her. She noticed new lines etched across the image's forehead and frowned at it, adding yet another line. "The child runs farther, dives deeper, moves faster than any child her age. She asks questions I cannot answer. I *dare not* answer. Yet there is no one in Selden Hame who does not love her. Excepting me. Oh, Great Alta, except me. I fear her. I fear what she may, all unwitting, do to us.

"Oh, Alta, speak to me, thou who dancest between the raindrops and canst walk on the back of the lightning." She held her hands up to the mirror, so that the blue on her palms was repeated. How new the mark looked, how old her hands. "If she *is* the One, how do I tell her? If she is not, have I done wrong in keeping her apart? She *must* remain apart, else she taints them all." Her voice ended in a pleading whisper.

The room was silent and Mother Alta leaned both palms against the mirror. Then she drew back. The moist shadow of each hand shimmered on the surface.

"You do not answer your servant, Great Alta. Do you not care? If only you would give me a sign. *Any* sign. Without it the decisions are mine alone."

She turned abruptly from the mirror and left the room just as the prints of her hands faded from the glass.

Mother Alta's room was crowded with sisters, light and dark, the only singleton being Varsa. Kadreen, as a Solitary, could not take part in the ceremony and, of course, the younger girls were not present.

The little fires in the lanterns blew about merrily and in the hearth there was a great blaze. Shadows danced across the ceiling and floor in profusion. Because the fresh rushes on the floor had been mixed with dried rose petals, the room was sweet with the smells of past springs.

Varsa, her hair crowned with fresh woodflowers, stood with her back to the hearth as if the fire could warm her. But Mother Alta knew she was cold and afraid, even though the flush of excitement stained her cheeks. She was naked, as naked as her sister would come from the dark the first time. *If she comes at all,* the priestess thought warily.

Mother Alta and her dark sister walked over to Varsa holding their right hands up in blessing. Varsa bowed her head. When the blessing was done, they removed Varsa's crown of flowers and threw it into the hearth. The fire consumed it eagerly, giving back another sweet smell. In past days, the girls' garments had been stripped from them in front of the fire and thrown into the flames as well. But that was in the days of great plenty. In a small, poor

Hame, there were many economies to be made, even at the time of ceremony. Mother Alta had made that particular change ten years before, to
only a small amount of grumbling from the sisters.

The priestess and her dark sister held out their right hands and Varsa
took them eagerly, her own hands sweaty and cold. They led her to the
mirror, between the rows of white-clad sisters, each holding a single red
blossom. In the silence, their steps through the cracking rushes seemed as
loud as thunderclaps. Varsa could not stop shivering.

Slowly Mother Alta and her sister turned Varsa around three times in
front of the mirror, and at each turn the watching women murmured, "For
your birth. For your blood. For your death." Then the priestesses stopped
the spinning girl, keeping their hands on her shoulders lest she fall. Often a
nervous girl ate little for days before the ceremony, and fainting was common. But Varsa, though she trembled, did not faint. She stared at her image
in the glass and raised her hands, her fear blotching her small breasts and
the flush creeping down her neck from her cheeks. She closed her eyes,
slowed her breathing, and opened her eyes again.

From behind her, Mother Alta and her twin intoned:

> Dark to light
> Day to night
> Hear my plea,
> Thee to me,

Varsa turned her palms toward her breasts and made a slow, beckoning
motion, reciting the chant along with the two priestesses. Over and over
and over she called, till first the dark priestess, then Mother Alta, dropped
away and only Varsa's soft importunings could be heard.

The room was tense with anticipation as the sisters all breathed in Varsa's
rhythm.

A slight mist began to form on the mirror, veiling Varsa's image, clothing
it in a mantle of moisture. Varsa caught her breath at the sight, swallowed
hard, and missed a beat of the chant. As she stopped, the mist faded slowly,
first at the edges and then contracting inward to a white, snowy spot over
the heart.

Varsa kept up the chant for another few minutes, but her eyes were
brimmed with tears and she knew with the others that it was no good. Once

the mist began to break up, all hope of the sister emerging that night was gone.

Mother Alta and her sister touched Varsa on the back, below the shoulder blades, whispering, "It is over for tonight, child."

Varsa lowered her arms slowly and then, suddenly, put her hands up to her face and wept aloud. Her shoulders shook, and though the priestesses whispered to her to stop, she could not. Her mother and her mother's dark sister came over and draped a green cloak around her shoulders and led her away.

Mother Alta turned to the others. "It happens," she said. "Never mind. She will call her sister another night, without the extra burden of the ceremony. It will be as good in the end."

Nodding and arguing among themselves, the women left the room to go to the kitchen, where a feast awaited. They would eat well, whatever the night's outcome.

But Catrona and her dark sister Katri waited. "It is never as good," Catrona said fiercely to Mother Alta.

Katri nodded, adding, "The bond is not the same."

Catrona touched her on the arm. "Remember Selna . . ."

"You, Catrona, you, Katri—you are never to say this to Varsa. Not ever." Mother Alta's hands were clenched. "The child has a right to believe in her sister. *You shall not say other.*"

Catrona and Katri turned and walked silently out of the room.

Varsa was still weeping in the morning, her eyes raw-looking, her nails bitten to the quick.

Jenna and Pynt sat on either side of her at the table, stroking her hands.

Pynt murmured, "But you will call her eventually. She will come. No one who calls has ever gone without."

Varsa snuffled and swiped at her nose with the back of her hand. "It is the worst thing that can happen. All those people staring and then my sister not coming. Nothing worse could ever happen in my whole life."

"Of course something worse could happen," said Pynt cheerfully. "You tell her, Jenna. Of course something worse could happen."

Jenna made a face at Pynt. "Some help you are," she mouthed.

"Well, tell her, Jenna," Pynt said.

Jenna thought a minute. "You could be without a mother. Or without friends," she said. "Or you could be Hameless. Why—you could live in a town and never even know about sisters. *Those* would be worse."

Varsa stood up, pulling her hands angrily from theirs. "What do you know? You have not even tried yet. Nothing could be worse." She walked away through the arch.

"Let her go, Jenna," said Pynt as Jenna started up after her. "She is right, you know. Nothing *could* be worse."

"Oh, there you go being stupid, Pynt. There is a lot worse. But she *is* right about something. We cannot know how she feels. Not yet."

"Well, I know one thing," Pynt said, "I am not going to make a mistake. I am going to get my sister the first time."

Selinda, sitting across the table, shook her head. "Why such a fuss? She will get her sister eventually." She spooned more porridge into her mouth.

But in fact it was Alna who understood best. "Right now it hurts her more than anything and of course she cannot think otherwise. And nothing we say will console her. I was the same when I had to choose the kitchen. And now—well—I cannot think of a better place to be." She smiled in satisfaction and cleared the table.

As soon as Alna left the room, Selinda spoke up. "How can she say that? She knows that being in the fields and gardens is the *best*. She, of all people . . . How can she say it?"

Pynt put her hand on Selinda's but Jenna laughed. "What is it they say? *Words are merely interrupted breath.* That is how she says it. By interrupting her breathing. Easy, quite easy, Selinda."

Selinda got up and walked away without speaking.

Pynt slid close to Jenna and whispered urgently, "You do not suppose we were the cause of her failure?"

"Because we watched from behind the door?" Jenna asked. "No one saw. No one heard. And we will know the ceremony ourselves in time. We hurt nothing."

"But suppose . . ." Pynt let the sentence hang.

"Varsa is slow and afraid of too many around her. That is what caused it. Not two extra pairs of eyes and ears. You saw her; you heard how she hesitated the moment she saw the mist." Jenna shook her head slowly. "She will find her sister. And soon."

"I know what happened last night to Varsa has affected us all. It happens, sometimes, that a girl does not call out her sister during the Night of Sisterhood. It does not happen often, but it does happen."

Jenna elbowed Pynt meaningfully.

"But you shall see," said Mother Alta. "All will be for the best." She raised her hands and held them in Alta's blessing over the girls.

They bowed their heads and closed their eyes.

"Sometimes Great Alta, she who runs across the surface of the rivers, who hides her glory in a single leaf, sometimes she tests us and we are too small to see the pattern. All we feel is the pain. But there *is* a pattern and that you must believe."

Selinda made a small, comfortable sound and Alna nodded her head, as if remembering her Night of Choosing. Pynt poked a tentative finger into Jenna's leg but Jenna ignored her, thinking, *there is something more. I feel it. She is saying something more.* For some reason she felt chilled and there was a strange emptiness in her stomach, though they had just come from the meal.

Mother Alta spoke the words of Alta's grace, the girls following in response. "Great Alta, who holds us . . ."

The girls answered, "In thy care."

"Great Alta, who enfolds us . . ."

"In thy bounteous hair."

"Great Alta, who knows us . . ."

"As thy only kin."

"Great Alta, who shows us . . ."

"How to call the twin."

"Great Alta, give us grace."

The girls repeated, "Great Alta, give us grace." Then they looked up at Mother Alta and began to breathe in her rhythm. After they had chanted the hundredfold breathing prayer and had worked for an hour, each in turn, in front of the great mirror, Mother Alta had them sit once more on the floor in front of her. She took the *Book* from its ornate wood stand and opened it to the place marked off with a gold ribband.

"It says in the *Book* that *Before a child becomes a woman she shall greet the sisters of her faith in every Hame, for a child who knows not of the world chooses out of ignorance and fear, just as the dark sisters before they came into the light.*" She looked up from the *Book,* smiling her smile of little warmth. "And what does this mean, my children?"

Jenna sat still. She no longer answered immediately, even though she knew the expected response, for the priestess always became angry when she spoke first. Now she held her counsel, reserving the last place to speak, summing up when the others were done, adding to it and refining.

"It means our mission," said Alna, clearing her throat halfway through the short sentence, a sure sign of spring.

Selinda, elbowed by Alna, added, "We go to every Hame in turn."

"Or at least as many as we can get to in the year," added Pynt.

Mother Alta nodded. "And Jo-an-enna—have you nothing to add?"

Jenna nodded back, holding on to her right braid as she spoke as a reminder to herself not to be sharp. "It is true, Mother, that we go from Hame to Hame, but not just to visit and play. We must go with open eyes and ears, mind and heart. We go to learn, to compare, to think, and to . . . to . . ."

"To grow!" interrupted Pynt.

"Very good, Marga," said Mother Alta. "And it is that growth the Mother of each Hame must be concerned with. Sometimes growth comes when all the girls go together and . . ."

Jenna felt the cold return. She pulled on her braid until it hurt in order to keep herself from shivering.

Mother Alta drew in a deep breath and instinctively the girls breathed in with her, all except Jenna. "And sometimes the growth comes when they are apart. It is my judgment therefore, as your guide and as the Mother of this Hame, that you will do best separated during your mission this year. Marga, Selinda, and Alna, you will begin by going to Calla's Ford. But you, Jo-an-enna . . ."

"No!" Jenna said, the word exploding from her. Startled, the other girls moved away from her anger. "Girls are never separated in their mission year if there be more than one girl ready."

"Nowhere does it say that in the *Book,*" Mother Alta said slowly, carefully, as if speaking to a very young child. "All the rest is mere custom and laziness, subject to change *at the discretion of the Mother of the Hame.*" She opened the *Book* to another page, one not marked by the ribband, but obviously often consulted, for the pages stayed open without any pressure from her hands. "Here, child, read this aloud."

Jenna stood and read the sentence underlined by Mother Alta's long nail. Her lips moved but no sound came out.

"Aloud, Jo-an-enna!" commanded the priestess.

Jenna's voice was strong as she read, betraying neither her anger nor her sorrow. *"The Mother's wisdom is in all things. If it is cold, she shall light the fire. If it is hot, she shall let air into the room. But all she does, she does for the good of her children."* Jenna sat back down.

"You see, my child," said Mother Alta, a smile starting in her mouth and ending up, for the first time, in her eyes, "you will do as I say, for I am the Mother and I know what is best for you, Jo-an-enna, and what is best for the others. They are like little flowers and you the tree. They cannot grow in the shade you cast."

Pynt's hand crept into Jenna's and squeezed, but Jenna did not respond. She willed the tears *not* to start in her eyes. She willed her heart to stop pounding so wildly. Slowly she brought her breath under control and stared at Mother Alta, thinking, *I will not forgive you this, not ever.*

Mother Alta raised her hands over the girls, and Selinda, Alna, and Pynt obediently bowed their heads to receive her final words. But Jenna stared up at her, dark eyes into green, and had the blessing of Great Alta flung into her upturned face.

They packed the next week, on a morning so filled with the trillings of birdsong, Jenna's heart ached. She had been silent about the priestess' ruling, but everyone else at the Hame was abuzz with it. The girls, especially, had been inconsolable and Pynt had cried herself to sleep every night. But Jenna nursed her sorrow to herself, thinking that way she would not double anyone else's, not realizing that her silence was more troubling to the sisters than any tears might have been.

Only once during the week did she refer to it. She pulled Amalda aside as the girls and their mothers went on the traditional walk around the Hame for departing missioners.

"Am I a tree shading everyone?" she asked Amalda. "A-ma, does nothing grow around me?"

Amalda smiled and pulled Jenna into the circle of her arms. Then she turned her around and pointed to a great chestnut by the path. "Look under that," Amalda said.

Jenna looked. By the roots of the tree grew white trillium and clumps of violets, all nodding in the breeze.

"Your friends are hardy little plants," said Amalda. Then she laughed. "And you are not yet a mighty tree. Another few years, perhaps." But she hugged Jenna fiercely and they walked in silence the rest of the way around the Hame.

Jenna remembered that silence as she packed, putting her best leggings at the bottom and her nightdress in the middle. She reserved the top space for the food she would get from Donya, and for her corn doll. She picked up the doll and was preparing to put it in the pack when Pynt stopped her.

"No," said Pynt. "Give me your doll, the light sister, and I will give you mine. Then we will not really be parted."

Her earnestness convinced Jenna, who traded dolls solemnly. Pynt stroked the cornsilk hair before setting Jenna's doll in her own pack.

Selinda gave Jenna a moon snail shell which had been a present from her mother on the day of her Choosing, and Alna gave her a posy of dried flowers.

"From the garden. I've always kept it by my pillow," she said shyly, as if it were a secret, though they had all known of it.

Jenna cut a lock of her hair for each of them and, as she set the white curl in her friends' palms, said quietly, "It is only a year. One year. And then we will be back here, together again."

She had meant it to sound brave and jaunty, but Alna turned away, and Selinda gave her a quick hug and ran from the room. Only Pynt stayed, staring down at the bone-white curl resting in her hand.

Down in the warrior yard, Catrona waited for them by the tabletop map. She stared at each of them in turn, noting Alna's reddened eyes, Selinda's pale complexion, the determined look on Pynt's face. Only Jenna seemed calm.

Folding her arms, Catrona said briskly, "Let us go over the way again. And then you must be off. Remember—*The sun moves slowly, but it crosses the land.* You must not waste the best part of the day. The trip is long enough as it is."

The girls moved closer to the table.

"Now show me the way," said Catrona.

Pynt started forward.

"Not you, Marga. You know the woods so well, I would have Selinda or Alna show me. *Just in case.*"

Alna's hand flew rapidly along the route, first west away from the sun, down the path toward the town of Slipskin, and along the river. At the mountain's foot she hesitated for a moment and Selinda's hand pushed hers off toward the south.

"And that," Catrona interrupted, "Jenna, is where you leave them. You must take the more northerly journey to Nill's Hame. Your markers are what?"

Jenna moved closer to the map, tracing the path with a steady hand. "The river has two paths. I go around toward the Old Hanging Man, the mountain with the high cliff shaped like a man's face, till I come to the Sea of Bells, the lily field."

"Good. And you others?"

"We go with our back to the Old Man, our faces toward the twin peaks of Alta's Breast," Pynt said.

They recited the rest of the route in like fashion, several times through, so that Catrona was finally assured. Then she gave them each a hug, reserving the final embrace for Jenna.

* * *

All the women of Selden Hame waited at the great gates. Even the outer guards had been alerted and had come in from their posts. They stood in silence while the girls knelt before the priestess for their final blessing.

"Hand to guide them," Mother Alta intoned. "Heart to shield them. Hold them in thy hair forevermore."

"Evermore," the watching women echoed.

Jenna lifted her face and stared at the priestess, but Mother Alta was already looking down the road.

The girls hoisted their packs and started off to the accompanying ululation of the watchers. The eerie quavering sounds followed them around the first three turns of the trail, but long after the sounds had died away, the girls were silent, thinking only of the path.

BOOK THREE

Sister Light, Sister Dark

THE MYTH

Then Great Alta shall touch her only daughter with a wand of light and the child will fall away from her down to Earth. Wherever the child steps, there will spring up flowers like bells that shall ring hosannas to her name. "O child of light," the bells will peal, "O little sister, O white daughter, O queen who is to come."

THE LEGEND

Once a shepherdess from Neverston went up the flank of the Old Man to tend her flock. But it was her first time up the mountain and darkness still stained his granite cheeks. The girl was young and afraid. Fearing to lose her way, she put a handful of white pebbles in her apron pocket and at every step she placed a pebble on a green leaf to mark her path.

All day she watched her ewes and lambs eating the sweet spring grass that was the Old Man's beard, and prayed for guidance for a safe return.

While the shepherdess and her flock remained on the high mountain, the pebbles slowly took root and became tiny white bells.

When it was evening and the sun had set behind the Old Man's head, the shepherdess led her flock safely home, following the sound of the tinkling bells. Or at least that is what they say in Neverston, where "lamb-bells," or Lilies of the Old Man's Valley, grow in great profusion.

THE STORY

It had been cooler along the water than at the Hame and the girls had stopped at the confluence of the two rivers to eat their noon meal and wash off some of the trail dirt. It was there they said their farewells to Jenna. Selinda and Alna had wept without restraint, but Pynt had laughed oddly and winked at Jenna. Shrugging slightly, Jenna winked back, but as she trudged up the twisting northern path alone, she was still puzzling over Pynt's odd behavior.

As she walked, Jenna swung her head from side to side as Amalda and Catrona had taught her. Just because she was thinking did not mean that her ears and eyes should be unaware. As Amalda was fond of saying, *You must set the trap before the rat passes, not after.*

She noted a pair of squirrels chasing each other through the treetops, the scat of a large mountain cat, and deer tracks. An owl pellet below a tree contained the skull of a wood mouse. There would be much to eat if she needed it, though she still had plenty in her pack. But she checked everything as a cook might check the larder.

Stopping for a moment to listen to the trillings of a wood thrush, Jenna smiled. She had been worried about being alone, but though she missed Selinda and Alna and especially Pynt, she realized with a kind of surprised elation that she did not *feel* alone. This puzzled her. She wanted to hold on to her anger, as if anger alone could make her strong enough, so she repeated as if it were a prayer, "I will never forgive her. I will hate Mother Alta forever." But the words seemed hollow. Spoken aloud in the joyous cacophony of the forest, the litany of hate had no power. She shook her head.

"I *am* the woods," she whispered. Then she said, more loudly, "The woods are in *me!*" She laughed, not because the thought was humorous but because it was true, and because Mother Alta, all unknowing, had sent her out to her true destiny.

"Or . . ." she said, hesitantly, *"did* she know?"

There was no answer from the woods, at least none that she could understand, so she put her fingers to her mouth and whistled like a thrush. It returned her call instantly.

* * *

Sunset came earlier than Jenna expected because she was still in the deep woods and in the massive shadow of the Old Man's western flank. She had hoped to come upon the white lily field by dark, having gotten the impression from Catrona that she should spend the first night there. But they had wasted so much time with their good-byes, and then she had not pushed herself along the trail, dawdling and enjoying her freedom. Now she would have to camp in the woods rather than the field.

In the gathering dark, she picked a tree with a high crotch, for the cat scat had been fresh. Not wanting to take chances with a cat in her face at night, she decided to sleep high up in the tree. It would not be comfortable, but she had been trained how to do it. And, as Catrona often said, *Better the cat under your heel than at your throat!*

She made a small fire below the tree and ringed it with stones. It would be only a small protection, none at all if the cat were really interested. But it might scare off one that was only mildly curious.

Then she climbed the tree and stashed her pack several feet above her head. She balanced her unsheathed sword in a branch just above the fork she had chosen to sleep in. That way she would be able to get to it quickly. Her knife she kept by her side.

The tree was smooth, not nubbly like the first tree she and Pynt had ever tried to sleep in. She chuckled to herself, remembering the uncomfortable bark. Both she and Pynt had had the print of that bark impressed on their backs. They had joked about it in the morning. Suddenly she missed Pynt unbearably, so she stretched up, took down the pack, and removed the doll from it. She held the doll tightly in her arms and imagined she could smell Pynt's hands on its skirt. Her eyes grew misty at the thought, so she looked up at the stars through the interlacing of limbs, and tried to name the patterns, as if naming them would keep away her tears.

"The Huntress," she whispered into the dark. "The Great Hound." She sighed. "Alta's Braid."

The sound of river water washing over stone lulled her quickly and she was asleep before the count was done, one hand slipping off her lap to dangle in the air.

In the morning, Jenna woke up before the sun had found the valley, cramped and with a tingling sensation in the dangling hand. But that disappeared as soon as she used it. The cramp in her right leg took longer to go away. She descended the tree with the sword, climbed back up for her pack, then stretched lazily before looking around.

The early birds were already heralding the dawn. She recognized the dry, rattling chatter of a mistle thrush and the peremptory *tew-tew-tew* of a pair of ouzels. She saw a flash of rusty brown she thought might be a nightingale, but as it was silent, she could not be sure. Smiling, she set about making her breakfast, using some of the grain she had carried with her in a leathern sack, the flask of goat's milk, and the pack of dried berries Donya had gifted each girl. It was a feast and she felt herself making a quiet chuckling sound way in the back of her throat like the ouzel, and the realization caused her to laugh aloud.

Before leaving her campsite, she checked carefully that there was no sign of her stay there.

Except for my smell, she reminded herself, for Catrona had always said a cat might be able to track one of Alta's hunters, but no one else should.

Belting on her sword, she hoisted her pack, patted the knife at her hip, and started off down the trail.

Around a great bend in the track that followed the meandering of the river, she came upon a meadow so broad she could not see the other side. Unexpected and beautiful, the meadow made her lose her breath. The expansive green was sprinkled with tiny white flowers.

Jenna sang out in delight, a high crowing that she turned into a song of triumph. *So, I had been that close all night long and had never known it. But to come upon it in the day, with the flowers open and the sun shining down, was much the best way to do it,* she thought.

Her song masked any other sound she might have heard, and that was why the hand on her shoulder startled her. She put her own hand to her knife, drew it, and turned in the same instant, bringing the knife up in the swift, clean motion she had practiced so often.

Pynt stepped back just as quickly, though Jenna's longer arms meant the knife slashed Pynt's tunic, up and over the heart.

"Some welcome!" Pynt said, putting her hand over the ripped tunic breast and breathing a sigh of relief when she realized the shirt beneath was still whole.

"You—you startled me!" was all Jenna could manage before dropping her knife and enfolding Pynt in a tremendous embrace. "Oh, Pynt, I could have killed you."

"No one can kill her shadow," Pynt said, her voice trembling and a bit muffled against Jenna's hair. She moved out of Jenna's embrace. "My fault, really. I should have known better than to come upon you that way. But I thought you knew I was behind you. Alta knows I made enough noise." She grinned broadly. "When I am in a hurry, I am a regular twig breaker."

"What are you doing here?" Jenna asked, a tinge of anger in her voice. "Is this another of your *secret* ways?"

"You did not expect me?" Pynt looked bewildered. "But I thought you agreed. When I winked, you winked back. You knew there was no way I was going to stay with those two and let you go off alone. Selinda stares off into space and plunges into rabbit holes every third step, and Alna chatters as endlessly as Donya." She paused. "Without you, I could not stand them. And . . ." She sighed. "I could not let you go off alone."

"Oh, Pynt, think. *Think!*" Jenna pleaded. "Use your head. Those two will never find the way on their own." She shook her head. "Selinda still thinks the sun rises in the west."

"Of course they will," Pynt answered. "It is all one trail, no turns, until Calla's Ford. All they have to do is follow the river. They can both use their knives, so there is no danger. And they have each other, you know. Often girls are sent out on their own because there are no others the right age ready to go."

"I could follow the way on my own, Pynt."

Pynt looked stricken. "You do not want me here?"

"Of course I *want* you here, Pynt. You are my dearest companion."

"I am your shadow," Pynt reminded her quickly, a bit of her old spark returned.

"You are a twig breaker," said Jenna. She punched Pynt lightly on the shoulder. "But you did not think this all the way through."

"I have been thinking about this since old Serpent Mouth said you had to go a separate way."

"Old Serpent Mouth?" Jenna put her head back and began to laugh.

Pynt joined her and soon the two of them were so helpless in their laughter, they had to unbuckle their swords and throw down their packs. They rolled in the meadow grass, crushing hundreds of white lily bells beneath them. Each time one of them stopped laughing, the other would think up a new name for the priestess, both scurrilous and silly, and the laughter would begin anew. They went on this way until at last Jenna was able to sit up, wipe a hand across her eyes, and breathe in deeply.

"Pynt . . ." she began seriously and, when Pynt still giggled, said more sternly, "Marga!"

Pynt sat up, sober-faced. "You have never called me that."

" 'Pynt' is a child's name. We are on our mission year. Now we must both be adults."

"I am listening, *Jo-an-enna.*"

"Marga, I meant it—about thinking things all the way through. What do you suppose they will do to you—to us—when they find out we disobeyed Mother Alta? Have you thought about that?"

"They will not know until we return in a year, and by then we will have done so many glorious deeds and become so grown up, *Jo-an-enna*, that we will be forgiven." She grinned at Jenna with a crooked smile and head cocked to one side that made her irresistible.

Jenna shook her head again. "You are impossible, Pynt."

They stood up, brushed each other off, and Pynt picked three white flowers out of Jenna's hair. Then, shouldering their packs, they buckled on their swords and started off through the meadow, singing jauntily.

THE SONG

Come, Ye Women

Oh, come, ye women of the Isles,
And listen to my song,
For if ye be but thirteen years,
Ye've not been women long.

And if ye be threescore and ten,
No longer women be,
Or so say all the merry men
Who count so cruel-ly.

But women we be from our birth,
And will be till we die.
Our counte is made so differently
To give the men that lie.

Oh, come, ye women of the Isles,
And listen to my song,
For we be women all through life,
Where life and love are long.

THE HISTORY

"Very little music from the early Alta worshippers survives today. Because of the destruction by fire of most of the Hames in the tragic period of the Gender Wars, there are no large manuscript sources before the Covillein Booke of the sixteenth century. Fragmentary sources from earlier periods contain a handful of lullabies, several mangled ballads, and one instrumental dance scored for the 'tembala,' an instrument no longer extant. From the scoring, the tembala appears to be a stringed instrument of the guitar family with five melody strings and two drones."—Arne von Tassle, Dictionary of Early Music, *Vol. A.*

It is clear from the passage above that Dr. von Tassle, the world's greatest authority on Early Music of the Isles, believes categorically that little music from the Alta Hames has survived till today. In flagrant disagreement, Magon—who readily admits that he is no music expert—cities modern Dales balladry and songs as proof positive that a vital and prolific musical heritage is preserved in the Highlands and Valleys. In yet another reference-poor monograph (*"Music of the Spheres,"* Nature and History, *Vol. 47), Magon insists that there were four major categories of Alta music: religious tunes, lullabies and everyday songs, historical balladry, and dialectics.

His thesis concerning the religious tunes is, perhaps, the only tenable one. Certainly songs (which he cites) such as the fragmentary plainsong "Alta," with its plaintive refrain "Great Alta, salve my soule," could possibly be traced to religious ceremonies. But the song itself is such a close relative to the seventeenth-century "Lyke Wake Dirge" of the North Country that it is more than likely a modern reconstruction of that old song.

When Magon tries to link the charming and famous "Catte Lullaby," which had been found scribbled on the battered flyleaf of a sixteenth-century ballad book, to the early Garunian period of the Hames, he is sailing in choppier water. It is almost certainly a composed song, though, like many others of the time, patterned closely on the old oral-tradition tunes. Magon does not, for example, seem to realize that the word "catkin" has no written source prior to the mid-sixteenth century and was certainly not used to mean "kitten" or "little cat" at that time, further invalidating his early dating.

The ballads that Magon cites in the section on historical balladry are of little interest tunewise, as they are derivative of famous standing ballads of *later composition. As to their historicity—well, he simply offers the same old shaky thesis about the White Goddess, the albino girl of exceptional height and strength who single-handedly both destroyed and saved the Alta worship system. Magon states this thesis but offers no more historical evidence when talking about the ballads except the internal evidence of the rhymes themselves, which any scholar knows is difficult to count on given the mutability of folk rhyme. We should as soon trust legends.*

As to the dialectic songs, such as the infamous "Come, Ye Women," with its preposterous pornographic double entendres on the words "counte" and "lie"—it has already been well proved by von Tassle, Temple, and others that this song is a nineteenth-century fake, composed at a time when feminist agitators were once more on the rise throughout the Isles, linking themselves backward in time with the Alta Luxophists.

So once again Magon's reputation as an academic and scholar has been proved to be a tissue of thinly woven cloth, the threads tattered and worn.

THE STORY

Walking through the meadow proved to be more work than either Jenna or Pynt had thought. If they went straight across, they would leave a trail of crushed lily bells that even a child might follow, and Catrona's first rule in the woods had been: *No tracks, no trouble.* Besides, the ground was spongy and it made loud sucking noises as they walked, noises which provoked Pynt to giggles. So they backtracked and went, instead, along the tree line that circled the enormous sward.

By the time the sun was directly overhead, they had gotten only a third of the way, and the flower-covered green still stretched endlessly before them.

"I have never seen an ocean," Pynt grumbled as they marched along. "But it cannot be any larger than this."

"Why do you think it is known as the *Sea* of Bells?" Jenna asked.

"I thought that was just a name, like the 'Old Hanging Man.' It takes a great deal of imagination to see a man's face in that rock," Pynt said.

"How would you know? You have not seen any men."

"I have, too."

"When?"

"When we were helping at Selden. At the flood. They are a hairy lot."

"Lumpy, too," Jenna said, walking with an exaggerated swagger.

Pynt giggled.

By evening they could see a faint smudge on the horizon which Jenna thought might be trees.

"The end of it, I think."

"I hope."

"We can camp here tonight and make it to the end of the Sea of Bells by midday tomorrow."

Pynt sighed. "If I never see a white lily bell again it will be too soon."

Jenna nodded her agreement.

"White is a boring color."

"Thank you," Jenna said, flipping the end of her braid into Pynt's face.

Pynt grabbed the braid and yanked it. "Boring, boring, boring," she taunted.

Jenna pulled back until the braid stretched between them, then suddenly stepped forward and doubled over, butting her head into Pynt's stomach. Pynt sat down on the ground quite hard, but as she had never let go of the braid, she pulled Jenna down with her. They both burst into laughter.

"Now . . . I . . . know . . ." said Jenna, in between deep breaths, "why the first thing warriors do after their final Choosing is to cut their hair."

"You could tuck it into your shirt."

"And then it would stick out of my tunic like a tail!"

They both began to laugh again.

Pynt tried to look serious and failed. "You could be known as the White Beast of Selden Hame."

Jenna shrugged out of her pack and unbuckled her sword. She stood up and crouched over, swinging her arms low enough so that her knuckles grazed the ground. "I am the Beast. Fear me," she said in a low, growling voice.

Pynt gave a high-pitched scream, like the squeak of a wood rat. "Oh, do not hurt me, White Beast," she cried out in mock fear. She dropped her own pack and sword, then began running around in circles. "Oh, help me! Help me! The Beast is here!"

Jenna chased her in ever-decreasing circles until at last they collapsed together in a tangle of arms and legs, with Jenna on top, laughing.

Jenna got up and pulled Pynt to her feet, giving her a fierce hug. "I *am* glad you found me, Pynt. *I am.*"

* * *

Later in the evening they camped on the ground because there had been no cat sign or bear sign or sign of anything larger than a rabbit. Pynt uncharacteristically talked of her fears as the small fire crackled and the thin line of smoke unwound like a gray thread from a skein.

"I am sometimes afraid that I will not be brave in a real fight, Jenna. Or that I will laugh at the wrong moment. Or . . ."

"I am sometimes afraid that you will never shut up and go to sleep," Jenna mumbled.

"I am sometimes afraid that . . ." Pynt continued, ignoring Jenna's comment. But when she realized that Jenna had fallen asleep, she sighed, turned her back to the fire, and went to sleep herself.

They rose to a morning so fogged over that they could not see the meadow, though they had slept not ten feet from it under the overhang of trees. The fog seemed to get inside of them as well. They found themselves whispering and moving about on tiptoe, as cautious as little animals in the undergrowth.

"No twig snapping today," Jenna said, her voice scarcely audible.

"None," Pynt agreed.

They collected their gear and buried the fire, brushing its remains into the dirt so that there was no sign of their overnight stay. Jenna rebraided her hair and Pynt ran quick fingers through her black curls. Then, squatting on their heels, knees touching they whispered their plans.

"It will be slow going until the fog clears," said Jenna, her voice hissing on the word *slow*.

"*If* it clears," answered Pynt.

"It will clear," said Jenna. Then, as an afterthought, she added, "It *has* to."

"Do you remember the story Little Domina told us?" Pynt asked. "We must have been eight or nine years old. When we camped out and she scared us so much, you got sick and threw up your dinner."

"And you wet your blanket and cried all night."

"I did not."

"You did. Only I was not sick and I never threw up."

"Yes, you did."

Jenna was quiet for a moment. "The story was about a Fog Demon. With a monstrous snout and wide horns."

"It strangled runners by stuffing streamers of mist down their throats," Pynt added.

"It was just a story," Jenna put in quickly. "We were silly to be so frightened. We were very young."

"Then if it is just a story, why are we still sitting here?" Pynt asked.

"We could walk," Jenna said. "And not run."

"Yessssss," hissed Pynt.

"It is *only* a story," said Jenna.

"And the fog will be lifting soon anyway," said Pynt. "It always does."

There was a sudden crackling sound from the woods, as if a number of twigs were broken at once.

"What was that?" asked Pynt.

"A rabbit?" Jenna's voice was uncertain.

"A Fog Demon?"

There was a scrabbling behind them. Neither of them dared to move. A red squirrel ran up to Jenna's foot, stood up on its hind legs, and chittered at her. Then it ran off, scurrying in a zigzag pattern back toward the woods.

"A squirrel," said Jenna, relief evident in her voice. She stood. "We are only frightening ourselves this way. There is nothing out there but the forest and . . ."

"And that boring meadow," said Pynt, standing and buckling on her sword. "Now, if only we knew which *way* the boring meadow lies . . ."

"That way," said Jenna, pointing.

"No, that way," said Pynt, pointing in the opposite direction.

They were still arguing when a slight breeze lifted the edge of the fog like a hand lifting a comforter and they could see the meadow's edge, with the weak sun, a ghostly white, sitting on the horizon's lip.

"That way," they said together, pointing in a direction that neither of them had guessed before, away from the sun, westward and slightly north.

But the fog did not disappear. In fact, it settled more firmly around them, tucking them in. The result was not comfort but a cold, continuing layer of fear. They stuck to the edge of the forest and whenever they halted, even for a moment, they set their swords down on the ground pointing in the direction they were to continue in, the only steady markers they had.

The birds were still or had long since flown out of the fog. The small animals had all gone to earth. A silent, motionless white world surrounded them and nothing they did seemed to make a difference. The silence was broken only by the shuffling of their feet through the leaves and the sound of their breathing. They walked shoulders touching, afraid to lose contact with each other, even afraid to stop talking, another tenuous link in the fog.

"I do not like it," Pynt said, every few feet.

After the tenth time, Jenna ignored Pynt's complaint, babbling instead about life back in the Hame and about her anger at Mother Alta. Pynt's antiphonal response broke in at regular intervals.

By lunch they still had not reached their goal, or at least they assumed it was lunch, for both their stomachs growled at once. It was a loud, unlikely noise in the fog.

"I have nothing left to eat in my pack," Jenna said. "And there is only a little milk in my flask. It is quite sour."

"I do not even have that," complained Pynt. "I was counting on ferns today, and mushrooms, and perhaps a squirrel for tonight."

"We will find nothing in this fog," Jenna said. "So we will just have to go hungry."

"In another day we could have cheese. From your sour milk!" Pynt tried to laugh at her own feeble joke, but the fog thinned the sound until it was but a hollow mockery.

They did not stop but walked on, their remarks to each other less and less frequent, as if a Fog Demon had, indeed, stoppered their mouths with streamers of mist.

Once Pynt tripped over an exposed tree root, falling heavily onto her knees. When she rolled up a pant leg, she clicked her tongue at the large bruise already purpling her right knee. Moments later, Jenna walked into a low, overhanging branch and spots, like black blossoms, bloomed before her eyes.

"You are too tall," Pynt whispered. "That branch sailed miles over my head."

"You are too small, so things on the ground rise up to meet you," Jenna answered.

It was their first exchange in almost an hour.

And still they walked.

The fog began to grow darker, as if it were nighttime instead of day. Their shirts were soaked and Pynt's curls had plastered in wet tendrils against her back. Their leather vests and leggings smelled dank and sour.

"Is it night already?" whispered Pynt. "How long have we been walking?"

"I have no idea," Jenna said. "And I do not—wait!" She put her hand on Pynt's arm, drawing her close. "Do you hear that?"

Pynt strained into the mist. "Hear what?"

Jenna was silent for a moment longer, turning her head back and forth as if trying to catch a sound. *"That!"*

There was a low, thrashing noise behind them and then, as if on the thrasher's trail, a high, faint *yip-yip-yipping.*

"A cat?"

"Too noisy."

"A bear?"

"Not noisy enough."

"Is that meant to be comforting?"

"It is meant to be truthful. *Hush.*" The sound had moved away from them and Jenna turned completely around trying to locate it again.

"Gone," she said. "Whatever it was, it is gone now."

"I counted two *whatevers,*" said Pynt. "Not one."

"Is *that* meant to be comforting?" Jenna asked.

"It is meant to be truthful," Pynt said.

They walked on.

When the sound came again, it was somehow in front of them. Or else they had gotten turned around. Neither of them was certain.

"There it is," whispered Jenna.

"There they are," Pynt said at the same time.

The thrashing was closer, as if twigs and brush, brambles and briars, were being knocked about with careless disregard for the trail. And along with the thrashing was the sound of heavy, frantic breathing. Farther away, something sounding very much like an enormous animal charging through the woods was accompanied by a thunderous cry. *"Garoooooom! Garoooooom!"*

Instinctively, Jenna and Pynt shrugged out of their packs and stood back-to-back, their swords in one hand, knives in the other.

"Oh, Jenna, I am terribly afraid," Pynt whispered.

"You would be stupid not to be," Jenna whispered back.

"Are you afraid?"

"I am not stupid," Jenna said.

Something larger than a cat and smaller than a bear scrambled out of the fog, tumbling at their feet, and breathing in high, sobbing gasps.

Jenna bent down, knife in her right hand leading the way. Her heart was *thud-thudding* so loudly in her breast, she was sure Pynt could hear it. She stared into the mud-stained face of a boy who could not have been more than fifteen or sixteen years old.

"Who . . ." she began, her tongue suddenly stuttering over the familiar syllables. Bright eyes, wide, frightened, and incredibly blue, stared back at her.

"Merci . . ." the boy cried. "Sisters of Alta, *ich crie merci. Ich am thi mon."* His voice was ragged and torn.

"What is it saying?" whispered Pynt from behind Jenna.

For a moment Jenna could not speak; then she looked over her shoulder at Pynt. *"It* is a boy. Slightly older than us. And he is speaking in the old tongue, though I cannot think why."

The boy sat up, his fear tempered by curiosity. "Isn't that how you Altites speak? That's what I was taught. And that if I ever needed aid from you, I was to say *Merci, ich crie merci, ich am thi mon* and you'd be forced by your vows to help me."

"We have not taken our vows yet," said Pynt. "We are only thirteen years old."

"Only thirteen? But she . . ." He gestured toward Jenna. "She looked older." He stared at Jenna, then shrugged. "My mistake. It must have been the white hair."

Pynt spat to one side. "You know nothing, boy."

"I know a lot," he argued. "And I'll know a lot more when . . ." He hesitated and let the sentence trail away.

"No one speaks in the old tongue except the priestess," Jenna said. "And in prayers. Or when we read from the *Book."*

"The *Book of Light?"* He seemed to have forgotten his fear in his excitement. "Have you seen it? Have you touched it? Have you read it? Or . . ." He seemed to search around for the right words, then shrugged and plunged ahead. "Or can you read?"

"Of course we can read," Jenna said with disgust. "Do you take us for savages?"

The boy shrugged again, this time in a kind of apology, and stood. Just as he got to his feet, there was a thunderclap of noise nearby, and an enormous double-headed horned creature burst out of the fog screaming indecipherable curses.

"Oh-oh!" muttered the boy, scrambling away from them and disappearing once more into the fog.

But Pynt and Jenna stood their ground.

"Back to me!" Jenna cried, and Pynt moved immediately to stand with her.

At Jenna's cry, the creature reared up once, towering above them, a black monster in the swirl of white fog. Then it charged toward them, a long, sharp weapon scything down from above.

"Duck!" Pynt screamed, scrabbling under the musky-smelling belly of the beast and coming up the other side. She thrust her sword toward the horned head of the creature. Leaping at the last, she hit something and crashed at the same moment into its huge, sweaty body. For a moment the breath was knocked from her and she fell backward onto her pack, spilling its contents. She pushed herself into a desperate somersault to get out of the way of the beast's flailing legs, and when she stood again, her sword was gone. Whether it was in the creature's neck or lying on the ground somewhere, she could not have said.

The great animal lay on its side, and all Pynt could see in the fog were its struggles to get up again. Then she heard the clang of steel on steel, and she made her way quickly around the beast toward the sound.

Jenna and another horned creature were in full battle. It was the ringing of their swords against each other that Pynt had heard. For a moment she did not understand, and then in sudden illumination realized that the horned creature had been the rider. What had fallen had been its steed, which was even now struggling to its feet.

But Jenna seemed to be losing the fight, for the demon was bigger and stronger than she. Forgetting her own fears, Pynt ran silently behind the hulking horned fighter, bent down, and threw herself against its knees. The backs of its legs were fleshy, but when she grabbed the front, she found they were unbending and hard, as if the creature wore leathern armor. She pushed against its knees again and this time it fell heavily backward on top of her. At the last minute, she reached around and knifed it in the thigh.

Jenna leaped on top of them both and thrust her sword unerringly into the creature's neck.

The demon shuddered once, made a small mewing sound, and was still.

"What . . . what kind of creature is it?" Pynt asked, when Jenna had rolled the heavy body off her. Her arms ached and both her legs felt as if they had weights attached. There was a sharp pain in her side. "Is it a Fog Demon?"

Jenna was breathing hard. Her sword still thrust awkwardly from the creature's throat. She squatted by the body, put her face in her hands, and wept.

Pynt crawled over to her and put her arms around Jenna's legs. "Why are you crying?" she asked. "Why now, when it is all over?"

"This was not like hunting rabbit or squirrel," Jenna whispered. "I do not think I can bear to look at him."

Pynt nodded, stood up, and went over to the creature's body. She thought to roll it over in order to hide the hideous brown snout and bulging eyes. But as she tugged at Jenna's sword, the edge of the blade slipped up through the brown flesh, severing the chin. Only then did she see that the

leathery brown face was no face at all but a mask. Slowly she peeled the
mask back, revealing the face beneath. It was an ordinary face, the beard
red and gray, the teeth broken and yellow, the right cheek crisscrossed with
old scars. Pynt ripped the mask away completely and the horns, part of an
elaborate helmet, came off in her hand.

"Jenna, look!"

"I cannot."

"It is not a demon, Jenna. It is a man."

"I *know* that," Jenna whispered. "Why do you think I cannot look?
Looking at a dead demon's face would be easy."

"His name," said a voice behind them, "is Barnoo." It was the boy, who
had returned silently. "He was known as the Hound. He'll hunt no more."
He knelt by the dead man but did not touch him. "Strange . . . even dead
he frightens me." Shivering, the boy reached out a tentative finger and
poked at Barnoo's hand. "Cold," he said. "So cold, so soon. I thought it
would take longer. But then, the Hound was always cold. Cold-blooded, he
and his brothers, and the master they serve." He stood up. "I think I'm
going to be sick."

Jenna stood up as well and shrugged meaningfully at Pynt. They listened
while the boy was noisily but efficiently sick somewhere in the bushes behind them.

At last the noises from the bushes ceased and the boy found them again,
looking somewhat drained but calm.

"I never thought it would be the Hound who would die. I assumed it
would be me," he said. "My only hope, in fact, was to lose him in the fog, a
small hope at best. He was known throughout the land as a great tracker."

"*The Hound*," said Pynt, nodding.

"How did you know about the fog?" asked Jenna.

"Everyone knows fogs are frequent around the Sea of Bells. So when I
found out he was on my trail, I headed straight here."

"*We* knew nothing about the fogs."

"And we know nothing about the Hound. Or about you," said Jenna
pointedly. "Why was he hunting you? Are you a thief? You do not look like
one. Or a cutthroat?"

"He looks even less like that," said Pynt.

"I'm . . ." He hesitated. "I'm Carum. I am—or was, at least, before I
had to run for my life—a scholar. Alive I'm a threat to Lord Kalas of the
Northern Holdings. Lord Kalas . . . who wants to be king!" There was
unhappiness in the boy's voice, and bitterness he tried to disguise. "I have
been running all spring."

Pynt reached out to touch his arm. At the last moment, they both drew back.

"We'd best bury him," the boy said. "Else his brothers will find him when the fog lifts and they'll make further black marks on my long tally sheet."

"Are his brothers as big?" Pynt asked.

The boy nodded. "And as ugly."

"And—they are very much alive," Jenna muttered to herself.

They began to dig a grave using their knives carefully, a long, time-consuming task. Carum stripped the dead man of a dirk at the belt and another in his boot. He also found a small spadelike ax in a throwing sheaf under the Hound's arm and they used it as well. When the digging was done, they rolled the Hound's body into the hole. The hole would have been too small for the carcass had not Barnoo curled up in his death throes and stiffened that way. He landed facedown in the hole.

Jenna breathed a sigh of relief at that, and tossed the mask after him. Then they threw in handfuls of dirt, aware of the heavy breathing and frequent huffing and stamping of the steed somewhere out of sight in the fog.

As the last clod of dirt was tamped down, Jenna whispered, "Is there something we should say to speed him on his way?"

"On his way where?" asked Carum.

"To wherever you believe he goes after death," said Jenna.

"I believe there's only Here," said Carum. "Nothing after."

"Is that what all men believe?" asked Pynt, astonished.

"That's what I believe," said Carum. "And all my reading has not changed my mind. But I can say a few words about what the Hound and his brothers believe, if you'd like."

"Do," Jenna said, "for I cannot wish him a place in Alta's cave or at her breast, which is where I expect to go when I die."

Carum's mouth twisted a bit, almost as if he were trying not to smile. Then he took a deep breath and looked down at the gravemound. "May the God of Fine Battles, Lord Cres, welcome you to his side in the great halls of ValHale. May you drink his strong wines and eat his meat forever, and throw the bones over your shoulder for the Dogs of War."

"What an awful prayer," said Pynt. "Who would want to go to such an unpeaceful place after death?"

"Who indeed," said Carum, shrugging. "Is it any wonder I don't believe it?"

Just then the steed gave a strange, low sound and marched over to them.

"What is that?" whispered Pynt.

"Never seen a horse before?" Carum asked.

"Of course." Pynt's answer came so quickly, Carum smiled.

"Of course," he said, his voice full of mockery.

"Well, once anyway," said Pynt. "And they were much shorter. What would we do with such a large beast on our small mountain trails?"

Jenna turned away from their argument and stared out into the impenetrable fog, remembering the two little foals they had helped rescue from the flooded Selden barn while the body of the mare had floated by, knocking against the pilings. She turned back suddenly. "Is it all right? The horse. Is it hurt? Can it be ridden?"

Carum's voice came to her from the fog. "If it's on its feet, it can be ridden. Kalas' horses are always strong and solid. He knows flesh, my uncle does." This time the bitterness in his voice could not be disguised.

"Can you catch it?" Jenna asked.

"Just grab its halter and it'll come. It's well trained, you know. All of Kalas' battle horses are."

"Well, you grab the halter, whatever that is, and then we can start off again," Jenna said, picking up her sword and pack.

"Which way?"

Jenna turned around several times, trying to pierce the fog.

Pynt, on her hands and knees, was too busy looking for the contents of her pack to offer a suggestion. When she found everything she could, she jammed it in and looked around again for her sword. Then she joined the other two, who were still trying to figure out the direction.

They huddled together, a small island in the midst of a sea of fog, arguing over the way. At last Carum sat down in disgust. Only the horse, its gray nose moist and its dark eyes unfathomable, seemed unworried.

"Shall we camp here until morning?" asked Jenna.

"Without food?" Carum's voice threaded up to them.

"And do you want to go off on your own in that fog in the hopes of a handful of mushrooms?" asked Pynt.

"What about a fire, then?"

"We'll go hand in hand to look for wood," Jenna said.

They found only a few dry bushes and made a small brushy fire, as far from Barnoo's grave as possible. The horse stood, silently, all night over the fresh gravemound, its only marker.

The three were asleep long before the fire went out. The horse, in its silent vigil, stayed awake much of the night.

THE BALLAD

Lord Gorum

Oh, where have ye been all day, Gorum, my son?
        The bull, the bear, the cat, and the hound,
Where have ye been all day, my pretty one?
        And the brothers have pulled me down.

I've been far afoot, with my staff in my hand,
        The bull, the bear, the cat, and the hound,
I have been out walking my dead father's land,
        And the brothers have pulled me down.

I looked in the mountains, I looked in the sea,
        The bull, the bear, the cat, and the hound,
A-looking for someone a-looking for me,
        And the brothers have pulled me down.

What have ye for supper, Lord Gorum, my son?
        The bull, the bear, the cat, and the hound,
What have ye for supper, my pretty young one?
        And the brothers have pulled me down.

I've nothing for supper, and nothing to rise,
        The bull, the bear, the cat, and the hound,
But fed on the look in my own true love's eyes,
        And the brothers have pulled me down.

What will ye leave to that true love, my son?
        The bull, the bear, the cat, and the hound,
What will she leave you, my handsome young one?
        And the brothers have pulled me down.

My kingdom, my crown, my name, and my grave,
        The bull, the bear, the cat, and the hound,

Her hair, her heart, her place in the cave,
And the brothers have pulled me down.

THE STORY

They awoke to birdsong and a sky the color of old pearl. Pynt laughed
aloud on rising but Jenna cast a suddenly shy glance at Carum, who had
rolled into a ball at her feet and looked at once young and grownup in the
lambent morning. He had long dark lashes that seemed to fan and shadow
his cheeks, and his right hand lay across his nose, the long, shapely fingers
hanging limp. Jenna was careful not to disturb him by stretching.

Pynt came over and stared down at him. "I thought . . ." she began,
but Jenna shushed her with a finger to her lips. Then Pynt whispered, "I
thought that men were all hairy and lumpy."

Jenna turned away, whispering over her shoulder, "That is because *he* is
still a boy." But her heart sent a different message as she walked into the
woods, casting about until she came upon some of the wild mushrooms that
Pynt loved best. She was especially glad she found Pynt's favorites, the
fleshy ones that were as good raw as cooked.

A twig snapped behind her, and Jenna turned. "See," she said to Pynt,
"here are the ones you like."

"I found some ferns," Pynt said. "If we only had water, we could cook
them up."

Jenna shook her head. "No fires and no time," she said. "Without the
fog to mask it, we cannot chance a fire and if the Hound's brothers are,
indeed, on his trail, we need to leave this place and its ghosts, quickly."

Pynt nodded her agreement, and they bent to the gathering of mushrooms. When their hands and their leather pockets were full, they stood
and headed back to the camp.

Carum was gone.

The ground was scuffed, but just a little. It *could* have meant a fight.

"What is it?" Pynt whispered. "The other brothers? Or Lord Kalas? Not
many, I would say."

"We should never have left him alone," Jenna said fiercely. She clenched
her hands, crushing the mushrooms. They dropped the food on the grass by
the fire. "He cannot have gotten far. Surely we have enough woodsense to

trail a scholar. And look, they have not taken the horse." She bent over, casting about for his track, and discovered a place where he seemed to have staggered off into the undergrowth, for the branches were broken and the trillium trampled underfoot.

They had not gone far when they heard a noise; both dropped to the ground as one. Inching forward, they saw the back of Carum's head, his light brown hair tangled. With one hand he was scratching his head and with the other . . .

"Alta's Hairs!" said Jenna disgustedly.

Pynt sat up and laughed.

Carum's head snapped around and he spotted them, his cheeks a bright flush. "Haven't you ever seen a man relieving himself?" Then he laughed, too. "No, I suppose not." He turned his head away again.

"We thought . . ." Pynt began.

"Explain nothing," said Jenna in a tight voice. She stood, stared at Carum's back with hooded eyes, then turned and stalked back to camp. "Come, Marga," she called.

Pynt scrambled to her feet and followed.

After their meager breakfast, they headed along the wood's edge toward the end of the lily meadows, taking turns on the horse. Its broad back stretched their muscles painfully and the heavy leather saddle rubbed sores on their thighs. After a try or two, both Jenna and Pynt decided to walk. But Carum chose to ride as if he were born to horseback, or as if the added height lent him courage in the girls' company.

"Tell me about the Brothers," said Jenna, one time that Pynt was astride the horse and she and Carum walked along together companionably. Carum was leading the horse by its halter. "So that I do not come upon them unaware." She had forgiven him the morning's scare and embarrassment—as long as he did not mention it.

"They really *are* brothers, of a single mother, though it's said they each had a different sire. One can readily believe that, seeing them together, for in all things but one they're as unalike as strangers. But in their devotion to Lord Kalas, they're as one. The Bull, the Bear, the Cat, and the Hound."

"The Hound I have met," said Jenna, keeping her voice calm and the memory of the dead man's back hunched over in his grave out of her mind. "What of the others?"

"The Bull is ox-strong and as stupid. He tries to do with his arms what his head cannot. He can work all day and not tire. I've seen him turn a mill wheel when the ox falters."

"And the Bear?"

"A hairy man, as large as the Bull, but smarter. A *little* smarter. His hair falls down to his shoulders, and his chest and back are likewise covered as if with a hair shirt."

"Attractive," said Jenna, half smiling.

"But the Cat, he's the one to be wary of. He's small and light on his feet. Once he leaped across a chasm, from rock to rock, with a pack of the king's hounds after him. The pack fell to its death. They cried all the way down. I heard them in my sleep for weeks." Carum's eyes squinted in the sun and Jenna could not read them.

"But though he's half the size of the others, he's the one I fear the most."

"More than Lord Kalas?" asked Jenna.

Carum shrugged as if to say they were to be equally feared.

"Then tell me about him, this dread Lord Kalas, so that I will know him if I meet him."

"You wouldn't want to meet him," Carum said. "He's tall and so thin they say he must stand twice to cast a shadow. His breath smells the sweet rot of piji."

"Piji?" Jenna asked.

"It is an addiction the poor know nothing of," said Carum.

"We are not poor," said Jenna.

"You don't know piji," Carum replied. "Therefore you are poor!"

"If that is a scholar's argument, then I am glad I know only the one book!" She laughed lightly and punched Carum on the arm. "What more of Kalas?"

"*Lord* Kalas," reminded Carum, ignoring the touch, though his cheeks seemed to grow pinker. "If you leave off his title, he'd as soon have you leave off your head."

"A pleasant man," said Jenna. "What more?"

"He has red hair and a red beard."

"The Hound had a red beard," mused Jenna. "Does red run in your family of villains?"

"No more than white runs free through the Alta Hames, I imagine," replied Carum.

Jenna nodded. "You are right. I alone have white hair. And I have always hated being so different. I longed to be just like the others and instead I have been called a tree overshading the little plants below."

"You *are* tall," said Carum. "But I like that. And your hair is . . . is marvelous. Promise me you'll never cut it."

"I will cut it when I take my vows," said Jenna. "A warrior cannot chance long hair in battle."

It was Carum's turn to muse and he was silent for a long while. Then he spoke in a strange, faraway voice. "There was a tribe of warriors—men, not women—in the East across the sea about . . ." He seemed to be calculating, bit his lip, then smiled. "About seven centuries ago. They wore their hair in long, single braids. They tied the scalp locks of their defeated enemies into the braids. Sometimes they used their hair to throttle their foes, when silence was the key. That's what the historian Locutus wrote. He added, *And in that way they were never weaponless.* They were called . . ." He hesitated again. "No, I've lost their names. But it'll come to me."

"You carry a great deal in your head, packed tight for travel," said Jenna, smiling.

"That, my lady," Carum answered, sweeping his arm in front of his body in an elaborate bow, "is a fine definition of a scholar: a bag of information packed tight for the road."

They laughed loudly and Pynt, from her high seat on the horse's back, called down, "What is so funny?"

"It is nothing, Pynt," said Jenna. When she turned back to Carum to smile again at him, she missed the look that passed over Pynt's face.

Pynt dismounted. "I do not want to ride anymore."

"Then I shall," said Carum, putting his hands on the horn of the saddle and swinging himself easily into the seat.

"How does he do that?" asked Jenna, her voice filled with admiration.

"*Why* does he do that?" muttered Pynt.

They reached the meadow's end by the time the sun stood straight overhead. Casting a glance backward at the great sweep of the Sea of Bells, Jenna sighed.

"Before we go farther, we need to take stock," she said.

"And find something to eat," reminded Pynt.

"And explain to my stomach that my throat hasn't been slit," said Carum. He slid off the horse's back and led it to the meadow's edge to graze. When he wandered back, Pynt and Jenna were in the middle of an argument, and Pynt was saying, "And *I* say we should leave him."

Carum pulled a smile across his face and said cheerily, "You don't want to leave me, because I know a shortcut to Nill's Hame."

"How did you know we were going there?" asked Pynt.

"Do not be stupid, Pynt. What other Hames are along this route?" said Jenna. She turned to Carum, all the while pulling on her braid. "Thank you, Carum, but we know the way. The map is up here." She pointed to her head. "And besides, you cannot come into the Hame. No men are allowed."

"I know that," Carum said, "but I'm going farther along the same road, to a place where *only* men are allowed. It's a place of sanctuary where even the Brothers and Kalas—"

"*Lord* Kalas," interrupted Jenna, stroking her finger across her throat. "Remember your head!"

He grinned. "Lord Kalas wouldn't dare violate those walls. I'll be safe there. So I can guide you and . . ."

"And we can keep you out of trouble!" said Pynt.

"*Three are better than one where trouble is concerned,*" Carum said gently. "At least that's what we say."

"We say the same," said Jenna. "Is that not strange?"

"Then I can go along?" His face betrayed his eagerness.

"After we eat," Jenna said. "But do not leave the horse out in plain sight. Just because we have not seen any trace of the Brothers does not mean they have missed us."

Carum nodded.

"We shall each take a different path, going only within ear of this place, to find something for our meal."

Carum collected the horse and by the time he got it tied to a limb of a middle-size oak, the other two had disappeared into the forest. He looked around, found a wide deer run, and followed along it as quietly as he could.

Not an hour later they met again near the horse and poured their woods' bounty onto a kerchief that Jenna spread. Pynt had collected several dozen mushrooms, not the great white puffs of which she was so fond, but a darker variety that had a nutty flavor. Jenna had discovered a squirrel's cache of nuts and a little dell of ferns, but she left the ferns since smoke from a fire for the boiling of them would have stained the bright, clear sky and given them away at once. Carum had filled his pocket with berries.

"Berries!" Pynt laughed.

Jenna explained. "*Spring berries are for dye and dying.* That is what we say in the Hame. The eating berries are not yet ripe and these others"—she counted through his meager store —"these are all poisonous. Though some —like this Bird Berry"—she touched a small hard black pebbly fruit—"can be steeped in hot water over several days for a strong purgative. And this"— She touched a larger, bright red berry—"which we call *Step-o'er-me-lady,* can be mashed into a greasy salve for burns."

"Berries!" Pynt laughed again.

Carum looked down at the ground.

"Oh, hush, Pynt," said Jenna. "Carum knows much more than either of us, just not what is here in the woods."

"And *what* does he know?" asked Pynt.

"He knows about warriors who use their braids to strangle their foes, which is what I shall do to you if you do not shut up." Jenna held her white plait between her hands like a noose and gave Pynt a wicked look.

"The Alaisters!" Carum said triumphantly, looking up with a grin.

"What?" Pynt and Jenna turned to him at the same time.

"That's the name of the tribe. The Alaisters. I knew I'd come up with it after a time."

Jenna squatted on her heels and picked up two mushrooms. Stuffing them into her mouth, she muttered, "Just don't eat the berries, scholar."

They ate quickly and quietly and when they were done, swept away any sign of their makeshift lunch. Carum went over to the horse and untied it.

"Bring the horse here," Jenna called.

Smiling, Carum led the cross-grained gray to her. "Do you want to ride now?"

"None of us will ride anymore," Jenna said. "We are going to send the horse across the meadow. That way." She pointed south. "He will make a wide trail and lead any followers away from us."

Carum looked over his shoulder nervously. "Have we been followed?"

Pynt laughed. "If we had, we would not now be standing here out in the open. Trust us."

"But there *will* be followers. Following you or following the Hound. And well you know it. I have worried all this morning about taking the horse with us, and you both should have been worrying, too. But I think, with Alta's help, we will use the horse to confuse the trail." Jenna threw her right braid over her shoulder for emphasis.

"*You* did not look worried," scolded Pynt.

"Why didn't you say something?" Carum's face clouded over. "It never even occurred to me . . ."

"That is because scholars worry about the past, Carum, while warriors must worry about the future. It is possible we will have no future if we keep the horse," Jenna said, her tone low and sensible. "So tell me, horseman, how do we best encourage the beast to ride off that way?"

Carum laughed. "Trust *me,*" he said. Dropping the horse's reins, he went over to a flowering bush, cut and stripped a switch. Then he came back to the horse, patted it once on its nose, and whispered into its ear. Turning it around so that its head was facing south, he brought the switch down hard twice on its flank, shouting, "Get on home!"

The horse shied, kicked out its rear feet, and missing Carum's thighs by a scant inch, galloped off across the meadow, leaving a swath wide enough to be read by even the most reluctant trailers. It did not stop until it was hundreds of yards away, where it put its big nose down and began to crop the grass.

"What did you whisper into its ear?" asked Jenna.

"To forgive me for the switching," Carum answered.

"I do not think it forgave," Pynt pointed out, "if its aim was any indication of its intent. Had it connected, I doubt there would be many new scholars of your line."

Jenna smothered a laugh and Carum scowled.

"I thought you Altites knew nothing of men," he said.

"We know we do not spring from flowers or cabbages or from the beaks of birds," said Jenna. "Our women give birth so we know where babies come from. *And* how they are made. We choose . . ." She stopped, for Carum's ears were beginning to turn red from embarrassment, but Pynt had no thought to spare his feelings.

"We choose to use men but not to live with them. To serve them for wages as guards if need be, but not to stay otherwise in their service." Although she said it with conviction, it sounded more like a litany, and Carum began to protest.

"Your mouth says that, but . . ." he began. Jenna put her hand on his arm to stop their argument.

"The horse has not moved on," she said.

Carum walked a few feet into the meadow and shouted, "Gee-up home, you misbegotten son of a she-ass!"

The horse lifted its head and, with a mouthful of grass and lilies still hanging from its jaws, took off south. Soon it was just a moving dot on the horizon.

"*Wonderful!*" said Pynt sarcastically. "Your shout should have alerted every follower within miles."

Carum ignored her pointedly and turned to Jenna. "There was no other way."

Jenna nodded and turned to Pynt. "What is wrong with the two of you? First you shout, then he shouts. You speak with fire and he answers with ice. We cannot go on this way."

"Then send him off," muttered Pynt, not entirely under her breath. She walked a few steps away.

Carum drew in a deep breath, then spoke softly so that only Jenna could hear. "Never mind, Jenna, we'll be at the Hame soon, and I'll be gone. And don't worry about the horse." He raised his voice at the end so that Pynt, hearing him, looked back. "Kalas' horses are well trained and he'll find his way home eventually."

"And home is . . ." Pynt's curiosity overcame her anger and resentment.

"North," Jenna said. "The Northern Holdings, you said. Alta's Hairs! That horse will be going the same way we are."

"No, Jenna," Carum interrupted, putting his hand on Jenna's shoulder. "That *was* home for Lord Kalas once. But now he's taken over the High King's palace in the South Downs and calls it after himself. The wine cellar my . . . king so loved has been made into a dungeon. And Kalas squats on the throne for the past year like a toad in a hole, waiting for a coronation that will not—if the gods forbid it—ever come."

"I thought you believed in no gods," said Pynt.

"I'll believe if there is no coronation sanctioned by the priests. But in the end, even that won't matter. A man who sits on a throne long enough even though he wears but a helm is still called *Your Majesty.* The people's memory is short when mercy and justice are short. I fear Kalas *will* be king ere long."

The girls stared at him as he spoke, for the words seemed to lay a mantle of majesty on him, though it was sorrowing majesty at best. When the wind ruffled his hair, he seemed, somehow, taller and yet—at the same time—stooped.

"Oh, Carum," Jenna said, and there was a real sadness in her voice, loss echoing loss.

Carum seemed to shake himself suddenly free of the oratory and shrugged. "Never mind me. We scholars sometimes invent an appropriate metaphor and, other times, we simply talk because we love to hear the sound of ringing words."

Pynt said nothing for the longest time, but at last she cast a glance at the lowering sky. "Where is that shortcut you promised?"

Where the meadow ended, the ground was boggy, sucking eagerly at footfalls. Jenna led them back into the woods so as not to leave a pattern of prints, and they came around the northern edge where the great oak and beech forest gave way to newer growth. There was a real track now on the meadow's far side, not just deer paths. The track was wide and well worn, with roadside bushes and flowers that bespoke a nearby civilization: the prickly raspberry patches, the yellow spikes of toadflax, and the tiny, pensive blue and purple heads of heartsease nodding in the rising breeze.

They found a clear spring, and bent over to drink one at a time, long eager draughts. Then the girls rinsed out their skin bottles carefully before filling them again with the water.

"We must stay off the road but close enough to it that we do not lose the way," said Jenna.

"Why not let Carum walk in the woods, keeping us in sight? No one is searching for us," Pynt argued.

"Because we undertook his guardianship," said Jenna. "He cried us *merci*. And though that is not something we have yet pledged, you and I, I guess it will be one of the seven vows we will take in less than a short year's time."

Pynt nodded, but muttered, "Could we not guard him as well from the road?"

Jenna shook her head.

"All right," Pynt said at last. "Into the woods, then." She turned abruptly and entered the woods first without snapping a single twig.

Carum followed after and Jenna, after checking the road both ways, came last.

They walked along as quietly as possible, all comments contained in the kind of hand signals the guards at the Hame used, which left Carum out of the conversation entirely. It was the road, not fifty yards to their right, that silenced them, but Carum did not seem to mind. He walked along almost oblivious of his surroundings, caught up in his own thoughts.

Single file, with Pynt in front and Jenna in the rear, they moved in a rhythm dictated by the density of the undergrowth. Twice Carum let a branch snap back into Jenna's face and, turning to apologize, received only a scowl and a dismissing wave of her hand. Once Pynt stepped in a small depression, twisting her ankle, though not severely. But the accidents, small as they were, served as warnings. Silently, they watched the ground as well as the branches, glancing only occasionally off to the right to check the road.

Brambles caught at their clothes and hair, slipping without incident off the rough skins that Jenna and Pynt wore. Carum, in loose weave, had the most trouble and often they had to stop and help him untangle himself from the thorns. But silently, always silently, the road so close by a stopper in their mouths.

The silence in the end was what saved them, and the fact that, for once, they were not moving ahead but standing in a knot trying once again to unhook Carum's shirt from a high raspberry bush. The sound of hooves galloping nearby was a thunder underfoot. They crouched down instinctively, huddled together, while a dust of riders raced by, going north.

As soon as the riders had passed, Pynt whispered, "Could you see?"

Jenna nodded. "At least a dozen," she said under her breath, "maybe two."

"There were twenty-one," said Carum.

Pynt and Jenna looked at him. "How can you be so sure?"

"I counted. Besides, a company of horse is always twenty-one, with a captain at its head."

"*And,*" Pynt said, the sarcasm a hard edge in her voice, "I suppose you also happened to notice who was in charge!"

Carum nodded. "The Bull."

"I do not believe it," said Pynt, her voice growing louder until Jenna had to silence her with a hand on her arm. Then Pynt whispered, "They went by too quickly and we were kneeling here on the floor of the forest."

"*You* were kneeling," Carum pointed out. "I was caught upright by the thorns."

"He is right," admitted Jenna.

"Besides," continued Carum, "only the Brothers ride those big cross-grained grays. And the Bull is so large, he towers over his men. *And* his helmet gave him away."

"His helmet," Jenna whispered, her face marking the memory of the other helmet and the sound it had made *thunking* down on the dead man's back. She was silent for a moment longer than necessary, then whispered fiercely, "We must move even deeper into the woods. If *we* can see *them*, then . . ."

She did not have to finish the thought. Both Carum and Pynt nodded, united at least on the danger. Pynt ripped Carum's shirt from the thorns without regard for the cloth, and led them further into the forest where some of the old, great oaks still stood sentinel.

Carum had promised them the trip to the Hame would take only a day, and they had hoped to get there by evening. But the woods, even the edge of it, slowed them down considerably. Twice more that afternoon a company of riders raced by, once from the north and once up from the south. The first had been a silent ride, all dark purpose. The next time the riders were shouting, though their words were lost in the dust and clamor of hooves. Each time the three in the woods moved deeper into the shadows of the trees.

"We will try and rest now," Jenna said. "And we will move only at night. Even if it takes an extra day or two. Carum must be kept safe."

Pynt nodded and, under her breath, muttered, "And we will be safer, too."

They found a hollow tree with a large enough hole that all three of them —with a bit of sorting out of arms and legs—could sleep as comfortably as kits in a den. Pynt reminded Jenna of a story they had heard in Selden Hame about a sister who had lived for a year in a hollow tree, and Jenna smiled at the tale. Carum fell asleep in the middle, snoring lightly.

THE HISTORY

We are more certain of the makeup of the armies of the G'runians than of anything else of that period, since the Book of Battles *is quite clear on the subject. The* Book of Battles *(hereinafter referred to as the BB) is the only extant volume discovered in the old script. It was translated by Doyle even before her monumental work on Alta-linguistics. It is best to remember, however, as Doyle herself reminds us in her Introductory Notes, that work on the BB is far from over. Many words are, as yet, untranslated and the idiomatic phrases are often puzzling. But the BB brings us closer to that dark period in the history of the Isles than any other single rediscovered object.*

The BB is dedicated to two gods: Lord Cres of the dark and Lady Alta of the light. This is the earliest literary reference to Alta, firmly placing her within the Garunian pantheon of gods where, as Professor Temple advises us in his book, "she reigned as a minor goddess of childbirth and song." Even more puzzling, then, her position as dedicatee of the BB, though it would be wrong, as Magon would have it, to conclude that it is "further indication of Alta's warrior status."

The BB begins its descriptions of the armies with the following invocation. (The translation is, of course, Doyle's.)

> *Come, lover of the light,*
> *Come, my strong right arm,*
> *Follow me down into the dark walkways.*
> *Be my sword, my shield, my shadow.*
> *Be my Blanket Companion.*

A curious prayer, and the most curious part of all is the phrase "*Blanket Companion,*" which Doyle translates badly, having—as she says—no notion of the idiomatic usage. She suggests, however, that the phrase has more to do with the homoerotic impulses of long-term soldiery than with actual battles, war, or the makeup of the armies.

The BB delineates three types of forces. Paramount was a warrior caste, a hereditary guard known as Kingsmen who "*ate before the king.*" (Doyle states that it is unclear whether this means the Kingsmen ate in front of the king—i.e., where they were placed at the table—or that part of their job was to serve as food tasters, so that they ate their food earlier than the king.) According to the BB, the sons of a Kingsman could choose to be in the guard, but the eldest had to become a member or forfeit his life. (The phrase "*offer his naked neck to the king's sword*" is used.) There has been much debate about the origins and the state of antiquity of this curious caste. Baum argues for the simple equation: nobles = Kingsmen in his treatise "*Might Makes Right: Noble Ranking and Noble Favors in the Early Dales*" (Nature and History, Vol. 58), while Cowan, always searching for a more intricate answer, holds forth the provocative idea that the Kingsmen represented the retention of arms in the hands of a conquering people who have, by their conquest, reduced an entire population to serfdom. (See her footnote #17 in the article "*Orbis Pictus,*" Art 99.) The Kingsmen were a mounted guard the only soldiers allowed horses, and they rode in groups or troops of twenty that were paired (perhaps Blanket Companions?) under a single leader. These leaders were known by animal names, such as the Hound, the Bull, the Fox, the Bear. (In fact the BB cites twenty-seven such names.) The leaders of this select horseguard were known, collectively, as the Brothers, and the men of the guard colloquially—and only amongst themselves—as the Sisters. (Which nomenclature, Dr. Temple points out convincingly, most likely gave rise to the mistaken belief that there were women in the armies.)

The second type of armed force was the provincial troops that served under a governor appointed by the king. These troops were called Queensmen, a sop perhaps to the matriarchal system so recently overthrown, though they owed their allegiance not to the queen but to the provincial governor(s). Arguably, this was a dangerous system, laying as it did the groundwork for insurrection. Several times in the early history of the Garunian rule of the Isles, according to the BB and corroborated by folk tradition, governors (or Lords) revolted against the king, and the basis of their power was the loyalty of the Queensmen. (See Cowan's "*The Kallas Controversy,*" Journal of the Isles, History IV, 17.)

The third type of armed force was the Mercs, or mercenaries, a small but *significant soldiery. Fearing to arm the conquered peoples of the Isles, the Garunians banned mass conscription, turning instead to hirelings from the Continent. These soldiers of fortune often made vast amounts of money fighting for the king, settling afterward on the land and raising families who were identifiable by their patronymics as sons and daughters of mercenaries. The BB cites several names as typical of such soldiery: D'Uan, H'Ulan, M'Urow, the initial letter identifying the company in which the mercenary had served.*

THE STORY

Jenna awoke first out of a shallow sleep and realized it was the moon that had awakened her. In only a day or two the moon would be full, and in the clear night sky it was a beacon. The hollow tree was on the edge of a clearing, so the clearing itself was well lit. Something dark and small moved past the tree cautiously, turned once, then seeing Jenna's movement, raced away.

Her first thought was to her stomach. They had eaten only handfuls of mushrooms and nuts for days. But a fire and hot food would be impossible, and she did not dare light a torch. It would be another long period of hunger before they came to the Hame.

She touched Pynt lightly on the shoulder, and the touch was enough to wake her.

"Hush, come with me," whispered Jenna.

Pynt was careful not to wake Carum, slipping her legs out from under his. She followed Jenna to the clearing.

"Are we leaving him now?" Pynt asked.

"What do you think?" said Jenna.

"Just checking." Pynt laughed quietly.

"While he sleeps a bit longer, we should see if we can find something to eat."

"Would you believe I have a pocket full of nuts?" Pynt asked.

"No," said Jenna.

"Just checking again." This time Pynt laughed out loud.

"Hunger makes you giddy," Jenna remarked.

"And it makes *you* sour," said Pynt. "For that alone we had better find some food."

They separated quietly, Pynt moving northward into the forest and Jenna searching the clearing's edge.

Pynt found five potherb plants and pulled them up. The root bulbs were small and round and sharp-tasting, but delicious. She nibbled one as she continued searching. She came upon thistle in the usual way—by backing into it. But she remembered Catrona's verse about it:

> *Downy head and thorny spine,*
> *On the roots you safely dine,*

which meant the young, tender roots would be good to eat. Avoiding the prickers, she cut away the roots and chewed thoughtfully on a piece. It tasted a great deal like celery.

Meanwhile, Jenna had found some birds' nests, all but one empty. There were three eggs in that nest and, hoping the young birds had not yet begun to develop, she stole the eggs. A handful of walnuts, still in their coverts, completed her share of the feast.

They met back at the tree and woke the sleeping Carum, who grumbled until they mentioned food. Luckily the eggs were liquid. After showing Carum how to bore a hole in the shell with a knife point, Jenna and Pynt each took an egg themselves and eagerly sucked out the contents. After only a moment's hesitation, Carum did the same.

"I never thought such a meal would taste good," said Carum. "But it's greater than any feast I've eaten."

Jenna smiled, and Pynt said, "At the Hame it is said that *Hunger is the best seasoning*. I do not think I ever understood that before."

Carum laughed. "I understand it, too." He chewed on the thistle root a while, then said, almost to himself, "In the moonlight you two look like shadow sisters, black and white."

Jenna clapped her hands. "We are," she said. "Did you know that Pynt is called 'shadow' in the Hame because . . ."

Pynt stood up abruptly, tumbling her share of the walnuts onto the grass. "It is time to go. Before—Jo-an-enna—you give away all our secret, private things." She threw a shell angrily and went back to the tree to pick up her pack and sword.

"She is tired and hungry and . . ." Jenna began.

"She is jealous," Carum said.

"Jealous of what?"

"Of you. Of me. Of us."

"Us?" Jenna looked puzzled for a moment, then said very slowly, "There is no *us.*" She stood up.

Carum reached up for her hand and she ignored it, so he stood on his own. "Jenna, I thought . . . I felt . . ."

"There is only a woman of Alta and a man who cried her *merci.* That is all." She turned her head away quickly, seeking out Pynt, who stood silently waiting by the tree.

The silence stretched out endlessly as they walked through the midnight forest, Pynt in the lead. They cast long shadows whenever they crossed open ground, the shadow limbs touching in intimate ways none of them dared consider. As if to underscore their silences, the forest seemed alive with small noises. Leaves dropped mysteriously to the ground, crackling. Little animals scurried unseen through the undergrowth, rustling the grass. A night bird called over and over from a low, overhanging branch, in ever-descending loops of sound. And their feet kept up a steady susurration.

They walked hours in the same speechless way, their mouths stoppered by their feelings. Jenna turned time after time to say something to either Pynt or Carum, and found she could not begin, sure that whatever she said would be wrong. So she continued to say nothing, her head down. Trudging through the woods, she scarcely noticed her surroundings until a single, high, fluting birdcall stopped her.

Carum, unalerted, continued walking and crashed into her back. They both leaped away, and Jenna fell against Pynt, who had already turned.

Pynt caught her and whispered, "It is too early for thrush. The sun is not yet warming the woods and there is no light save the moon."

Jenna nodded, signaling to Carum to be still.

The birdcall came again, tremulous, insistent.

"Ours or theirs?" Pynt's question threaded directly into Jenna's ear.

Jenna's response was to put her hand to her mouth and whistle back a darting, twittering reply.

"Good call!" whispered Pynt.

A shadow unwound behind them and hissed. "Sssslowly. Turn slowly so that I might identify you."

Jenna and Pynt obeyed, raising their hands and making the goddess sign quickly with their fingers, but Carum did not move.

The shadow laughed and when it came full into the moonlight, resolved itself into a tall, youngish woman with a vivid brown scar running down her right cheek. Her hair was cut in a high crest and she was wearing the skins of a warrior. Unnocking the arrow, she put it carefully into the quiver on her back in a single fluid motion. Then she struck her breast with her fist. "I am Armina, daughter of Callilla."

"And I am her dark sister, Darmina."

Carum turned to look behind them and there was a second woman, almost a twin of the first, with her hair in a high black crest and a dark scar on her left cheek.

Armina spoke again. "You two are, I think, missioning. But who is this scarecrow you have with you? A boy but not a boy. A man almost. Quite pretty."

Darmina laughed. "For a scarecrow."

"He might be fun in the dark," Armina said.

"Or with a candle by the bed," her dark sister added.

"If he is a bother to you, we could—" Armina stopped speaking suddenly but her grin continued.

"He *is* a bother," said Pynt.

"But a bother we take on willingly," Jenna added quickly.

Armina and Darmina nodded.

Pynt struck her own chest in imitation of Armina's greeting. "I am Marga, called Pynt, daughter of Amalda."

Jenna followed suit. "Jo-an-enna, called Jenna. Daughter of . . ." She hesitated, swallowed, then began again. "Daughter of a cat-killed woman, daughter of Selna."

Pynt added, *"And* daughter of Amalda, too."

"He is Carum," Jenna said, gesturing with her head.

Armina and Darmina walked around Carum several times, clicking their tongues against the roofs of their mouths as they did.

"Close enough to make him interesting, sister," said Darmina.

"There are several in the Hame who like bull calves," Armina replied. "But—alas—he cannot come in. Too close to a Choosing."

"What a pity," Darmina said.

"Pity, my pretty," Armina added.

Jenna pushed between them. "Leave him alone. He cried us *merci.*"

Carum laughed. "They're only teasing, Jenna. I like it. No one has ever admired me for my body before, just my mind!"

"Merci?" Darmina shook her head.

"You have not taken vows yet," said Armina. "Am I right?"

Pynt nodded.

"So—it means nothing. Just a boy and a couple of girls at play. But if you two have spoken for him already . . ."

Pynt looked over at Jenna, and Jenna's face was stone. "We may not be fully vowed yet, but we of *Selden* Hame take such pleas to Alta's altar seriously. We have killed a man for him already."

"A Kingsman," Carum added suddenly.

"Are you sure?" Armina asked, rubbing her hand up through the crest of her hair.

Darmina echoed her. "A Kingsman?"

"If Carum says it is so," Jenna told them, "it is so. He is a scholar and he does not lie."

"Think you scholars do not lie, little sister?" asked Darmina.

Armina chuckled. "One may lie by saying or by *not* saying." She glared at Carum. "Tell us of this Kingsman, boy."

Carum squared his shoulders and stared back at her. "He wore a helm and rode a cross-grained gray. He carried a sword and a dirk at saddle and at knee. Does *that* identify him for you?"

Armina looked over at Pynt. "True?"

Pynt nodded.

"And what did the helm look like?" Armina asked.

"It had antlers," Pynt said.

"Antlers?" Armina shook her head. "I know of no Kingsman who wears an antlered helm."

Jenna interrupted. "From afar they looked like antlers. But I held the helm in my hand and can say different. Not antlers but the great chewed ears, lifted, of a giant hound. With a snout and snarling fangs."

"The Hound!" The sisters spoke together.

"So *he* said." Pynt's head jerked at Carum for emphasis.

"You killed The Hound!" Darmina's voice was low.

Jenna nodded. "We did, Pynt and I. It was not . . . pleasant."

"I can believe that," Armina said. Her mouth worked without sound for a moment, the scar stretching and bunching in an ugly fashion. "So you killed The Hound. Well, well, young missioners. Such news you bring. We must go to the Hame, and at once."

Darmina put her hand on her sister's. "What of the Choosing? And bringing *him* in?"

"We will take him directly up to Mother Alta's chamber by the back stairs. She will know what to do." Still clutching her sister's hand, Armina turned to Jenna. "I wonder, young missioner, what terrible thing you may have brought to our doorstep. And I wonder, too, whether we but compound it by bringing you in. Come."

She threaded her way through the forest, with Darmina, visible only when the moonlight pierced the canopy of trees, right behind. Pynt followed after. Jenna, leading Carum by the hand, made up the rear.

It was fully light by the time they reached the Hame, and only Armina was there to guide them. Where the forest ended, there was a wide clearing rimmed around with berry bushes and several plantings of herbs in straight, marked rows. A wide road ran by the wood-and-stone gates, but it was empty of travelers and the dirt, hard-packed, not recently disturbed.

They walked quickly to the gate and Armina called up a password in the old tongue. Slowly the gates were pulled inward, but not before Jenna had gotten a good, long look at the ornate carvings on the front.

"Jenna," whispered Pynt, "it is the same scene as the tapestry in Mother Alta's room. Look—there is the game of wands, and there Alta collects the children, and there . . ."

They were ushered inside and the great gates slammed shut behind them. Now they stood in a vast, almost deserted courtyard. Only one sister hurried across it, her back to them, holding a full basket of breads heaped high. From the corner of her eye Jenna could see another yard, somewhat smaller, off to the right where three girls her age were lined up with their bows. The steady *thunk-thunk-thunk* of arrows hitting an unseen target squarely came to her, but Armina had already disappeared through an archway on the left. Pynt pulled Jenna to the door and pushed her through.

"Come on," Pynt urged.

Carum followed without a word.

They trotted after Armina through a maze of halls and rooms, more than four times the number at Selden Hame, and climbed two flights of stairs as well. For Jenna and Pynt this was a new experience, for Selden Hame was all on the flat, and they exchanged delighted glances. But Carum mounted the twisting stairs with an air of knowing.

"Castle-born," Pynt muttered at his back, as if that were a curse.

Jenna was still marveling at the complexity of the Hame when Armina stopped suddenly before a door and signaled them with a raised hand. They moved cautiously up to the door, which was even more ornately carved than the outside gate. Only instead of figures, the door was inscribed with symbols: apple, spoon, knife, needle, thread . . .

"Eye-Mind!" Jenna said. "Look, Pynt, the signs are all from the Game."

Pynt traced around the knife sign with her finger.

"Now we go in," Armina said, nodding at them, and her great crest of hair swayed slightly. "In to speak with the Mother."

Jenna drew in several long breaths, ending the Spider breath with which she had climbed the stairs and beginning the deeper *latani* breathing. It soothed her. She could hear Pynt matching her breath for breath.

Armina smiled. "Frightened? Of the Mother?" She pushed through the door into a darkened chamber and dropped to one knee so quickly Carum stumbled into her. The girls, still breathing deeply, walked in more slowly and knelt by Armina's side.

Jenna peered into the dimly lit room, trying to follow Armina's gaze. Between two covered window slits was a large chair. Something—someone—stirred in the chair.

"Mother, forgive me this intrusion, but I come with three whose presence may be in danger. It is for you to say."

There was a long hush. Jenna could hear Carum swallowing. Pynt swayed a bit by her side. Then the figure in the chair gave a sigh.

"Light the lamps, child. I was just napping. Your sisters damp them when I sleep—as if day or night has meaning for me. But I can smell that the lamps are out. And I like the small, hissing sounds they make."

Armina stood and lit the lamps with a torch she fetched from the hall, then drew aside the cloth from each of the windows as well. The light revealed a small, dark figure in the chair, as small as a child, but old. Older, Jenna thought, than anyone she had ever seen, for the woman's face was as brown and wrinkled as a walnut, and crowned with thin, white hair. Her blind eyes were the color of wet marble, gray and opaque.

"Forgive, Mother?" Armina said, but her question carried no deference.

"You scamp, Armina, I always forgive you. You and your dark sister. Come here. Let me feel that foolish head." The old woman smiled.

Armina moved over to the priestess and knelt before her, lifting her face to the old woman's touch. "I am here, Mother."

Mother Alta's fingers, like little breezes, brushed across Armina's face, ran down the scar, and then floated up to the brush of hair. "Who have you brought me? And what the danger?"

"Two girls on a mission, Mother, and a boy they say cried them *merci*," Armina replied.

"The girls, from what Hame?" the old woman asked.

Armina turned and looked at Jenna.

"Selden Hame, Mother," Pynt said before Jenna could answer.

"Ah, the small Hame in the Borderland Hills. How many there now?" She stared at them as if she could see them.

"Forty light sisters, Mother," said Jenna.

"And forty dark," Armina said, chuckling.

"Thirty-nine," Pynt said quickly, delighted to have caught Armina out. "One, our infirmarer, is a Solitary."

"And four missioners and five girls," Jenna finished.

"We have four hundred, light and dark," Armina said. "And many, many children. Many missioners, too, though I doubt they go to so small a Hame as Selden."

"We have only once or twice seen a missioner," admitted Jenna. "But we know about missioning. We know about . . ."

"Girls!" Mother Alta said sharply, and raised her hands, which had been hidden in the voluminous sleeves of her robe. Jenna saw with a kind of fascinated horror that each hand had a sixth finger stretching straight out from the side. She could not keep her eyes off the hands. They seemed to be weaving dark fantasies in the air.

"Now, Armina, you are the older by several years, for your mission is five years gone. Act as a guide and a guard; be my eyes. If there is danger, we must be ware afore time." Her hands disappeared again into the cave of sleeves.

Armina's face darkened for a moment from the scolding; then the mischievous grin reasserted itself. "Mother, the taller one is the one with the lower voice. She stands nearly as tall as I do."

"Taller, since you have that crest," said Pynt.

"That, then, is the smaller one?" asked the priestess.

"Yes, Mother, she is smaller in all but mouth. Slight and dark. Like a woman of the Lower Dales. The boy is reasonably good-looking, fine-featured, none of your barbarian stock. They say he is a scholar and in danger, though what danger a scholar could possibly get into, only Alta knows. Reading the wrong volumes, I suppose. But he is *himself* the danger to our Hame. The girls have killed the Hound in his cause."

The old woman's head came up and her hands flew out of the sleeves again. "The Hound? Are you sure?"

"We . . ." Jenna began, but Carum's hand reached out and touched her on the arm, silencing her.

"Mother Alta," Carum began, his voice strong, *"I* am sure because I knew the Hound well."

"Did you?" murmured Armina.

"How did you?" asked Mother Alta.

"I . . ." He hesitated and darted a quick glance at Jenna. "He was seeking me because I am . . ." He stopped again, drew in a deep breath, and finished, "I am Carum Longbow, a scholar and the king's youngest son."

Jenna's eyes opened wide and Pynt elbowed her in the side. Jenna moved away from her, staring at Carum.

"*So!*" said Armina.

"The Hound hunted for a vicious master," said Carum.

"He hunted for Kalas," Mother Alta said, head nodding.

"You know!" His head began to nod in rhythm with hers. Putting his hands in front of his chest, he said, "Mother, *ich crie thee merci!*"

"It seems, young Longbow, that scholars do not know everything." Her smile added wrinkles. "You have already cried to one Altite, and one is surely enough. If they have killed the Hound who hunted you, indeed what more could they do?"

"These girls have not yet taken their sacred vows, Mother," reminded Armina. "And a vow to a king's son must be . . ."

"We did not know he was a king's son," Jenna said, sharply.

"If we had . . ." Pynt added, but let the rest of her sentence trail off, for she did not know what they would have done.

Neither one mentioned that the Hound had been killed because *he* had attacked *them*.

"What is a vow, Armina, my child," asked Mother Alta, "but the mouth repeating what the heart has already promised? These two young hearts will be no stouter next year, nor their mouths any more truthful after their vows than before. Carum Longbow cried them *merci* as a man, not as a son of this person or that. And they have killed in his cause, because they took on his protection. What can be more binding than blood? What can be more sacred than that? The Goddess smiles."

Armina looked down at the floor and was silent.

"Now, imp, do not sulk. I can hear your angry short breaths. Bring us food that we may sit and gossip of the Hames." Mother Alta chuckled. "And you will share with us, Armina, child of my child."

Armina looked up. "But, Mother, what of the danger?"

"Think you that Kalas' men will look for the boy here? We will dress this young cock in hen's feathers and if he is as fine-featured as you say, if he is young enough to be beardless yet . . ."

"I am, Mother," said Carum. Then he flushed, realizing that it sounded as if he were praising himself.

They all laughed then, Carum a beat behind.

"Now, Armina, get us that food. And some sweet wine. And do not forget a savory for after. But ware—not a word about our guests save that they be missioning. I do not want this young bull calf amongst the heifers undisguised. I wish to discover what I can without the added danger of tongues wagging. If we have one fault here in this Hame, it is that we can keep nothing secret."

"I will say nothing, Mother," Armina promised, "and I will get the food at once." She rose directly and went to the door, where she turned. "There is rhulbarbe pie, your favorite." Then she left, whistling.

Mother Alta sighed. "If she keeps her promise, it will be the first time." Then, bringing her hands once more out of her sleeves and gesturing to them, she said, "But come, my children, closer to these old ears. And tell me how you met and what has transpired since."

A succession of kitcheners left food outside the door on platters decked out with red and gold flowers. Pynt and Jenna helped Armina bring in the plates but ate so eagerly, they scarcely noticed the decorations. And so intent were they on the tales they were spinning for the priestess that the profusion of sweet breads, tangy rabbit stew, and salads of spring lettuce and small onion bulbs went down without comment. The priestess ate with quiet precision, scarcely moving.

They found themselves admitting everything to her, even Pynt's disobedience, even Jenna's disgust at the killing, even their worry at Carum's disappearance into the forest to relieve himself.

After the third time Pynt made excuses for deserting Selinda and Alna, Mother Alta sighed with annoyance.

"Enough of your excuses, child. You have told me not once but over and over that you are Jo-an-enna's shadow and that dark must follow light."

"Yes, yes," Pynt answered.

"Dear child," Mother Alta said, leaning forward in her chair, "though loyalty is prized, Great Alta reminds us that *A foolish loyalty can be the greater danger.* You will find understanding from me but not expiation. We do not yet know what your loyalty will cost."

"Did she actually say that?" Carum asked, breaking into the conversation. It was his first entrance in many minutes. "Great Alta, I mean. Did she actually say that? Or is it written?"

"If she herself did not utter those words, still they are well said," the priestess answered, her mouth twisting with private mischief. "But the words are written down in the *Book of Light,* chapter thirty-seven, verse seventeen, in a quite ordinary hand." She raised her left hand and wriggled all but the sixth finger.

"There is nothing ordinary about that hand," Carum said.

"Ordinary—extraordinary," mused Mother Alta, her head nodding down. Then she looked up, her marble eyes shining. "We are—do you not all feel it—at a moment in history, a nexus, a turning where the ordinary *is* extraordinary. I *know* these things. There is a light in the room, a great light."

"But, Mother," protested Pynt. "You are blind. How can you see a light?"

"I do not *see* it, I feel it," Mother Alta said.

"Like the feeling in the forest right before a storm?" asked Jenna.

"Yes, yes, child. You understand. And do you feel it, too?"

Jenna shook her head. "Yes. No, I am not sure."

"Well, never mind. It is gone now, that feeling," Mother Alta said, her voice whispering off. "Fading . . . fade . . ." Her head nodded once and she was asleep.

"Come," Armina said, standing, "we must leave her to her rest."

"Is she all right?" Carum asked.

"She is old, old past counting, Longbow," Armina said. "And sometimes she is not quite lucid. But today she was—somehow—transformed. Visitors are always good for her, but you three seem special somehow. I have not seen her so—so *animated* in a long time." She bent and quietly began replacing the dishes onto the trays. "She will want to talk to you later, I know."

They helped carry out the trays with as little noise as possible, but nothing seemed to disturb the old woman, who sat upright, eyes closed and mouth slightly open, fast asleep in the chair.

As the door closed behind them and they placed the trays against the wall, Jenna asked, "But should we not move her to her bed? Will she not fall out of the chair?"

Armina shook her head and the great crest of hair waved. "She is tied into the chair. She will not fall."

"Tied! But that . . . that is . . ." Pynt fumbled for the right word.

"*That* is her own request," Armina said, her voice gentle in the extreme. "For if she fell, she could not help herself. She cannot walk, you see."

They went to Armina's room by a dark back stairs, passing no one on the way. It was a pleasant, open room, with a narrow window through which afternoon sunlight streamed. A large bed, its head under the window, the covers rumpled, filled much of the space. On one side of the bed stood an oaken wardrobe, on the other a table with a lamp. Half a dozen piles of clothes were on the floor.

Armina went over to one pile and pulled out a pair of baggy brown britches. From another she chose a red shirt; after holding it to her nose for a moment, she discarded it on a third pile and picked instead a loose blue shirt and a blue scarf.

"There," she said. "These should do. Put them on."

Carum looked around. "Here? With you watching?"

"*Over* your other clothes," Armina said. "I shall want them back when you are gone, and we cannot leave you running naked down the halls of refuge—" She stopped and laughed. "Though it *is* a thought."

He slipped into the trousers and shirt and looked helplessly at the scarf. Armina tied it expertly around his head. The blue brought out the color of his eyes.

"There," she said as she stood back to admire him. "No one would ever guess you are a prince." She looked over at Jenna and Pynt, who had watched the whole thing from the bed. "And no one will guess he is a man, either, not with those long lashes and those eyes."

"Enough!" Carum said, snatching the cloth from his head. "It's bad enough that I have to wear these things. I won't be laughed at."

"Laughter, dear boy," Armina said, turning to him, "is called the goddess gift in this Hame. And it is well known that women can laugh at themselves, whereas men . . ."

"The first thing a scholar learns," Carum said, "is to beware of any sentence that begins *It is well known!*"

"And the last thing a scholar learns is humor," said Pynt.

"Enough," Jenna said. "All of you. Enough. *Wicked tongues make wicked wives.* And that bit of wisdom comes from the Lower Dales."

"Upper, actually," Carum said.

"If you think my tongue is wicked, wait until dark. Darmina's tongue is twice as fast as mine." Armina stopped, tried to catch control of her thought, then exploded into laughter. When she caught her breath again, she shrugged and winked at Jenna and Pynt. "Private joke. *Her tongue is twice as fast!*" She began to laugh again, and the girls looked wide-eyed at her and completely mystified.

Carum's eyes narrowed. His shoulders went down and his head up. "I don't mind women making randy jokes," he said, "but . . ."

"Alta's Hairs!" Armina ran her hand up through her hair. "He is a prude as well. What fun we shall all have."

Carum finished thoughtfully, " . . .their jokes *and* their curses should at least have the grace of originality. Come on, Jenna, Pynt. We're going."

"But where?" asked Pynt.

Jenna stood and pulled Pynt up beside her. "Carum is right. We must go and find Mother Alta and tell her it is time to get Carum to his refuge. Hospitality is one thing, safety another."

"He is safe here," said Armina.

"But is the Hame safe with him here?" asked Jenna.

Pynt thrust her chin forward. "He is *our* pledge, after all. He cried *us merci.* We must go on." She grinned. "But we could pack some food. That rhulbarbe pie was wonderful."

Armina shrugged. "I did not think you even noticed. Very well, I will take you back to Mother Alta. You will never find the way on your own."

"You are talking to three who got through the Sea of Bells in a fog," said Pynt.

"That is child's play compared with the maze of this Hame. Why"—and Armina smiled—"they say there is one young missioner from Calla's Ford who was lost twenty years ago in our halls." Her voice got very low. *"And she has never been found."*

"Can you never be serious?" asked Carum.

"What for?" Armina asked, shrugging again. *"Laugh longer, live longer,* the hill people around here say. But, Longbow, before we go out into the halls, put the scarf back on. It is what makes you look the part. Besides"— and she laughed again—"it goes so well with your eyes." Her laughter was so completely without malice that they were forced to laugh with her, first Pynt, then Jenna, and at last, though reluctantly, Carum.

They followed her out of the room and swiftly traversed the mazing hallways, nodding pleasantly at the women they passed. Armina led them up a broad flight of stairs and past many rooms, until they stood at last before the priestess' carved door once again. The trays of food they had left in the hall were gone.

"There, would you have found it?" Armina asked.

"You took us a different way," said Jenna. "We might have found the old route."

"We *would* have found the old route," said Pynt.

"Or we could have gotten lost *and never found,"* Carum put in, in the same sepuchral tones Armina had used before.

"You see," Armina said with a broad grin, "now Longbow will live longer!" Her face turned suddenly serious. "But mind, you must sit there quietly until she wakes on her own. She is not so sweet-tempered if you wake her beforetime. *I* know!"

* * *

But the old priestess was already awake when they went in, being fussed over by two older women who were arranging her robes and combing her hair, not without some resistance from Mother Alta.

"Leave me," she said to them, dismissing them imperiously with a wave of her hand. The blue priestess sign in her palm showed plainly. "I would talk with these three missioners alone. Armina, guard the door. I do not wish us to be disturbed." Her voice now held an edge of authority. All three women jumped to do her bidding.

When the carved door snicked shut behind them, Mother Alta's hands once more disappeared into the sleeves of her dark robe. She nodded her head and her voice was the same soft burr as before. "Come, children, and sit. We must talk. I have been giving your problems much thought."

"But you were asleep, Mother," Pynt said.

"Is it not written that *Sleep is the great unraveler of knots?* And do not ask in what volume, young Carum. I forget. But this I know, I do my best thinking there, where color and line explode behind my sightless eyes. All becomes clearer to me, as a traveler sees his own home more clearly in a foreign land."

They sat by her feet and awaited instruction.

"Let us first breathe the hundred-chant," Mother Alta said. "And you, Longbow, follow as best you can. It is an old Alta exercise that calms the mind and frees the senses, making one fresh for the new work ahead. With it, the Goddess smiles."

As the deep breathing began, Jenna felt strangely lightened, as if her real self had been pulled free of the body to float above it. The chanting moved into the twenties and thirties, and she seemed to range around the priestess' room without moving, her mind remarking upon the furniture she had not noticed before: the slat bed with its two pillows; a large wooden wardrobe incised with goddess signs; a copy of the *Book of Light* on a stand, its raised letters casting strange shadows in the fading light of day; and a mirror covered by a red-brown cloth the color of dried blood. The chanting bodies below her moved toward the seventies and eighties, and Jenna found herself ranging over them, her translucent fingers reaching down to touch each upon the very center of the skull, where a pulse beat beneath the shield of skin and bone. At the touch—which only she seemed to notice—Jenna found herself drawn down inside each of her companions in turn. Mother Alta was as cool as a well, and as dark. Armina was all sparkling points, like the bright flames and embers of a wood fire. Pynt, on the other hand, was a windstorm, blowing hot, then cold, then hot again in quick and dizzying succession. Carum was . . . She was drawn down and down and down to his center, passing pockets in him, some restful, some fretful, some filled with a wild, engulfing alien heat that threatened to entrap her. She pulled herself away and fled up into the air again, turned, and faced her own chanting self. That was, somehow, the strangest of all, to watch herself, unaware, a secret mirror of . . .

The hundred-chant ended and Jenna opened her eyes, almost surprised to find herself anchored once again in her own flesh.

"Mother," she began huskily, her voice scarcely above a whisper, "a strange thing has just happened. For the time of our hundred-chant, I was —somehow—free of my flesh. I floated above the room, searching for something or for someone."

Mother Alta spoke slowly. "Ah, Jo-an-enna, what you feel is the beginning of womanhood, the beginning of true twinning, though you are much too young if you are only now missioning. Such *enlightness* happens on the Night of Sisterhood, when the soul ranges for a moment, finds the mirror, and plunges into the waiting image. Light calls dark, the two parts of the self are made whole. Did you find the mirror, child?"

"It . . ." Jenna looked around the room and saw that the mirror was, indeed, covered. "There is a cloth over it."

"Then how . . . strange, my child. Strange that you are so young for this. That it is daylight. That the mirror is masked." Her chin touched down on her chest and, for a moment, she seemed to sleep.

Armina stood and quietly went out the door.

"What did it feel like, Jenna?" whispered Pynt. "Were you frightened? Was it wonderful?"

Jenna turned her head to answer, but Carum's hand was on her arm.

"The Mother wakens," he said.

The priestess' opaque eyes were open. "I do not sleep," she said, "but I *do* dream."

Pynt whispered into Jenna's ear, "Armina said she is sometimes not lucid. Is this one of those times?"

"Hush!" Jenna commanded.

"More lucid than ever I was, dear Pynt," the old woman said. "Remember, child, that one who has no sight is gifted extra hearing. It is nature's way."

"Forgive me, Mother," Pynt said, her head lowered. "I meant no . . ."

Mother Alta's hand crept from her sleeve and swept away Pynt's embarrassment with a quick gesture. "We must all think, now. What brings us together?"

"We came back, Mother, to tell you that we must get Carum away from here," said Pynt.

"I fear I am a danger to your Hame. We saw riders . . ." Carum began.

"Oh, there is more to the puzzle than these few pieces," Mother Alta said. "Something is missing. The Game is incomplete. I cannot recall all the parts." She began to mumble to herself. "Light sister, dark sister, needle, spoon, knife, thread . . ."

Pynt elbowed Jenna.

The old woman's head snapped up. "Come to me, Pynt, and tell me of yourself. Not *what* you have done, for that I know. But *who* you are." The old woman gestured to her.

Reluctantly, with Jenna pushing her, Pynt inched closer to the priestess and knelt so that her head was within reach of the six-fingered hands.

"I am Marga, called Pynt," she began, "daughter of the warrior Amalda, whose dark sister is Sammor. I have chosen the way of warrior and hunter. I . . ." She giggled as the priestess' hand ran down her face.

"Good, good, child. My eyes are in my fingers. They tell me you, Marga called Pynt, have dark, curly hair and a quick smile."

"How do you know I have dark hair? The eyes in your fingers cannot tell you that."

"By the coarseness of the strands. Dark hair is always coarser than light. Light hair has a fineness to it, and red hair often confuses."

"Oh."

The old woman smiled. "Besides, Armina told me you were dark like a woman of the Lower Dales. I may be old, but my memory is still sharp. *When* I am lucid."

Pynt's cheeks flushed and the old woman laughed.

"Are you embarrassed, child, or are you disappointed that my magic has such a mundane explanation?"

Pynt did not answer.

"Never mind. Go on, child."

"I have a scar on my right knee from wrestling with Jenna when we were seven, right before the Choosing. And my eyes are dark."

"Almost violet," put in Jenna.

"And . . ."

"And you have a fine scar under your chin. More wrestling, Pynt?"

"I fell in the kitchen in a game of Seek and Find. It bled forever. At least it seemed so at the time."

"Good. That is all I need to know of you now. Jenna?"

Jenna slid over to Pynt's place. In passing, Pynt winked and whispered, "It tickles."

"I am not ticklish."

Carum cleared his throat but said nothing.

The priestess' fingers started over Jenna's face. "Speak, child."

"I am Jo-an-enna, called Jenna, daughter of a cat-killed woman and fostered to Selna, the great warrior of Selden Hame, and her dark sister Marjo. I am named for her, I think."

"You think—you do not know?"

"They died when I was but an infant."

"And then who fostered you at the Hame, thrice-mothered child?"

Her voice faltered. "No one."

"*Our* Mother Alta would let no one else foster her. It was the shame of Selden Hame," Pynt put in. "My mother, Amalda, would have had her gladly. But there was something awful that happened when her foster mother died. Something so awful, they were not allowed to talk of it. And . . ."

"Enough, Pynt," Jenna said.

"Let her tell," said Mother Alta.

But Pynt bit her lip and was still.

The priestess' hands returned to Jenna's head. The right hand made the goddess sign over her; then the sixth finger of the hand caught in Jenna's hair.

"Are you dark, too, Jo-an-enna? Your hair is not fine enough for light, yet Pynt calls you her light sister."

"And I call her White Jenna," Carum put in. "At least I call her that to myself."

"*White* Jenna?" The priestess was suddenly still, as if listening to a song no one else could hear. At last she asked quietly, pausing between each word, "And . . . is . . . your . . . hair . . . pure . . . white?

"Yes, Mother," Jenna replied.

Mother Alta smiled triumphantly. "The final piece of the Game!" she said. "And if I were not blind, I would have known it at once." She sang out a low plainsong of five lines in a voice that rang clearly through the room.

THE SONG

Prophecy

The babe as white as snow,
A maiden tall shall grow,
And ox and hound bow low,
And bear and cat also.
Holy, holy, holy.

THE STORY

When the song ended and the echo of it was gone as well, Jenna started up. "I am *not* the White Babe. Our Mother Alta said I was, but I reject that utterly. Look at me. Look!" She turned to her friends, her voice pleading. "Do I look like something from a prophecy?"

Carum reached up and pulled her down beside him. "Hush, Jenna," he said, stroking her hand. "Hush. This is just an old woman's whim. Let *me* deal with this. It is scholar's work." He spoke to the priestess. "That is a Garunian prophecy, Mother. The white babe and the bowing of hound and ox and the rest. But no one takes it seriously, no real scholar." He smiled.

"Ah, young Longbow, and did you think you were the only scholar, the only *real* scholar, on the Isles?"

Carum's cheeks flushed. "Of course not. But I surely didn't expect to find one here."

"Here, in this backwater, you mean? Amongst the warrior maidens? But we are not all warriors here, much as I must look the part to you." She chuckled pleasantly. "Some of us must cook and some of us must clean and some of us must keep the rota of events, just as it is amongst you of the outer world. And *some* of us"—she leaned forward—"*are* real scholars."

Settling back in her chair, she continued. "Who knows what I might have been in your world, Carum, for I am a daughter of a Garun lord. Yes, even I. But look at my hands, look deep into my eyes, and you will see the signs of my abandonment." She held her six-fingered hands before her face. "I was a babe wrapped in cloth of gold and left on a heath long years after white-haired Alta had reaped the hillsides. Still the women of the Hames, to honor her, culled that forbidden crop. I was brought to this Hame and raised up to lead. Years later, when my father's line had come to its barren end, a messenger sought out all the Hames to ask whether a blind child with twelve fingers had miraculously weathered the years. But my foster mother and sisters would not give me up, nor would I have gone if asked. I had pledged myself to Alta, and Alta's I remain." She stopped and tapped a finger to her mouth.

"It was clear to all that I was a strange child bound for a stranger destiny than death on a hillside. Yet no one knew what role I would play. I chose to study, and was curious about my father's world, learning of it as I had learned all else, with my ears, the good, strong daughters of the mind. I have learned—through these ears, Carum—more than you shall ever through your eyes."

"I apologize for my thoughtlessness, Mother," said Carum, striking a fist against his chest.

"It is youth's privilege to be thoughtless," Mother Alta replied. "But also youth's privilege to learn. Think, Carum Longbow. You and I *may be* kin in blood, but we are kindred souls. We seek connections, we look for links. You see, I know the Garunian prophecy."

"Only the plainsong, Mother. And it is much discredited."

She laughed. "You think I know only the plainsong, child? No, indeed. I know the entire prophecy: about the virgin in the winter, though we say here at the Hame that *virgin* is just another word for a girl. So it could be that the babe's mother was more or less a child herself. And I know about the mothering three times. And all the rest. Know you Alta's prophecy so well?"

He shook his head. "I don't know it at all," he said. "Much of Alta is closed to outsiders."

"And so we desire to keep it," she answered. "But I can tell you this much: what our prophets wrote is the light sister to your dark. We hold—and we believe it utterly—that there will be a child as white as snow, as black as night, as . . . what color are your eyes, Jenna?"

"Black, Mother," Jenna replied. "But . . ."

"As white as snow, as black as night, as red as blood."

"What is red about her?" asked Carum.

"Do I know all? The language of prophecy is the language of puzzles, is the language of riddles, is the language of dreams. What is said is not always what is meant. Often we come to understanding long after the events have occurred. Perhaps the red was the Hound's blood. Perhaps it will be Jenna's first flow. But like the Garunians, we say clearly that this one shall be queen above all and she shall begin the world anew. The one great task laid upon Mothers of every Hame is this: to wait for her, to look for her, the white child, the Anna."

"The *Anna*," mused Carum. "The white babe, the great white goddess."

Nodding, Mother Alta continued. "Many thought I was marked for the Anna myself, for my hair turned white overnight when I was eighteen. And to look upon me was to be sure I had been touched by Alta's heavy hand. Long we waited and nothing more occurred, till at last my sisters pitied me for being naught but an unnature, a freak. Yet I, alone, never lost hope that I might be part of the workings-out of the prophecy. If not the Anna herself, at least her forerunner, her guide, the one who sings her praises. *Holy, holy, holy.* And now the Anna is here."

"No, Mother. Not here. Not me," Jenna cried. "I am not that white babe. I am only Jenna of Selden Hame. When I have a cold, my nose runs. When I am hungry, my stomach growls. When there are beans in the stewpot, I make a stink. I am no Anna. I am just a girl."

"The signs cannot be ignored, my child," Mother Alta said. "Much as you would like to. Though it is true there have been thrice-mothered girls before. And there have been white babes with hair the color of snow and eyes like watered wine. But the Hound bowed down. That cannot be forgot —the Hound bowed down."

"He did not bow, Mother. He died," Jenna said. "With my sword in his throat and Pynt's knife in his thigh."

"And what greater obeisance?" Mother Alta asked.

"Might as well say the white-haired babe will have red hair," Jenna said unhappily. "Might as well say a goat and a horse will bow to her."

"Might as well," murmured Pynt.

Mother Alta chuckled, a low, cooing sound. "Prophecies speak to us on the slant, child. We must read them through slotted eyes."

"*You* read them," Jenna said. "I will not."

Carum, who had been listening to the exchange with a faraway look in his eyes, suddenly turned to the priestess. "Mother Alta," he said slowly, "the prophecy also says that the white babe will begin the world anew. That's the point of the whole thing, isn't it? But to do that, one must first . . . must first . . ." He hesitated.

"Spit it out, boy!"

"First one must destroy the old, and that I can't see Jenna doing."

"Ah, Longbow, on the slant. See the world on a slant . . ." she murmured and fell asleep with a strange smile on her face, as quickly and as quietly as an infant taking a nap.

They looked at one another and, as if on a signal, all stood, opened the door carefully, and slipped out into the darkening hall.

Armina was outside the door. "Well, what did she say? Is she still asleep?"

"She . . . she asked us about our lives. Who we were. And—yes—she is asleep. But she said we must . . . must find refuge for me," Carum said.

Jenna and Pynt said nothing, their silence conspiring to agree with him.

Armina looked puzzled for a moment. She blew air into her cheeks and the dark scar puffed out. Then she smiled. "Refuge. Of course. But first we must all eat. It will be a long trip otherwise. I will take you back to my room and bring the food there. No one else must know our plans. When it is dark, we will start out and that way I shall have Darmina for company. It is the last night before the full moon."

They followed her down the stairs. The wall sconce sent shadows bouncing along behind them, and they were silent for the entire time. Feeling like conspirators, they entered Armina's room and sat uncomfortably on her bed, and stared up guiltily. She smiled at them from the door.

"I will be back soon. With the food." Then she closed the door behind her. Instead of the comfortable snick, the door let out a strange, ratcheting sound.

Jenna leaped up and ran to it, trying to push it open. She turned back to her companions with a stricken look. "She has barred it. She has barred the door. It will not open." Then she turned again to the door and hammered on it, shouting, "Armina, what are you doing? Let us out."

Armina's voice strained through the thick oaken barrier. "You did not tell me the truth, sisters. Mother would never send you elsewhere for refuge. Not without telling me. I will speak with her when she wakes. Until then, stay quiet. *This* is a place of refuge. No harm will come to you here."

Jenna put her back to the door and looked at her friends. "And what do we do now?"

In the end they did nothing. The door was impassable and the single window, while wide enough for Pynt, was too narrow a slit for either Jenna or Carum. Besides, it was too high for escape, even with all the bedclothes and Armina's few leggings knotted together. What appeared to be the second floor was really the fourth, for the back end of the Hame was built on a cliff which fell off abruptly into swift-flowing river. Neither of the girls could swim.

It was well after dark, with the moon grinning through the window slits, when Armina returned. She and her dark sister opened the door and barred it with their swords, sliding the tray of food into the room with their feet before speaking.

"Mother still sleeps," Armina said. "You will see her first thing in the morning. Your visit tired her. So eat well, and rest."

Darmina smiled at them. "The bed is wide enough for two—or three, if you are so minded."

Armina looked at the window, where the bedclothes were still knotted and the end wound several times around the sconce. She laughed. "I see you have used your time well. When I was younger, I used to slip out of the window and dangle over the river. It was what we all did, before we were allowed to play at the Wands. But in those days we were on a lower floor and the drop was not so deadly. Except . . ."

Darmina took up the narrative. "Except there was one girl, a silly twist named Mara, who had wet hands and a weak heart."

"It matched her chin. She let go. She screamed all the way down until the water covered her mouth." Armina's free hand ran up through her crest of hair.

"She could not swim," Darmina added.

They ended together, *"And her body was never found."*

"Another one of your ghost stories?" asked Carum.

"Call it a warning tale," Armina answered. "Besides, there are guards."

"Why, Armina?" asked Pynt. "Why not just let us be on our way?"

"Twice this evening Kingsmen have been to our gates asking about Longbow, calling him by name and describing him by a few choice birthmarks."

Carum blushed.

"Twice we have sent them away knowing nothing," Armina continued. "They are not singling *us* out. They are asking the same questions in all of the villages as well. But Longbow cried us *merci,* and so we must shield him."

"He cried *us!*" Jenna pointed out.

"And in so doing, cried us all," Darmina said. "Did not Mother Alta tell us that?"

"But you . . . you were not there this afternoon when she spoke with us," Carum began, looking first at Darmina, then at Armina. "Or at least I think it was you." He pointed to Armina, who smiled.

Darmina took up that smile and answered him. "Do you not understand yet, *scholar,* that what my light sister knows, I know?"

Armina lowered her sword a fraction of an inch. "We wait for Mother to awaken. She will tell us what we must do. My mother, Callilla, says there is a secret passageway out of here, through the priestess' room and down along the river. But only Mother Alta knows the way."

"Then for our sake, or Alta's sake, or the sake of the Hame," cried Carum, "wake her."

Both sisters shook their heads.

"We cannot," said Darmina. "The Mother is exhausted. If we wake her before time, she will be muddled and it will avail us not. And soon enough it will be morning." She gestured with the sword toward the window, where the moon had already traveled beyond the window slit. "So sleep. And sleep well. We will have much to do tomorrow."

So saying, the sisters backed out of the door, slammed it, and slid the heavy bolt across it once more.

"What do we do now?" asked Pynt.

"What *can* we do?" said Carum.

"We can eat!" Jenna said. "And worry after."

They broke for the tray and sat around it, and, after the first few bites, relaxed enough to eat the meal slowly, savoring the steaming pigeon pie, the pickled eggs, and the rose-colored wine. When there was nothing left but a few slivered bones and the gillyflower that had decorated the platter, they stopped.

Pynt belched daintily and lay down on the bed. Jenna crawled up next to her. Carum looked longingly at the empty side of the bed, then lay down on the floor, under the window, and covered himself with a piece of the knotted blanket. He was conscious of the sound of the girls' breathing, steady and sighing, from the bed. The floor was hard under him. He thought he could feel a nail unevenly hammered into the boards. Just when he had resigned himself to a sleepless night, he slipped reluctantly into a dream. It concerned Jenna, who was tied to a chair, her long, white hair blowing across her face as if stirred by a sea wind. She was crying out to him, but the voice was an infant's, high, frantic, wordless, and thin.

They were awakened not by the sliver of morning sun through the window slit but by Armina's voice.

"Mother Alta is awake and asking for you. It is a good sign. She remembers all. Come."

They roused quickly, and Pynt and Jenna took turns with Armina's combs. She had brought them water in a pitcher and a bowl. The scented water felt cool on their faces. With his back to them, Carum waited until they were done, then ordered them outside.

"Men seem to take forever cleaning themselves," remarked Pynt as they waited.

"Perhaps they have more to clean?" mused Jenna.

Armina laughed. "I take it, then, you spent a *quiet* night."

"We slept," Jenna said.

His face clean and his hair combed, Carum stepped out into the hall. "What I'd give for a real bath," he said.

"That can be arranged," said Armina. "In daylight or at night?"

"As long as there's plenty of hot water, I don't care about the time."

"*Not care?*" Armina laughed out loud. "Oh, you *are* innocent of Alta's ways, boy."

Pynt and Jenna giggled and Carum blushed furiously.

"But we have no time for baths or . . . other things. Mother wants us now." Armina led them quickly up the back stairs.

Mother Alta's door was open and the old woman was waiting for them. "Come in, come in quickly. We must talk of Jenna's future."

"But what of my future, Mother?" asked Pynt, settling herself down at the priestess' feet. "And Carum's?"

Mother Alta reached out toward her and Pynt shrank back from the touch. "Child, if Jenna is who I say she is, then her future is all of ours. She is the rushing river and we are carried along. But you, dear child, must learn to think before you speak, not to push ahead. Use your head in front of your heart, else you will have no future at all."

Pynt's lips pursed, and she shrugged away from Mother Alta's words.

"Pynt," Jenna began, "do not be hurt. That is no more than what A-ma has always said to you."

"And you, Anna," Mother Alta said, shifting slightly in her chair. "You must learn to listen more to the musings of your heart, to lengthen yourself by your own shadow. Heart and head working together is always the best way."

"Mother, for the last time, I am not the Anna. I puzzled it over all this past night, praying to Alta for guidance. And . . ."

"And?" The old woman leaned forward in her chair.

"And I found no greatness in me. Only the memories of an ordinary childhood."

"What do you think the Anna should have?" asked Mother Alta. "Thunder and lightning at her birth? An animal in the woods to nurse her?"

"Something," Jenna begged. "Something out of the ordinary."

"And would you recognize it, Jo-an-enna, if this something extraordinary happened to you? Or would you excuse it, lopping off the unwieldly parts to fit it into your ordinary life? Do not worry. When you and I are long in the Cave, there will be poets and storytellers who will gift you such a birth."

Jenna looked down, unable to meet those marble eyes. She tried to concentrate on the priestess' words, but there was an awful pain in her stomach, almost as if she were hungry. And an angry buzz in her ears. Then she realized the buzz came from the window. She glanced over at it.

Mother Alta, too, had stopped to listen.

Noting their attention, Pynt stood up and went over to the window, standing on tiptoe to see out.

"What is it, child?"

"A knot of men and horses, Mother, in front of the gate. They are shouting, though I cannot make out their words. The guards atop the gate are shouting back. One man is on a gray horse and . . ."

Carum leaped up and ran to the window. "Oh, the gods! Kingsmen! And that is the Bull himself. Now we're for it."

"The Bull," said Pynt, "has a spear and is shaking it at the guards."

"There's something on the spear tip," said Carum.

"I see it! I see it!" Pynt said excitedly. "Oh, Alta's eyes!" She dropped down from the window and turned slowly, a strange look on her face. Then she found their packs where they had left them the night before, upended her own, dropping the contents on the floor. Pawing through her meager possessions, she gave a horrified cry.

"What is it, Marga?" asked Mother Alta.

Jenna ran over to the window slit herself. Tall enough to see out without straining, she stared at the scene below. "I see him. I see the Bull. What is it? Oh, Pynt, no!" She turned. "It is my light doll, Pynt. The one I gave you."

Pynt's voice was an agony. "I cannot find it, Jenna. It must have dropped from my pack."

"When, Pynt, when?"

"I cannot remember. I had it . . . I had it when I was first trailing you. I slept with it in my arms."

Jenna said nothing, remembering vividly how she had spent the night in the crotch of the tree with Pynt's doll wrapped in her embrace.

"And I never took it out again, just jammed it on top of the pack. And then we met Carum and . . ." Pynt stopped, horror written all over her face. Putting her head in her hands, she shuddered.

Though Mother Alta's eyes could not read Pynt's face, she understood the sudden silence. "You remember, child."

Pynt looked up. "In the fight with the Hound, I tripped over my pack and it spilled. I gathered everything up after we buried him. At least I thought I gathered everything up. I must have missed the doll in the fog."

"Oh, you *twist!*" said Carum in disgust.

"Quiet, Longbow," Darmina said. "She was fighting in your cause."

Jenna took up the tale in a quiet voice. "We could not stand to sleep close to the grave and so we moved on a bit and did not look back in the morning." She hesitated.

"Yes, that is what must have happened," said Mother Alta, nodding. "Those men, Kingsmen, came upon Carum's old trail and followed it to the site of the fight and the grave with its dreadful contents. And there was the doll nearby. Who but a young Altite would have a doll so deep in the woods? Surely not the boy they were seeking! We at Nill are the closest Hame, so of course they came here."

"Mother, I am sorry . . ." Pynt began.

"There is no blame, daughter," Mother Alta said. "No blame at all. You are simply playing out your part in the prophecy. What will be was written long before you were born."

Pynt began to weep openly.

"Now listen to me, my children, it is clear there will be a battle. These men are in no mood to be cozened. And they are no fools. We must try to buy some time. In the daylight our forces are halved. And—"

Carum interrupted. "You don't *really* mean the dark sisters aren't here until night?"

Armina laughed. "Why do you men have such trouble believing that?"

"It is mere superstition. There are other tribes, down in the Dales, who believe that their mothers are filled by the god of the river and they give birth at the flood. And the Besarmians say that the son of their god comes down once a month in the shape of a bee to . . ."

"Darmina is no superstition. She is real. You saw her. You talked to her, you . . ."

"Children, we have no time for this. Carum will believe what he will. So it has been through the years. Men see and do not understand. Their minds belie their ears and eyes. Come, now, Armina, I need you to go down and tell Zeena to keep the gate closed no matter what. And bring the little ones here to me." Mother Alta stopped and ran her curious hands across her eyes. As the door closed behind Armina, Mother Alta suddenly cried out, "Oh, that my blindness brought us to this place. If I had guessed earlier, I might have . . . I might have . . . I am old, my children. And blind. And helpless." Two large tears ran down her cheeks. Then she looked up at them with her sightless eyes. "No—not *so* helpless. For the *Anna* is here. So the ending begins. But so, too, the beginning."

Jenna and Pynt looked at each other, shaking their heads. Carum put his finger to his temple and touched it, nodding.

"Come here, Jo-an-enna," commanded Mother Alta.

Jenna glanced at her companions once more, then moved closer to the priestess, who reached out to touch her hands.

"Listen carefully, for if this is indeed the end, you must understand what lies ahead. The prophecy says that you shall be queen and not queen, and that you shall carry three babies."

"Mother, I am but thirteen years old," Jenna said.

"And not yet to your woman time, I suspect," Mother Alta said, cocking her head to one side as if listening for the sound of Jenna's nod.

"Not yet," Jenna whispered, blushing furiously.

"But if you are to be a queen, then you must know a king. I suspect your meeting with this young Garun princeling Longbow is no coincidence but further proof."

"Mother," Jenna whispered urgently, "he is but fifteen or so." She took her hands away from the old woman's and held them swiftly at her side.

Carum cleared his throat. "I am seventeen, Jenna."

"Does he look at you?"

Jenna was silent, embarrassed.

"You tell me so with your silence."

"I am Alta's own."

The old woman chuckled. "So am I. So are we all here. Yet still there are babes in our cradles, and not all are fostered. The girls go down into the towns for long nights. The world turns ever and the sun goes east to west. *Queen and not queen.* What can that mean but that you will bear a king sons but not sit on the throne. Sometimes prophecies are easy to unriddle. Sometimes."

"But the fight, Mother. What shall we do?"

"You shall get the boy from here. The Kingsmen must not find him at Alta's door. Better that they not suspect you are the white one spoken of in their own prophecy, the one before whom Hound and Ox and Bear and Cat bow down. Take him from here, you and your dark sister."

"Pynt? You mean Pynt is in the prophecy, too?" Jenna grabbed onto the old woman's hands thankfully, almost tugging her from her seat.

But Mother Alta looked away, as if listening, and Jenna listened, too. The sounds outside were louder, angrier.

"Quick, my child, take this ring." She slipped the great agate ring from her tiny bird-talon finger. It barely fitted on Jenna's pinkie. "You must go from Hame to Hame to warn them. Say this: *The time of endings is at hand.* Say it to the Mothers. They will know what to do. Repeat it."

In a little voice Jenna said, *"The time of endings . . .* oh, Mother Alta, I am not who you think I am."

"Say it!"

She whispered, *"The time of endings is at hand."*

"Good. There is a map of all the Hames. Can you read maps?"

"We both can," said Pynt.

Mother Alta ignored her and spoke to Jenna alone. "Go to the mirror." She gestured with her head to the great covered mirror. "Touch the goddess sign, turning it to the left. A small drawer will open and in it will be the map. Every Hame is outlined in red."

It was Pynt who leaped up first, crossing to the mirror. A sliver of morning light touched the cover. She took off the cloth and stepped back, shocked at her own blanched reflection. Then she found the carved goddess sign and moved it to the left. There was a loud click and the sign leaped open, disclosing a little dark cubbyhole. Reaching in, she found a piece of parchment and removed it.

"I have it, Mother," she said.

"Give it to the Anna."

Pynt handed it to Jenna, who opened it. It was a map outlined in spidery black writing. The names of the seventeen Hames were in red. Jenna folded it back along the deep creases and slipped it into her tunic.

"Let no one else take it," Mother Alta said. *"No one."*

"Not even Pynt? You said she was my dark sister."

"Only if you are dying. Only then."

"Only then," Jenna whispered, though she could not quite take it in. Dying? How could she think of it? Even when she had been fighting the Hound, she had not thought about the possibility of death, only what it might feel like to be wounded. "Only then," she whispered.

"Now go."

"What of you, Mother?"

"My children will care for me. And I care for them. So go now. The time grows short."

Jenna nodded and started toward the door. "Alta's blessings, Mother," she said, looking over her shoulder. She signaled the others to her.

"Wait," Carum said. "Armina said there was a secret passage. We could go out that way."

"There is no such thing," said Mother Alta. "Armina has these . . . little tales she likes to tell. Her own fancies."

"So we have learned," said Carum.

"Will we meet again, Mother?" asked Jenna.

"We will surely meet again in the Cave," the old woman said. It was her only benediction.

Jenna turned and went out the door, the others following her. As they went down the stairs, the thread of Mother Alta's reedy voice followed them to the first landing, singing the song of burial.

> *In the name of Alta's cave,*
> *The dark and lonely grave . . .*

They met Armina on the landing. She was carrying an infant in each crooked arm and there were two little ones clinging to her jacket. Behind her trailed a dozen or so girls past the age of First Choosing, each holding a sleeping babe. Beyond them were five older girls and they, too, carried babes not quite at the toddling stage.

Jenna, Pynt, and Carum put their backs to the wall to let the processional pass.

Armina smiled. "The Mother wishes to bless them," she said as she went by. "And to keep them from any fighting."

The children were silent as they filed past the landing; one golden-haired little one in the arms of the next-to-last girl waved to them. Jenna waved back.

"I've never seen such quiet children," remarked Carum.

"Alta's babes are ever so," said Pynt.

At the final turning, they came into the Great Hall, a high-ceilinged, light-filled room with great vaulted wooden ribs that held up the roof. Candelabra hung on long chains from the roof beams, swaying slightly.

The room was abuzz with women at work on weapons. A group of them squatted in a semicircle, honing knives rhythmically and chanting. Over to the side, in a small alcove hung with bows, a group of ten women was testing bowstrings and nocking arrows. They were speaking softly to one another, and one had thrown her head back and was laughing. By the great hearth, small knots of three and four women huddled together, talking intensely as they plaited ropes.

"We will be in a *real* battle this time," Pynt remarked.

"Was the slaying of the Hound not real enough for you?" Jenna asked.

"You know what I mean, Jenna."

"Well, I don't," Carum said. "Blood is blood."

Pynt turned on him. "You do not know? I thought scholars knew everything. I mean sisters side by side, the way the ballads tell of it." She began to recite the first lines of *Krack's Ride:*

> I sing the arrow's song,
> The eager, whistling flight,
> I sing the sword's sharp tune,
> And sisters side by side . . .

"You are like that arrow," said Carum. "Too eager."

"What do you know of it, who loses his meager dinner over a killing?"

Jenna put her hand on Pynt's shoulder. "He is right, Pynt. We should not be so eager for killing. Who knows—we may be the ones killed."

"And what if we are?" asked Pynt. "Then we will go directly to Alta's cave." She glared at Carum.

"Where you will throw the bones over your shoulder for the Dogs of War, I suppose," he countered.

"Shut up, *scholar,*" said Pynt. "I say only what we all say before a battle."

"Then you say it because you are afraid. Not because you believe in the beauty of battles."

"Of course we are all afraid," Jenna said. "We would be stupid to be otherwise. And *that* is what all this bickering is about. But the battle is not ours. You both heard the Mother. We must get you away from here, Carum, and when you are safe, our task is to take a long route around to warn all the Hames."

Pynt turned her head away and stared at the floor. "If it were our own Mother Alta, I would disobey her again. But this one is no Serpent Mouth, is she?"

"No, Pynt, she is not. And Carum cried us . . ."

" . . . *merci,* I know. But could we not get him to his refuge and hurry back here for the fight?"

Jenna shook her head.

"Then we will do what Mother Alta says. But still, I feel we will be in the thick of things and they will sing of us long after we are gone," Pynt said.

Carum snorted. "You'd like that! *The Battle of Pynt and White Jenna*, accompanied by nose flute and tembala."

"No, scholar, I think it will be called *How the Dark Warrior Marga Saved a Princeling's Insignificant Skin.*"

"I will write one myself," said Jenna, "though I have no gift for balladry, and I shall call it *The Day Jenna Knocked Heads.*"

Carum laughed and, to her surprise, Pynt laughed, too, and when Carum held out his hand, Pynt took it.

"But which way will we go?" Pynt asked.

As they were puzzling that over, a tall, long-nosed woman came over to them.

"I am Callilla," she said, "the mother of Armina. There is a back door Mother Alta wishes you to know."

On the landing, Armina turned to the little ones. She pursed her lips and whistled once, stopping them all.

"Soon Mother Alta will speak to you and you must listen without comment. What she says, you must do—as always. Big ones, help the little ones. There may be dark times ahead, and fearsome. But we are Alta's own. We will not be afraid." She nodded at them.

The girls nodded back, solemnly.

Armina led them to the carved door and pushed it open with her foot. The children filed into the room in front of her. Then Armina entered and kicked the door shut behind.

"We are ready, Mother," she said.

Mother Alta smiled at the children, who stood waiting for her command. She lifted her arms. "Sit, my babes, and I will tell you a story."

They sat at her feet.

"Once, long ago, before you were born, the first Mother Alta of Nill's Hame was told in a dream of a great battle to come. She dreamed that all the children were saved because they lived like little creatures in a warren. And so she had a secret tunnel built against that time." She smiled again and put her finger against her lip.

Some of the littlest children imitated her gesture.

"Today is a special day," said Mother Alta, "for we are going to find that secret tunnel. It will be your safe passage. Armina shall lead you there and there you shall wait. Food has been placed on shelves and you shall stay in your warren, eating when you are hungry, sleeping when you are not. Some of you shall be little rabbits, who shall it be?"

Only seven of the girls raised their hands.

"Good," said Mother Alta, as if she had counted them with her sightless eyes. "And we need some little moles, too."

Two girls raised cautious hands.

"And some little jumping mice?"

A host of other hands went up.

"And you older girls will be foxes and hedgehogs to keep the little ones in line. Do you understand?"

They nodded and she heard the movement of the air where they had agreed.

"When the food is gone, one by one the foxes shall emerge and check to see if all is safe. If it is not, return to the warren until you are called. One shall save you. You will know her by her white hair. She is the Anna, sent by Great Alta."

"But, Mother," piped one of the four-year-olds, the golden-haired child with the sunny face. "We have seen the Anna already. She was on the stairs."

"You will see her again," promised Mother Alta. "She will come for you with a sword of fire and a heart of flame."

"Will you come, too?" persisted the child.

"The warren is only for little creatures."

"But you *are* little," the child said.

Armina hissed through her teeth to shut her up.

Mother Alta smiled again. "I will not enter your warren, but I will guard the way."

The children nodded.

Mother Alta leaned forward in her chair. "Armina, line the children up before my mirror."

It took no more than a minute for all the children to be so aligned.

"Now touch the goddess sign and turn it to the right."

At Armina's touch, there was a loud, groaning sound and the floor beneath the mirror's carved legs slid open, disclosing a dark stair.

"Look into Mother Alta's glass once, where someday you shall find your dark sisters, then go down the stairs. Armina shall lead you and light the way."

Armina took the lamp from the wall, lit it, and—first looking into the glass—led the children down the stairs. As the last of them disappeared,

Mother Alta sighed and brushed away the tears that had pooled in the corners of her marble-colored eyes.

THE LEGEND

There was once a noddy old woman of Nilhalla's Crossing who had so many children, she kept them in an underground warren as if they were rabbits or mice. No one knew the children were there, indeed no one even suspected it, for the woman was as ugly as early spring and twice as windy.

One day the old woman died. Of distemper, some said; of pure meanness, said others. When the guardsmen went to bring out her body for burial, they found the warren entrance and lifted up the great wooden door barricading it.

Thirty-seven half-starved children of all ages scattered out, but they had lived so long under the ground in the dark like animals, they were blind, every one. And their long, unkempt hair had turned white. Ever since, Nilhalla's Crossing has been known as the Home of the White Babes.

This is a true story. It was told by Salla Wilmasdarter, whose great-grandfather had been a guard at the Crossing around the time the old woman's warren was uncovered.

THE STORY

Callilla led them across the Great Hall, threading a line between the busy women and into the kitchen, which was three times the size of the kitchen at Selden Hame.

Pynt gasped at it, but Jenna kept her eyes on Callilla's back. Carum trailed behind.

"Jenna," Pynt whispered, "they are heating great vats of oil."

"And water," said Jenna.

"You did not look."

"On the slant, Pynt. You have to use your woods' eyes everywhere."

"Do not lecture me, Jo-an-enna."

"Then do not be stupid, Marga."

"And do not call me stupid."

Suddenly Callilla turned right and stopped before a plain door. "Here," she said.

They clustered around her.

"This door opens onto a narrow, steep path that goes down to the Halla."

"That's the river," Carum said.

Callilla nodded. "The Halla is swift and unforgiving, so you must take care."

"I cannot swim," said Pynt.

"Nor I," admitted Jenna.

"Well, I can," Carum said.

"No one needs swim the Halla," Callilla said, "though all our girls are taught early to traverse it at its calmest points. The path may be steep, but it is well trod. Our guards patrol it daily. No one else knows of it. Once you get down to the river, you must simply follow its line until you come to a stand of birch. Turn east, and you will come, in the space of a full day's journey, to Bertram's Rest."

"My refuge," Carum added.

"And will it really be safe for him there?" asked Jenna.

"Bertram was a great saint of their religion, a fighter who gave up fighting. His sanctuaries are never violated by the Garunians, whatever the provocation. They are a strange people, and their gods are bloody, but they are honest for all that. However, women are not allowed in their sanctuary halls, so you will have to leave him there and go on about your missioning. It will be a hard year for you if this is but the first of it."

"We have a greater mission now," Pynt said.

Jenna touched her tunic over the breast and could feel the map crackling beneath, but said nothing.

"What about food?" asked Carum.

"You will find what you need in the woods," Callilla said. "We have no time for provisioning beyond these." She bent down and picked up three full wineskins from the floor. "And I found some goat cheese for you. Bread also." Reaching into a deep tunic pocket, she brought out a leather-wrapped packet and gave it to Carum. "It is but a day's journey. How hungry can you get? For the rest . . ."

"We know," Carum said. "Nuts, mushrooms, and roots. No berries."

Callilla smiled reluctantly. "Good. Then you shall need for nothing." She pulled open the door. "Alta's blessings on you, hand and foot."

The girls nodded and slipped through the door, but Carum turned and whispered loudly. "And may the eyes of Dark Morga see you long after and may his fins stoke the water over your back."

Callilla looked blank.

Carum grinned. "A safewell blessing from the Morganians. They live on the southern coast of the Continent and eat only what comes from the sea at low tide. Strange people. Nasty diet. But honest!" He turned and disappeared after the girls. Callilla's short, barking laugh followed him.

The path began at the door, for, farther up, the sheer wall of the Hame and the cliff met in a single steep drop. Even on the path there was little room between the wall on their right and the drop-off to the Halla on their left. They walked carefully, listening to the low growling of the river far below them, surging angrily between its banks.

Pynt slipped suddenly on some loose pebbles and fell backward, catching herself at the last moment and hurting her wrist. She got up and angrily brushed off the back of her clothes despite the pain.

They could hear the tumbling shower of dirt and rock for only a moment before the noise of the river overwhelmed it.

Once they were past the Hame's steep wall, the path widened a bit, though there was still a small cliff, half again as tall as a man, on the right. Then the path took an abrupt right-hand turn and before them was a twisted fir tree jutting out across the path. Its roots held deep into the cliffside like the fingers of a clutching hand, and the fanning branches obscured the way ahead.

"Under or over?" asked Jenna.

Pynt peered under the tree. "Under. There is enough room."

Unbuckling her sword, Pynt pushed it under the tree, then followed it, crawling along on her belly. Jenna was next, and Carum last, the food packet in his hand. As he started to stand up, Pynt put her hand out.

"Hush. Wait. I hear something."

"That's just the river," Carum said.

"I hear it, too," Jenna whispered. "Hush!" She drew her sword from its scabbard. In the sunlight it seemed to catch fire.

"Probably the Hame guards," Carum whispered back. "Callilla said no one else knows the path." He stood and began to brush off his clothes.

"Get behind me," Pynt said softly.

"I'm already behind you," Carum said. "I've been behind you all the—"

But he did not get to finish his sentence, for there was a high whistling and an arrow whizzed by his shoulder to embed itself in the tree.

"There they are!" came a shout. "Three more of Alta's bitches."

"Those aren't guards," Carum said. "They're . . ."

Another arrow flew by, this time passing through his shirt and pinning him to the tree.

"Damn!" Carum shouted, pulling himself loose by ripping the shirt.

"Duck!" screamed Pynt. She pushed Carum toward the tree, nearly sending him over the cliffside instead. He scrambled under the gnarled trunk, then turned. Pynt's sword hand and arm were partway under, but she had stopped. He grabbed her hand, careful of the sword, and pulled her through, surprised at her dead weight. When she was on the other side, he saw the arrow sticking out of her back, broken off halfway.

"Pynt!" he cried, drawing her to him.

She did not answer.

He picked up her sword and straddled her, waiting.

A sword and then a hand emerged from under the tree. Carum raised his sword to strike, then saw it was Jenna's arm and stopped. She scrambled the rest of the way under the tree.

"It's Pynt," Carum cried. "She's been hit. An arrow under the left shoulder."

"Alta's Hairs," Jenna cursed quietly. She bent over Pynt's body. "How bad is it?"

"I don't know. But she doesn't move."

"Oh, Pynt, say something," Jenna begged.

Pynt groaned.

"She needs water," said Carum. "And that arrowhead has to come out. And . . ."

"She needs to be back at the Hame."

"She's not heavy. I could carry her."

"You get her back there," Jenna said, "and I'll cover your retreat."

"No—you get her back there. I'll cover *your* retreat."

"I am better with a sword," Jenna said.

"And you think I'm better at retreating?"

"Why are we arguing?" Jenna cried.

"I don't want anything to happen to you."

"It is a narrow cliff and I have the advantage of that tree," said Jenna. "Just take Pynt. Now. If she dies, I will never forgive you."

Carum hefted Pynt's body onto his back. She cried out once and then was still. He heard the shout of the men on the other side of the tree and started back up the path as quickly as he could. Pynt seemed heavier at every step, but still he ran. Pebbles shot out from under his feet, skittering over the cliff. He ran until he came to the Hame door and, balancing Pynt on his back, pounded on the door with both fists. A peephole slid open, then shut, and then the door began to move. Carum and his burden fell inside.

Someone took Pynt from him and when he stood again, he saw that the door was shut.

"But Jenna is out there," he cried. "Open the door."

No one moved and so Carum ran over to the door and tried to open it. Locked, it did not move.

"Move this god-rotted door!" he shouted.

Callilla played with a lock and the door opened. Jenna fell toward Carum, her sword dragging, something bloody and horrible clutched in her left hand.

"I do not know . . ." she began, trying to catch her breath. "I do not know if this was the hand that sent the arrow into Pynt's back, but it is a hand that will surely do no more damage to Alta's own." She flung it down, her eyes wild. "He foolishly put it under the tree first as he tried to crawl through."

Callilla pushed the hand with her boot. "Not so foolish, perhaps. It might have been his head!"

Carum stared at the hand. With the dark hairs on its back and the crabbed fingers, it looked like some strange, bloody creature. On the middle finger was a great ring with a K engraved in the middle. Looking up, Carum stared at Jenna wildly. "It's the Bull's ring, Jenna, with Kalas' crest. Many a time I had a buffet from it. The Bull was my swordmaster before he joined his brothers in Kalas' service. Jenna, don't you know what this means? Now Ox and Hound have both bowed down. Ox and Hound. Mother Alta is right. The prophecy *must* be true. You *are* the White Babe, the Anna."

The women began to murmur, but Jenna ignored them and knelt by Pynt's side. The infirmarer, short and stocky, with gray flecks in her hair and worry lines etched across her brow, was already looking at the wound.

"It is deep," she said to no one in particular. "And badly placed. Near the heart."

"Will she die?" asked Jenna, her voice breaking.

The infirmarer looked over at her, as if surprised to find she had been talking to someone. "I cannot say with any certainty. But for now I must get her up the stairs to my hospice and clean the wound. The arrowhead must be removed. After that I might be able to say with more accuracy."

Pynt coughed and groaned almost at the same time. She tried to sit up but the infirmarer pushed her down with a gentle but firm touch.

"It is you who are being stupid now, Jenna," Pynt whispered hoarsely. "I will not die. How can I? You would be lost without your shadow." Then her eyes rolled back and she was still.

"Is she dead?" Jenna cried.

"She has only fainted," said the infirmarer, "for the pain is great and that is nature's way of easing it. Now she must go upstairs and"—she looked at Jenna—"she is to have no visitors. Trust me, child, you cannot do her any good right now."

At the infirmarer's signal, three of the younger women gathered Pynt up and carried her away. Then the infirmarer turned and pointed at the hand which still lay on the floor. "Get that thing away. It will soon gather disease to it and it might frighten the children. We who are Alta's heirs do not revel in such bloody keepsakes."

Carum bent down and tugged the ring off the stiffened hand. "I will keep this until I can fling it at Kalas' feet. We Garunians, unlike you Altites, revel in such reminders." He put the ring into his pocket and turned away quickly, hoping he had been fast enough so that no one could see the color of his face, which he knew had whitened at the feel of the dead hand.

But Jenna had seen. She touched him on the back, whispering, "Carum, do not be ashamed at your disgust. If I had not been blood-crazed, I would never have brought that hand into this hall. But battle fever had hold. I did what I did without thinking. You, though—you think too much."

He turned around, his face composed at last, but before he had time to answer he caught sight of Callilla behind her, anger and fear fighting in her face.

"We must talk. And quickly. Before those men gather their courage and try this door."

"The door is well defended," said Carum.

"It can be," admitted Callilla. "But do we keep it ready to be opened for our guards, or do we barricade it?"

"We saw no guards," Jenna answered.

"No bodies either," added Carum.

Callilla nodded grimly. "The Halla has cradled Alta's own before."

"The men who chased us cried out, *Three more of . . .*" Carum stopped.

". . . *of Alta's bitches,*" finished Jenna.

Callilla turned to two women standing nearby. "Who stood guard to-day?"

"Mona," said one.

"And Verna with her."

"Oh, sweet Alta, salve them," murmured Callilla. "And Verna just past her seventeenth spring. Their mothers must be told. I fear the worst."

The two women nodded solemnly and left.

"How many men?"

Carum shrugged. "We didn't wait to count them."

"At least three," said Jenna. "And one of those now sorely wounded."

"He was the leader," Carum added. "Which might slow them down."

"Or might provoke them further. There is never any way of knowing which, so we must prepare for a swift attack." Callilla looked beyond them and shouted, "Clea, Sari, Brenna—to me."

Three young women came running.

"Is it true, Callilla? About Verna?" asked one.

She nodded.

"Hush, Clea. Do not ask more," the larger of the three girls said.

Callilla said quietly, "Remember what Alta, in her great wisdom, reminds us. *Not to know is bad, but not to wish to know is worse.*"

The girls all looked at the floor, waiting.

"Now you must do this. Sari and Brenna, you barricade the door and stand watch here until you are relieved. Clea, you must alert all the door wardens that the time of a great fight is at hand. We all know what to do." Callilla dismissed them with a wave of her hand, then turned to Jenna. "It is written in the *Book* that *The day on which one starts out is surely not the time to begin one's preparations.* You will find this Hame well prepared."

"I can see that," Jenna said.

"Then we must prepare also for another escape route for the two of you. I will send Armina to you when she returns from Mother Alta. Tonight you will go by a road even the watchers outside our gates will not guess at or follow. Darkness will be our helpmeet."

"The moon is all but full, Callilla," Sari said over her shoulder as she struggled with Brenna to move a large chest in front of the door.

"Then they shall have both dark and light to aid them." She signaled to Jenna. "Meanwhile, you two can help us with our fortifications."

They worked all afternoon ceaselessly, helping the Hameswomen set strong barriers against the other doors and nail shut the narrow first-floor windows. Carum took a long turn at fletching new arrows, while Jenna helped haul up water from the courtyard well.

"If there are fires," she explained to Carum, "the Hame will be well prepared."

Only once did they try to visit Pynt in the upstairs hospice, but were turned away by the infirmarer at the door.

"She sleeps," they were told. "But I have gotten out the arrowhead, which, by luck, was not poisoned. She has taken a tisane I brewed which will help her sweat out any fever the wound produces. The wound itself I have treated with a poultice of figwort, which we call HealAll. You may believe I have done everything in my power to make her comfortable."

"Comfortable!" Carum said. "That's what the physician said of my mother for the month it took her to die."

"Will Pynt die?" asked Jenna.

"We all die at the last," said the infirmarer. "But do not measure the shroud before there is a corpse. Your friend is in Alta's good and gentle hands, those same hands that hold a nestling and take the fawn from the doe." The lines in her forehead deepened as she spoke.

"I hope," Carum whispered to Jenna as they left, "that she is more original with her medicines than she is with her words." He held tightly to Jenna's hand, which lent comfort to them both.

There was an early dinner in shifts in the kitchen. Jenna and Carum ate during the second round, sitting with Armina and two of her friends. Armina finished picking at the drumstick on her plate and pushed away the bones. Turning her back on her friends, she spoke urgently to Jenna.

"When the attack comes or night falls, whichever is first, I will take you upstairs. There is another way, more difficult of course than the back path, but surely no man will find you there."

Carum interrupted. "Why didn't we go there first?"

"You will see."

Jenna pushed the uneaten fowl around on her plate.

"Battle does not make you hungry," Armina commented. "It makes me starved."

"My stomach argues both ways," said Carum. He was reaching for another wing piece when there was a flurry of shouts from the Great Hall and the muffled *thud-thumps* of someone hammering on the gates.

"This is it, then," Armina said, rising. "They will be busy at the front for a long while. Those doors are a foot thick at the least and there are wicked spikes on the tops of the walls."

"Armina, are you coming?" asked one of her friends.

"I have charge of these two," Armina said, nodding at them.

"Alta's luck, then."

"You, too."

"You know," Carum murmured, "they'll have rams, the Kingsmen. And a great sling for boulders. The gates won't outlast such implements of war."

"We know," said Armina. "A number of our women have served in the king's armies. Your way of fighting is not unknown to us."

"Blanket Companions!" said Carum.

"My mother, Callilla, was one. I am the result." Armina smiled faintly. "But the walls will buy us time. And if they are breached, still the men will find us no easy prey." She stood.

"But the children . . ." Carum said. "And the wounded."

"We have a place for them. Never fear. Come."

They followed her out of the kitchen, through the Great Hall, and up the wide front stairs to the second floor. She turned right, then left, then right.

"I'm lost again," Carum whispered to Jenna, who did not answer.

Armina stopped, flung open a door, and went in. They followed at her heels and were surprised to find themselves in a kind of playroom, with toys for young children scattered across the floor.

"We have nothing like this at Selden Hame," murmured Jenna, looking at the half-dozen small wands and jumping ropes, hoops, and balls.

"The windows aren't boarded up," Carum said. "Isn't that dangerous? Kalas' men could come in that way."

"Think you so? Then look!" commanded Armina.

They peered out. It was a sheer drop down to the Halla, tumbling nearly a hundred feet below.

"Oh, no," said Jenna immediately. "I cannot swim."

"I can," said Carum.

"I shall rope you together," Armina said as she knotted together four of the jump ropes, testing each knot by pulling against it. "These are very strong. And you shall each carry a kicker."

"Kicker?"

Armina went over to a standing wardrobe, pulled the doors open, and searched through the contents of an upper shelf. She turned back with two large pieces of wood the shape of shovel heads, though twice as big. "We use these to teach our little ones how to swim. They are held so." Gripping the flat edge, she raised the kicker overhead. "And then you kick with all your might. The wood floats, you see. As long as you hold on to it, you will not go under."

"*I* will go under," said Jenna.

"Even should you do so, remember, you will still be roped to Longbow, and he can swim."

"A little," admitted Carum. "In quiet pools and in the palace baths. I have never tried a swift river. An *unforgiving* river."

"You must *jump* in," Armina said. "There is no other way."

Carum turned to Jenna. "It has to be all right, Jenna. The prophecy doesn't talk about the Anna dying. She's to become queen and . . ."

"For the goddess' sake, I am no Anna," Jenna said angrily. "But I *am* a warrior of Great Alta's. And as I have pledged myself to your safety . . ." She drew in a deep breath and looked steadily at Armina. "We will jump."

"First we must get the ropes ready to tie around your waists. Carum, you mount that window and I the other," said Armina. "Then I shall fling you an end outside."

Carum climbed onto the windowsill and, straddling the spanning bar, leaned out. Meanwhile, Armina had climbed up onto the other and flung the rope toward him. It took three tries before he could catch it, but at last he drew the rope in and secured it loosely to the bar. Armina did the same with her end, then jumped back down.

"Now, we must fasten your sword to your side, Jenna. The river is a grasping sort. It will take it from you if it can."

"I can do that," Jenna said. She found another jump rope and began to twine it around herself and the sword, knotting it securely.

Armina picked up the kicker boards and set one by each window. "There is not much danger in this, really. It is more frightening than anything else. We older girls—as a test of courage—often come up and leap into the Halla. *Without* the kickers."

"So you told us. And of the girl who was never found," said Carum.

"That was just a tale. To frighten you."

"You've succeeded," said Carum.

"The only real danger," Armina said, "is that you might not get out of the river in time. There are some rapids after a bit."

"Rapids?" asked Jenna.

"Rough water, great whirlpools and eddies. And then there is a waterfall. You must be sure to get out early enough *and* on the right side."

"And how will we know when these rapids are approaching?" asked Jenna.

"You will know."

"Then we'd better go," said Carum. He looked at Jenna, who nodded.

"I am ready," she said, then added, "I think."

"Carum is right. You must go quickly. Carum, you get up first and tie the rope to your waist. Then, Jenna, you do the same. Less time to worry that way. I shall hand you up the boards and then count to three. On three, leap together. Oh, and you must leap at the same time, or one will drag the other." Armina thought a minute. "There is one other thing."

"Now she tells us," said Carum.

"Do not leap straight down or you shall hit the rocks. Leap out."

"Anything more?" asked Carum as he climbed up and stepped over the spanning bar.

"Do not scream. It might alert any Kingsmen about. It is getting dark and they will not be close enough to see you leap, but why take chances? And may Alta hold you both securely in her hair."

Jenna nodded, climbing onto the windowsill. "And to you, too, Armina. And all in this Hame. May you fight bravely and may I see you again." She turned, stepped over the bar, untied the rope, and secured it around her waist with a double knot.

Armina handed them each a board and began the count. "One . . . two . . ."

Jenna felt something hot and hard in her stomach, and her mouth tasted salty. She knew that a woman of a prophecy would never feel such fear.

". . . three!"

Jenna leaped slightly ahead of Carum but not so much that the rope pulled taut between them. She felt the rush of wind by her ears and a strange scream flew all unbidden from her mouth. There was a thin echo of that scream and Jenna realized, only as she plunged into the icy water, that Carum had been yelling as well. She hoped they had not been heard.

Water rushed suddenly into her open mouth and the board leaped like a wild thing from her hands. Flailing about, she tried to find the surface of the river, but with her eyes closed it was all guesswork. Then, thinking she was out, she breathed in and swallowed a mouthful of water, and then everything was black and full of cold bubbles. Just as suddenly her head was in the air, and Carum was pushing a board into her hands. She heard, as if from far away, his shout, "Breathe, Jenna, please breathe." She gulped in air and coughed out water almost at the same time. Then she pulled herself partway onto the board, conscious of its solidity under her, but she was too weak and confused to kick. Carum put his arm around her, lifting his body partly onto hers, and kicked for them both.

After a while, Jenna's eyes cleared of the film of water and she could see again. Her heart, while still pounding, was no longer racing quite so madly, and the fear that had inhabited her throat and bowels no longer threatened to spew forth. Breathing deeply, she called to Carum over the noise of the river in a raspy voice, "We . . . we are alive!"

"Of course we're alive," he shouted back. "I told you I could swim. Now kick, Jenna." He slipped away and she was suddenly conscious of the loss of his body on hers. "Kick, I say!"

Jenna began to kick and the board moved noiselessly through the water ahead of her. "It works!" she cried, turning her head toward him.

Carum swam by her side, as graceless as a waddling pig, but still managing to keep pace with her and her board. They were both helped along by the force of the river, and the banks on either side hurtled by with frightening speed. Scarcely had they sighted one possible landmark when they were beyond it.

"How will we know when we are nearing the rapids?" Jenna shouted.

"Armina said we'd know," he called back.

The noise of the river was such, they barely made out one word in three, but after several more tries they understood each other. Then they rounded a turn, and suddenly the noise of the river seemed to double while the water boiled about them with white pockets of foam.

"I think we've found it," Carum shouted.

"What?"

"I think we've found it."

"What?"

With an effort, he kicked closer to her, grabbed her shoulder, and headed her toward the right side.

"Just go over there."

They were nearer the left bank than the right, the east bank, but they fought toward the right with the last of their strength. The river drew them steadily forward. Suddenly Carum was spun away from Jenna and the rope went taut between them. He was turned around several times into a deep eddy that drew him down and then popped him up again like a cork till the rope snapped him back to Jenna's side.

Just as he found a footing on the rocks, Jenna was spun about in the same swirling water and the board was torn from her grasp. It shot straight up in the air and splashed down inches from Carum's head. He ducked, nearly fell back into the channel, then steadied himself and hauled on the rope between them, dragging Jenna toward him. She was so exhausted he had to half lift, half drag her to the shore.

They flopped down on the slippery grassy slope, breathing heavily. Jenna coughed up water twice without lifting her head from the bank. Then she sat up suddenly, turned a greenish face toward Carum, and was sick in the grass. She lay down again, unable to move away.

"There . . ." Carum said, breathing deeply between words, "now . . .

we . . . are . . . even . . . for . . . my . . . getting . . . sick . . . in . . . the . . . woods."

It took Jenna a full minute to answer. "Not . . . amusing," she muttered.

"I'm only trying to laugh and live longer," he replied.

This time she did not bother to respond.

Carum sat up slowly and looked around. Then he crawled on his hands and knees up and over the embankment. Ahead of him was a long meadow pied with the pensive blue, purple, and yellow faces of heartsease. Off to the right was a copse of graceful, white-barked trees, almost ghostly in the fading light.

"The stand of birch!" Carum called down to Jenna. "The birch that Callilla said to watch out for."

Jenna sat up at last and tried to wring the water from her braid, but her hands had no strength yet. "We could have passed hundreds of such stands while we were drowning," she said.

"Do you have a better idea of where we are?"

"None at all."

"Then let's assume we are only a day's journey to Bertram's Rest, Jenna, because that way we'll both sleep easier."

Jenna shook her head. "How can either of us sleep easily, knowing that Pynt may die, knowing that the Hame is in danger, and knowing that we have no idea where we are or that we may be found by the Kingsmen at any minute?"

"I don't know, Jenna," Carum said, "but I'm going to try."

She nodded, too tried to argue, and in fact they both fell asleep within minutes on the riverbank, in plain view of any passersby.

THE HISTORY

The Garunian religious practices are much more thoroughly documented than any other group of the Dales from that period. There are two reasons for this. First, the Continental ancestry of the Garunians provides us with a broad base from which religious history explorers may make their speculative forays. After all, though only two authenticated Garunian documents have been found in the diggings in the Dales, there are at least twenty such (including a book of gnomic sayings) discovered by Dr. Allysen J. Carver during her twenty years of barrow work in the Continental border towns. Second, of the two Dalite documents, one is the famous essay "Oblique Prophecies" (or, as Magon persists in calling it rather too colloquially, "Prophecies on the Slant," thus diminishing its considerable power) by the scholar-king Langbrow II, in which the system of refuges, or Rests, is mentioned.

These walled monasteries, which were part religious retreats, part sanctuaries, part prisons, were considered sacrosanct by the Garunians, and many a wanted man apparently holed up in them, possibly (though not probably) for years. Langbrow cites a number of proverbs, some too obscure for parsing, but two seem clear enough: In the wrong, in the Rest *and* Better in the Rest than in the Battle. *Both Magon and Temple, for once, agree on the meaning, that felons and army deserters alike took advantage of the immunity such Rests offered. Magon further hypothesizes—a bit freely considering that the length of the document is but three pages—that once a man was hounded into a Rest, he was often there for life.*

THE STORY

They were, in fact, less than a day's journey away, for they began, after seven hours of sleep, with the moon still overhead. Following close by the path, they did not stay directly on it; caution, an old habit, claimed them.

So it was a bit past noon, the sun ripe above them, when they crested a small rise and saw Bertram's Rest in the valley below. The Rest was a series of low stone buildings in the shape of a broken cross with neat gardens and fruit trees nestled in each crook, the whole surrounded by a set of double walls. While smaller by far than Nill's Hame, the Rest was still larger than Selden.

"That's it!" said Carum. "All Rests are built that way, in the bent crux sign." He started to stand and Jenna pulled him down by the shirttails.

"Wait!" she said. "We always say *They stumble who run ahead of their wits.* Let us watch a moment or two."

He knelt down again and as they watched, a troop of horsemen raced out of the western woods and gathered restlessly before the gates. Long minutes later the horsemen, on some signal, spun around and sped away toward the rise where they were huddled.

Jenna grabbed Carum by the arm and pulled him into the densest part of the underbrush, careful not to leave a trail that the seasoned traveler might read.

Farther on they came upon a small cliff with a tiny dark cave pocking the face. They pressed in, though it was barely big enough for the two of them. It was full of animal droppings and sour-smelling, but they stayed in it until darkness had wrapped around the woods, and the riders, whoever they were, were long gone.

A full moon rode high in the sky and the valley was starkly illuminated.

"We might as well have crossed by day," Carum said, "for the moon is as strong as the sun."

But without a hope for clouds, and under a sky bright with a powerful moon and the scattering of stars, they raced across the grassy meadow. Luck was with them; if there were watchers, they slept at their posts.

The walls of the Rest were higher than they had seemed from the hill, so high it would take a scaling ladder to mount them. They were topped by cruel-looking spikes.

"A welcoming sort of place," Jenna commented.

"Remember, it's got to keep people out as well as in," Carum said.

"I thought your people respected the sanctuary."

"My people are not *all* people," Carum said.

The gates were wood set into the stone walls with iron brackets. They were good, solid, unadorned gates, the only decoration a peephole about halfway up.

Carum hammered on the door with both hands while Jenna, sword unsheathed, stood guard. For a long time nothing happened.

"They cannot want to help those in need very much if they do not open their doors," Jenna said.

"Jenna, it's the middle of the night. They'll all be asleep."

"All? Are there no guards?"

"Why should there be guards? No one in the Dales would dare violate a Rest."

"I would have thought no one would violate a Hame filled with women and children. But Pynt has an arrow in her back, and Verna and the other sister are missing, and we have had to swim an unforgiving river."

"*That* was a Hame and *this* is a Rest," Carum said.

"And you are a king's son who had to cry me *merci* from his own kind."

Carum looked down. "I'm sorry, Jenna. You're right. That was a stupid thing to say. A wicked, un—"

"Unthinking?"

"Unthinkable thing to say. And there should be someone up. Or we can get someone up." He turned and hammered on the gates again.

At last there was a grinding noise and the peephole cover slid aside. They could see a single eye staring through. Carum moved in front of Jenna and shouted up at the eye.

"We seek sanctuary: I for what time I need, and my companion for the rest of the night."

The door opened slowly, drawn inward just a crack, and an old man, with deep creases around his mouth like parentheses, stood in their way.

"Who asks?"

"I am Carum Longbow, the king's . . ."

"Ah, Longbow. We have been wondering if you might make your way here."

Carum stared. "How did you know?"

The old man's head moved back and forth like a clockwork doll. "Your brother Pike, who lies within, had hopes. And there were Kingsmen here just hours ago asking of you. Of course we sent them on their way."

"Pike here? And you say *lies*. Does he sleep—or is he wounded?"

"Wounded, but nowhere near dying."

Jenna stepped forward. "Please let him in. You can talk once the gates are closed behind."

The old man peered closer at Jenna. "This is the companion you spoke of?"

"Yes."

"But she is a woman."

"She is an Altite warrior who pledged herself to save me."

The old man made a *tsking* noise with his tongue. "Highness, you know we have no women here."

Carum drew himself up. "She stays. I am the king's son."

"But not yet the king, nor likely to be unless your brother dies. And only the king can make that request. She cannot tarry here. It is the law." His head went back and forth again, more like palsy than an answer.

Jenna put her hand on Carum's arm. "Go inside, and quickly. My charge is done, Carum Longbow. You are safe now, and I am free of my vow to you."

"Free of the vow but not free of me, Jenna."

"Hush, Carum," she said. "We both have other missions now, I to my sisters and you to your brother. And to your life. We were companions because danger tied us one to the other with bonds as strong as the ropes that held us in the Halla."

"I won't let you leave so quickly. Not like this."

"Carum . . ."

"At least kiss me good-bye."

"Why?"

"Why not?"

"Because . . . because I have never kissed a man before."

"You said I was a boy."

"I have never kissed a boy before."

"That's not a good enough reason. I never ate bitter roots before I met you. You never swam a river before you met me." He smiled, and held out his hands.

She nodded imperceptibly and moved into the compass of his arms. His lips touched hers softly and when she thought to move away, his hands were on her arms, steadying her, so she moved, without quite meaning to, even closer to him until their bodies were pressed together and she began to tremble. She pulled back a little and took her mouth from his.

"What is this?" she whispered.

Carum smiled ruefully. "I'd call it love."

"Is that . . . is that a scholarly definition, Carum?"

"It's a guess," he said. "I've never kissed a girl before. But from what I've read . . ."

"What have you read?" Her voice was still a whisper.

"That the Carolians, who worship only under an open sky, say that *love* was the first word God memorized."

"What a strange god."

"No stranger than this," Carum said, kissing her once again without touching her anywhere but on the lips. Then he stepped back. "We *will* see each other again, my White Jenna."

"Oh," Jenna said, unable to say more until the door had closed between them, and then all she could manage was to whisper his name.

It was only when she got back to the forest's edge and drew out the map that she found it had been ruined by the water. Knowing no other route to a Hame but the ones she had already traveled, she knew she had to turn back toward the river and retrace her steps. At Nill's Hame they would give her another map or at least set her on the track to the next mission Hame.

Without Carum, she did not feel the need to leave the path. One person alone, she reasoned, could disappear quickly into the woods. One person alert, she convinced herself, would hear an army on the road.

She moved swiftly, stopping infrequently, gathering what edibles grew along the path. She slept only a few hours, a sleep that gave her little rest, for she dreamed of Carum, who fell to his knees and cried out, "Holy, holy, holy," refusing her embrace.

By midmorning she found herself back by the fir tree that groped across the path like a disfigured hand. A dark stain, half under the tree, the size and shape of a serving plate, was the only reminder of the violence that had occurred there. Crawling under, she held her breath, for she feared what might wait for her on the other side. But when she came through, she was alone.

There was a strange silence, broken only by the river's surging, though in her mind she heard again the screams and cries that had last accompanied her at this place. Those voices haunted her, and she ran quickly to the Hame's back door. She pushed against it and it was solid and unmoving and, though she breathed thankfully for that—it meant no Kingsmen had gotten through this way—she did not hammer on it in case the enemy were inside.

Instead, she went back down the path, scrambled once more under the tree, and ran along the path until she came to the place where the cliff was lowest. Hand over hand she climbed up the face, her sword banging against her legs and threatening, at every move, to entangle them. It took her a long time to achieve the top, where she lay panting and grateful on the grass, waiting to catch her breath. Then, slowly, she began to crawl through the high grass toward the front of the Hame, conscious all the while that she could be seen from the tops of the walls.

As she crawled, she realized that everything except the grass right around her was still. Too still. Surely there would be the sounds of voices or the cries of cocks or the bleating of goats floating on such still air. Fear trembled through her and for a moment she did not dare move again.

To calm herself, she took three deep *latani* breaths, no easy task lying on her stomach, then pushed herself to her knees. In a crouched-over position, she ran to the wall and put her hand on the stone. Its very solidity lent her courage.

Turning the corner carefully, she gasped, her stomach knotting, a strange metallic taste flooding into her mouth. The carved gates were in splinters, the walls breached. Tumbled about like fruit from a bowl, the heavy stones had their dark, hidden faces up to the sun.

Jenna waited, hardly daring to breathe at all, for minute after minute, straining for some sound. But that deathly pall lay over all. Three more deep *latani* breaths, and she moved forward at last, stepping carefully between the fallen stones.

There were bodies scattered everywhere throughout the courtyard: men in full battle armor, women in their warrior skins. She stopped at one body after another, brushing impatiently at the flies, hoping to find someone, some*thing*, alive.

Everywhere, she thought distractedly. *They are everywhere.*

The women who died facedown she turned over, looking for someone familiar—Armina, Callilla, or the priestess herself.

Near the well, her hand over her face as if shutting out the sun, lay a young women in trews. There was a small hole in her throat. Jenna stared down at her.

Such a small entrance to let in death, to let out life, Jenna thought.

She knelt and pushed the hand away and recognized Brenna, though she had seen her only the once.

"Alta's mercy," she whispered, wondering where that mercy had been scant hours before. She felt more for that one corpse suddenly than for all the others. "I swear, Brenna, I shall give you a burial if I can find someone to show me your Hame's Cave."

She stood and continued to search through the courtyard, her shadow dancing oddly by her side, until she realized she was moving in peculiar starts and stops. That was when she first knew she was incapable of taking it all in, the heartbreaking horror of it. There was simply too much of it, too much death. And she realized, too, that she was terrified to go inside the Hame.

She forced herself to squat down and breathe deeply, though the air was filled with a sweet-sharp smell. The sun beat down on her and she began the hundred-chant, trying to steady herself for what further horrors lay ahead. As she counted, she felt again the strange lightening, and she was pulled slowly from her body to float above the courtyard. She looked down as if from a great height at the chanting figure swaying slightly in the midst of the scattered corpses. But when she sailed down to touch one body after another, she found no entrance, no living self to be drawn into. At last she spiraled down, down, down toward her chanting self just as the final number was reached.

Standing again, she walked purposefully toward the broken door into the Hame.

* * *

She found Callilla in the kitchen, her throat slashed, and five dead men around her. Armina was on the main stairs, an arrow in her back and a broken sword at her feet. Behind her were three men whose faces had been scored by her nails and whose throats had been pierced with a knife.

Jenna sat on the step by Armina's head and stroked the crest of hair. "Laugh longer, live longer," she whispered hoarsely. And only then the tears came, gushing out of her eyes, along with great gulping sobs. She wept uncontrollably, not only for Armina, but for all of them, her unknown sisters who had died defending themselves against the Kingsmen. The Kingsmen, who wanted Jenna for the killing of the Hound, and Carum for . . . she realized for the first time that she did not even know why they wanted Carum. Only that they did. They wanted him so badly they had slaughtered an entire Hame of women to find him. And to find her. This horror, then, was their fault, Carum's and hers. Just as Mother Alta had said: she *was* an ending. An entire Hame gone.

An entire Hame! And Pynt, too! Jenna leaped up and, turning, took the stairs two at a time, trying desperately to remember where the hospice room was. Somewhere on the second floor, that much she knew. She could not make herself believe the men would kill a wounded girl lying in a hospice bed.

She opened door after door, stepping over corpses of women and their pursuers, for the women of Nill's Hame had taken more than their own number into the dark Cave.

A tall, bearded man with a face as seamed as wood and a bloody throat lay against a closed door, blocking it. Jenna kicked him aside.

"And are you throwing bones over your shoulders for those bitter dogs now?" she shouted. "May they rip your throat out again." She opened the door and saw it was the hospice. Three dead women lay on the cots and one, her eyes bandaged, was under a table. None of them was Pynt.

"Pynt!" Jenna screamed. The room echoed with the name but there was no answer.

She raced out the door, leaped over the dead man, and ran down the hall, flinging doors open and shouting wildly into each room. One door was already ajar. When she looked in, she saw it was the playroom from where, two days before, she and Carum had leaped into the icy flood. She went over to the windows and stared down at the Halla below, coursing mindlessly between its banks. When she turned back, the scattered toys looked like the corpses of playthings.

Slowly something else teased into her mind, something beyond the horror and the blood.

"The children!" she whispered. "I have seen no dead children!"

Leaning against the window frame, she tried to remember what it was Armina had said to them about the children, but when she tried to picture Armina speaking, she could only see her body stretched out along the stairs.

"I must think," she said aloud. "I *must* remember." She forced herself to recall the dinner and the fatal hammering at the doors. That was when Armina had told them something about the children. But what was it she had said?

And then she remembered. ". . . a place for them. Never fear." The children, she had said, and the wounded. Jenna bit her lip. She had seen the wounded murdered on their cots. No safety there. Then she said, speaking her thoughts aloud, "But surely not *all* the wounded. In a battle of this size, things would have gone on for hours. So there *must* have been others, moved earlier. To the place Armina mentioned. If only she had named it!" She thought, suddenly, *Perhaps Pynt is there as well.*

Afraid to hope too much, she nevertheless allowed herself a faint glimmering. Leaving the playroom, she finished her search of the second floor and then, finding the back stairs, mounted to the third.

There were fewer bodies here, as if the fighting had not reached so far or, she thought grimly, as if there had been fewer fighters left. And then she came to Mother Alta's carved doors. They were shattered, split down the middle. Cautiously she stepped inside.

It was here some sort of stand had been made. The last of the wounded were clustered at Mother Alta's feet, almost stacked up, their bandages soaked in newer blood. The infirmarer, her own head encased in a linen binding, had fallen across the priestess' lap. Mother Alta's fingers were entwined in hers, the sixth finger alone outstretched. The priestess' marble eyes were wide open and staring.

But Pynt and the children were gone. The realization came to Jenna suddenly. The men must have taken them, taken the screaming, hysterical children and . . . Here her imagination failed her utterly. She simply could not guess what grown men would do with several dozen children, some still babes in arms.

For the rest of the day Jenna carried the corpses of the women down to the kitchen and the Great Hall. She carried them reverently, as if by doing so, somehow, she could excuse her guilt. She laid them side by side, leaving room between for their dark sisters. The last one she brought down was Mother Alta, the small, twisted body weighing less than a child.

She knew that she could not bring them all to the Cave, had she even an idea of where the Cave lay. Instead, she planned to set the Hame afire. It would serve as a fitting memorial for the battle brave.

It was deep into the night by the time she brought Mother Alta down, setting her gently atop the kitchen table and arranging her shrunken legs. She kissed each finger on the six-fingered hands before crossing them over the old woman's breast. Jenna's eyes had grown used to the almost-dark. She lit lamps only at the far turnings of the stairs, for otherwise she would have been burdened with the dark sisters as well as the light. But once she had Mother Alta's body arranged, she lit a candle and placed it at the priestess' head, watching with quiet satisfaction as the corpse of Mother Alta's dark sister appeared, her flickering sixth finger resolving in the full light.

"Sisters side by side," Jenna whispered. Then she lit all the kitchen lamps before proceeding into the Great Hall. Making sure all the corners of the room were well lit, she nodded as corpse after corpse appeared next to their light sisters. Unbidden, the words of the grave prayer came to her lips.

> *In the name of Alta's cave,*
> *The dark and lonely grave . . .*

And she thought that those dead sisters would *not* be lonely this night. The memory of the last time she had heard those words came to her: Mother Alta's reedy voice following them down the stairs.

Mounting those stairs one last time, Jenna was suddenly aware just how exhausted she was. She headed directly for the priestess' room, for she had already decided to bring down two final tributes to the courage of the Nill's Hame sisters—the *Book of Light* and the mirror. Standing before the broken door, she took a single deep breath, then went in.

She snatched the cloth from the glass, momentarily startled at her reflection. There were blades of grass in her hair and her braid needed replaiting. Black smudges seemed to be growing under her eyes. She had either lost weight or grown unaccountably taller. Blood spotted her clothing and there was a smear of it across her right cheek. It was a wonder Carum had ever wanted to kiss her.

At the thought of him, she put her fingers to her lips, as if some trace of the kiss still lingered there. *And he is gone, too,* she thought. *Gone to a place where I cannot go.*

She raised her hands toward her mirror self as if pleading, and whispered hoarsely, "Thee to me. Thee to me," the only part of Night of Sisterhood she could remember. "Thee to me."

She meant Carum and Pynt and the children and all the dead women of the Hame. She meant her stepmother A-ma and her foster mother Selna and her real mother who had been cat-killed. And even Selden's Mother Alta. Even her. All the ones who had been part of her life and were gone from her now. "Thee to me." Knowing they were dead or too far for her recalling, still she called. "Thee to me." Tears ran hot down her cheeks, washing away the bloodstains. "Thee to me. Thee to me."

The moon silvered through the window and a small breeze stirred the tendrils of hair at her forehead and neck. In the mirror a mist seemed to form, as if there were moisture in the air, clouding the glass. But Jenna's eyes were so teary, she did not really see it.

"Thee to me," she whispered urgently.

The mist shrouded her reflection slowly, from the edges in, and all the while her hand moved in its beckoning motion and the chant, taking on a life of its own, ran its course.

"Thee to me."

The image, mimicking her motions, whispered back, "Thee to me."

As if in a trance, Jenna stepped forward until she was almost on top of the mirror. Palms out, she placed her hands upon the glass. Instead of the hard surface, her hands touched warm skin, palm to palm. She closed her fingers about the image's fingers and drew the other from the glass.

"It took you long enough," said the image. "I could have been here days ago."

"Who *are* you?" Jenna asked.

"Your dark sister, of course. Skada."

"Skada?"

"It means shadow in the old tongue."

"Pynt is my shadow." Mentioning Pynt's name out loud made Jenna's throat hurt.

"Pynt *was* your shadow. Now I am. And I will be closer to you than Pynt could ever be."

"You cannot be my dark sister. You look very little like me. I am not that thin and my cheekbones are not that prominent. And . . ." She ran her hand nervously down her braid.

Skada smiled, touching her own black plait. "We none of us know how others see us. It is one of the first warnings taught in my world: *Sisters can be blind.* I am dark where you are light. And perhaps I am a bit thinner. But that will change."

"Why?"

"You can eat better in this world, of course."

"Your world is different from ours?" Jenna was confused.

"It is the mirror image. But image is not the same as substance. We must wait your call for that."

Jenna shook her head. "This is very different than I expected. *You* are very different than I expected."

Skada shook her head as if mocking Jenna. "What did you expect?"

"I do not know. Someone . . . softer, maybe. Quieter. More pliant."

"But, Jenna, *you* are not soft, quiet, pliant. And though I am many things, I am not what you are not. *I am you.* And what you keep yourself from being." She smiled and Jenna smiled back at her. "I would not have waited so long to let Carum kiss me."

"You saw that?" Jenna felt her cheeks flush.

"Not exactly *saw*. But it happened at night under the moon. So your memories of that are mine."

Jenna touched her fingers to her lips, remembering, and Skada did the same.

"And there are other things I would do differently," said Skada.

"Such as . . ."

"*I* would not have hesitated to claim being the Anna. So that means some part of you desires it, too."

"No!" Jenna said.

"Yes!" Skada answered.

"How can I believe you?" Jenna asked. "How do I know you are not simply a woman of the Hame?"

"Shall I tell you what Carum said? How he carried you out of the Halla? That was at night, too. Moon nights I share with you, Jenna. Forever."

"Forever?" Jenna's voice was scarcely a whisper. "You will not leave?"

"I *cannot* leave," Skada whispered back. "You called and I came and it is done. Sister called to sister, need to need."

Jenna sank down on her haunches and stared at the ground. Skada did the same. "My need . . ." Jenna muttered. Then she looked up to find Skada staring back at her. "My need is to find where the children have been taken. And Pynt."

"I will help you every moonlit step of the way."

"Then first help me take the mirror down. And the *Book*. I want to put the *Book* by Mother Alta's head and the mirror at her feet. But I will break the glass first just in case. No man shall ever find the secret to our sisterhood." She nodded her head at Skada.

Skada nodded back. "You begin the task, sister, and I will have little say in the matter."

Jenna smiled ruefully. "I forgot."

"It will take some getting used to," Skada said. "For me as well. In my own world, except at a mirror or pond, my movements were my own."

Jenna stared at her. "Do you resent me for that?"

Skada returned that stare. "Resent you? You make me—how shall I put it —whole. Without you I am indeed a shadow."

Jenna stood and touched the left side of the mirror. Skada touched the right.

"When I give the signal, lift with me," said Jenna.

Skada almost smiled. "When you lift, that will be signal enough," she said.

"Oh, I understand. Strange—I have been around dark sisters all my life, but gave them little thought."

"Soon you will give me as little. I shall just *be*," Skada answered. "Lift the mirror, Jenna. You talk too much."

Jenna spread her legs apart and bent her back to the task, and Skada heaved with her, but the mirror would not move, as if it were attached, somehow, to the floor.

"That is strange," said Skada.

"Very strange," Jenna agreed. She straightened up for a moment, then bent back to the task, Skada following her every movement. "Let us try again." As she tried to heft the mirror, Jenna's hand was on the goddess sign and her hand moved it slightly to the right. There was a loud, groaning sound and the floor under Jenna's foot began to move. Jenna leaped away from the mirror in alarm and Skada did the same. Jenna pulled her sword from its sheath with a single swift motion and was momentarily startled when Skada's sword flashed back. The moonlight touched the steel and, for a moment, both seemed bathed in a cold fire.

The floor continued its groaning motion, and slid open until it disclosed a stair going down. There was a strange, high cry from below and a child climbed out, blinking in the moonlight. She looked around, first at Skada, then at Jenna.

"The Anna," she cried. "Mother Alta said you would come."

She turned, gave a loud, piercing whistle down the stairs, then turned back and flung herself into Jenna's arms.

The children boiled out of the tunnel like rats from a hole, all trying to talk at once. Even the babies gabbled for attention. Jenna and Skada hugged and petted them each in turn, then gathered them in a large semi-circle.

"Is that all of you, then?" Jenna asked. "No more hidden down those dark stairs?"

"Just one, Anna," said one of the older girls. "But she is too sick to come up herself."

Jenna gasped. "How sick?"

"Very sick," said a smudge-faced girl with tangled brown hair.

"Why did none of you bring her up?" asked Skada.

"She is too big for us to move," the brown-haired child replied.

"*Too* big!" Jenna whispered. Pushing hope down, she stood. "Skada, help me."

"Then someone must bring a lamp," Skada said.

The oldest child there, a twelve-year-old with dark braids and a deep dimple in her cheek, lit a lamp. "I will."

They went down the stairs and through a series of dark, dry rooms with cots lined up along the walls. The remnants of food tins were scattered about. The rooms were close and smelled dreadfully.

"Too many babies and too few baths," whispered Skada.

Jenna wrinkled her nose but did not reply.

In the last room, the child cried out, "There she is."

There was a cot against the wall and the figure in it had dark hair, but her back was to them.

"Pynt," Jenna whispered. "Pynt, is it you?"

The girl on the cot stirred, but she was obviously in too much pain to turn over. Jenna ran to the bed and, with Skada's help, turned the bed around.

"Hello, Jenna," Pynt said. Her eyes were dark hollows.

Jenna could not contain her tears. "I said I would be back," she whispered. "In my heart, I said it."

"I knew you would," Pynt said. She smiled up at Jenna, then looked at Skada.

Jenna noticed the look. "Pynt, this . . ."

"Your dark sister, of course," Pynt said hoarsely. "I am so glad for you, Jenna. It would not do for you to be alone, and I will not be shadowing you for a while. Not for a long while." She closed her eyes and was still.

"Not . . . not dead," Jenna whispered to Skada.

Skada smiled. "Well, they say *Sleep is death's younger sister*. No wonder you are confused."

"Oh—sleep!" Jenna said, and grinned.

They hefted the bed between them and carried it carefully through the dark rooms and up the stairs, setting it in front of the half circle of children.

"But where is Mother Alta?" asked the girl with dark braids.

Jenna squatted down so as not to tower over the children, and Skada squatted right by her side. "Now listen, little ones, what you will find below will break your hearts if you let it. But remember that your mothers are all with Great Alta now, where they wait for the day we can all be together again."

A four-year-old began to snuffle. One or two of the others started to cry. The girl with the dark braids made a strange moaning sound.

"All?" she asked. "Not all."

"All," Jenna said as gently as she could and wishing there were some comfort in it.

A baby, unused to the light and the sound of all the crying, took it up in a thin, high wailing.

Pynt opened her eyes. Without moving more than her mouth, she began to speak, her voice surprisingly strong. "Hush! Hush! You are young warriors of Alta. You are the Mother's own. Would we trouble the mothers' rest in Alta's cave? They are happy there, playing at wands with the goddess herself and taking their nourishment from her breast. Would we make them miss a cast with our cries? Would we disturb their suck? No, no, my babies. We must be strong. We must remember who we are, always."

The snuffling cries stopped at her voice; even the baby was still, soothed by her tone.

When it was quiet, Pynt whispered to Jenna, "They will cry no more. Not a one of them cried in the warren, even when the candles gave out. And I know none of them will cry outside. Lead on, White Jenna. Lead on, Anna. Lead on and we will all be your shadows."

They broke the mirror with the butt end of Jenna's sword and set fire to the kitchen and the Great Hall. Jenna let only the older girls help. She could not bear for the babies to see the bodies and all the blood. So the children waited by the back door.

Then, with the smoke spiraling behind them, Jenna and Skada carried Pynt's cot, followed by the single line of children.

They chopped through the twisted fir tree that lay across the path, clearing the walk for everyone. And when they came to a low embankment, the children scrambled over easily. With ropes they hauled Pynt's cot up and then, at Jenna's signal, turned toward the Sea of Bells where, beyond, Selden Hame waited. It was the only place Jenna knew of that would take so many children in. Once she got them safely there, she swore she would find another map and warn the Hames.

THE MYTH

And so Great Alta made the Anna, the White One, the Holy One, out of fire and water, out of earth and air.

"This One that I have made," quoth Great Alta, "shall be sundered and yet shall be whole. She shall be drowned and yet she shall live. She shall burn and yet not be ashes. She shall go down into the earth and up into the air and yet shall not die. She shall be the end of all things and the beginning."

BOOK FOUR

The Anna

THE MYTH

Then Great Alta took up the hair that bound the dark and light sisters to her and with a great shears severed the braid. It fell between them into the sinkhole of night.

"Even as I have done, so you must do," quoth Great Alta. "For a child who is wrapped in her mother's hair, a child who wears her mother's clothing, a child who lives in her mother's house, that one remains a child forever."

So the queen of shadows and the queen of light departed, but not before they each took a single hair from the braid, twining it about their wrists, as a token of their love.

THE LEGEND

The day that Mairi Magoren was playing at Counters, she looked up and saw an old woman trotting down the road with her head going back and forth like this, tok-tok, tok-tok. Behind her was a long line of dirty, nasty children calling after her.

"Old woman, old woman," said Mairi, "and where are you going so fast?" For she was thinking that she might give her a drink or a chair to rock in or a kind word, and let the gang of children go by.

But the old woman trotted along without a sound, her white-haired head moving back and forth, tok-tok, tok-tok. And her shadow on the ground made the same motion, tok-tok, tok-tok. And those ragged children kept pace behind.

And then Mairi saw that the children were bound together with ropes of hair and that she could see right through them to the trees beyond.

That was when Mairi knew she had seen the Hanna Bucca, the Hanna Ghost or Devil, who stole naughty children from their cradles and lured them

*from their beds and forced them to dance behind her till their clothes were in
rags and their shoes in patches and their mothers long dead in their graves.*

THE STORY

They traveled by night, but not because it was safer. How a troop of
thirty-three children, ranging in age from infancy to twelve years, hoped to
obscure their tracks was beyond even Jenna's fine woodcraft. But they traveled in the moonlight because Skada could be there to help haul Pynt's cot.
Once into the deep woods, though, Skada's movements were not to be
counted on, and Jenna relied more and more upon dark-braided Petra.

Petra seemed extraordinarily composed for a girl on the edge of missioning, and Jenna was not surprised to discover she had chosen to follow the
priestess' way. Jenna tried to remember herself just a year past, but what she
recalled mostly was the sound of doors slamming, the angry scraping of
chairs being pushed from tables, and endless moody self-examinations. Petra seemed troubled by none of these, being equally at home with the babies
as with the still-feverish Pynt. She also had an endless store of tales and
songs which she recited in a voice that reminded Jenna more and more of
the six-fingered Mother Alta.

They had taken as much food from the Hame as they could pack. Each
of the older girls carried sacks or baskets crammed with breads, cheeses, and
dried fruits. The younger ones had leather pockets full of *brod*, the hard-
baked crackers Nill's Hame was famous for. Jenna had slung a half-dozen
wineskins over her back which she planned to refill with water whenever
they were near a stream.

"Even if we never make it to Selden Hame," Skada had remarked, "we
will never go hungry."

The children had cheered then, the first sound they had made since
leaving the Hame, though Jenna had shushed them quickly.

Outlined by the moon, the Sea of Bells seemed an endless realm of closed
white flowers and dark, shadowy grass. Jenna was thankful there was no fog.

She and Skada led the children straight across the great meadow, heedless of the matted track they left behind. More important than any trail was
speed. The children needed mothering, Pynt needed nursing, and regardless

of Skada's joke, there was hardly enough food for more than a few days. Besides, Jenna's head was never long without Mother Alta's voice saying to her, *"You must go from Hame to Hame to warn them. Say this: The time of endings is at hand."* Every repetition brought with it a memory of the horror that had been Nill's Hame, with body and after body in the court-yard and on the stairs, and after the thin smoke trailing up from the funeral fires like an unwinding skein of souls.

The first morning they picnicked by the eastern edge of the lily bell meadow. The infants, who had slept all night in the arms of their carriers, were wide awake. But the others were exhausted from their night of walking and fell asleep in the grass, heedless of the babies' happy babblings.

Jenna and Petra took turns standing guard during the day, though there was, thankfully, little to see except a family of red foxes playing some hundred feet away from the sleeping children and a V of wild geese honk-ing northward overhead.

In the evening they all shared a meal of cheese and bread, water and a cache of nuts Jenna had found during one of Petra's turns at the watch. The fruit was saved for treats along the way.

After the meal, Jenna got them all to their feet, saying, "Come, my warriors. Come, my fine woodswomen. Petra will tell us a story and then we will be on our way."

Petra told them the ever-stirring ballad of *Krack's Ride,* singing the chorus:

> *Hallo, hallay, King Krack does ride,*
> *And with him, sisters side by side*

and all the children joined in. Even the infants seemed to take part, waving their arms at the last three words just as the older girls did.

Remembering Pynt's recitation of the opening lines of the poem, Jenna knelt by her cot.

"And how are you doing, my shadow?" she asked.

Pynt managed to raise her head. "I believe I am healing, Jenna. Who would have credited it? Bouncing along between you and Skada, packed in like a pound of *brod* and cheese. But my fever broke in the night and the wound aches only a little, like a tooth gone rotten."

Jenna put her hand on Pynt's head and found it cool, though a bit damp.

She tucked the covers gently around Pynt's shoulders as Petra finished the last lines of the poem.

Pynt whispered the chorus along with the children. *"And with him, sisters side by side.* That is a good one, Jenna. It will get them moving quickly, and without fear."

"So she hoped," Skada said, materializing by Jenna's side.

Glancing quickly to the horizon, Jenna saw the moon making its slow way. She nodded, as if to herself, and said in a low voice, "You are here. Now we can really go."

The moon was no longer full, its edges sloped and faded, but Skada seemed as crisp as ever, her laughter piercing Jenna's moodiest moments. So the first time Jenna tried to hush her along the long march, she would not be still.

"If I quieted, Jenna, you would say the very same things inside your mind, but they would not be half as amusing. Admit it."

"Hush, Skada, I hear something," Jenna said, stopping, her head cocked to one side. Skada stood in the same attitude.

"How you can expect to hear anything beyond the tramping of sixty-six little feet, Great Alta alone knows," Skada said, though she listened as well.

"Will you hush?"

"I am still. You are the one who is flapping."

As soon as they stopped, the line of children stretched out behind them came to a halt. After the last child had quieted, there was still a shallow echo of sound, a crackling of twigs from the line of trees.

Pynt whispered from her cot, "A cat?"

"Too noisy."

"A bear?"

"Not noisy enough."

"Is that meant to be comforting?"

"That is meant to be—oh, Pynt, we have had this conversation before."

Pynt grinned despite the fear.

"How can you joke at a time like this?" Jenna asked.

Pynt pushed herself up onto her elbow. "Jenna, you are always asking *me* to think. You think this time. Think about the last time we heard such a noise, and in the fog."

"It was Carum." Jenna's voice was suddenly soft.

"But it was not Carum now. Still, that is a noise made by someone equally human. *One* someone. Surely we outnumber whoever is there."

Jenna nodded and drew her sword. Skada followed suit.

A voice called out from the bush, "Put up your sword Jo-an-enna. If I had wanted to surprise you, you would never have heard me."

Pynt sat all the way up on the cot, her smile disguising the cost of such effort. "A-ma!" she cried.

Amalda stepped out of the shadows and, as she did, her dark sister Sammor materialized by her side.

Jenna slipped her sword silently back into its sheath, nodding as Skada did the same. They stepped aside so that Amalda and Sammor might get to the cot.

"What has happened to you, child?" asked Amalda.

"I spoke too soon and went first," Pynt said wryly. "Just what you warned me about. I think that *this* time I may have learned my lesson. But, A-ma, why are *you* here?"

Sammor held Pynt's right hand, Amalda her left. "You brought us here, imp," they said together.

"When a runner came from Calla's Ford to say that you had not gotten to the Hame with the other two—" Amalda began.

"See, Jenna," Pynt interrupted, "I told you they would make it on their own."

Unruffled, Amalda continued. "We could not stay at home knowing you had acted so foolishly, knowing that you might have put your life—and others'—in danger. Marga, you went *directly* against the Mother's orders."

"They were bad orders, made to hurt, not to heal," Pynt said.

"They were the Mother's orders," said Amalda, "no matter what your heart told you. In the Dales they say: *The heart can be a cruel master.* And look how cruelly it has served you." She and Sammor fussed at the bandage around Pynt's shoulder and back.

"Even more cruelly served were the women of Nill's Hame," Jenna whispered. She gestured at the exodus fanned out around them, the children waiting quietly for their next instructions.

Pynt bit her lip and looked down.

"We wondered who they were," said Sammor. "They have the quiet containment of Alta's own babes."

"That is quite a reaping of hillsides, Jenna," Amalda added.

Jenna nodded.

"Where are their mothers?" Amalda asked.

"Dead," Jenna said.

"All of them?"

Jenna said nothing.

"All." Skada spoke for the first time.

Amalda and Sammor turned and stared at her.

"But . . . but you are . . ."

Skada and Jenna both nodded and moved closer together so that their shoulders touched. Seen that way, their twinship could not be denied.

"I do not understand," Amalda said, coming over to stand before them, Sammor following. "You are at least a year away from your Night of Sisterhood. Surely the women at Nill's Hame had no time to set you before the glass. You had no training. You had never even *seen* the rites."

Jenna shrugged. "It just . . . just happened," she said.

Skada's shrug was more generous. "Need called to need," she said. "And I answered."

They were all silent for a long moment; then a four-year-old broke from the ring of children and came over to tug at Jenna's sleeve. "Anna," she whispered urgently, "we have heard the cough of a cat nearby. Some of the little ones are frightened."

"And you are not frightened?" asked Jenna, kneeling down beside her. Skada flanked her.

"No, Anna. You are here."

"Why does she call you Anna?" asked Sammor. "That is not your name."

"The Anna is . . ." Amalda began.

"I know what the Anna is," said Jenna, "but I no longer know who I am." She put her arm around the child on one side, and Skada did the same on the other. "Tell me again, sweet heart."

"We heard a cat in the woods. It coughed like this." The child gave a remarkably good imitation of a cat's rough voice.

"The tale will keep," said Sammor. "The cat will not. We will kill it for you, Amalda and I, and one of your babes will sleep in a skin warmer than her own tonight." Without another word, they slipped away from the group.

"Tell the others," Jenna said to the child. "We will wait here until they return. But no one is to worry further about the cat. At our Hame we say: *A cat who boasts once is a cat who boasts once too often.*"

"We say that, too, Anna," the child said, clapping her hands before she hurried back to the circle of children. Trotting around, she gave them all the message and they sat down in the grass to wait.

"That cat is not the problem," Jenna said to Skada.

"Nor is the telling of the tale," Skada added.

"Time is the problem," Pynt said from her cot. "Every minute we wait here is a piece of moon time lost."

"Moon time matters no longer," said Skada. "A-ma will help with the cot now. You will be able to travel by day, too, if you wish."

"If it were just Amalda, Pynt, and me, we would go both day and night. But the children are exhausted. Little food and less sleep is not a healthy rule."

"They are young. They will recover," said Skada.

Jenna looked over Skada's shoulder at the trees, dark and untidy in the moonlight. "I wish we were gone from this place. It is too close to bad memories."

"And a rough grave," added Pynt.

It was less than an hour, with the moon still climbing, when Amalda and Sammor returned, the cat's skin carried between them.

Jenna smiled thinly. "A small time," she said.

"A small cat," Amalda answered. "And only roughly skinned. It will stink, but we will clean it better once we are home. We worried about the time, you see."

"We worried, too," Pynt said.

They dropped the skin on top of Pynt's feet, and the children gathered around to touch it, jostling one another slightly to get a better look, their infant sisters forgotten for the moment in the high grass.

"One touch," warned Petra, "and that is all. Then we must go."

Silently and solemnly, the little girls touched the catskin; then they turned back to the grass where their sisters lay, and picked up their burdens before forming two straight lines.

Amalda and Sammor nodded toward the south. "That way is quickest. *And* it avoids a certain place."

"What place?" asked Jenna.

"A grave with a snarling dog's helm glowering over it from a broken cross," Sammor said.

"But I threw that helm into the grave," Jenna blurted out.

"And whoever uncovered the grave the first time gave him a proper burial according to their own rites," Amalda said.

"First?" Pynt asked, her voice thin.

"We uncovered it second," said Sammor. "We tracked the two of you with an ease that belittles our training. You trod a path in circles with frequent back-treading."

"There was a fog," Jenna said. If it was meant as an explanation, neither Amalda nor Sammor took it so.

"When we trailed you to that dirt-packed clearing and found the new grave, we feared the worst. But all we found in the grave was a big, ugly lump of a man," said Sammor.

"A man killed twice," added Amalda, "if we read his wounds right. Once in the thigh and once . . ."

Jenna made a small sighing sound.

"Please," Skada said, "Jenna has no stomach for such tellings. She scarcely had any stomach for the doing."

"I did what had to be done," said Jenna. "But I will not take joy in it, neither once nor again. The children are waiting. Can we go?"

They walked on and on, sharing out the last of the *brod* and fruit with the children, giving the infants drinks of water flavored with the honey that Amalda and Sammor had carried with them.

Along the road, first Pynt and then Skada recounted the horror of the Nill's Hame slaughter as starkly as they could, reciting just the facts so that Jenna's blanched face might find its color again. Amalda and Sammor knew better than to interrupt the telling and thus make it longer. And when it was done, they were all five silent, for there were no words for comfort after such a tale. They were careful, though, not to let the children overhear any of it, leaving them to Petra's gentle chivying.

At last the southern road turned into the woods, and Skada and Sammor disappeared, so that the cot had to be carried between Amalda and Jenna. They were silent far into the morning, when they led the children beneath a cliff into a great circling encampment with Pynt's cot at the center. They slept there, at the base of the Old Hanging Man, whose broad, rocky face watched over them until dusk.

The children were hungry and one or two even complained of it, despite Petra's warnings and the many songs she had them sing. The children all were ragged from the long, steady, unending march, and finally Jenna and Amalda let several of the smallest take turns riding on their shoulders. Pynt cradled a few of the infants at a time in the cot by her breast and at her feet, freeing the older children from their heavy burdens. In this way the band of thirty-six straggled up to the gates of Selden Hame at dawn on the fifth day, flanked by two silent Hame guards who had not asked questions, fearing to delay them further.

The gates were opened at once, for the doors of a Hame were never shut to children, and the women of Selden boiled around them, lifting the children into much-welcomed embraces. Then they guided the ragtag crew into the kitchen for food.

Jenna knew that the Hame baths would be kept steaming long into the afternoon, and she could already feel the laving of the waters over her tired legs and back. She put her arm around Petra.

"Come, my good right hand, after we cram some hot stew down you and clean you up, you and I will have to go and speak to the Mother." She said it jauntily, though her own stomach knotted at the thought. When she looked down at Petra, to her surprise, the girl had tears in her eyes.

"Are we safe here, Anna?" Petra asked in a whisper.

"You are safe here, Petra," Jenna answered. "And the children, too, because of your good shepherding."

"The Goddess smiles," Petra said, her voice a small echo of the six-fingered priestess.

Jenna turned away slightly and under her breath, so that Petra could not hear, muttered, "The Goddess laughs, and I do not know if I like the sound."

"What did you say?" Petra asked.

Jenna did not answer, but guided her to a chair in the kitchen, where Donya set two steaming mugs of stew before them and a platter of thick bread slices slathered with melted butter and cloudberry jam.

Amalda had let no one question them while they were eating, then took Pynt to see the infirmarer. Kadreen checked Pynt's shoulder and back while she gulped down a second mug of stew.

"A good piece of work," Kadreen said, her mouth in its usual thin line. "You will not lose the use of the arm, which is often the case when a wound cuts across muscle. But you will have to exercise that arm as soon as you are able."

"When will that be?" Pynt asked.

"I will tell you," said Kadreen, "and it will be sooner than either you or your arm will want. We will work on it together, you and I."

Pynt nodded.

"There will be a nasty scar," Kadreen said.

Amalda smiled. "I will trace it for you myself, Marga. A warrior's scars are the face of memory, a map of her courage."

Pynt hesitated a moment, then looked up at her mother. "I am a warrior no longer, Ama. I have seen enough death for twenty warriors, though my hand struck but one, and he only in the thigh. Yet was I a bringer of death, as surely as if I carried some contagion."

Amalda's face blanched. "But . . ."

"My mind is made up, A-ma. And it is not to shame you. But at my

Night of Sisterhood, I will choose to tend the children, like Marna and Zo. I am good with them, and surely with so many new ones in our Hame, there will be need of me."

Amalda started to speak again, but Kadreen put her hand up. "Listen to her, Amalda. There are some scars that we cannot see and they heal slowly if at all. I know. I have such scars myself."

Amalda nodded and looked again at Pynt. "You are tired, child."

"I am tired, my mother, but that is not the reason I say what I do. If you had seen them in the end, all the beautiful, strong women of Nill's Hame: *sisters side by side.* Jenna pulled my cot into the kitchen and the hall that we might bid them farewell. She said—and I shall carry it with me always— that we must remember. For if we forget, then their death has no meaning. *Sisters side by side.*" She turned her face down and stared at the cot as if she could read some picture there, pushed the mug away, and wept.

Amalda sat down on the cot and ran her hand over Pynt's curly hair. "If that is your wish, heart of my heart. If that is your wish, child whom I carried beneath my breast. Then that is what shall be. You always were a stubborn little thing. Hush. Hush and sleep. You are safe here."

Pynt turned back and stared up at her, eyes still brimming with tears. "But, A-ma, you do not understand. I shall never ever feel safe again. That is the worst of it. Yet I shall dedicate my life to the safety of those little ones so that they do not have to feel as I do. Oh, A-ma . . ." She sat up suddenly and threw her arms around Amalda, without regard for the pain in her shoulder and back, and held on as if she would never let go.

THE BALLAD

The Ballad of White Jenna

Out of the morning, into the night,
Thirty and three rode off to fight
To put the dreaded foe to flight,
Led by the hand of Jenna.

Thirty and three rode side by side,
And by the moonlight fortified,

"Fight on, my sisters," Jenna cried,
"Fight for the Great White Alta."

The blood flowed swift, like good red wine,
As sisters took the battle line.
"This kingdom I will claim for mine,
And for the heart of Alta!"

Thirty and three rode out that day
To hold the dreaded foe at bay,
But nevermore they passed this way,
Led by the hand of Jenna.

Yet still, some say, in darkest night
The sisters can be heard to fight,
And you will see a flash of white,
The long white braid of Jenna.

THE STORY

The bath had been soothing and Jenna even fell asleep for a moment in the hot, scented water. Her white hair, free of the confining braid, fanned out around her like strands of bleached seaweed.

Petra picked at a single strand that had floated across her breast, silently waiting for Jenna to speak. At last, unable to wait longer, she asked, "What is your Mother Alta like? I shall be studying with her."

Jenna opened her eyes and stared at the wooden ribbing of the roof. She was a long time answering, and the silence stretched between them like a taut rope.

"Hard," she said finally. "Unbending. A rock."

"A Hame needs a solid rock upon which to build," Petra said slowly.

Jenna did not answer.

"But one can bruise oneself against unyielding stone," Petra said with a little sigh. "Our Mother always said that a priestess should not be rock but water. That there is an ebb and flow to a Hame. Our Mother Alta . . ."

". . . is dead," Jenna said very softly. "And the fault is mine."

Petra shook her head. "No, no, Jo-an-enna. There is no fault. *No blame, no shame*, Mother Alta always said. And she told me about the Anna. To study to be a priestess is to learn prophecy. If you are the Anna . . ."

"Am I?"

Petra tried to smile. "I believe you are."

"But do you *know?*"

"I will know a hundred years from now," said Petra. "I will know tomorrow."

"What kind of an answer is that?" Jenna asked disgustedly. "It is priestess talk, all words and no meaning." She slapped her hand against the water, splashing them both.

Petra rubbed the water from her eyes as she answered. "It is what Mother Alta said. She meant that we must act now for now, and leave the answers to those who come after. And so I believe."

Jenna stood and the water came up only to the sharp ridge of her hipbone. Her body, with its covering of fine white hair, seemed to glow in the darkened room. "I wish I could believe so simply. I wish I *knew* what to believe."

Petra stood next to her, the water past her waist. "Jenna, a prophecy only suggests, it does not tell. It can be read accurately only long after. We who live it must read it on the slant."

"Those were Mother Alta's words."

Petra shook her head. "Not just words, Jenna, but the heart of it. If you *are* the Anna, then there is much for you to do. If you are not, you must still do it, for events will happen whether you believe or not. The Hames must be warned." She put her hand on Jenna's arm. "And this Hame must be warned, too."

Jenna wrung her hair between strong hands, then quickly braided it up, tying a ribband around it, and flinging it over her shoulder. She smiled wryly. "I had hoped to put it off."

"Put what off?"

"Speaking to the rock."

"I will be there, Jenna. And I will be water over stone for you. You will see."

"Water over stone," Jenna mused. "I like that."

They slipped into clean clothes that had been left for them and, arm in arm, went into the hall. But the hot water had drained them both of any strength after the long nights of walking, and before they could be summoned to see Mother Alta, they had both fallen into a deep sleep across

Jenna's bed. Jenna awoke only once all afternoon, when Amalda came to fetch them and instead tucked Petra into Pynt's old bed.

Amalda sat uneasily in the priestess' room waiting for Mother Alta to speak, wishing it were night and Sammor by her side. She had explained about the girls' exhaustion and had, in their stead, told Mother Alta the tale. Her recitation had been stark and uninterrupted. Though there were gaps in what she knew—and gaps in what she understood—she had told it without a warrior's usual flourishes, knowing that this was a time for truth and not balladry. Mother Alta listened with her eyes closed, a bad sign, nodding or shaking her head in unreadable glosses. Amalda could not tell if she was angry, sad, or pleased with the story. All that was certain was that she was making a judgment. Mother Alta always made private judgments, and the decisions she rendered afterward were as if written in stone. Amalda had never challenged those judgments aloud, though some, like Catrona, had often exchanged harsh words with the priestess.

Matching Mother Alta breath for breath, Amalda tried unsuccessfully to summon up a fragment of the chant to calm herself. But all that came to her mind were the words of the chorus of *Krack's Ride* and a vision of Pynt's agonized face.

"Amalda!" Mother Alta's voice, sharp and commanding, brought her back to the moment. "We shall hear all this tale tonight from the mouths of the three who lived it: Jo-an-enna, Marga, and this young Petra. We will listen for the truth and to discover what you may have—all inadvertently, I am sure—left out."

Amalda nodded miserably, trying to remember what she might have omitted in the telling, and could not recall a word of what she had said.

"The others, the infants and the children," Mother Alta continued, "shall go to bed and watch over one another while we speak. All shall know the horror and the shame of this. All."

Mother Alta's face seemed to have taken on a feral look, reminding Amalda of a fox on hens. It made her increasingly uncomfortable. She wanted to argue, but without Sammor to back her, she felt unequal to the task. So she said nothing and waited for some signal to indicate the priestess had finished speaking. After a moment of silence, Amalda stood.

Mother Alta made a dismissive motion with her hand and Amalda left the room, grateful to be away from the confines of those particular walls.

As soon as the door had closed after Amalda, Mother Alta stood. Smoothing down her long woolen skirt, she took a deep breath and turned toward the mirror. She snatched the covering from its face and stared at herself for a long moment. A familiar stranger stared back.

"Do I believe her?" she asked the mirror. "Why should she lie?" Shaking her head slowly, she considered the question. "No, Amalda does not lie. She has not the wits for it. She says only what Jenna has told her, a shameful tale. But what if there *is* a lie somewhere in the story? An untruth or a not-saying? The *Book* is clear, that *One falsehood can spoil a thousand truths."* She waited, as if expecting the mirror to answer her, then reached out and touched the glass, palm to palm. The blue mark doubled itself before being covered, and around her hand the mirror fogged, making ghostly finger-prints.

"Oh, Great Alta, thou who dancest from star to star, I believe and I do not believe. I want to be the Mother of the Anna, but I fear the ending that comes with it. I have led a good life. I have been happy here. *It is a fool who longs for endings, a wise woman who longs for beginnings,* as you say in the *Book.*

"If I deny her, will I be wrong? She is but a girl. I have watched her grow. I have seen some strangeness there, true. But where is the crown of glory? Where are the voices crying, 'Holy, holy, holy'?

"To choose wrongly is to declare myself a fool. And like the fool in the tale who learns the game after all the players have gone home, I will be laughed at if I am wrong. Laughed at. By the women I command. Thou knowest, Great One, that I am no fool." She took her hand from the glass and watched as the moist prints slowly dried.

Staring at the ceiling, she cried, "I have waited fourteen years for an unambiguous sign from thee. Now, *now* is the hour. Give me that sign."

But it was a clear day and there was neither thunder nor rainbow, nor a voice from the sky. If the Goddess spoke to her, it was in whispers. Mother Alta put her hands over her eyes and tried to weep, but no tears came.

Up first, Petra brushed her long dark hair and braided it into a crown, which she pinned atop her head. Her dress was badly wrinkled, since she had slept in it, and there were creases on her right cheek still where the bed linen had marked her. Yet she seemed remarkably alert and cheerful none-theless.

Jenna, on the other hand, felt as if someone had beaten her about the head and shoulders before flinging her onto the mattress. The bed looked as bad, the covers rucked up by the foot. She came awake slowly.

"Amalda was in, though you did not hear her," Petra said when Jenna began to move. "There is to be a meeting tonight at dinner and we are to tell the story then."

"Mother Alta will be there?"

"And Pynt. And all the women."

"And the children? I would not like to tell the story of Nill's Hame before them. They will know it soon enough, but not from my lips," Jenna said.

"They are to go to bed in one another's charge." Petra came over and sat beside Jenna on her bed. "But I am to be at the meeting. That way we can tell the sisters everything. *Everything,* Jenna."

Jenna looked down at her hands and wondered that she was twisting and winding them together.

"Do not be afraid of your destiny, Anna," Petra said, putting her hands over Jenna's.

"It is not destiny I am afraid of," Jenna said sharply, drawing her hands away.

"Then why are you angry?"

"I am not angry."

"Look at your covers," Petra said, pointing. "Look at your mouth."

Jenna stood and went over to the water basin and stared down into the still, silvered face. Her dark eyes seemed echoed by dark smudges on her cheeks. The cheeks themselves were hollowed. Her mouth was thin and sour. Touching her lips with her right hand, she suddenly felt as if her mouth had forgotten everything, even Carum's kiss. "I look like our Mother Alta," she said.

"Water over stone," Petra reminded her.

Jenna smiled at that and the face in the water basin smiled back. Turning, Jenna said to Petra, "I am ready. I think."

Petra held out her hand. "Sisters," she said, "side by side."

THE HISTORY

Folktales and myths about women warriors, either avatars of their god-desses or female incarnations of the godhead, abound in all the religions of the world. The Greeks, according to Herodotus, knew of such women who— he claimed—lived on the northern coast of Asia Minor in the city of Themis-

cyra. The man-hating Indian princess Malayavati was another such unnature, commanding like-minded females. In Brazil, the Makurap of the Upper Guaporé River told of a village of women even farther afield who kept all men at bay. And so forth. (For an extensive monograph on the subject, see J. R. R. Russ' "The Amazon Explosion," Pasden University Monograph Series #347.)

So it was not unusual for the folk of the Upper and Lower Dales to have conjured up a White Goddess, an Anna (which in the old tongue means "white" or "the white one," according to Doyle), a female hero. But their Amazon warrior differs in several important respects from the classic mythos.

For example, the Altite Anna was not worshipped as a mare or in any other way associated with horses, as her Continental and Eastern counterparts were. In fact, in the few snippets of narrative which have been positively identified as part of the ancient Anna Cycle (see Dr. Temple's chapter on these stories in Alta-Natives: *"Tongue-tied in the Dales"), the Anna is seen as afraid of horses or at the very least puzzled by them. In one battle she mistakes a horse for a monster (". . . the two-headed demon of the fog-gee . . ." is a line from a modern ballad that scholars agree is a remnant of the Cycle). In another she falls off a cross-grained gray mare into a puddle at the feet of her human lover. The modern Anna songs found today in the Dales are not heroic at all, but rather mock-heroic or even antiheroic. In some cases they are downright humorous. (Cf., "Krick's Horn," "The Battle of Anna and the Catte," and "How the Warrior Anna Knocked Heads.")*

Also, the Altite Anna was in no way a man-hater. A number of the ballads are love songs that detail her rather lusty affairs with an amazing variety of men, most notably (and anachronistically) King Langbrow. There is one homeoerotic song, a rather wistful melody, about her best friend, Margaret, dying of love for her as the Anna strides off into battle once again.

It is safe to say, though, that the Anna of the Dales was not a historic personage but merely a popular mythic figure. That such a one as Anna or Jenna or Jo-hanna ever actually lived and fought pitched battles for the sake of her warrior sisters (as Magon in his sentimental essay "Anna of a Thousand Years," Nature and History, *Vol. 41, would have it) is patent nonsense. It is true that the word* history *contains the word* story, *but every good scholar knows better than to confuse the two. We must, therefore, look deeper than the mere rota of events for the real meaning of the Anna of the Dales. We must probe into the very psyche of the Isles before we can begin to understand what needs brought forth a folk creature of such staying power as the Amazonian White Goddess during the time of the brutal and devastating Gender Wars.*

THE STORY

There was a tension throughout dinner that would not dissipate. Even the chatter of the children did nothing to dispel the dark mood. Everyone knew that Jenna, Pynt, and the girl Petra had much to tell. But the word from Mother Alta's room had been to wait. Wait until the meal was over and the children put to bed; wait until the moon rose to bring forth the dark sisters. They had heard tantalizing pieces of the story from the children themselves, and from Amalda.

Donya and her kitcheners had done their best. Slabs of venison made tender by beating, and early spring salads freshened with the sharp wines Donya had laid down from the year before, were at every place. But the meat and the crisp vegetables and the saucy wine did not perform their usual magic. The tension in the dining hall was as palpable as the mist around the Sea of Bells. And the women were as silent as if a Fog Demon had, indeed, stoppered their mouths.

Jenna and Petra sat at a small side table apart from the others. Jenna pushed the food around the plate the way a cat plays with its catch. Petra did not even bother trying, keeping her hands in her lap and silently watching Jenna's display of nerves.

At the three long tables where the rest of the women gathered, only the occasional *clink-clank* of foodsticks on platters marked the passage of time.

But at last the meal was over and Donya, disgusted at how little had been eaten, directed her girls to clear the places, muttering about the waste of food, saying, *"It is better to eat when the food is before you than to be hungry because the food is behind you,"* a piece of folk wisdom she had picked up from one of the men in the Dales. She used it all the time and no one paid her any mind.

Mother Alta had chosen to eat in her room, something she often did before a meeting. She knew how to use the tension to her own advantage; when to enter the dining hall and when to leave it. This time she timed her entrance so that the moon was just rising and the dark sisters slowly coming into view.

Standing in the doorway, side by side with her own dark twin, hair plaited with spring flowers, Mother Alta raised her hands in a blessing. Her sister did the same. The motion was sharp and commanding and all the women in the hall bowed their heads, save Jenna.

She stared into the priestess' face and was just opening her mouth to speak when Skada appeared by her side, the misty edges of her outline quickly brought into focus by the moon and the fluttering torches.

The look in Mother Alta's eyes was one of complete surprise. Jenna realized that Amalda—whatever else she had told Mother Alta—had left Skada out of her telling. Jenna smiled and her dark sister smiled, too.

The priestess' eyes slid away from Jenna's and she recited the blessing in a voice made wooden by surprise. "Great Alta, who holds us . . ."

The hall echoed with the response. "In thy care."

"Great Alta, who enfolds us . . ."

"In thy bounteous hair."

"Great Alta, who knows us . . ."

"As thy only kin."

"Great Alta, who shows us . . ." And for the first time the priestess' voice faltered.

But only Jenna seemed to notice, for the women countered immediately with the proper response: "How to call the twin."

Recovering, Mother Alta finished the blessing emphatically: "Great Alta, give us grace."

The answer resonated through the hall. "Great Alta, give us grace." Then the women looked up, anticipation shining in their faces.

Only a few of them noticed Skada at first, but soon the room was abuzz with it. Mother Alta moved in a slow, stately manner toward her great chair by the fire, as if the appearance of an unnamed sister were of no consequence. Her own sister enthroned herself in a slightly smaller chair by her side. They summoned the women from the tables to them with a slight wave of hands.

Pushing the benches away, the women of Selden gathered in a semicircle by the hearth. Some sat on the floor. Others, like Marna and Zo, leaned against the fireplace stones. Jenna led Petra to a place directly opposite the priestess' chair, with Skada trailing slightly behind. They waited for Mother Alta to speak.

There was another slight flurry of excitement when Pynt came into the hall, escorted by Kadreen. She leaned heavily on the infirmarer's arm, but walked upright. When she saw Jenna and Skada, she winked at them. Then Kadreen led her to the fire and Amalda and Sammor brought over a chair with a deep cushion for her, which Pynt sank into gratefully.

For a moment after that the only sound was the crackling of the fire and a *thud-pop-pop-pop* as a half-consumed log slipped down into the blaze. Jenna strained to make out the sighing breaths around her. Looking about the half circle, at all the dear, familiar faces, she suddenly saw the features of the slaughtered sisters of Nill's Hame slip over them like masks. Like the hound's helm over the engorged face of the dead Kingsman. Reaching out, her hand found Skada's and she laced her fingers through her sister's. Only that touch kept her from tears.

Mother Alta began speaking in a low voice. "It has been two weeks since our young sisters, our four missioners, went forth. And in that time such events have transpired that will shake the foundations of our cozy Hame. But it is not my story to tell. It must be told by those who know it best: Jo-an-enna and Marga and Petra of Nill's Hame." She smiled her serpent smile, and though she looked as if she tried to put some warmth in it, Jenna saw none there.

So Jenna began the story, starting at the confluence of the two rivers where she and Selinda, Alna and Pynt, had said their good-byes. She spoke movingly of her feelings as she had walked away from them, and how the woods had seemed more beautiful because of their parting. When she got to the section of the story where Pynt had come after her, Pynt herself interrupted the account.

"I disobeyed the Mother's wishes," Pynt said. "I saw myself as dark sister to Jenna's light. You remember—I was always called her shadow. And so I became it in truth. I could not let her go on without me. I thought what Mother Alta had asked was too great a sacrifice. So I followed Jenna. If there is any fault in all of this, it is mine alone."

Mother Alta smiled broadly for the first time, and Jenna saw wolfish teeth.

By her left side, Petra muttered, *"No blame, no shame."*

As if Petra's comment spurred her on, Jenna took over the narrative again. She told them of the fog and the strange, low calling that had turned out to be the Hound hunting Carum. Deliberately, she did not describe Carum in any detail beyond the fact that he was a prince. If anyone noticed her omission, the sister did not say. But Pynt looked down at her lap during that part of the recitation, with a silly, knowing grin.

When Jenna got to the telling of Barnoo's death, she hesitated, and it was Pynt who entered the story again. Swiftly, as swiftly as a knife across a throat, and plainly she told it. Jenna stared up at the ceiling through that part, her hands remembering the feel of the sword and the awful sound it had made going into the man's neck. Then Pynt's voice got ragged and Jenna picked up the thread of story again at the burial of the Hound.

She introduced them to Armina and Darmina; she led them with the tale to the gates of Nill's Hame. As she spoke of the carvings, Petra interrupted.

"We were so proud of those gates," she said. "Oak and ash they were. And carved over a hundred years ago by . . . by . . ." She could not go on. Biting her lip, she folded her hands one around the other, the right gripping the left so tightly the knuckles went white.

Marna and Zo, who had been standing close by, their backs against the hearthstones, moved as one to her and enfolded her in their arms. It was the act of tenderness that undid Petra, and she began to cry in earnest. Her weeping made the warriors so uncomfortable, they did not know where to look. Though they did not speak to one another of it, most suddenly found themselves staring either at the high, ribbed ceiling or at the rushes on the floor. Mother Alta was still, unaccountably, smiling.

Jenna thought that if she continued the story, everyone would watch her and Petra might get control of her tears. So she quickly sketched out the buildings at Nill's Hame. Those who had visited the Hame on their own missioning nodded their heads at the memory. Then Jenna told them of the back stairs and described the six-fingered, blind priestess who ruled the Hame.

The rest of the tale tumbled out quickly: Pynt's wounding, the severed hand of the Ox, and the great leap into the Halla in which she and Carum almost drowned. She mentioned everything but Carum's kiss, though she brushed her fingers unthinkingly across her mouth when she told of their farewell before the walls of Bertram's Rest. Skada's hand, she noticed from the corner of her eye, seemed to linger on her own lips longer than was quite necessary.

And then she told them about her return to Nill's Hame and all she had found there. By the time she was done, even some of the warriors were weeping, and those who did not sat stone-faced or shook their heads slowly back and forth, as if by their denial they could make it not so.

Jenna stopped speaking at the moment in the story when she had brought the tiny Mother Alta, the last of them, down the stairs in her arms. A deep sigh ran around the room, but the priestess was not part of it. She leaned forward in her chair and her dark sister moved with her. "Tell me how you called your shadow forth, how one so young managed it. I understand this much: that you thought you had lost one shadow and needed another. But I need to know *how* you did it. For if you can do it, perhaps others can. It is a breach that must be repaired."

Jenna gasped. She had not thought of it that way—that having lost her dark Pynt, having lost Carum, she had needed a replacement. Was Skada only that? A poor substitute? But Skada's shoulder suddenly touched hers and she turned her head slightly, looking slantwise at her.

"Be careful," Skada whispered. "Or you will bruise yourself on that flinty heart."

Jenna nodded and Skada nodded back, a movement so slight no one could have noticed.

"I called and she answered," Jenna said to the priestess.

"I would have come sooner had she asked sooner," Skada added.

Then Jenna told of finding Pynt and the children in the hidden rooms and leading them away from the slaughterhouse, over the meadows, under the nose of the Old Hanging Man, and home.

Now dry-eyed, Petra spoke up. "Jo-an-enna has told you *what* has happened, but not *who* she is. My Mother Alta named her. Now your Mother must tell you the same."

Mother Alta turned her head by moving her entire body slowly, as if a mountain had turned. She stared angrily at the girl, but Petra stared back defiantly.

"What do you mean?" Donya asked Petra.

But Catrona turned to the priestess. "Tell us, Mother." There was a strange challenge in her voice.

"Tell us," the other women echoed.

Sensing she was losing control of them, Mother Alta leaned back slowly and held up her hands so that the blue goddess sign showed. Her sister followed suit, and their four palms flashed the powerful signal to quiet the room.

When she had their complete attention, she waited a beat longer, then began. "What young Petra means," she said, letting her voice linger on the word *young,* "is that there is a story about the Anna, the white avatar of the Goddess, that is still told in some of the more backward Hames."

Petra shook her head. "Nill's Hame was no backwater community. And the Anna is no story, Mother, as well you know. It is a prophecy." She took two steps into the semicircle, looked around at the women to gather in their attention, and began to recite the prophecy in that singsong voice priestesses affected for such things.

> *The babe as white as snow,*
> *A maiden tall shall grow,*
> *And ox and hound bow low,*

And bear and cat also.
Holy, holy, holy.

No one moved as Petra continued. "Was Jenna not a white babe now grown straight and tall? Have not both the Bull and the Hound already fallen to her?"

There was a low grunt of agreement from some of the women. Before they were fully quieted, Petra went on.

She shall bring forth the end,
And sever friend from friend.
The brothers all shall bend,
And we begin again.
Holy, holy, holy.

"What is that verse?" Mother Alta asked. "I have never heard those five lines."

"Do you think I made them up?" asked Petra. "And me so young?"

The women's low mutterings began again.

Petra leaned toward the priestess and spoke as if to her alone, though her voice rang clearly in the room. "Never was there more of an ending than Nill's Hame, where sister from sister, mother from daughter, was severed. Surely Jenna was the harbinger of that end."

"I reject it!" Mother Alta roared above the women, who were now openly arguing. "I reject it utterly. I have asked for a sign from Great Alta and she has given me none. The heavens do not roar. The ground does not open up. All this was promised in the writings." She looked around the hall, her hands up, no longer signaling but pleading. "Did I not seek out the truth of it myself? It was I who, fourteen years ago, followed backward Selna and Marjo's trail. Yes, I, a priestess, who read the woodsign. In the town of Slipskin I found a farmer who spilled out his tale into my arms. This girl, this child you claim a wonder, was his, born from between his wife's dead thighs. Jo-an-enna killed her mother. Is that the act of an avatar of Alta? She killed the midwife as well. And she was the cause of her foster mother's death. Tell me, all you women who have born or fostered a child, is this the One you would follow?"

"Would you blame the infant for its mother's death? Would you shame the innocent? *No blame, no shame*—it is written in the *Book,*" Petra said. But her voice, being still a child's, was weak compared with the full modulations of Mother Alta's.

The priestess stood, and her sister rose beside her. "Would I withhold from you such a miracle? Would I keep from you such a savior?" Seeing the women wavering, she pressed her advantage. *"Who is she?* I will tell you who she is. She is Jo-an-enna, a girl of this Hame. You watched when she spit pap from her baby mouth. You changed her soiled pants. You nursed her through rosy fever and dabbed at her dripping nose. She is your sister, your daughter, your friend, that is who she is. What more would you have her be?"

Jenna looked around slowly at the rolling sea of faces. She could not read what lay written there. Pulling into herself, she began the breathing chant and within a space of ten counts once again started to feel the strange lightening. Slipping the gross bonds of her body, she lifted above it to survey all who quarreled below. In that other state, all was silent and she could see each woman purely. Most clearly of all she could see herself. She wondered at the still, white center she found there. Her body was like the others, yet at the core there was a difference. Did that make her a savior, an avatar, the Anna? She did not know. But what seemed clear now was that Petra was right. Events would move forward whether she believed or not. She could be swept along, possibly drowned, like a child in the Halla. Or she could dig a channel to control the waters as the townsfolk of Selden had done with their flood. It was that simple.

She let herself slip back into her body and opened her eyes. Moving into the center of the half circle, she raised her right hand. Skada did the same.

"Sisters," she began, her voice trembling, "Listen to me. *I am the Anna!* I am the Goddess' good right hand. I go to warn the Hames that the time of the endings, the time of the beginnings, is here. I am the Anna. Who goes with me?"

For a long moment there was silence and Jenna suddenly feared that the priestess had won and that she was cut off from all of them, now and forever.

Then Pynt said, "If I were fit, I would go with you, Anna. But my place is here, here helping with the children even as I heal."

"I will go with you, Anna," cried Petra, "for I know prophecy even though I do not know how to use a sword."

"And I," called out Catrona. "With my sister by my side." Her dark twin nodded.

"We will go, too," Amalda and Sammor said together.

Jenna looked at them and shook her head. "No, my fourth mothers. You must stay. Selden Hame needs to ready itself for what comes soon. The time of endings. Your arms are needed here. I will go with Petra and Catrona and, at the moon times, we shall have our dark sisters with us. We are messengers, after all, not a mob." Then she turned and spoke to the priestess. "We would go with your blessing, Mother, but we will go whether you give it or not."

Slumped against her chair, Mother Alta suddenly looked old. She waved her hand in a feeble sign that might have been a blessing. Her dark sister's motion was feebler still. Neither of them spoke.

"I know the way to most of the Hames," Catrona said. "And I know where there is a map."

"And I know all the words to be said," Petra added.

Jenna laughed. "What more can a savior want?"

"A sword would be helpful," Skada said. "And perhaps a sense of the absurd."

It took no more than an hour to arm and provision them, and Donya outdid herself with the parcels and packs. It was as if she were supplying an army, but they could not tell her no.

Skada whispered to Petra as they watched the food being packed, "Was it not strange that Mother Alta was unfamiliar with the second part of the prophecy?"

Petra smiled. "Not strange at all," she said. "I made it up. It is my one great trick. I was famous for reciting poems to order at Nill's Hame."

And then they were off on the road from the Hame into history, a road that glistened under the waning moon in a night lit by the flickering of a thousand thousand stars. As the five of them strode down the path, the women of Selden Hame cried out behind them in a long, wavering ululation that was part prayer, part dirge, and part farewell.

THE MYTH

Then Great Alta set the queen of shadows and the queen of light onto the earth and commanded them to go forth.

"And you two shall wear my face," quoth Great Alta. "And you shall speak with my mouth. And you shall do my bidding for all time."

Where the one stepped, there sprang fire and the earth was scorched beneath her feet. Where the other stepped, there fell soothing rains and blossoms grew. So it was and so it will be. Blessed be.

Here Ends Book 1: *Sister Light, Sister Dark.*

THE MUSIC OF THE DALES

Prophecy

The babe as white as snow, A maid - en tall shall grow, And ox and hound bow low. And bear and cat al - so. *rit.* Ho - ly, ho - ly, ho - ly.

Lullaby to the Cat's Babe

Lord Gorum

Plaintively

O where have you been all day, Go-rum, my son? The
bull, the bear__, the cat and the hound, (2.) I
Where have you been all day, my pret-ty one? And the
broth-ers have pull-ed me down.__

2. I've been far afoot, with my staff in my hand,
   The bull, the bear, the cat, and the hound,
   I have been out walking my dead father's land,
   And the brothers have pulled me down.

3. I looked in the mountains, I looked in the sea,
   The bull, the bear, the cat, and the hound,
   A-looking for someone a-looking for me,
   And the brothers have pulled me down.

4. What have ye for supper, Lord Gorum, my son?
   The bull, the bear, the cat, and the hound,
   What have ye for supper, my pretty young one?
   And the brothers have pulled me down.

5. I've nothing for supper and nothing to rise,
   The bull, the bear, the cat, and the hound,
   But fed on the look in my own true love's eyes,
   And the brothers have pulled me down.

6. What will ye leave to that true love, my son?
   The bull, the bear, the cat, and the hound.
   What will she leave you, my handsome young one?
   And the brothers have pulled me down.

7. My kingdom, my crown, my name, and my grave,
   The bull, the bear, the cat, and the hound,
   Her hair, her heart, her place in the cave,
   And the brothers have pulled me down.

The Ballad of White Jenna

With spirit

Out of the morn-ing, in-to the night, Thir-ty and three rode off to the fight To put the dread-ed foe to flight Led by the hand of Jen-na.

2. Thirty and three rode side by side,
   And by the moonlight fortified.
   "Fight on, my sisters," Jenna cried.
   "Fight for the Great White Alta."

3. The blood flowed swift, like good red wine,
   As sisters took the battle line.
   "This kingdom I will claim for mine
   And for the heart of Alta!"

4. Thirty and three rode out that day
   To hold the dreaded foe at bay,
   But never more they passed this way,
   Led by the hand of Jenna.

5. Yet still, some say, in darkest night,
   The sisters can be heard to fight
   And you will see a flash of white
   The long white braid of Jenna.

Alta's Song

With great feeling

I am a babe, an on - ly babe, Fire__ and water and all__, Who in my moth - er's womb was made,

[1,2,4: take; 3,5: save]

Great Al - ta {take__ / save__} my soul.__

2. But from that mother I was torn,
   Fire and water and all,
   And to a hillside I was borne,
   Great Alta take my soul.

3. And on that hillside was I laid,
   Fire and water and all,
   And taken up all by a maid,
   Great Alta save my soul.

4. And one and two and three we rode,
   Fire and water and all,
   Till others took the heavy load,
   Great Alta take my soul.

5. Let all good women hark to me,
   Fire and water and all,
   For fostering shall set thee free,
   Great Alta save my soul.

The Ballad of the Selden Babe

with great expression

Do not go down, ye maid-ens all who wear the gol-den

gown, Do not go to the clear-ing at the edge of Sel-den

town, For wick-ed are the men who wait to bring young

1.-6. 7.

maid-ens down.   span, And a good and long life span.

rit.

2. A maiden went to Seldentown,
   A maid no more was she,
   Her hair hung loose about her neck,
   Her gown about her knee,
   A babe was slung upon her back,
   A bonny babe was he.

3. She went into the clearing wild,
   She went too far from town,
   A man came up behind her
   And he cut her neck around,
   A man came up behind her
   And he pushed that fair maid down.

4. "And will ye have your way wi' me,
   Or will ye cut me dead,
   Or do ye hope to take from me
   My long-lost maidenhead?
   Why have ye brought me far from town
   Upon this grass-green bed?"

5. He never spoke a single word,
   Nor gave to her his name,
   Nor whence and where his parentage,
   Nor from which town he came,
   He only thought to bring her low
   And heap her high with shame.

6. But as he set about his plan,
   And went about his work,
   The babe upon the maiden's back
   Had touched her hidden dirk,
   And from its sheath had taken it
   All in the clearing's mirk.

7. And one and two, the tiny hands
   Did fell the evil man,
   Who all upon his mother had
   Commenced the wicked plan.
   God grant us all such bonny babes
   And a good and long life span.

Come Ye Women

Jauntily

1. O come ye wom-en of the Isles, And lis-ten to my song,
2. But wom-en we be from our birth And will be till we die,

For if ye be but thir-teen years ye not be wom-en
Our count is made so dif-f'rent-ly To give the men that

long.__ And if ye be__three score and ten, No long-er
lie.__ O come, ye wom-en of the Isles, And lis-ten

wom-en be, Or so say all the mer-ry men Who
to my song, For we be wom-en all through life, Where

count so cru-el-ly, Who count so cru-el-ly.__
life and love are long, Where life and love are long.__

WHITE JENNA

For Beth and Tappan
and new beginnings

SYNOPSIS

For years, the birth of a girl child in the Dales had been no cause of great rejoicing. After the first of the Garunian Wars, when the patriarchal tribes from the mainland had sailed across to slaughter the men and conquer the island country, there had been a surplus of women in the Dales. Forced into polygamous marriages or forced to expose excess girl babies on the hillsides, a woman's lot was not enviable. However, early on, a few of them had begun to reap the hillsides of the grim harvest, saving the infants and raising them in small, walled communities called Hames.

The centuries passed and the Hames were left alone. Eventually there were seventeen such separated communities filled with women, worshippers of Great Alta, the Goddess who had once been the ruling deity of all the Dales before being supplanted by the Garunian pantheon of gods. As the population regained its balance, the Hames became sanctuaries for dissident women.

The Altites, as they were called, continued to take in the few fosterlings brought them, but to keep up their ranks often went outside the walls to breed themselves, leaving any male babies with the fathers and carrying the girl children back to the Hames. Women of the Hames also went outside as skilled warriors-for-hire, fighting in the king's army for a few years, thus honing their own skills and learning the latest in tactics and weaponry.

However, the young girls were kept away from the outside as much as possible, until puberty and their mission year when they traveled to several other Hames as part of their education.

What went on behind the Hame walls was a mystery to the commonfolk of the Dales as well as to their Garunian overlords. Though the commonfolk still spoke of Alta, worshipping her as the consort of Lord Cres, who was the dark warrior god of the Garunians, and as the goddess of childbirth and the homey virtues, the only pure Alta worship belonged to the Hames. Yet as much as the commonfolk of the Dales mentioned Alta in their prayers, they could not even come close to guessing the secret She had gifted the Altite women. Trained from childhood in special breathing exercises, memorizing the words of their goddess as set down in the *Book of Light*, the Altites had learned how to call up their dark sisters, their shadow souls, when they reached puberty. Ever after, these dark sisters would appear with the moon or in candlelight or firelight, walking and talking, fighting and making love, side by side with their light counterparts.

There was persistent prophecy, rumor, and myth about one white-haired girl to be born to three mothers, all of whom would die giving her birth. This White Babe, as she was called, would become a warrior queen, a goddess, known alternately as the White One or the Anna, an old Dale word meaning "white." The prophecy, with typical gnomic misdirection, said that the child would be both white and black, both light and dark. She would conquer ox, hound, bear, and cat, signaling the end of an old era and heralding in a new.

The Garunians, who had carried a similar prophecy across the sea with them, feared such a phenomenon as a threat to their rule. So to confound the locals, they named their warlords Bull, Hound, Bear, and Cat. The Dalites told frequently quoted cante-fables about the White One's coming. And the Altite priestesses had a clear charge: nurture the White Babe and warn the other Hames when she is born.

So when a child, white-haired, dark-eyed, and seemingly preternatural in her abilities, was born to a Dale farmer's wife who died in childbirth, the story of *Sister Light, Sister Dark* was begun. The midwife, upon instructions of the farmer crazed by his bereavement, took the child to be fostered at Selden Hame, the Hame closest to their town. On the trip, the midwife herself was killed by a cat, and the cat, in turn, killed by a pair of Selden Hame light/dark sisters who were out hunting. They took the child to foster, but it was a late and first fostering for this particular pair. They grew to quarreling, a quarrel which eventually led to the light sister's exile and then the pair's death. Three mothers, and all dead, because of the strange white-haired child.

That child, Jo-an-enna, called Jenna, was mothered by the entire Selden Hame, for the priestess, Mother Alta, suspected the child was the prophecy's fulfillment, and wished to have a hand in any glory.

Young Jenna grew up beloved in her community by all except the suspicious and jealous Mother Alta. Instead of choosing to be a priestess, Jenna chose the warrior/hunter path, going through training with her special best friend Marga, called Pynt. Little, lithe dark-haired Pynt was called Jenna's shadow, and indeed the two were inseparable.

At thirteen, Jenna did not understand the priestess' enmity nor why she was sent to a different Hame for the beginning of her mission year. Resentful, angry, alone for the first time in her life, Jenna was forced to leave her friends and take a different path. She headed toward Nill's Hame, across the Sea of Bells, a great meadow pied with lilies-of-the-valley.

But despite orders to the contrary, Pynt deserted Selinda and Alna, the other two mission-going girls, and tracked her best friend. The two were reunited halfway to Nill's Hame in the dense fog that settled almost daily over the Sea of Bells. Startled by a strange baying, fearing it to be the Fog Demon they had been warned about in tales, they stood back-to-back, swords drawn, waiting.

The strange howling chivvied a young man into their path who, it turned out, was the third son of the true king. This boy—for he was only a few years older than they—was Carum Longbow, in training as a scholar. He cried them *merci*, using the old formula. They pledged his safety and, in the fog, Jenna killed the man who had been trailing him, one of the usurper Lord Kalas' dread warlords known as the Hound.

Burying the Hound in a shallow grave, with his fearsome Hound's helm thrown on top of his body, the three made their way out of the forest to Nill's Hame. It was a strange trio: Pynt jealous of Carum's attention to Jenna and Jenna's attention to Carum; Carum falling under the spell of the tall, white-haired girl; Jenna befuddled by her own conflicting emotions.

Men were not allowed in a Hame, so Carum was disguised. As he was yet beardless and—while tall enough—was not very muscular, the disguise was accomplished with marginal success, despite his grousing. The three were led up to the room of the priestess of Nill's Hame, a strange, powerful Mother Alta who was blind, crippled, with six fingers on each hand. She recognized Jenna as the Anna of the prophecy, having once been thought to be that prodigy herself. Mother Alta showed Jenna how she had already fulfilled the beginning of the prophecy: being white-haired, with a dark companion, burying three mothers, making "the hound bow low." Jenna alone was unconvinced.

As the girls had promised to take Carum to safety to one of the walled "Rests," sanctuaries that even Lord Kalas did not dare violate, Jenna, Pynt, and Carum started out the back way from the Hame. But they were set upon while still in reach of the walls of the Hame by Lord Kalas' men who had tracked them from the Hound's hasty grave.

Pynt was mortally wounded and carried back to the Hame by Carum. Covering their retreat, Jenna cut off the hand of one of Kalas' men. When she got back into the Hame carrying this grisly trophy with her, Carum recognized the ring on the hand as belonging to the Bull. Jenna had made the bull/ox "bow low" as well. Surely now she had to admit she was the White One. But Jenna would have none of it. She insisted she was just an ordinary girl caught up in extraordinary events.

Leaving Pynt to the ministrations of the infirmarer, and with instructions as to the location of the Rest by a water route, Jenna and Carum leaped from the third floor of the Hame straight down into the treacherous river below, linked together by a child's play rope.

Almost drowned, they managed to make it to shore and find their way to Bertram's Rest. Being a woman, Jenna could not enter the men's sanctuary, so she left Carum at the gate. He kissed her tenderly, promising everything in that one kiss, and Jenna returned to the Hame by the back route.

But it was silent at the Hame. Too silent. When Jenna came closer, she saw why. All the women had been slaughtered; many of them lying next to the men they had killed. The courtyard was filled with them, the stairs, the halls. Jenna raced desperately through the Hame to discover anyone alive, to find her wounded friend Pynt. Eventually, she came upon the place where the brave women of Nill's Hame had made their last stand: in the priestess' room. All the women of Nill's were dead and the children— including Pynt—were gone.

Sorrowing beyond measure, Jenna spent the entire day carrying the bodies of the women down to the kitchen and the Great Hall, laying them out side by side, with enough room between for their dark sisters. Then she returned to the priestess' room to bring down the great wood-framed mirror. Standing before it in the priestess' room, Jenna unknowingly recited part of the ritual of Sisterhood which called forth the dark sisters. Though a year too young and untrained in the proper rites, Jenna's great need and the intensity of her calling brought her own dark sister Skada out of the mirrored world.

Skada—as dark-haired as Jenna was light. Skada—who spoke the things that Jenna had never dared speak. Skada—who urged Jenna to deeds that Jenna never dared dream.

Jenna and Skada together tried to lift the mirror to bring it downstairs for the funeral pyre. But when they moved it, they triggered a secret door which opened under Jenna's feet, exposing a passageway where the children of Nill's Hame had been hidden from the marauding men. Pynt was there, too, bedridden and still desperately ill from her wound, but alive.

Jenna, Skada, and the young priestess-in-training Petra set the funeral pyre. Then they led the troop of children, some only babes carried by their older sisters, along the Sea of Bells and back through the woods to Selden Hame.

There the story of their adventures was told and Jenna lay claim to the title of White Goddess, not because she believed in it, but because she felt it would help the cause: *the other Hames must be warned.* Suddenly afraid of what Jenna's title might mean, the priestess denied her; but, with Petra's help (she invented prophecy in instant rhyme), Jenna convinced the rest that she was indeed the Anna of whom it was written that she *is the beginning and the end.*

Accompanied by Skada, Petra, and the twinned older warriors light Catrona and dark Katri, sworn enemies of Selden's Mother Alta, Jenna went forth on the road.

Prophecy

And the prophet says a white babe with black eyes shall be born unto a virgin in the winter of the year. The ox in the field, the hound at the hearth, the bear in the cave, the cat in the tree, all, all shall bow before her, singing, "Holy, holy, holiest of sisters, who is both black and white, both dark and light, your coming is the beginning and it is the end." Three times shall her mother die and three times shall she be orphaned and she shall be set apart that all shall know her.

BOOK ONE

Messengers

THE MYTH

Then Great Alta looked down upon her messengers, those whom she had severed from her so that they might be bound more closely to her. She looked upon the white sister and the dark, the young sister and the old.

"I shall not speak to you that you may hear. I shall not show myself to you that you may see. For a child must be set free to find her own destiny, even if that destiny be the one the mother has foretold."

And then Great Alta made the straight path crooked before them and the crooked path straight. She set traps for them and pits that they might be comforted when they escaped, that they might remember her loving kindness and rejoice in it.

THE LEGEND

It was in the town of Slipskin, now called New Moulting, soft into the core of the new year's spring, that three young women, and one of them White Jenna, rode out upon a great gray horse.

His back was as broad as a barn door, his withers could not be spanned. Each hoof struck fire from the road. Where his feet paced, there crooked paths were made smooth and mountains laid low, straight paths were pitted and gullies cut from the hills.

There are folk in New Moulting who say it was no horse at all, but a beast sent by Alta herself to carry them over the miles. There are footprints still near the old road into Slipskin, carved right into the stone. And downriver, in the town of Selden, there are three great ribs of the thing set over the church door that all might see them and wonder.

THE STORY

The road was a gray ribbon in the moonlight, threading between trees. Five women stood on the road, listening to a ululating cry behind them.

Two of the women, Catrona and Katri, were clearly middle-aged, with lines like runes across their brows. They had short-cropped hair and wore their swords with a casual authority.

The youngest, Petra, stood with her shoulders squared. There was a defiance in the out-thrust of her chin, but her eyes were softer and her tongue licked her lips nervously.

Jenna was the extremely tall girl, not yet a woman for all that her hair was as white as the moonlight. Whiter, as it had no shadows. The other tall girl, but a hairbreadth smaller, and a bit thinner, and dark, was Skada.

"I will miss the sound of their voices," Jenna said.

"I will not," Skada answered. "Voices have a binding power. It is best for us to look ahead now. We are messengers, not memorizers."

"*And* we have far to go," Catrona said. "With many Hames to warn." She drew a map from her leather pocket and spread the crackling parchment upon the ground. With Katri's help she smoothed it out and pointed to a dark spot. "We are here, Selden Hame. The swiftest route would be there, down the river road into Selden itself, across the bridge. Then we go along the river with our backs to the Old Hanging Man, never losing sight of these twin peaks." She pointed to the arching lines on the map.

"Alta's Breast," said Skada.

"You learned your lessons well," said Katri.

"What Jenna knows, I know."

Catrona continued moving her finger along the route. "The road goes on and on, with no forks or false trails to this Hame." Her finger tapped the map twice and Katri's did the same.

"Calla's Ford Hame," said Jenna. "Where Selinda and Alna have begun their mission year. It will be good to see them. I have missed them . . ."

"But not much," murmured Skada.

"Is it the best place to start?" Jenna asked. "Or should we go farther out? Closer to the king's court?"

Catrona smiled. "The Hames are in a great circle. Look here." And she pointed to one after another, calling out the names of the Hames as if in a single long poem. "Selden, Calla's Ford, Wilma's Crossing, Josstown, Calamarie, Carpenter's, Krisston, West Dale, Annsville, Crimerci, Lara's Well, Sammiton, East James, John-o-the-Mill's, Carter's Tracing, North Brook, and Nill's Hame. The king's court is in the center."

"So none will complain if we visit Calla's Ford first," Katri said, her finger resting, as did Catrona's, on the last Hame. "As it is closest."

"And as our own Hame's children are there," added Catrona.

"But we must be quick," Jenna reminded them all.

Catrona and Katri stood simultaneously, Catrona folding the map along its old creases. She put it back in the leather pocket and handed it to Petra.

"Here, child, in case we should be parted from one another," Catrona said.

"But I am the least worthy," Petra said. "Should not Jenna . . ."

"Now that Jenna has seen the map once, she has it for good. She is warrior-trained in the Eye-Mind Game and could recite the names and places for you even now. Am I right, Jenna?" Catrona asked.

Jenna hesitated for a moment, seeing again the map as it had lain under Catrona's hands. She began to recite slowly but with complete confidence, outlining as she spoke with her foot in the road's dirt, "Selden, Calla's Ford, Wilma's Crossing, Josstown . . ."

"I believe you," said Petra, holding out her hand. "I will take the map." She tied the leather pocket's strings around her belt.

They started off down the road, walking steadily, each an arm's length apart. There was little sound in their going and Catrona on the right and Jenna on the far left kept careful watch of the road's perimeter. Only young Petra, in the center, seemed in the least uneasy. Once or twice she turned to look behind them, back toward the place where the long, low cry of the Selden Hame farewell had echoed.

The SONG

Anna at the Turning

Gray in the moonlight, green in the sun,
Dark in the evening, bright in the dawn,

Ever the meadow goes endlessly on,
    And Anna at each turning.

Sweet in the springtide, sour in fall,
Winter casts snow, a white velvet caul.
Passage in summer is swiftest of all,
    And Anna at each turning.

Look to the meadows and look to the hills,
Look to the rocks where the swift river spills,
Look to the farmland the farmer still tills
    For Anna is returning.

THE STORY

They stopped only once in the woods to sleep under a blackthorn tree by a swift-flowing stream. Taking turns, they kept the night watch, leaving Petra the shortest time, and that near dawn when she would have awakened anyway. Besides, as Catrona reminded them, with the moon they watched in pairs and Petra was alone.

There was nothing to disturb their rest except the mourning of owls back and forth across the stream, and the constant murmur of the water. Once on Jenna and Skada's watch, there was a light crackle of underbrush.

"Hare," Jenna whispered to her dark sister, alert for more.

"Hare," Skada agreed. They both relaxed. Slightly.

By early eve of the next day they had passed the outlying farms of Slipskin, neatly tilled land, well cleared of rocks and roots by generations of farmers. Each acre was gently fuzzed over with green. In one field twenty horses were pastured on blue-green grass.

"There," said Catrona, "a man who sells horses. Probably supplies the king. We could *borrow* one or two and he would never know the difference."

Petra shook her head. "We had horses and flocks at my Hame. Believe me, our shepherds knew every beast by name."

Catrona snorted. "I know that, child. Just testing."

"I will *not* ride a horse again," Jenna said. "Once was enough."

"I doubt we could get three off him anyway," Catrona said. "But if we could get one, one of us could ride ahead. We need swiftness whatever the cost."

Unhappily, Jenna had to agree.

"Let me do the talking," Catrona added. "I have spent much time among men and know what to say."

"I have spent no time at all with them," admitted Petra.

Jenna said nothing, but her finger strayed to her lips and she was glad that it was still daylight and Skada not there to remind her just what she had—and had not—said to Carum when he had kissed her. Two men she had known: one she had kissed and one she had killed. She knew as little as Petra. "Yes, you speak," she said to Catrona. "We will wait behind."

"But mind you, look fetching," said Catrona.

"Fetching?" Jenna asked, genuinely puzzled.

"Men like that." Catrona threw back her head, laughing loudly.

Although they weren't sure what Catrona meant by *fetching,* both Jenna and Petra managed to smile at the farmer when he opened the dark wood door. He stared at them for a moment, as if unsure of what he was seeing, then called over his shoulder, "Martine, Martine, come quick."

"What is it?" a voice called from the room behind him.

He did not speak again until his wife, a rosy giantess, stood next to him, a full head higher than his own balding crown.

"There, the big girl, look at 'er. Look, woman."

She stared as well.

"We are Alta's own," Catrona began, stopping when she saw that they were paying no attention to her but were rather staring at Jenna. She spoke again, loudly. "My name is Catrona, from Selden Hame. My sisters and I . . ."

"By the blessing, Geo, you are right. Who else could it be," the farmer's wife said, her cheeks bright red. "Except for the hair, she's the spit of my poor dead sister."

Catrona suddenly understood. "You think Jenna a fosterling from your family? Of all houses, that we should have stopped here."

"Naaa, naaa," the farmer said, shaking his head and sounding remarkably like a penned beast. "She has eleven sisters, and all the same. Not fifty years ago the hillsides would've been full of 'em. But we got low on girls 'round here and so now girls is a commodity. You be thinking of staying, I could set you up with good husbands." He shook his head again. "Well, the niece, maybe, and the little one there. We need breeders, you know. That's why Martine's sisters, they all got spoke for early. Good stock. Not a holding this side of the Slip don't house one of 'em. *T'would be harder to miss one than find one,* as they say of blackbirds in a flock. It would be . . ."

Martine pushed her husband aside and walked past Catrona to Jenna's side. Together, their relationship was obvious. "She has the Dougal height, the Hiat eyes, remember Geo like you said when we was courtin', my eyes was *dark eyes of a spring.* And my sister Ardeen went white afore she was fifteen, and my sister Jarden afore she was twenty. Give your aunt a hug, girl."

Jenna did not move, her mind whirling.

"Her mother was bringing her to us to foster, out in the woods when a cat killed her," Catrona said. "My own sisters gave yours a decent grave and said the words you like over her. Her fosterer died, or I would tell her of you."

"Nonsense!" Martine said, turning from Jenna to speak directly to Catrona. "Her mother died at birth. Lay there bleeding like a pig stuck for market while the midwife bore the child away. If your sister fostered her, then . . ." She stopped a minute and counted on her fingers. "One for my poor dead sister, two for the midwife, and three be your sister. Oh, my Blessed be!" She dropped suddenly to her knees, her hands covering her mouth. "The White One, triple mothered. Of my own flesh and blood. Who could have guessed?"

Her husband went down more slowly, as if he had been pole-axed, and buried his face in his hands.

Jenna rolled her eyes up and sighed. She heard Petra's quick intake of breath and priestess voice behind her.

> Mothered Three,
> Blessed be.

"Stop that," she hissed back at the girl.

From her knees, Martine heard only the rhyme. She put her hands up, palms together, and cried out, "Yes, yes, that's it. Oh, White One, what can we do? What can we say?"

"As for what you can do," Catrona said quickly, "you can give us three good horses, for we are on a great mission of mercy and it would not do for the White One to walk. And as for what you can say, you can say *yes* to us and *no* to any man who asks."

"Yes, yes," Martine cried again, and when her husband did not answer fast enough, she elbowed him.

He rose, still not looking again at Jenna, and mumbled, "Yes, yes, I can give you three. And they will be good. Anyone says Geo Hosfetter gives not good horses is . . ." He sidled out of the door still talking. They could hear his footsteps going away at a run.

"I will go and help him choose," said Catrona.

"Let the White One stay a moment more," begged Martine. "She is my own flesh, my own blood. Let her tell me her own tale. I have tea. I have cakes." She gestured in toward the neat, well-lit kitchen.

Jenna opened her mouth to accept and Petra whispered by her ear, "Dark sisters will be there. Let me talk." Jenna closed her mouth and looked stern.

"The White One does not break bread with any. She fasts on this mission and has taken a vow of silence until it is done. I am Her priestess and Her mouth."

Jenna rolled her eyes up again, but kept silent.

"Of course, of course," Martine said, wiping her hands on her apron.

"Better that you tell Her all you know so She may weigh its significance."

"Of course, of course," Martine said again. "What shall I tell? That my sister, the White One's mother, was tall and red-haired and made, we all thought, like the rest of us for easy birthing. But something was twisted up there. She died giving the child life. And then that wicked midwife stole the babe away, afore any of us got to see it. We knew the child was a girl because she told her own daughter she was taking it to one of the . . . you know . . . Homes."

"Hames," Petra corrected automatically.

"The closest one. Up the road and into the mountains, it was."

"Selden Hame," Petra prompted.

But the woman could only tell the story in her own meandering way. "Selling the babe, most likely. Some midwives be like that, you know." Suddenly afraid she might have offended them, she added quickly, "Not that you Alters buy children. Not that."

"We reap the hillsides; we do not pay the sowers," said Petra.

"I meant that. Yes, I did." Martine's hands wrangled with one another.

"And the father?"

"Died not a year later. Heart broken. Lost wife and child all to once. And crazed. Saw Alter women everywhere, he did. On the farm. At the hearth. In his bed. Two at a time. Double crazed he was." She shook her head. "Poor man."

"Poor man," Petra echoed, her voice soothingly soft.

Jenna bit her lip. *Her* mother. *Her* father. She tried to credit it and could not. Her mother had not lived under such a cozy, thatched roof, dying with her thighs covered in blood. Her mothers—and there were many of them— lived in Selden Hame. And *they* would not die in blood if she could help it. She turned abruptly and left Martine of the wrangling hands to Petra's comforting. Striding quickly across the farmyard, she headed toward the barn.

The sky above was a steely blue, and a bright pink sat on the horizon behind the barn and the fields. Once the sun slipped below the world's rim, there would be another hour before dark. And then there would be a moon. With the moon, the dark sisters Skada and Katri would reappear. Petra had been right to warn her about going into the candle-lit kitchen. Hearthlight and candlelight could also call the sisters out. No need to frighten these poor, silly strangers. *Strangers!* Jenna tried to force herself to think of them as her aunt and uncle. No, there was no blood between them. None at all. It was a mistake, that was all. But a mistake that was bringing them three horses. *Horses!* She never wanted to ride one of those broad-beamed, hard-on-the-rear, teeth-rattling beasts again.

Just as she thought of them, from behind the barn came Catrona leading three sleek mares, two reddish brown and one almost pure white. The farmer strode behind her looking, somehow, relieved. When Catrona spotted Jenna, she grinned, then quickly composed her mouth into a more respectful expression.

"Do these meet your approval, White One?" she asked Jenna.

Jenna nodded. The snow-colored mare threw her head back and whinnied.

"The white is yours, Anna," said Catrona. "The man insists on it." She held out the reins. "And he takes no coin for them."

Jenna drew in a deep breath, willing herself to like the horse. Reaching for the reins, she pulled on them gently and the horse took a few steps toward her. She patted it on the neck and the horse nuzzled her ear. Jenna smiled tentatively.

"See, White One," Geo Hosfetter said, still not looking directly at her, "the horse knows that she is yours." He bobbed his head twice. "Her name is . . ."

"Her old name does not matter," Petra said suddenly from behind Jenna. "She shall have a new one. For, as you know, it says in the prophecy:

> *The White One, the Anna,*
> *Shall ride, shall ride,*

> *And sisters with Her*
> *Side by side.*
> *The horse She sits on*
> *All astride,*
> *It will be called . . . DUTY!"*

"Oh, yes, oh yes," Martine said, hurrying up to them, "I know that. Duty, that's the name. Of course. Duty."

"Duty!" Jenna said, laughing, once they had ridden away from the farm. "What kind of a name is Duty?"

"And where did you learn that prophecy? I never heard it," Catrona said.

"It was the best I could do at the moment's spur," Petra admitted. "I apologize for that sixth line. It was a bit . . . well . . . shaky."

"You mean you *made it up?*" Catrona shook her head.

Petra, nodding vigorously, smiled.

"It is a special trick of hers," Jenna said. "She was famous for it at Nill's Hame. Prophecies and poetry on the moment. But, Petra—*Duty!*"

"Never mind," Petra answered. "They will tell their neighbors and the story will grow and grow. By the time you hear it again, you will be mounted on *Beauty* or on *Booty* and the tale will add that the White One, Blessed be, rode off, pockets ajingle with coin or followed by one hundred men all crying out with love."

"Or they will call the horse *Dirty*, which she will surely be, for we will have little time to keep her clean." Jenna pulled on her right braid. "So why did you get me a *white* horse, Catrona?"

"*He* insisted on it. 'The white one for the White One,' he said. 'And a pair of matched bays for her servants.' "

"Servants!" Petra shouted. At her voice the little bay mare startled and tried to bolt and it took a mighty sawing on the reins to control her. When the horse was steady again, Petra shrugged ruefully at her friends.

"I would not trust *that* horse in a fight," Jenna said.

"But she *should* run like the wind," Catrona pointed out. "Look at her legs. And as they say in the Dales, *The gift horse is the swifter.*"

"Then let her show us her heels," said Jenna. "We have no more time for talking."

Catrona nodded.

They kicked their mounts into trots.

*   *   *

They were just through the town of Selden, with its neat little houses lining the cobbled lanes, and starting over the new bridge, when the partial moon rose. By its light, Skada and Katri reappeared, riding double behind their light sisters.

Jenna knew Skada was there by the familiar breath behind her; the horse knew sooner because of the added weight. It slowed its pace to accommodate the second body but did not flinch.

"Fine horse," Skada whispered in Jenna's ear.

Turning her head slightly, Jenna said, "What do you know about horses, fine or otherwise?"

"I may know little, but at least I am not set against them for no reason."

"No reason!" Jenna said. "Ask my bottom and ask my thighs about reasons." But she said no more and focused her attention on the long bridge as they clattered across.

Once they were on the other side, Catrona signaled them to stop. They dismounted and left the horses to graze on the roadside grass.

"Why did we stop?" Petra asked. In the moonlight her face had a carved look. Her hair, which had been tightly braided and crowned, had shaken loose of its pins and the plaits now fell down along her spine. There were dark circles under her eyes, but Jenna could not tell if they were from weariness or sorrow. She put her arm around the girl's shoulder and Skada, like a parenthesis, closed her in from the other side.

"Horses, like humans, need to rest," Jenna reminded her. "It would not do to kill them on the very first day."

"Nor ourselves," Catrona said, stretching. "It has been a long time since I have ridden a horse. Those are not muscles I exercise regularly." She bent over and put her palms on the ground and Katri did the same.

"My horse is not tired," said Petra.

"He carries one. Ours will have to carry two through a night of strong moonlight," Skada said. "Unfortunately no one has ever trained horses to call up their shadows."

"Are there horses where you come from?" Petra asked.

"We have what you have," said Katri. "But we leave it behind to come here."

Catrona rubbed her horse's nose and the horse responded by nuzzling her. "We will go another few hours and then sleep." She held the horse's head between her hands and blew gently into its nostrils. "This rest is just for breathing."

"And for bottoms," Jenna and Skada said together.

Petra laughed, but Catrona and Katri stared up at the sky.

"Look," Katri said. "See how the moon sits on the Old Hanging Man's brow."

They looked. The cliffs, with their wild jut of stone, seemed crowned with the moon. A shred of cloud was just beginning to cross the moon's spotty face.

"I think it will cloud over soon," Catrona said.

"That will be for the good," added Katri.

"But then you and Skada . . ." Jenna began.

". . . will be gone," Catrona finished. "But since we are just riding, not fighting, the horses will have an easier time of it."

"As will we," Skada said.

"No sore bottoms." Jenna laughed.

"No sore . . ." Skada started to say, but just then the cloud covered the moon and she was gone.

"Mount up," called Catrona, vaulting onto her horse's back.

Jenna and Petra had slightly more trouble climbing back on theirs. Finally Jenna held the bay's reins while Petra got on. Then she caught her own horse and handed its reins to Petra.

"Steady her," Jenna said.

"Talking to your servant?" asked Petra.

"Please," said Jenna.

"Duty awaits," Petra joked. "So, Jenna, go to your Duty!"

"Enough," Jenna said. When she was up at last, the reins gathered back in her own hands, Jenna looked down the road. Catrona was already around the first bend, Petra halfway there. Jenna kicked her heels into Duty's white sides, and the horse started bouncing along. Gritting her teeth, Jenna kicked harder. This time the horse took off at a gallop, sending clouds of dust behind them, obscuring even the dark silhouette of the Old Hanging Man.

THE SONG

Ballad of the Twelve Sisters

There were twelve sisters by a lake,
Rosemary, bayberry, thistle and thorn,

A handsome sailor one did take,
*   And that day a child was born.*

A handsome sailor one did wed,
*   Rosemary, bayberry, thistle and thorn,*
The other sisters wished her dead
*   On the day the child was born.*

"Oh, sister, give me your right hand,"
*   Rosemary, bayberry, thistle and thorn,*
Eleven to the one demand
*   On the day the child was born.*

They laid her down upon the hill,
*   Rosemary, bayberry, thistle and thorn,*
And took her babe against her will
*   On the day the child was born.*

They left her on the cold hillside,
*   Rosemary, bayberry, thistle and thorn,*
Convinced that her new babe had died
*   On the day the child was born.*

She wept red tears, and she wept gray,
*   Rosemary, bayberry, thistle and thorn,*
Till she had wept her life away,
*   On the day her child was born.*

The sailor's heart it broke in two,
*   Rosemary, bayberry, thistle and thorn,*
The sisters all their act did rue
*   From the day the child was born.*

And from their graves grew rose and briar,
*   Rosemary, bayberry, thistle and thorn,*
Twined till they could grow no higher,
*   From the day the child was born.*

THE STORY

"I am sorry," Jenna said. "I have acted foully since we left the Hame. It is as if my tongue and my mind have no connection. I cannot think what makes me act this way."

They had stopped for the night, scarcely a hundred feet off the road, in a small clearing only slightly larger than a room. There was a rug-sized meadow with great oaks overarching it, branches laced together like a cozy roof. Still, Catrona would not let them light a fire for fear of alerting any passersby.

They ate their dark traveling bread and the last of the cheese in silence. Nearby the horses grazed contentedly, hobbled by braided vines. When they had first dismounted, Catrona had shown them how to twist the green rope and secure it to the horses' front feet, tight enough to keep the horses from running off, slack enough so that they did not stumble.

Jenna decided, after much thought, that the slow, steady crunching progress the horses made was a comforting sound, not annoying. But she felt neither steady nor particularly happy about her own progress the past few days. An apology was necessary, and so she offered it.

"What is there to be sorry about?" asked Catrona. "You have slept little and seen too much this past fortnight. You have been torn from and shorn of much you know. Your young life has been turned completely upside-down."

"You speak of Petra, not of me," Jenna said, shaking her head. "And yet her mood remains sunny."

"What is it they say in the Lower Dales? That: *A crow is not a cat, nor does it bear kits.* Jenna, if you were Petra, you would be sunny despite all. It is her way. But you are Jenna of Selna's line . . ." Catrona said.

"But I am *not* of Selna's line," Jenna interrupted. "Not truly." Appalled at the whine in her voice, she buried her face in her hands, as much in shame as in sorrow.

"So. That is it." Catrona chuckled. "How can White Jenna, the Anna, the mighty warrior who killed the Hound and cut off the Bull's hand, as in the prophecies; who has ridden off to save the world of the Hames with her companions by her side; how could *she* have been born between the thighs of a woman like that." She jerked her head back to indicate the direction from which they had just come. "But, Jenna, it is bearing, not blood, that counts. You are a true daughter of the Hames. As am I."

"Do *you* know *your* mother?" Jenna asked, her voice quiet.

"Seventeen generations of them," Catrona said placidly. "As do you. I remember you reciting them, and never a hesitation."

Petra spoke for the first time. "And I can say my lines, too, Jenna, though my birth mother left me at the Hame doorstep when I was not yet weaned, with a note that said only, 'My man will not abide another such as this.' "

"I know," Jenna said, her voice a misery. "I know all the tales. I know that half the daughters of the Hames come there abandoned or betrayed. Or both. And it never bothered me until now."

"Until that silly woman and her sillier husband claimed you," Petra said, moving next to Jenna and stroking her hair. "But their claim is water, Jenna. And you are stone. Water flows over stone and moves on. But the stone remains."

"She is right, Jenna," Catrona said. "And you are wrong to worry over such nonsense. You have more mothers than you can count, and yet you count that story more than all the rest."

"I will count it no longer," Jenna said. She stood, brushed the cheese and bread crumbs from her breast, and stretched. "I shall take the first watch." She looked up at the heavy lacings of the oak and the one small patch of cloud-covered sky, then sighed and stared down at her hands. The ring on her littlest finger, the one the priestess had given her to use as identification, was a reminder of her task. She should think of that, and not of this other silliness. *At least,* she thought, *Skada is not here to bruise me about it.*

But the watch seemed longer without Skada's company, and despite her promise not to think about Martine and Geo Hosfetter—their names as silly as their manners—she could think of nothing else. If she had stayed with her true mother, her birth mother, she would surely have been as awful as they. She spent her watch braiding and unbraiding her long white hair and musing about a life she had never lived.

Morning began with a noisy fanfare of birdsong from a dozen different tiny throats, mellow and chipping, thin and full. Jenna sat up for a moment and just listened, trying to distinguish one from another.

"Warblers," Catrona whispered to her. "Can you tell them?"

"I know the one that Alna called Salli's, that one, there." She raised her hand, finger extended, at a single, melodious call.

"Good." Catrona nodded. "And what about that one, with the little *brrrrrup* at the end."

"Maybe a yellow-rump?" Jenna guessed.

"Good twice. Three times and I will admit you are my equal in the woods," Catrona said. "There—that one!" The call was thinner than the last two, and abrupt.

"Yellow throat . . . no, wait, that is a . . ." Jenna shook her head. "I guess I am not yet as good as you are."

"That was a Marget's warbler, after which Amalda named your best friend. It is good to know that I am still needed in the woods." She smiled. "Wake Petra while I see what there is to offer for hungry travelers." She disappeared behind a large oak.

Petra, who had had the middle watch, was curled up in her blanket, the waterfall of her hair obscuring her face. Jenna shook her gently.

"Up, mole, into the light. We have much traveling yet."

Petra stretched, bound up her hair quickly into two plaits, and stood. She looked around for Catrona.

"Food," Jenna said, motioning to her mouth.

As if the word itself had summoned her, Catrona appeared, but so silently, even the horses did not notice. She carried three eggs.

"One each, and there is a stream not far from here. We will water the horses and fill our flasks. If we ride quickly, we will make the Hame by midday." She gave an egg to each girl, keeping the smallest for herself.

Jenna took her throwing knife from her boot and poked a hole in the top of the egg, then handed the knife to Petra. As Petra worked the blade point into her egg, Jenna sucked out the contents of her own. It slid down easily and she was hungry enough not to mind the slippery taste.

"I will lead the horses," Catrona said. "You, Jenna, and you, Petra, pack up the rest of the gear. And do what you can to make it hard to read our signs. With horses that is difficult, I know."

She led the three horses away. Using branches as brooms, Jenna and Petra followed right after. There were no fire remains to disguise, but much evidence of the horses and their browsing which could not be totally erased. Still, the signs *could* be confused, and Jenna did what was possible. Perhaps an incompetent tracker might think a herd of deer had grazed through.

At the stream they washed quickly, less for the cleanliness and more for morale. Jenna filled their leather flasks while Petra kept a watch on the horses. Catrona went ahead to scout to make sure their return to the road would not be noted.

When Catrona came back, they pulled the reluctant horses from the water, mounted up with more facility than grace, and started off, Catrona in the lead once more.

* * *

The sun was high overhead and they had passed no one on the road. The one small town they had ridden through had been strangely deserted. Even the mill by the river had been empty of people, though the water kept the wheel turning on its own.

"How odd," had been Catrona's only comment.

Jenna's thoughts were darker than that, for the last time she had been where all motion and sound had seemed to stand still had been at Nill's Hame when she returned to find death the only occupant. Yet there were no bodies lying about the town, no blood spilling along the millrace. She breathed slowly, deliberately.

Petra's face was unreadable and Jenna said nothing, worrying more about her friend's silence than the silence in the town.

They rode on, till they came to the ford after which Calla's Ford was named. The pull-line ferry waited on the far side of the river but there was no ferryman in sight. Together Catrona and Jenna hauled on the thick line and the flat-bottomed ferry slowly moved across the water on its tether.

When it grounded, they walked their horses onto the boat in silence. Even with the weight of three horses and three women, the boat rode high in the water.

Built for more than that, Jenna thought. The silence was so oppressive, she kept the thought to herself. But she wondered, all the time that she and Catrona pulled on the water-slicked rope, whether the twenty-one horses of the king's troop could cross on such a boat. Twenty men, and the Bear. Or the Cat. Or Lord Kalas himself.

The little ark plowed across the river quickly, grounding itself with a grinding sound on the shore. The horses got off with more promptness and less urging than they had gotten on. This time both Petra and Jenna remounted with ease.

Jenna urged Duty into the lead, and the horse began an easy gallop along the well-worn road. Behind, Catrona's and Petra's bays took up the white mare's challenge. Jenna could hear their quickening hoofbeats and smiled wryly. For a moment nothing existed but the wind in her hair, the sound of the galloping horses, and the hot spring sun directly overhead.

If I could capture this moment, she thought. *If I could hold this time forever, we could all be safe.*

And then she saw what she had feared: a thin spiral of smoke scripting a warning against the sky.

"The Hame!" she cried out, the first words any of them had spoken in an hour.

The other two saw the smoke at the same time and read it with the same fear. They bent over their horses' necks, and the mares, with no further urging, raced toward the unknown fires.

As they rounded a final bend in the road, the road suddenly mounted upward. The horses labored under them, breathing heavily. Jenna could feel her own heart beating in rhythm with Duty's heaving breaths. Then they crested the rise, and saw the Hame before them, its great wooden gates shattered and the stone walls broken.

Petra reined up at the sight and gave a little cry, flinging her hand to her mouth. But Jenna, seeing movement beyond the walls, stood in the stirrups hoping to distinguish it. Perhaps it was fighting, perhaps they were not too late. Pulling her sword from its sheath and raising it overhead, she called to Petra, "Stay here. You have no weapon."

Catrona was already racing forward. Without giving further thought to the consequences, Jenna turned Duty toward the broken stones and, with a great kick, impelled the horse to leap the fallen wall.

There were three men and a woman bending over. They scattered before Duty's charge. One man, tall and ungainly, like a long-limbed water bird, turned and stared. Jenna screamed sounds at him, not words, and was about to strike when the woman ran between them and raised her hands.

"*Merci,*" the woman cried, desperation lending force to her thin voice. "In Alta's name, *ich crie merci.*"

The words penetrated Jenna's fury and slowly she lowered her sword, her sword arm shaking so hard, she had to reach over with the other hand to steady it. She noticed what she should have noticed before. The tall storkman was not armed. Neither was the woman. "Hold, Catrona," Jenna called out.

Catrona's voice came back strongly, "I hold."

"Please," the woman said, "you must help, if you be Alta's own."

"We are," said Jenna. "But who are you? And what has happened here?" She looked around as she spoke, not directly at the woman. Expecting to see bodies, she saw none. Yet the gates and walls were thrown down, shattered as if by a great blast. There were weapons scattered throughout the courtyard: several bows, dozens of swords, a number of knives, three rakes, even pieces of wood that might have been makeshift cudgels.

The woman clasped and unclasped her hands. "We be from Callatown. To south. If you rode that way."

"We did," Catrona said. "And none there to greet us. Nor at the ford."

"My husband Harmon, here, be ferryman at't ford. He and I and all our neighbors been here two day, burning dead."

The tall man, her husband, put his hands on her shoulders and spoke to Jenna from behind his wife. "Grete speaks true, girl. I went out to ferry when a troop of king's horse came by. They tied me up and Grete, bless her, be down in root cellar getting it spring cleansed. She could hear their coarse mouths and kept hid, waiting till they be gone."

Grete interrupted. "It wouldna done any good to come out and fight. I knew that much."

"She does, too." Harmon had taken his hands from his wife's shoulders and swept off his brown cap, kneading it between his long fingers. "She come up later, after they be gone over the water, and cut ropes. Look, the mark be still on my wrists." He held one hand up but if there was a mark there, Jenna could not see it.

"A hundred or more they be," said a second man, coming over. "That's what Harmon said. A hundred or more."

"This be Jerem the miller and his boy," Grete said, gesturing at the two. "They was let be for they give the troop grain for horses."

"But the rest of the town, they be tied up or kilt," said Jerem. "Exceptin' the girls. Them they took. My boy sneaked out to see that night."

"Mai," said Jerem's boy. He said it quietly but his dark eyes were defiant under his thatch of yellow hair.

"Mai be his sweetheart," explained Grete, "and she be gone with the rest. And they be promised to one another."

"Why are you *here?*" It was Petra, who had dismounted upon hearing the voices. She led her horse through the maze of fallen stone. "You had your own sorrows, then. Did you come here for help?"

"For help?" Grete repeated, shaking her head.

"Bless you, girl," Jerem said, "we came *to* help. They be our mothers and our sisters and our nieces and our aunts. They came among us to give us sons."

Harmon added, "Jerem, he ground their grain and they paid him well, in crops and in strong arms. And when I be took last year with the bloody flux, didn't a pair of 'em work all day pulling ferry for me. And four of 'em at night. And another doctored me, and two nursed me in the even."

"And takin' no payment for it. None. Not ever. It be their way, you know." Grete's thin voice rose and fell oddly.

"So we come quick as we could. When we knew what went on in town." Harmon's hands still pummeled his hat.

"But we be late," Jerem said. "We be hours too late. And they be all dead or gone."

"But where . . ." Jenna began, her hands still trembling on sword and reins.

Grete nodded toward the central building of the Hame. "We been cartin' 'em to Hall. My sons in there be helpin', though it be strange for men to work there. That be never allowed. Us women, yes, we came sometimes. To help bring in harvest, or our girls for training some. But the boys wanted to do for the sisters, settin' 'em side by side. The old lady, that Mother A, she be not quite gone when we got here, the blood all bubbling out of her like kettle to boil. She told us what to do. 'Side by side,' she said."

Jenna nodded slowly. That explained why the women's bodies were not scattered through the yard. "And . . . and the men?" she asked at last. "Surely there were some wounded, some dead."

Catrona added, "Surely they took some of them with them in such a fight."

"They drug their own wounded away. Or killed 'em on spot," said Harmon. "The men be all dead, some thirty of 'em. We burned them there." He pointed outside the broken wall, away from the road. "Foreign-looking, they be. Dark skin. Staring eyes."

"Young," Grete said. "Too young for such deaths. Too young for such killings."

"But dead all the same," said her husband, putting the hat back on his head. "And don't they say: *The swordsman dies by't sword, the hangman by't rope, and the king by't crown.*" He turned, looking over the ridge of his shoulder, and spoke to Jenna. "We be obliged for your help."

Jenna nodded, but it was Petra who spoke, her voice shaky. "We will help."

"We must be gone soon," Catrona said in an undertone to Jenna. "The others must be warned."

Jenna nodded at that, too, thinking to herself that her head must be on a string, so easily did it bob up and down. Then she whispered back, "But one hour surely will not matter. Let us find Selinda and Alna and bid them farewell."

"An hour can spare a life," Catrona said. "It is something we learned many times in the army." But she gave in all the same. "For Alna and Selinda. An hour. That is all."

* * *

As Grete had promised, the sisters of Calla's Ford lay side by side in the darkening Hall. Jenna wandered up and down the many lines, kneeling occasionally to tidy a lock of hair or to close staring eyes. There were so many women, she could not count them all, but she refused to cry.

Petra, standing in the doorway, wept for them both.

"This be the last of 'em," Jerem said, pointing to an elderly woman in a long dress and apron, lying by the far door.

"Be they right?" Grete asked Catrona. "Be they in't form?"

"We will see them all right," Catrona said. "But best you leave us for now so that we may give them the proper rites."

Grete nodded, and turned to speak to the rest of the townsfolk who had gathered by the entryway, silently waiting. Her hands shooed them out like chickens toward the courtyard. She herself was the last one through the door, calling out in a whisper, "We will wait."

Jenna stared across the Hall. In the gray light the bodies of the women almost looked like carved stone. Though they had been cleansed of the blood on their hands and faces by the hard-working townsfolk, their shirts and aprons and skirts and trousers were stained with it. But the blood was black, not red, in the graying room. The bodies lay on rushes scented with verbena and dried roses, but the sharp, unmistakable smell of death overpowered the flowery bouquet.

"Shall I light the torches now?" Petra asked, her voice so quiet, Jenna had to strain to hear it. "So that their dark sisters might accompany them?" Without waiting for an answer, she went by the back hallway into the kitchen, came out with a lit candle, and proceeded to light the candles and torches that were set in the walls.

Slowly, in between the bodies, the corpses of the dark sisters took form and soon the room was crowded with them. It was as if a great carpet of death lay wall to wall.

Strangers, thought Jenna, *and yet not strangers to me at all. My sisters.*

"We must fire the Hame now," said Catrona. "And then go."

"But Alna and Selinda are not here," Jenna said. "Nor any of the younger girls. They may be hidden away like the children of Nill's Hame. We do not dare set the flames until we find them."

"They were taken," Catrona said bluntly, "you heard what Grete and her husband said. Taken. Like the girls of Callatown. Like the boy's sweetheart."

"Mai." Petra said suddenly, still lighting the torches.

"No!" Jenna shook her head violently, her voice echoing loudly. "No!

We cannot be sure. Why would they want the girls? Why would they need them? We *have* to look."

Catrona put her hand out toward Jenna just as Petra put the candle to a sconce near them in the Hall. Katri appeared by Catrona's side and put her hand out as well.

"They *always* want women," said Katri. "Such men do."

"They have not enough of their own." It was Skada's voice right by Jenna's ear. "That is what Geo Hosfetter said."

Jenna did not turn to welcome her. Instead she insisted, "We must search the Hame. We could never forgive ourselves if we did not."

It took an hour of searching to prove to Jenna that the girls were not to be found. They even overturned the mirror in the priestess' room, ripped down tapestries, and knocked endlessly upon solid walls in the hope of finding a secret passage. But there was none.

In the end even Jenna had to agree that the girls were gone. This time she did not ask why.

"And what of the *Book?*" Petra asked, her hand atop the great leather volume in the priestess' room. "We cannot leave it here for anyone to read."

"We do not have time to bury it," said Jenna, "so it will have to be burned with the rest."

Petra cradled the *Book* in her arms, carrying it back down to the Hall where she placed it between the priestess and her dark sister. She set their stiffened hands on top of the volume, palms up so that the blue Alta sign showed, tying their wrists together with her hair ribbands. Then in a voice eerily familiar, she began to recite:

> *"In the name of Alta's cave,*
> *The dark and lonely grave,*
> *Where we dwell twixt light and light . . ."*

"I will not cry," Jenna promised herself. "Not for death. Not ever for death." She shook her head violently to keep away the tears. Skada did the same.

They did not cry.

THE LEGEND

There were twelve sisters who dwelt in Callatown, by the ford, each one more beautiful than the last. But the loveliest of them all was the youngest, Fair Jennet.

Jennet was tall, with hair the color of the Calla's foam, and eyes the blue of a spring sky.

One day the king's own sons rode into the town, twelve handsome youths they were. But the handsomest was the youngest, Brave Colm. Colm was tall, with hair the color of dawn, and eyes as brown as bark.

Twelve and twelve. They should have been fair matched. But a king's son is like the cuckoo: he takes his pleasure where he will, then leaves to love again.

When the king's twelve sons had left, eleven sisters flung themselves into the Calla, above the ford. But the last, Fair Jennet, stayed to bury them, then she rode to the king's hall. She sang her sorrow at his table, before climbing the stairs to the highest tower. There she cast herself into the wind. As she fell, her cry was the cry of the woodcock rising to its mate.

Colm heard her and raced outside. He held her poor, broken body cradled in his arms, singing back to her the song she had caroled at his father's feast:

> "Eleven sisters side by side,
> Each one a dishonored bride,
> Married to the ebbing tide,
> And I wed to the wind."

At the song's end, Fair Jennet opened her eyes and called Colm's name. He kissed her brow before she died.

"I am the wind," whispered Colm, drawing his sword from his sheath and plunging it into his breast. Then he lay himself down by Jennet's side and died.

They say that every year, at the spring's rind, the folks of Callatown build a great bonfire. Its light keeps away the spirits of the eleven who rise like mist above the Calla waves, trying to sing every man down to his death. And they say that Colm and Jennet were buried in a single grave whose mound rises

*higher than the ruins of the king's tower. On that mound—and nowhere else
in the Dales—grows the flower known as Colm's Sorrow. It is a flower as
light as her hair, with an eye as dark as his, and it rains its petals down like
tears throughout all of the long spring days.*

THE STORY

The fires burned quickly and the long, thin column of smoke wrote the
sisters' epitaph against the spring sky. Catrona and Jenna stood dry-eyed,
watching the curling smoke. But Petra buried her face in her hands, sobbing in soft little spurts. The townsfolk wept noisily. Only Jerem's boy was
still, staring off to the west, where the sky was clear.

At last Jenna turned away, walking toward Duty who had waited so
patiently by the broken wall. She patted the horse's nose with great concentration, as if the soft nostrils were the only thing that mattered in the world.
She inhaled the heavy horse smell.

Catrona came over and put a hand on her shoulder. "We must go now,
Jenna. And quickly."

Jenna did not look up from the horse.

"Do you go to fight?" It was Jerem's boy, who had come up behind
them. Small, wiry, he had a look of passionate intensity.

Catrona turned. "We go to warn the other Hames," she said sharply.

"And fight if we must." Jenna spoke softly, as much to the horse as the
boy.

"Let me go with you," the boy begged. "I *must* go. For Mai's sake. For
my own."

"Your father will need you, boy," Catrona said.

"He be having less to do now that so many be gone," he answered. "And
if you do not let me go with you, I go anyway. I be your shadow. You be
looking behind at every turning and at every straightaway, and I be there
following."

Jenna, her hand still on Duty's nose, stared at him. The boy's dark green
eyes bore into her own. "He will, too," she said softly to Catrona. "I have
seen that look before."

"Where?"

"In her mirror," Petra said joining them.

"And in Pynt's eyes," Jenna added.

Catrona said nothing more but strode to her horse and mounted it with swift ease. Then she jerked on the reins and the startled mare turned toward the fallen Hame gate.

Petra's horse stood still while she climbed up, its withers trembling slightly, like ripples on a pond.

Jenna ran her hand along Duty's head and down her neck with slow deliberation. Then suddenly she grabbed hold of the saddle's horn and pulled herself up in a single, swift motion.

"*Hummmph!*" was Catrona's only comment, for she had turned in her saddle to watch the girls mount, but a smile played around her mouth before resolving itself in a frown.

They sat, motionless, on their horses for a long moment. Then Jenna leaned down and held out her hand to the boy. He grinned up at her and took it. Pulling hard, Jenna lifted him onto the saddle behind her. He settled easily as if well used to riding double.

"Jareth, boy, where be you going?" Jerem ran over, grabbing onto the boy's right knee.

"He rides with us," Jenna said.

"He cannot. He must not. He be but a boy."

"A boy!" Catrona laughed. "He was promised in marriage. If he is man enough to wed, he is man enough to fight. How old do you think these girls are?" Her voice carried only to Jerem's ears. It was Petra, standing up in her stirrups, who addressed the rest of the villagers.

"We ride with the Anna, the White One, She who was thrice mothered and thrice orphaned."

The Calla's Ford folk gathered around to listen. Grete and her husband stood in the front, Jerem still by his son's knee. They were silent, staring at Jenna.

"We follow Her," Petra continued, pointing dramatically. "For She has already made both hound and ox bow down. Who would deny Her?" She paused.

Feeling that it was her turn to speak, Jenna drew her sword from its sheath and raised it above her head, wondering if she looked foolish, hoping she appeared noble. "I am the ending and I am the beginning," she cried out. "Who rides with me?"

From behind her Jareth called, "I ride with you, Anna."

"And I!" It was a dull-haired, long-legged boy.

"And I!" Standing by him, one who might have been his twin.

"And I!"

"And I!"

"And I!" The last was Harmon who, caught up in the moment, had snatched off his hat and thrown it into the air causing Petra's horse to back away nervously. The commotion gave Grete time to put her hand forcefully on her husband's shoulder, and he sank back, hatless, against her.

In the end, three boys volunteered. Jareth was given his father's blessing and Grete and Harmon's two sons took a loan of their father's spavined gelding. Riding double, they tracked behind the mares down the darkening road toward the west.

THE MYTH

Then Great Alta said, "You shall ride to the North and you shall ride to the South; you shall ride to the East and you shall ride to the West. And there great armies will rise up beside you. You and your blanket companions shall match sword with sword and might with might that the blood shed between you shall wash away the stain left by the careless men."

BOOK TWO

The Long Riding

THE MYTH

Then Great Alta reached into the sinkhole of night and drew up three boy babes. One was light, and two were dark, and they were weak and pulling in the sun of her face.

"And you shall grow and grow and grow," quoth she, "until you are like giants in the land. You shall ride over the world that evil may know fear."

Then Great Alta pulled them by the hair and by the bottoms of their feet until they were as large as towers, until they were giants in the land. She set them down by the fordside and sprinkled their foreheads with water and their feet with ashes that they might better endure the long riding.

THE LEGEND

Three heroes rode out of the East. One was light as day, one as bright as noon, one as dark as eve. And their horses were caparisoned the same: one in silver as the dawn, one in gold as midday, and one in ebon as the night. They carried crown and collar and ring.

Their swords flashed as they rode and the woods rang with their battle song:

> *We serve the queen of light*
> *We serve the queen of night*
> *On the long riding.*

Wherever they rode, they dealt death to the enemies of the White One, the Anna. And they were known as The Three.

The tapestry in room 4/Town Hall/Calla's Cross (pictured above) is from the Great Renascence in the Weaver's Gift Period. Legend has it it was finished the week after The Three had ridden by, a patent impossibility. Such tapestries were often years in the weaving. Note especially how it pictures three knights in full armor, swords upraised, riding straight toward the viewer. One is in silver armor on a gray horse; one is in black armor on a black horse; and one is in gold armor on a horse whose skin is the color of old gold. Their visors are up and one can see their eyes. They seem to be laughing.

THE STORY

Night came quickly and they were only scant miles down the road, but Catrona pulled them all up with a hand sign.

"You, boy!" she called to Jerem's son.

"Jareth," Jenna reminded her, even before he could speak for himself.

"Jareth, then," Catrona said. "Climb down from behind the Anna now and give her poor horse a rest. Best you ride for a while with Petra there." She pointed.

The boy pushed himself off the rear of the horse, landing as lightly as a cat, and went over to Petra's mare. Petra reached down to help him up, but he shook off her hand, went behind the horse, gave a little run-jump, and was behind her, grinning.

"I be handling a lot of horses," he explained shyly, "when the owners came to grind their grain. One told me a horse be making a giant of a small man. That's when I knew I had to ride."

Catrona nodded, but Jenna slipped her horse between them and leaned over, speaking softly. "Why have him switch now? Duty is not tiring."

Looking up at the darkening sky, Catrona whispered back. "The moon will be up soon and our dark sisters here. No need to frighten the boys or overburden Duty."

"I forgot." Jenna bit her lower lip. "Alta, how could I have forgot?"

Catrona smiled. "You are but days new to having a dark sister share your life. And even I, who have lived side by side with Katri for thirty years, sometimes forget. Not Katri, not the *fact* of her. But sometimes I forget to be prepared for her. She is ever a surprise, though she is the better part of me."

"Then we must warn the boys," Jenna said. "But what do we say?"

"We say to them what we always say—in the army or in bed—for a man hears and sees what he wants," Catrona said. "Do not worry so. In the Lower Dales they say *A man's eye is bigger than his belly and smaller than his brain.*" Laughing, she turned her horse toward Petra and the gelding upon which Grete and Harmon's boys sat, legs dangling down.

"Soon we will be met by two sisters of the night," she began, in a voice of easy authority. "They are friends of ours who will travel along the way with us. But they come when they will and they leave when they will and they are not fond of the day. As long as they decide to remain with us, they will be our dearest allies, our boon companions on the road." She looked carefully at the boys. "Do you understand?"

The boys nodded, Jareth quickly and the other two with a bit more caution, as if it took them more time to sort through what Catrona meant.

"We be seeing such night sisters afore," Jareth said. "They be helping my Da once at mill and Sandor and Marek's Da at ferry. They be there when we needed them though never when we called."

Sandor and Marek nodded.

"Good. Then you will not be frightened or confused when these two appear. Their names are Katri and Skada. Katri is the older." She smiled. "Even older than me."

"Catrona!" It was Petra who seemed shocked.

Catrona smiled mischievously. "Well, maybe only a little older."

"We be neither confused nor frightened," said Jareth solemnly, "for we be in the presence of Anna."

Sandor shook his head. And Marek, like his brother, shook his head as well. Otherwise they did not move, staring at Jenna with worshipful eyes.

"Let us dismount and feed the horses. And ourselves." Catrona climbed off her horse.

"But there be no food," Sandor said.

"None," added Marek.

Jenna laughed, a short barking sound. "We have the woods as our larder," she said. "So we can never starve."

THE SONG

The Long Riding

Into the valley, come riding, come riding,
Into the meadow and into the dell,
Into the moonlight where shadows are gliding,
Into the forest where enemies hiding,
Riding, riding, Three come ariding
Into the mouth of hell.

Into the village come riding, come riding,
Into the hames where the sweet women dwell,
Into the rests where the men are abiding,
Into the forest where enemies hiding,
Riding, riding, Three come ariding
Into the mouth of hell.

THE STORY

They showed the boys how to search the woods for food, and Jareth discovered a bird's nest with three eggs. The other two boys came up empty-handed, but Jenna found a ring of tasty mushrooms and Catrona a stream whose bank was dotted with cress. Petra, who had waited with the horses, came upon the greatest cache of all, a stand of nettles which stung the back of her hands. She was still complaining about them when Jenna reappeared, trailed by Jareth.

"Nettles!" Jenna said. "Then we can have nettle tea."

"But we dare not be making a fire, Anna," Jareth reminded.

"We can make a small fire in a deep tunnel," she said, "just enough to heat water to steep tea if your friends can find leaves that are dry enough."

They had cress salad sprinkled with hard-boiled egg, mushrooms, and half the tea, a feast.

"The rest of the tea I will store in my water pouch," Catrona said as they buried the tunneled fire. "Nettle tea is as good cold as hot. *And* I have a surprise." She reached into her leather pocket and pulled out a rough-weave cloth packet. Slowly she unwrapped a large piece of journeycake.

"Where . . ." Petra began.

"From the Hame kitchen," Catrona said quietly. "I knew they would have had us take it. Any old soldier knows that in battle one takes quickly and saves regrets for the morning."

They nodded, one after another, and held out their hands for a share.

The dark sisters did not come for the moon had finished its full phase and, without fire, the small light of the stars was not strong enough to call them forth. Jenna lay on her blanket staring up at the patterns in the sky, counting their names to herself in the hope that the roll call would lull her to sleep: Alta's Dipper, Hame's Horn, the Cat, the Great Hound. But she could not sleep and at last stood up and walked, barefooted, to the place where the white horse and its companion bays slept standing. When she placed her hand on Duty's soft nose, the horse blew through its nostrils lightly, a sound at once strange and comforting.

"Anna?" It was a soft voice.

Jenna turned around. Jareth was moving toward her quietly.

"Anna, be that you?"

"Yes."

He reached the horse and touched it lightly on the nose, careful to keep the horse's head between them. "I be on watch and heard you. Be there something wrong?"

"No. Yes. I could not sleep."

"You be thinking about Calla's Ford Hame?"

She hesitated, then nodded. "I am thinking about *all* the hames, Jareth. But that is not why I am restless."

"Can you tell me, Anna?"

"Do not, for Alta's blessed sake, call me that," she said, her voice edged with anger.

"Call you what?"

"Anna. That is not my name. My name is Jo-an-enna. My friends call me Jenna."

Jareth was quiet for a moment. "But I be thinking you be . . . I mean, *she* said you be . . . that be . . ."

"It seems I am," said Jenna. "Or may be. But that is only a title, something put *upon* me. It is not what I am in truth."

Jareth thought about that a minute, then whispered, "Then who *be* you? In truth?"

"Just a girl. And the daughter of many mothers."

"That be what they say of Anna. That she be thrice mothered."

"And so I was."

"And white-haired."

"And so I am."

"And the hound and ox . . ."

"So they did. But I eat like you. And I pass wind if there are beans in the pot. And when I have too much to drink, I must find a place in the woods to . . ."

"Anna," Jareth said, reaching across Duty's nose to touch her arm. "No one be saying that Anna be not human. No one be calling her a goddess without water or wind. She be . . . she be linchpin, axletree, link between old carriage and new wheel."

"But linchpins and axletrees are made by humans," Jenna said. "Not by Alta."

"Exactly," Jareth answered. "It be prophecy that be the Goddess' own."

Jenna was silent a long time, thinking about what Jareth had said. At last she sighed. "Thank you, Jareth. I think . . . I think I shall be able to sleep now."

"You be welcome," he answered, coming around to the front of the horse. "But I be afraid you get no sleep yet. It be your turn at watch." He laughed, holding out his hand, "Jenna."

She took his hand. It was as firm in her own as Catrona's. Or Skada's.

They left before morning light, going out of the forest and crossing three towns in quick succession where no lamps were yet lit and their horses' hooves the only sound. In the last town, Jenna, Petra, and Catrona waited by the edge while the boys found them food, for Jareth had cousins there.

Once they stopped to wash the trail dirt from their faces in a small, meandering stream. Five or six times they stopped to relieve themselves and let the horses graze. They slept fitfully through a night that spit intermittent rain, soaking them despite a lean-to of split saplings. Otherwise, they remained on horseback all that day and into the next.

"I smell of horse," Petra complained mildly at their waking.

"You smell no different than a horse," Jenna amended.

They laughed heartily at her words, the first such since finding the devastation at the Hame. After that their mood was somewhat lighter, even though their muscles ached and both Marek and Sandor had saddle sores.

On the eve of the second day they crested a small hill where the beginnings of a great forest spread out below them. Mile after mile of unbroken woods lay on either side of a winding road.

"That is King's Way," Catrona said, pointing to the road. "There is no other through this wilderness. Wilma's Crossing is on the other side."

"Be it not dangerous to stay . . ." Sandor began, running his fingers through his matted hair.

". . . on the King's Way?" finished his brother.

"There is less danger on it than off. This wold is known to only a few and the few are the Greenfolk. They"—Catrona spit between her second and little fingers—"they are not likely to help us. More likely to take our heads. Or our fingers. They like the small bones. Wear them dangling from their ears."

Marek and Sandor looked nervously at one another, but Jareth laughed.

"My Da be speaking often of the Greenfolk. The Grenna, he be calling them. He be saying no such thing about taking bones. They be to themselves," Jareth said. "And that be all."

Catrona smiled at him. "True, they are to themselves. They call this forest their own and do not favor intruders."

"There is no bone-taking in that," Jenna said.

"It was a joke," Catrona said.

Jenna shook her head. "And not very funny."

"Tell us more about these Greenfolk and this road," Petra said, adding quickly, "But no more jokes. You are frightening some of us unnecessarily."

Catrona nodded. "When the good queen Wilma built this road, long before the G'runians broke apart our land, she made a pax with the Greenfolk's council. They have no queens nor kings."

"And probably better off for it," Jenna muttered.

Ignoring Jenna, Catrona went on as her horse trembled restlessly beneath her. "The pax was this: we would leave the rest of the woods to the Greenfolk if they would leave the road alone."

Jareth leaned forward eagerly. "My Da never be telling me this. What be sealing the pax?"

"Wilma offered them iron or steel or gold but they would have none of it."

"None of it?" Marek and Sandor said together, Sandor adding, "Then what *could* seal it?"

"They sat in a great circle on the highest hill," Catrona said. "And . . ."

"Pah! There is no hill," Jenna said. "So much for stories." She swept her hand expansively from east to west. "I see no hill. Just woodland, green and rolling."

"Look at things on a slant, Jenna," Petra said. "That is what my Mother Alta taught me. On a slant."

"That is how the story goes, Jenna," Catrona said. "I tell it the only way I know. They sat on the great hill—*that Jenna cannot see*—and ate bread together, swearing that the pax was engraved on their hearts and in their mouths. They hold all their history on the tongue. They do not have writing." Catrona stood up in her stirrups and stared down at the way.

The others copied her movement, dark sisters to her light.

"It is a chancy pax at best. And never more so then now, when the last three kings of the G'runs renamed the Way and promised to build fortresses and inns along it."

"I see no buildings," Jenna said.

"Not yet. But they will come." Catrona sat back down. "It was often spoke of when I was in the army. The men all favored it. *'Stand in the way of a cart,'* they said, *'and you will have wheel marks across your face.'*"

"It is a terrible thing," said Jenna, "to break pax with those who still hold it."

"If I be king . . ." Jareth began.

"And if horses could fly . . ." Petra said, laughing, "we would be across the wold and at Wilma's Crossing before nightfall."

"But we cannot fly." Catrona's face was stern. "And we dare not be stuck on that road with the stars our only protection. Let us find a quiet place off the road, camp the night, and be up before sunrise. It will be a long riding, whether we meet with anyone or not."

THE HISTORY

The Greenfolk, the Good Folk, the Grenna, the Faire, are all names given to the Dalian equivalent of the Garunian brownies or little people. Though histo-archaeologists, like Magon, they desperately to prove there was an actual race of pygmy-like wood-dwellers who occupied the Old Forest above the Whilem River, frequent diggings in the area have turned up nothing. (See my monograph "Woods-Folk or Would-be Folk: An Investigation into the Whilem River Cross Dig, Passapatout Press, #19.)

Carbon dating has proven beyond a shadow of a doubt that the remains of encampments found throughout the region were at least a thousand years earlier than the dates for the Gender Wars. The few human bones lay scattered rather than buried in gravemounds, proving the hunting-gathering tribes were so primitive that they had no sense of an afterlife. What tribes there were had to have been long gone by the time of the rule of Langbrow.

Yet the persistence of stories about the "folke all greene," as the ballad goes, has caused even such worthies as Temple and Cowan to consider the possibilities. Legends of the Greenfolk's generosity toward the followers of the White Goddess are legion in the industrial towns of the Whilem River Valley. Certainly Doyle's work on the Whilem names (Green As Grass: The Unnatural Occurrence of Color Names Along the Whilem, *Hanger College Press), with its suggestion that any forest communities would have a preponderance of woods/green surnames, is persuasive. Magon's rantings to the contrary, that certainly makes more sense than to say there was a small, proto-human race of faerie folk living in pre-literate splendor, supporting their candidate for queen with magicks and mysteries by the roadside and carrying away folk for rites under the nonexistent Whilem Hills.*

THE STORY

The King's Way was well pounded down, as if recent travelers had been many and recent rains few, but the forest grew right up to the edge of the road. Brambles, nettles, briars, and brush vied for space between the rangy trees. The varieties of green were numberless.

They pushed the horses unmercifully for the first few hours, but when the gelding stumbled in a hidden, dust-covered hole, nearly throwing Sandor and Marek, Catrona signaled a halt.

Dismounting, they led the horses to the road's brushy edge and Catrona picked up the gelding's left forefoot.

"I do not think he pulled anything," she said after a moment's careful examination.

"Perhaps we should rest him," Petra said. "Just in case."

"And eat," Jareth suggested. The other boys nodded.

But Jenna shook her head. "No. We need to move on. We must reach Wilma's Crossing Hame before . . ." She hesitated, decided not to say what they all were thinking. "Besides, I have had the strange feeling . . ."

"That we have been watched?" Catrona asked quietly.

"Something like that," Jenna said.

"And for many miles now?"

Jenna nodded grimly.

They mounted quickly, ignoring their hollow stomachs, and urged the horses forward. As if sensing danger, the horses responded at once. The gelding raced ahead, proving itself fit. Catrona managed to overtake it, but Jenna held back to guard the rear.

When she looked over her shoulder, she saw nothing but forest and the layers of green. But then she thought she heard a low drumming sound accompanied by a high whistle. It was at least a mile farther before she realized that what she was hearing was the sound of the horses' hooves on the King's Way and the wind racing past her ears. Only that—and nothing more.

Alternately walking and galloping, they rode for several more hours, before Catrona signaled another halt. This time they moved the horses well off the road and into the cover of a grove of trembling aspen.

"I do not like this," Catrona whispered to Jenna. "We have passed no one the entire time."

"I thought that was to the good," Jenna replied.

"This is usually a well-traveled road. Carts, trains of wagons, individual travelers. Even walkers. We have come across none of them."

"We must tell the others."

Catrona put a hand on her arm. "No. Wait. Why trouble them before trouble is here?"

"I was told at Nill's Hame that *Not to know is bad, but not to wish to know is worse,*" Jenna said. "These are our friends, Catrona. Our companions. We must trust our backs to them."

"They are hardly fighters," Catrona said wearily. "I trust my back to Katri and to you."

"They are all we have," Jenna pointed out.

Catrona sighed. "Yes, they are. More fools we." She put her fingers to her mouth, and whistled the others to her.

Gathered in a close circle, they listened as Catrona spelled out her fears. Jareth's forehead wrinkled in concentration, but Sandor and Marek rocked back and forth, as if the movement helped them understand what she was saying. Petra's whole body was still, and she breathed slowly, using *latani* breathing. Jenna matched her, breath for breath, but once settled into the rhythm of the expirations, she felt the familiar lightening as her real self pulled free of her body to float above it.

Catrona's voice was like a buzzing of insects as Jenna ranged over them. Her translucent fingers reached down to touch each in turn on the skull's center where the pulse beat under the fragile shield of skin and bone.

At that touch, as she had done before, Jenna felt herself being drawn down inside each of her companions in turn. Catrona was a strong fire, the hottest point in the center; Petra, a spill of cool water over a rocky race. The brothers were lukewarm, like milk fresh from the cow. But Jareth reminded her of Carum for he seemed to have pockets of fire and ice, pockets of alien heat, though she was not moved by them as she had been when centered on the young prince.

She pulled herself away, fleeing back into the air, and suddenly saw pinpricks of light in a great circle around them; dancing lights coming closer and closer. Flinging herself down into her own body she slipped into it as if into familiar clothes. "Back to mine," she cried.

On the signal, Catrona unsheathed her sword and stood back-to-back with Jenna. Jareth understood almost as quickly.

"Your knives!" he called to Marek and Sandor.

They drew their knives and stood with Petra in their center, waiting. For a long minute they could hear nothing: not a snap of twig nor rustle of grass. It was as if the forest itself had stopped breathing.

Suddenly Jenna's head went up with a jerk. "There!"

They looked around. At first there was nothing to be seen. And then— there was. A circle of some thirty mannikins surrounded them, dressed all in green, jerkins and trews, as if they had metamorphosed from the trees or brush. They were half the size of a man, with skin a greenish cast, like a translucent glaze, over fine bones. Yet they did not give the impression of fragility. It was as if the land itself had been thinned down to its essence and given human form.

Duty whickered nervously, followed by the bays. Only the gelding was silent, pawing the ground over and over with a dull thudding.

One of the green watchers moved forward, breaking the circle, and stood not three feet from Jenna. She could have leaned over and touched him on the top of the head but she did not move. He raised his hand in greeting, speaking in a strange, lilting tongue.

"*Av Anna regens; av Anna quonda e futura.*"

"Speak so we can understand," Jareth cried out, his voice cracking like a boy's.

"I can understand him," Petra said quietly. "My Mother Alta required I learn the old tongues. He says, *Hail, White Queen; hail White One now and forever.*"

Jareth grunted, but Marek spoke. "That be all right, then. Our Da be saying: *If a man call you master, trust him for a day; if he call you friend, trust him for a year; if he call you brother, trust him for all ways.*" It was the longest speech any of them had heard from him.

"But he called me none of those," said Jenna. "He called me Anna. So how would your Da say he can be trusted?"

Marek started to work out an answer, but the little man held up his hand and the boy was strangely still.

"For as long as the forest, Anna," said the little man, suddenly speaking their language, his voice only slightly accented.

"Why . . ." Jareth began, but Jenna hushed him.

"For as high as the heavens," the little man continued. "We have waited since the beginning of this time for you, cocooned in the time. Your birth has been told around many fires, your reign under many stars. First the Alta and at last the Anna, so the circle can close."

"Since the beginning of this time . . ." Jenna murmured to herself. *"And the closing of the circle . . . What does that mean?"* Out loud she said, "You have called me by a title, but I am called Jenna by my friends. Are you my friend?"

The little man grinned broadly, his even white teeth white against the green of his face. Bowing, he said, "We are your *brothers.*"

"All ways!" Marek said triumphantly.

"May be," Jareth whispered under his breath. "May be not."

The little man ignored them, speaking only to Jenna. "You may call this one Sorrel. That is not this one's true name, but your mouth would not be able to shape it nor your heart hear its sound."

"I understand," Jenna said. "I have a hidden name as well. So, Sorrel, are you king of these green folk?"

"We have neither king nor captain. We have only the circle."

"Then how is it you speak for your . . . circle?" Catrona interrupted.

"This one is first this time by the circle's leave," Sorrel said.

Nodding, Jenna sheathed her sword. "I put my weapon away *this time.* As does my sister, Catrona."

Catrona raised one eyebrow and, very slowly, replaced her own sword.

"And my men will put away their knives," Jenna added. She bit her upper lip, the only betrayal of her nervousness.

With a slight frown, Jareth slipped his knife into his boot. When Marek and Sandor hesitated, he growled at them, "Come on. Come on."

"We do this," Jenna said slowly, "because you carry no weapons against us."

There was a strange titter that ran around the circle of little men. Sorrel bowed again.

"We must tell you truly, we carry no weapons ever but these, Anna," Sorrel said. He held up his hands. His fingers were extremely long, the nails a paler green.

"And how potent are they?" Petra asked, her voice overly polite. *"Potentas manis qui?"*

He giggled, a sound like a bird's trill. *"Trez.* Very, Little Mother. Very potent indeed." He reached out suddenly and snapped off a greenwood stick, stripping it and twisting it quickly into a noose. Still smiling, he threw the noose away.

Catrona made a *tching* sound between her teeth and Jenna turned to her quickly. "These are our brothers, Catrona. *For the moment."*

Catrona nodded slowly, her eyes never leaving Sorrel's hands.

"With our sisters, our hands are as the sweet weed, the althea, smooth and soothing," Sorrel said. "See." In one liquid movement he was at Duty's side. He stroked the horse's nose. She sighed deeply, an odd sound, and leaned into his hands.

"Why have you been trailing us for so long?" Catrona asked suddenly. Her hand rested uneasily on the pommel of her sword.

Startled, Sorrel looked up at her, then as quickly hooded his eyes.

"Oh yes," Catrona said, pleased to have surprised him. "You are not the only ones who can read the woods. We sisters of the Hames are known for it."

"We have heard that," Sorrel said. "It brings us closer. Brother to sister."

"I ask again," Catrona said emphatically. *"Sister to brother.* Why trail us as if you are our enemy if—as you claim—you are our friends."

"Not *friend. Brother!"* Sorrel said. "We must watch and see who you are, riding through our woods. We must be sure it is the Anna. The stars tell us it is the time the circle closes. But many ride our path. We must be certain before we greet the Anna." There was a confirming murmur from the rest of the Greenfolk, as if punctuating his sentence.

Petra and the boys looked around at the sound; it came from all around them, like a noose of noise.

"Why do you surround us?" Petra asked, turning slowly, looking at each of the mannikins.

"Is the circle not the perfect form, Little Mother?" Sorrel asked. *"Perface.* In it no one is higher. No one is lower. No one is first. No one is last."

"Are you not first in this circle?" Jenna asked, casting her voice low so as not to give offense. She repeated his odd phrase: *"This one is first this time . . ."* and folded her arms across her breast. "Who else in the circle speaks but you?" She smiled.

Petra whispered in the old tongue, *"Quis voxen?"*

"The question does not suit you, Anna. Nor you, Little Mother. Such questions better fit the mouth of the Old Cat there, or her young Toms." He gestured toward Catrona and the boys.

As if on cue, Catrona spoke loudly, using the words Petra had used. *"Quis voxen?"* Her pronunciation was abominable.

"This one speaks today. Tomorrow another. The circle moves on."

Jenna stepped closer to the little man. Though she towered over him, instinctively she knew better than to kneel. To do so would demean them both. She inclined her head slightly, the only acknowledgment of his size she would allow herself. "Are we a part of your greater circle, Sorrel?"

He nodded. "As is all life."

"Yet you singled me out. You called me *Anna,* you called me queen."

"Regens," Petra whispered. "Good question, Jenna!"

"We have waited for you from the beginning," Sorrel said. "Your coming is part of the circle. You herald the end, the close." He held his forefingers and thumbs together to make a circle sign. Jenna saw that his long, thin fingers had an extra knuckle each.

"What end?" she asked. "What end do I herald?"

"The end to what we know," Sorrel said. "This time."

"Be he meaning the end to what he and the Greenies be knowing?" asked Marek aloud, clearly puzzled.

"Or the end to what *we* be knowing?" added Sandor, looking at Marek.

"We go. You go with us," Sorrel said.

"No," Jareth said. He reached down and pulled his knife back out of his boot. "The Anna be going to rescue her sisters. And we with her. We do not go with you. *My* Da told me: who be going with the Grenna, stays with them. Years later and all the folk we know be dead and the grass be growing over their graves. You be saying it yourself; we all be hearing you. *Cocooned,* you be saying. *In time,* you be saying."

"Jareth." Jenna stretched her hand toward him. "Those are but tales."

"Nevertheless . . ." Jareth began, "we must not be forgetting the sisters." The hand holding the knife began to shake. He steadied it with his left hand on the wrist.

Jenna looked at Sorrel. "He is right, you know."

Sorrel shook his head. "You are too late to help those sisters. Any of them, Anna. The only way is the circle. You will leave stronger than you come."

"Too late!" Jenna's voice shook. To calm herself, to help herself think, she took three deep *latani* breaths and tried to concentrate on matching Sorrel breath to breath. She was shocked to find his expirations so slow, she became dizzy in the attempt. Closing her eyes, Jenna considered his words. *Too late to help those sisters.* She knew he spoke the bald truth. But there were fifteen more standing Hames, including her own. Fourteen that needed to be warned. She could not leave them unready. She opened her eyes and stared at Sorrel. His woods-green eyes stared back, the gaze unwavering.

"Too late for *any* of them, Anna," he said as if reading her mind. *"Malas propas."*

She lifted her chin. Twisting the ring on her left hand, she remembered what Mother Alta had said to her when she had given Jenna the ring: *The time of endings is at hand.* In that instance she made up her mind. "We go with the Grenna."

"But, Jenna . . ." Jareth began.

Petra touched his shoulder. "We go quietly for we are few and they are many."

"They be many," Jareth said, "but they be small. Smaller than I. I have a knife. I be not afraid to die for Anna."

"I have a sword," Catrona said. "And I have never been afraid to die for my sisters." She purposely drew the sword from its sheath in such a way that it made a loud, angry scraping sound.

"We go with Sorrel," Jenna said, "into his circle. I would have none of you die for me. Sorrel called me sister and queen. And he promises strength. We need great strength for the coming days. I trust him."

"For how long?" Jareth whispered hoarsely. "For how long be you trusting him, Jenna? A day? A year? Or all ways? Or until another be speaking from out his circle?"

"I trust him until this thing is done, however long it takes," Jenna said. "Are you with me, Jareth? If so, speak."

He was silent, but Marek and Sandor answered as one.

"We be with you, Anna."

"And I, *regens*," said Petra.

After a moment Catrona added, her voice so soft Jenna had to strain to hear it, "And I." She did not sheathe her sword.

At last Jareth sighed heavily. "I be going only because you be asking, Jenna. You—not *them.*" He gestured over his shoulder at the circle of green mannikins.

Jenna nodded and turned to her horse. Slipping the reins over Duty's head, she pulled the mare along, grateful that the beast gave her no argument. She followed the green of Sorrel's back, wondering that she did not lose it in the myriad of greens in the forest. She could hear the others following close behind, the sound of their footsteps like an echo repeating *"Too late to help . . ."*

THE TALE

There was once a girl named Jenny who was walking behind her sheep over the grassy lea. When the sheep stopped to graze, young Jenny braided a crown of daisies and placed it upon her head. But thinking the daisies too plain, she plucked a single wild rose and was about to twine it into the crown as well when there was a shock of lightning without there being clouds.

Jenny leaped to her feet. Before her stood a handsome young man dressed in green.

"Who be ye?" she cried.

"I be the king of the lea," he said. "I have come at your call."

"But I called you not," said she.

"You plucked the rose, and that is the sign that calls me out from the green land."

He took her by the hand, his all green and cold, and led her under the hillside. There they sang and danced until the dawn turned dark and the stars fell like snow behind them and Jenny cried out, "I must go back to my sheep."

He let her go and she made her way back, across the long lea. But her sheep were all scattered and gone.

Sadly she made her way down the hillside to her home to report the loss. But when she got there, the village was changed beyond her knowing it. She stopped at the first house and knocked on the door.

"Who be ye?" cried the old man who answered.

"I be Jenny, daughter of Dougal and Ardeen. Be they here?" she asked.

"Alas," cried the ancient, "I be Dougal's only descendent. And as for Jenny, that poor lass be her mother's death. Ardeen died of sorrow when her Jenny never came home with her sheep. A hundred year or more it's been."

Jenny shook her head and cried:

> *"The King of the Lea, the King of the Lea,*
> *A hundred years he married me.*
> *A hundred years in but a day*
> *I've sang and danced my life away."*

Then she disappeared back over the hill and was never seen again.

This tale is from the Whilem Valley. Twenty-seven variants have been collected.

THE STORY

They trailed the Grenna for long hours, until the sun went down and even the shadows seemed green. No one spoke. It was as if the forest drained them of words. Except for the words in Jenna's head, which kept repeating, *"Too late . . . too late for any of them."*

She wondered if he meant too late to warn them or too late to help them; if he meant too late for the older sisters who would die unmourned or for the younger sisters carried away; if he meant only all the sisters in Wilma's Crossing or all the sisters in the land. But she did not ask him. She was afraid to know the answer. *Not to know is bad, but not to wish to know is worse.* She was tired of such wisdoms invented when need was smallest. She was tired of cryptic omens and signs to be read on the slant. She wanted only the wind in her hair again and . . . and Carum's mouth on hers. She closed her eyes and stumbled along into the gathering dark hoping that she had chosen the right way.

"Jenna!"

Her name recalled her to the woods. Opening her eyes, she looked around. They had come to a great black hole that led right into a cliffside. A pair of round, oaken doors stood ajar, looking like barrel covers cut in half.

"Jenna, look at the doors!" It was Petra who had spoken.

Jenna looked.

The doors were intricately carved: river, apple, berries, flower, stone, bird, crescent moon, rainbow, tree, fish. All familiar signs. Jenna touched each one in turn.

"Eye-Mind," she whispered.

Catrona's voice echoed hers, adding, "Why here?"

The circle of the Grenna were gone through the doors, leaving only shadows behind. Duty whickered softly and the sound seemed to go past the doors and into the black, stopping abruptly, as if cut off by an ax.

Jenna and Catrona hesitated at the gaping doors and the others gathered around them.

"We could be turning back," Jareth whispered. "You and Catrona and Petra could be riding for the Hame. Marek and Sandor and I could be holding the doors shut."

The other two boys nodded.

"For how long?" Catrona asked mockingly. "For a day? A year? Or all ways, Jareth?"

He made no answer, but his mouth twisted and he glared furiously at her.

"Old Cat!" Marek whispered to Sandor, approval in his voice.

"*Malas propas,*" Petra said, her voice low. "That is what Sorrel said: *malas propas.* It means too late. But it also means unfavorable, inauspicious, bad luck."

"We must make our own luck," Catrona said. "And three unseasoned boys have neither the luck nor strength to hold two doors against such as the Greenfolk. Besides, we do not know if there are other doors to this hole. They might be like ferrets. Close them here, they boil out there." She pointed to the right of the doors. "Or there." She pointed to the left.

Jenna slowly touched each of them in turn: Petra on the cheek, Catrona on the shoulder, Marek and Sandor on the top of the head, and Jareth on the hand. She let her fingers linger on his for a long moment. He smiled up at her.

"All we have is one another," she said. "We do not dare separate now. Are we afraid to trust? Are we afraid of the dark? Come, give me your hands. We will go down into this black hole together and gather great strength from the journey. So the Grenna have promised."

Catrona placed her hand directly on Jenna's. Petra's came next. Last Marek's and Sandor's. Jenna felt the pressure of those hands and their comfort. She took a deep breath and passed the comfort down to Jareth's hand that still lay beneath hers. Then hands together, warmed by the touch, they moved as one into the dark.

It was not a black dark but a green one; what light there was came from phosphorescent patches on the rock walls. For a long time there was no choice to the direction they were to travel. There was only one tunnel and it led inexorably down, too narrow to allow them to change their minds and turn the horses.

No one spoke; the close dark precluded conversation. Even the horses were silenced except for the dull *thud-thud* of their hooves on the rock floor. Jenna took some small comfort in the regularity of the sound; it was like a heartbeat.

All of a sudden the single narrow tunnel branched into three wider ones. Confused, Jenna and Catrona stopped and the others behind them stopped as well. They whispered together hurriedly, their words sounding a peculiar *swee-swashing* in the echoing space, making understanding difficult.

Finally Catrona pointed to the right. "Only that one has the green patches," she said.

In silent agreement they turned, following the right-hand path as it continued in an ever-steepening descent.

Once Jenna put her hand to the tunnel wall, but it was slippery and cold. She did not like the feel of it, like the insides of something dead, a fish or a snake or an eft. She had tried to eat an eft once, on an overnight in the woods with Pynt near their Hame when they were young. It had not been a pleasant meal. Shuddering, she wiped her hand on her sleeve. But even after she could feel the damp wall as if it had impressed itself on her palm, as if it had left a mark she would have forever.

Suddenly one of the horses snorted, a sound so loud in the confines of the tunnel that they all let out little squeaks of dismay, except for Catrona who *humphed* through her nose, sounding just like her mare. For a moment the explosion of sound and the echoes nearly deafened them. Then Jenna shushed them, pointing.

Ahead the tunnel dipped down and then ascended steeply, widening at the end into a strange light green glow.

"I will go first," Catrona whispered. "Petra, hold my reins."

Before Jenna could tell her no, she advanced on silent feet, down into the dip and then up to the very edge of the green light, her sword in her hand. They saw her quite clearly silhouetted by the light, an even paler green haloing her body. She raised her sword, in challenge or in greeting, and then in an instant she was gone. Not jumped over the edge or killed by a sword or fallen—just gone.

"Catrona!" Marek and Sandor cried out together. The walls sent her name back to them a hundredfold. They called out again but could not seem to move.

It was Jareth, shouting as he ran, who followed Catrona into the green light, one minute haloed at the edge and the next minute vanished into a million particles of light.

"Wait!" Jenna said, her voice less an authority than a plea. "Wait." She put her hand out to the rest of them. "We must think."

But one by one, Petra, Marek, and Sandor, leading the horses, moved toward the light as if drawn by it. One by one by one, as Jenna watched, they were translated into little brilliant green dust motes that were swallowed by the whole.

Jenna put her hand on Duty's nose. She blew into the mare's nostrils. "My Duty," she said. "My duty is with all of them. I cannot command you to follow when I do not know where it is I go." She turned and walked toward the light.

As she neared the edge, she heard a fine., high singing in her head. The light dazzled her. Vaguely she heard the horse's hoofsteps behind her but she could not bring herself to look away and warn the mare off. There was only the calling light, pulling her forward; it seemed to her that there was nowhere else in the world that she wanted to be. And then she reached the top of the climb. She teetered there for a moment, with her toes curling over the ledge, and was suddenly enveloped in the light. It was warm and cool at once; soft and crystalline; smelling of sweet flowers and the pungent cabbage of the swamp. She closed her eyes to savor it all, and when she opened them again, she was hovering over a bright green grassy meadow pied with lilybells and daisies and dotted around the edges with the blood-red of trillium. *Hovering.*

Then she was down in the soft grass on her hands and knees, jarred as if she had just fallen from a high place. When she turned around, Duty was beside her, grazing contentedly. There was no high ledge, no cave, no borders to be seen. Only a rolling meadow stretching to a hill on the far horizon, and broken sporadically by small stands of trees, a land of elegant, timeless peace.

From the closest copse a thin spiral of smoke threaded its way up against a blue-green sky. She stood and walked toward the trees, slowly, as if traveling through a dreamscape.

When she reached the first trees, she saw Petra and Catrona on the right, the boys on the left, all waiting to enter.

"You be going first, Anna," Marek said.

"We be going after," Sandor added.

She nodded and started in.

There were trees of every kind in that small grove, as if each had been planted singly: aspen and birch, larch, poplar, hawthorn, rowan, ash, willow, and oak. The trees stood tall, like pillars in a great hall, and Jenna was reminded of the *Song of the Trees* which she had sung so often as a child in the Hame, a song it was said Great Alta herself had composed, with its chorus:

> *Of all in green jerkin and all in green gown*
> *The trees in the forest they all bear the crown,*
> *The trees in the forest are cradle and hall,*
> *The trees in the forest are fairest of all.*

with the long alphabet of trees for the verse.

She picked out each tree as she walked, surprised to find they matched the song completely. If this was a dream, she told herself . . .

and then stopped for, from the center of the grove, where the single line of smoke had emerged, someone was singing the same song in a low, lyrical voice.

Jenna raised her hand and they all stopped. She cupped her ear, calling them to listen.

It was Catrona who spoke. "That voice . . ." then trailed off into silence.

Jenna turned and gathered them to her. "That is not the voice of a Grenna," she whispered.

One by one they nodded.

"Do you know this song?" Catrona asked Jareth.

"It be like a lullaby my mother be singing," he said. "Like—and not like." He whispered:

> *"Of all in green jerkin and all in green gown,*
> *'Tis my baby Jareth who carries the crown . . .*

least my mother be singing *Jareth*. Another's might be saying . . ."

"*Marek,*" said Marek. "And *Sandor,* when he be born."

Sandor nodded. "And both when we be sick with the pox together."

"What do we do?" Jenna asked Catrona.

"I know how to fight and how to live in the woods," Catrona said. "I am a fine blanket companion and a good provider. But this is beyond my knowing. It is priestess-work."

Petra shook her head. "I know that song from the Hame. And my Mother Alta taught me the meaning of each tree in the alphabet for so it is written in Alta's own *Book of Light*. Ash is for remembrance, birch for recovery, larch for the light, and the rest. But where we are and who is singing, I do not know. Perhaps only the Anna herself knows."

"The Anna herself is as puzzled as you," Jenna said, and muttered, "unless I am not the Anna."

"You be," Jareth said. "Even the Grenna be calling you so."

"Then who . . . ?" Jenna bit her lip.

"There is only one way to find out," Catrona said, raising her sword.

Jenna put her hand upon Catrona's. "Whoever she is, she sings a song known to the sisters and to them as well." She nodded at Jareth, Marek, and Sandor. "She means to tell us she is both sister and mother to us."

"To us all," Petra added.

"And who is that but Alta herself," Jenna said.

"I said you would know." Petra smiled.

"It is a guess. And a poor one at that," Jenna said. "Let me go first and we will see."

"We be going together," Jareth said.

And they did, crashing through the underbrush, the horses trailing behind them.

As they rushed forward, the trees seemed to extend upward till they touched the sky and arched over, their branches laced together in a roof of green through which the sunlight shone in filtered rays. The trunks of the trees became mottled pillars of marble with dark green veins running from the top. The ground beneath their feet became a floor upon which the pattern of grass and petal and leaf remained.

In the very center of the hall was a great hearth with a green cradle standing before it. Rocking the cradle was a woman dressed in a light green silk gown with darker green leaves embroidered on the hem of the skirt and gold vining twined upon the bodice. Her hair was pure white and plaited in two braids. She wore a crown of sweetbriar, a wristlet of wild rose, and a collar of thistle intermixed with annulets of gold. Her feet were bare.

"She . . . she be your mother, Anna," whispered Marek.

"She be having your hair and your eyes," added Sandor. "And your mouth."

Jareth just stared.

But Petra had already knelt before the woman, offering up her palms which were as yet unincised with the blue priestess sign. Catrona, too, had knelt, placing her sword by the woman's bare feet.

Jenna shook her head. "No. No, you are not my mother. I was never cradled in that." She went to the green crib and tore away the veil of vines.

The cradle was empty.

"I was born in blood between the thighs of a Slipskin woman. I was borne off by the midwife and rescued by a sister of Selden Hame. That much I believe. That much I can accept. I killed a man called the Hound more by accident than design. And I cut off the hand of one named the Bull. If that fulfills prophecy, then so be it. But do not ask me to believe this . . . this counterfeit." She could feel the skin tighten across her cheekbones. She was too angry to cry.

The woman smiled slowly, reached down, and raised up both Petra and Catrona. She pulled Petra to stand by her right side and Catrona to stand by her left. Then she looked directly at Jenna.

"Good. Good. I would have been disappointed if you had accepted all this." She waved her hand around the hall which turned back at once into a simple grove. "Accepted it without question."

Jareth let out a loud breath.

"Without question? I have *hundreds* of questions," said Jenna. "But I do not know which one to ask first. Who are you? Where are we? Why are we here? Where are the Greenfolk now? And . . ."

"And what about your sisters?" the woman asked.

"That most of all," Jenna said.

"Come, sit, and I will tell you all I can," the woman said.

"But what be we calling you?" asked Jareth.

The woman smiled and held out her hand to him. "You can call me Alta," she said.

He shook his head. "No. Like the Anna, I be not believing . . ."

She smiled. "Really," she said, shrugging, "that *is* my name." She gestured to the ground and sat down herself. The others followed her lead. "I was named, of course, after the Goddess, as were many of the girls of my day."

"When *was* your day?" Jenna asked, pushing away Duty who had come to nuzzle against her ear. The mare shook her head vigorously and plodded away to stand near the open fire.

"You will have to suspend your suspicions, Jenna," Alta said.

"How do you know my name?"

"How did the Grenna?"

Jenna was silent. She plucked a blade of grass and put it into her mouth, chewing absently.

"I am that Alta who harvested the hillsides and set up the system of the Hames. I wrote the *Book of Light*. And I brought the wisdom of the breathing and the Eye-Mind and the mysteries of the dark sisters to the Hames," Alta said quietly.

"Then you are Great Alta herself," whispered Catrona.

"No, no, my Cat," Alta said. "I dance over no rainbows nor can I walk over a bridge of light. I was a woman wed to a king and unable to bear a child. So he put me aside and took another wife. And another. In grief, I began to gather the forgotten girl children left to die on the hills of the Dales. I fashioned little carts and towed them behind me, more in madness than with any goal in mind.

"The Grenna found me wandering, crazed, pulling seven carts full of mewling, stinking babes and brought us down here—to the Green World. They taught me how to care for the children: how to play at the wand, how to see in the woods. They told me what would be in the world to come. They showed me how to control my breath and call up my twin. And when they had done all that, they sent us back into the Dales. But it was not one day or one month or even one year that had passed. It was a hundred. And my disappearance from the Dales had become a story, a tale to frighten children at the hearthfire. *Be good or the Alta will get you.*

"When we returned, a new story began and unwanted women—the barren and the homely and the lonely—came to our aid. We built the first Hame near here."

"Wilma's Crossing," Petra said.

"Yes, Wilma's Crossing. And the rest came after. I wrote down what the Greenfolk had taught me, or at least what I could remember of it, intermixed—I suppose—with the wisdoms of the Dales. I called what I wrote the *Book of Light*. And then . . ." She sighed deeply.

"And then you returned here?" Jenna asked.

"That was much later," Alta said. "When my work was done; when I was ready to die. My women brought me to the doors of the cave as I instructed and left me. When they were gone, I came down into the core. And I have been here ever since."

Marek sat up. "But, Alta, that be . . ."

". . . hundreds of years," finished Sandor.

"Time moves differently here," Alta said. She reached up and took off the briar crown, setting it by her side. "And I had to wait until the Anna came."

"Be others coming afore?" Jareth asked.

"A few. And they saw the hall and the cradle. They heard the song. They ate my bread and drank my wine. And then they left to find themselves alone and pale on the hillside, their loved ones long in the grave. But they knew *me* not. They knew only their own dreams." She took off the thistle collar and set it upon the crown.

"Why me?" asked Jenna. "Why us? Why now?"

"Because what I began must now end," Alta said. "The time has come for the world to turn again. Core to rind, rind to core. The Grenna call it the world's paring. It happens every few hundred years."

"Every few hundred years!" Jenna was both astonished and outraged.

Alta laughed. "Do you think we of the Dales are all there is in the world? We are but one apple on a vast tree. One tree in a vast grove. One grove in . . ." She pointed beyond Jenna.

Remembering the other groves in the meadow that extended to the horizon, Jenna whispered hoarsely, ". . . in a vast green."

"Yes, Jenna. You want to be and not to be *The* Anna. But there are many Annas. Have been many. Will be again. Oh, they will not all be called *Anna.* Their names will be a multitude." Alta touched Jenna's mouth with her finger. Her finger was cool. "But you are *The* Anna for *this* turning. And you have many things yet to learn." Standing, she said in a voice that, while sweet, could not be denied: "Come." She stood, taking crown and collar with her.

They rose and followed her straight toward the fire, Jenna by her side and the others in a line behind. As they approached the fire, it seemed to recede before them.

"So it is with time here," Alta commented, continuing on toward the flames. At last, having reached some particular destination known only to her, she stopped and gestured around them.

Looking carefully, Jenna saw they were in a cozy kitchen just like the one in Selden Hame. Any minute she expected to see Donya, Doey, and their helpers come bustling through the door. There were metal sconces on the wall with tallow candles shedding a brilliant light, a roast on a spit turning of its own accord over a well-set fire. Yet as sharp as the central image was, the edges were soft and unfocused as are things seen out of the corner of the eye. And for all the hominess, there was a strangeness, an aloneness at the heart of the place. Jenna felt uneasy. She drew in three deep breaths.

At last she spoke. "This is not real either. No more than the cradle; no more than the hall."

"Not real?" Marek said, disappointment clear in his voice. "But it be like our Da's house."

"*Just* like," added Sandor.

"It is nothing but glamour and seeming," Jenna warned. "Look at the candles. Look at the fire. There are no shadows here."

"And no dark sisters," Catrona said.

"You are right." Alta nodded solemnly. "You are right *in a way*. And you are wrong as well. This *is* only a seeming but it is constructed out of your memories and your desires and your dreams. It is not meant to tempt or distract you. It is meant to comfort and remind you."

"It is too odd here," Jenna said, shivering. "I feel no comfort, only a strange hollowness."

"Let it come to you," Alta said. "Sit—and allow it room in your heart."

Petra sat down first, drawing up a solid-looking oaken chair with inlaid panels of wood. The chair was so large that when she sat back, her feet barely touched the floor, only enough to stir up the rushes that had been sweetened with dried roses and verbena.

Jenna breathed in the familiar scent, remembering. Just so the Great Hall at her Hame had smelled. Just so. She shook her head vigorously and remained standing.

The boys all sprawled suddenly on their bellies by the hearth, like puppies after a long run. Sandor took a stick and began poking at the fire and Marek stared dreamily into the flames. Jareth put his chin on his arms but his eyes still moved restlessly around the room.

Sighing deeply, Catrona lowered herself into an armed chair with a deep cushion, stretching her legs toward the fire. She put her head back and stared at the ceiling, smiling.

Jenna's fingers traced the design on the back of Catrona's chair. Alta's sign was encised there: the circle with the two peaks that almost met in a cross. *It was too perfect,* she thought. She distrusted perfection. In the Dales they said *Perfection is the end of growing. In other words—death. I did not bring them all here to die in comfort.* Out loud she said, "You told us we had many things yet to learn. Teach us—and then let us go."

Alta smiled. "Much I have to teach you, you know already, Jenna. The Game of Eye-Mind that trained you for the woods. The game of wands that trained your sword arm. And you have called your sister even before your first flow. You love both women and men, and that, too, makes you ready for what is to come. But Jenna, Jo-an-enna, you are still so much a child. You fear your destiny. You fear to hold power. You fear to reach beyond your own hearth."

"I do not fear that. After all, I am here." She shifted back and forth uneasily from foot to foot.

"Annuanna," Alta said sharply.

Jenna stood perfectly still. It was her secret name, that only her foster mothers—and they long dead—and the priestess of Selden Hame knew. She felt herself trembling, not on the outside but on the inside; not with fear but with a kind of readiness, like a cat after its prey.

"When you are in the world beyond the green, you must remember how my fire always goes ahead, expanding as far as I let it, always beyond reach and yet by my hand. So must your dreams be, so must your desires be."

The trembling inside stopped, replaced by a sudden icy calm. *Riddles,* Jenna thought angrily. Then she said the word out loud: "Riddles."

"Not riddles," said Alta, shaking her head. "But like the wisdom of the Dales, which you and your companions so love to quote, merely a useful tool for understanding. For remembering. Remembering is what you must do most of all, Jenna. Remember my fire. Remember the green world." She waved her hand across the table and it was suddenly crowded with goblets, platters, and plates.

As if wakening from a deep dream, Petra, Catrona, and the boys came to the table and began to eat noisily and with gusto. There was pigeon pie, salads of cos and cress, platters of fruit. There were ewers of wine, both deep red and golden white, and the soft rosy-colored wine that Jenna fancied most of all.

"And will this faery food sustain us?" Jenna asked abruptly, reaching over and picking up a loaf of braided bread. She waved it toward Alta.

"It will," Alta said. "Just as my fire warms you. Just as my chairs give your legs rest."

Downing a second cup of the dark red wine, Catrona added, "Just as this wine strengthens my heart."

"That wine . . ." Jenna began, putting her hand on Catrona's arm, "does you no good. You know it eats away at your stomach. We cannot have you sick for days with the flux."

"This wine will not harm her," said Alta. "It will strengthen her for the coming fight."

Jareth pushed himself away from the table with such force his cup over-turned, spilling wine along the grain of the wood. In the flickering candlelight, the wine picked up the color of the oak, looking then like old blood until it dripped over the table in a golden fall. "What be this fight?" he asked harshly. "You be knowing more of it than we. Tell us. Finally."

"It is the fight that began in my time and must end in yours," Alta said. Her voice was so soft, they all had to strain to hear it. "It is the fight that goes on and on in this circle. The fight to bring light and dark together. The fight to bring men and women together."

"And if we win it," Jenna asked as quietly, "will it be won for all time?"

"One apple on a vast tree, Jenna," Alta reminded her. "One tree in a vast grove."

"One grove in a vast green," Jenna said. "I remember. I remember, but it does not make me glad." She stood, and the others stood with her. "Is there more to learn?"

"Only this," Alta said. She took off the wristlet of rose, and set it alongside the collar and crown on the table. "Take the crown, young Marek."

When he held it gingerly between his palms, Alta put her hands over his. "And you shall crown the king."

Then she looked back at the objects on the table. "Sandor, take up the wristlet."

He bent over, picked up the wristlet, letting it sit in his right palm. Alta covered his right hand with hers. "And you shall guide the king's right arm."

Alta herself picked up the collar from the table. She held it for a long moment without speaking, staring at Jareth as if weighing her words.

Jenna felt something inside go hot and then cold. She bit her lip. If Marek was to crown the king—whoever he was—and Sandor to guide his arm, then what could the collar mean? Slave to that unnamed king? Or a noose around his neck?

Not Jareth, she thought. *Not my good friend.* She put out her hand to stop Alta's words.

"No!" she cried. "Do not give it to him. If it is to be his death, give it to me instead."

Alta looked up and smiled sadly. "What you and Catrona and Petra must do is written in your hearts. You learned it from the *Book of Light* when you were children. You carry it inside. But for the men who do not understand it yet, there must be these reminders. And the collar has been waiting for the last of the heroes. I must give it to him, Jenna. I must."

"I be not minding, Anna," Jareth said, his eyes steady on hers. "And I be not afraid. I be following you, and you already bringing me to a stranger destiny than I might otherwise know, safe in the mill beside my old Da. That Anna be willing to take my death for me be enough."

Not Anna—Jenna, she wanted to say. But she saw that for such courage she had to be the Anna for him. So she kept silent.

Alta placed the collar around his neck and it turned into a band of purest green.

"You shall not speak again until the crown is in place and the king's right hand has won the war. After that, all that you speak shall be accorded great honor. But if this collar is broken before time, what you say could shatter the fellowship, lose the throne, and the circle would remain unclosed forever. For with this collar, you will have read the hearts of men and the minds of women and none likes to be reminded of what they think and feel by another."

Jareth put his hand up to his throat, turning slowly to gaze at each of his companions. His eyes grew large and small, like moons, as he stared at them. At last he looked at Jenna, until she dropped her glance, uneasy with his fierce examination.

"Oh, my poor Jareth," she whispered, putting her hand out to him.

He opened his mouth as if to speak, but no words came out, only a strangulation of sound. He did not touch her hand, pulling away to stand instead shoulder to shoulder with the other boys.

"And now," Alta said, "you must go. I will give you bread and wine for the journey, for it is a long riding between here and tomorrow. And if you speak of what you saw and heard in this green world, you will be believed no more than if you spoke with Jareth's voice. Farewell." She raised her hand and, as if they had been commanded, the horses trotted over to her. She picked up their trailing reins, holding them out.

One by one Jenna and her companions walked to their mounts. Jenna got up first. Next Catrona, her unsheathed sword in hand. Jareth got onto the bay mare, then reached down to help Petra up. Last of all, Marek and Sandor leaped onto their horse.

"Will we see you again?" Jenna asked Alta.

Alta smiled. "You will see me again at the end of your life. Come to the doors and they will open for you. You—and one other."

"One other?" Jenna whispered the question. When there was no answer to it, she turned her horse and headed in the direction Alta pointed, toward the far horizon.

The others followed.

* * *

At the beginning they rode slowly, as if reluctant to leave Alta's meadow. Then one at a time they kicked their horses into a gallop. First the sun, then the stars, fell behind them like snow, though it was neither day nor night but a kind of eternal dusk. As they rode summer followed spring, winter followed fall, and yet the road remained the same. They rode on and on toward the place where land and sky met.

Once Jenna glanced back. She saw Alta standing by her grove, in a circle of Grenna. When she looked again, Alta, the mannikins, and the grove were all gone.

THE MYTH

And then Great Alta said, "The crown shall be for the head, for one must rule with wisdom. And the wristlet shall be for the hand's cunning. But as for the collar, which surrounds the neck, it shall be for the tongue, for without tongue we are not human. How else can we tell the story that is history; how else can we hymn or carol; how else can we curse or cry? It is the collar that is the highest gift of all."

BOOK THREE

Blanket Companions

THE MYTH

Then Great Alta drew apart the curtain of her hair and showed them the plains of war. On the right side were the armies of the light. On the left side were the armies of the night. Yet when the sun set and the moon rose they were the same.

"They are blanket companions," quoth Great Alta. "They are to one another sword and shield, shadow and light. I would have you learn of war so you may live in peace."

And she set them down on the bloody plain for their schooling.

THE LEGEND

There is a barren plain in the center of the Dales, where but one kind of flower grows—the Harvest Rose. Little grass, and it quite brown; little water, and it undrinkable; only dust and gravel and the Harvest Rose.

It is said that once the plain was a forest of great trees, so tall they seemed to pierce the sky. And the cat and the coney lived in harmony there.

But one day two giants met on that plain, their heads helmeted but their bodies bare. For three days and three nights they wrestled with one another. Their mighty feet stomped the good earth into dust. Their mighty hands tore trees from the ground. They flailed at each other with the trees as though with mere cudgels or sticks. And at last, when the two of them lay dying, side by side, they ripped off their helmets only to discover they were so alike, they might have been twins.

The blood from the battle watered the torn and dying earth. And at each drop grew the Harvest Rose, a blood-red blossom with a white face imprinted on the petals, each and every face the same.

THE STORY

When they emerged from a final copse of trees lining the great meadow, the moon was full overhead.

"The moon?" Jenna was puzzled. "When we left it was not moon time."

"It has been more than one moon since you left, sister," a voice whispered in her ear. Jenna turned slightly. Skada was sitting behind her. Her face was a good deal thinner than Jenna remembered. And older, somehow.

"Just how many moons . . ." Jenna began, then glanced past Skada to stare at the rest of her companions.

Catrona and Katri on the bay mare stared back. There was a streak of white running through Catrona's short cap of hair, a matching streak in Katri's. Jareth, with his green collar tight across his throat, had a leaner look and Marek a downy moustache feathering his lip. Sandor's cheeks were sprinkled with the beginnings of a beard. But it was Petra who had changed the most. She was no longer a girl but a young woman, with a soft curve of breast showing beneath her tunic.

Jenna put a hand up to her own face, as if she might feel any change there, but her fingers held no memories.

"Look at us! Look!" Marek said, his voice booming into the night.

"I . . ." Sandor began and then, as if surprised by the depth of the syllable, stopped.

Opening his mouth, Jareth strained for a sound. When none came, he closed it again, shaking his head slowly at first, then faster and faster, banging his fist on his thigh in frustration.

It was Petra who spoke for them all. "The legends are true. *Cocooned in time,* the Grenna said. But they did not say how much time. How long . . ." her voice trailed off.

Jenna got off her horse, followed by Skada. Turning to her dark sister, she asked: "How many more than one moon, Skada?"

"I do not know. Many. After a time, I lost the count."

"Yet we ate not nor did we sleep," Catrona said. "We hold no memory of those passages through time. How can that be?"

"It is because of Alta," Petra said.

"And the Grenna," Catrona added.

"It is because of Anna," Marek and Sandor said together.

They all dismounted and the boys were quickly introduced to Katri and Skada. But the dark sisters' arrival was only a small, familiar mystery inside the larger one. It was the question of time that consumed them all.

"Is it one year or . . ." Catrona hesitated.

"Or hundreds?" Katri finished for her.

"Hundreds!" Marek seemed surprised at the possibility. "It be not hundreds. What about our Ma then?"

"And our Da?"

"What about our sisters?" Petra asked. "And the warnings?"

Jenna twisted the priestess ring around her little finger. She was not heedless of the sisters. But she had to know first where they were—what time and what place. Staring at Jareth, she whispered, "You have not mentioned his Mai." She did not add her own names: Pynt and A-ma and all the sisters at Selden Hame. What use was such a tally when they were so lost? She would not even *think* of Carum, would not conjure his face now. But Skada knew. She reached out and touched Jenna's hand.

They were not tired, but they thought it best to rest the night. In the daylight they might discover the path, might recognize some familiar landmark. Besides, the horses would fare better in the day without the added burden of the dark sisters. And they all needed to think.

"To focus," Catrona said, using the very word and tone Jenna remembered from their days in Selden Hame when Catrona had taught her about living in the woods.

As part of that focus, they taught the boys how to match them breath for breath around a small campfire. Catrona felt the need for light far exceeded the danger. She told the boys the story about the five beasts who quarreled before they discovered that breath was the most important part of life. Jenna recalled Mother Alta telling that tale, and how it sat heavily in the priestess' sour mouth. Catrona's telling was far more sprightly. The boys laughed when she was done, even Jareth, though his laughter was silent.

After the story, Marek and Sandor regaled them with rhymes their Da had taught them, all about pulling the ferry across the water. *Teaching rhymes,* Catrona called them.

"Every craft and every guild has them," she said. "The baker, the herdsman, the miller . . ."

Jareth interrupted by placing his hand on Catrona's. He gestured to himself.

"A miller . . . a miller," muttered Katri.

They were all embarrassed into silence until Petra began to sing a lullaby in a sweet voice that soon had them all rubbing their eyes.

"We will rise with the sun," Jenna said.

"Before the sun," Catrona amended.

THE SONG

Sisters' Lullay

Hush and sleep ye,
Shush and keep ye,
Safe within the
Hame's strong walls

Naught shall harm ye.
We shall charm ye
With the song the
Night bird calls.

> *Sisters strong shall*
> *Keep the cradle*
> *Sisters long shall*
> *Watch the way*

> *Sisters all shall*
> *Guard and guide ye*
> *Till ye wake at*
> *Break of day.*

Hush and sleep ye,
Shush and keep ye,
Alta watches
From above.

We will praise ye,
We will raise ye,

*Light and dark in
Alta's love*

THE STORY

They drifted into sleep one after another until only Jenna and Skada were
awake, side by side on Jenna's blanket.

"I have missed you," Skada said. "And missed this world, so bright and
deafening."

"Which have you missed more?"

"In equal measure." Skada laughed. Then she whispered, "But it has
been hard on you."

"It has been harder on the others," Jenna said. "And the fault . . ."

". . . is not yours, dear sister," Skada said. "This is a time when a circle
closes. That you are the clasp is not a fault, merely an accident of time."

"Jareth said I was a linchpin."

"We will miss his clear voice."

Jenna thought about that. It was what she had been feeling, but had not
dared to say aloud. "I . . ."

"*We.* Is it so difficult to accept that you are not alone, Jenna? That we all
share the burden?"

Suddenly Jenna remembered Alta's words: *You want to be and not to be
the Anna.* How easily Alta had said it. How hard it was to accept. She
wanted to be the center, the clasp, the linchpin, but she did not want the
enormous weight of it. Yet she could not have the one without the other.
How much easier to share. Not *I* but *we.* She reached out and touched
Skada's hand. They did not speak again, just lay there hand in hand until
sleep finally claimed them.

"Jenna! Jenna!" The voice seemed far away, a dying fall of sound. Jenna
awoke with a start to a day bright with birdsong. Catrona was shaking her
by the shoulder. She sat up, almost reluctant to leave the comfort of sleep.

Looking around, Jenna saw the horses cropping grass by a well-worn
roadside, the others still asleep.

"Catrona, I had the strangest dream," she began. "There was a vast
meadow and . . ." She stopped. A wide streak of white ran through Ca-

trona's hair and the runes across her brow were deeper than Jenna remembered.

"No dream, little Jen. The meadow, the grove, the hearth and hall. No dream. Unless two can dream the same."

Jenna stood slowly. Two might possibly dream alike but that did not explain the age creeping across Catrona's face. Or the fact that Duty, who had just lifted her face from the grass, had a dusting of white hairs on her nose. Or that Jareth, beginning to stir, wore a collar of green around his neck.

"No dream," Jenna agreed. "But if it is true, then where are we? And *when* are we?"

"As for where," Catrona said, "that I know now. This is the road to Wilma's Crossing Hame. It has not changed that much in the thirty years since I was last here."

"Thirty?" Jenna asked.

"I was a girl missioning here," Catrona said. "It was my last stop—and a dare."

"Why a dare?" Jenna asked.

"Because it was so far from my own Hame and across the famous forest of the Grenna and because it was the very first Hame. And because I had boasted too much about not being afraid to come."

"And were you afraid?"

Catrona laughed. "Of course I was afraid. I may have been a bit of a boaster, but I was no fool. I never saw any Grenna, of course. Doubted they existed. But fog and mist and men I found plenty. As for the men, well, I kicked my way out of several encounters and marched with a black eye but my maidenhead intact into Wilma's Crossing Hame." She chuckled at the memory.

"And . . ."

"And they laughed at me and gave me a hot bath and told me the facts of a woman's life, which somehow I had neglected to listen to when my Mother Alta imparted them. I got my flow that next week and had a man on the way back to my own Hame. Katri never forgave me for not waiting for her."

Jenna blushed furiously.

"Yes, this is the road to Wilma's Crossing. There the road goes back through the forest." She pointed to the long, empty path. "And there are Alta's Pins." She pointed ahead to a pair of rolling hillocks, grass-covered dunes that stretched for almost a mile. "Nothing like them in the whole of the Dales."

"Thirty years," Jenna mused. She combed through her hair with her fingers, then braided it up, twisting a dark ribband around the bottom to hold the plait in place.

"Thirty—or more," Catrona said.

"How much more?"

"I would tell you if I knew, child. I puzzled all night on it." Giving Jenna a swift, sure hug, she added, "As for that dream we both had, I recall there was food in it as well." She went to her own blanket and the saddlebags that she had used for a pillow. Opening up the flap of one, she rummaged around. "Yes, here. Quite a dream, that can supply such as this." She pulled out two loaves of a braided bread and a leather flask. "Come, girl, *First up, first fed*, we used to say in the army." She broke off the heel of the bread and handed it to Jenna. "In fact, *First up, finest fed*. As I recall, you were always partial to the ends, even as a babe."

Jenna took the bread gratefully and started chewing. At the first bite, a sharp burst of some sweet herb filled her mouth. She sighed.

Smiling at her, Catrona took a long draught from the flask, then grinned. "The red. She gave us the red. Bless her."

At that, Jenna laughed. "Only you, Catrona, would bless someone for wine." But she reached out and took a sip herself. She was careful not to mention to Catrona that the wine was not red at all but the gentle rosy drink that she preferred. Either Catrona was losing her judgment, or there was a strange magic at work here. It was not worth mentioning either way.

The others were up soon after, finishing off both loaves of bread and the flask which, though no one remarked it greatly, supplied milk for Petra and some kind of dark liquid for each of the boys, which Jenna thought might be tea.

They saddled the horses and were away just as the sun climbed between the rolling hills Catrona had called Alta's Pins.

"As I remember it," Catrona told them, "it is but a morning's walk from here to the Hame."

"Then it will be a short ride with the horses fresh," said Jenna.

Following Catrona, they threaded their way in a single line through the Pins and across a boggy meadow that was full of spring wildflowers, white, yellow, and blue. Quite soon they saw the wreckage of several buildings jagged against the clean slate of sky.

"Too late," Jenna whispered to herself as they neared the ruined Hame. She braced herself for the inevitable bodies and the horrible smell of death. "Too late for any of them." The whisper took on Sorrel's accent and she cursed herself and her companions for spending the time they had in Alta's grove.

Dismounting at the broken gate, they wandered through the silent ruins. Vines twisted up between fallen stones. The weedy arberry had taken root in the cracks. There was a scattering of linseed along the pathways, the blue flowers bending in a passing wind. But there were no bodies; there were no bones.

"This be not happening yesterday," Marek remarked cautiously, his fingers smoothing down his new moustache.

"Nor the day before that," Petra added. She plucked up a yellow flower and crushed it against her palm. "How long . . ." her voice trailed off.

Squatting, Catrona smoothed her hand across the gravelly ruin of a side wall. "A year. Or two. Or more. It takes a season at least for arberry and linseed, tansy and hound's tooth, to take hold in a waste. A season at least for vines to begin to twist up through the walls."

Sandor's eyes grew wide. "And see how high they go."

Jareth measured the vines and they were five times the width of his hand, from little finger to thumb. He spread his hand, counting silently. *Five.*

Sitting down heavily on a great stone, Jenna drew in a deep *latani* breath. When she finally spoke she hoped her tones were measured. "We find out what year it is. Whether one has passed or . . ." Glancing at Jareth, whose hand still silently tallied the length of the vines, she finished her thought. "Or five. We must know how long since we rode out."

"And then find out what damage to the Hames," Petra said.

Jenna nodded. "And then . . ."

"Hush! Now!" From her squatting position, Catrona had flung herself onto the ground, ear down, listening. For a moment she was still. Then suddenly she sat up. With a sweep of her hand, she whispered, "Riders!"

"Our horses . . ." Jenna cried, but she threw herself down on the ground and felt the pounding of the earth under her cheek. The riders were close. Saying no more, she drew her sword from its sheath and lay on the ground, waiting. All of her anger, unhappiness, and fear were focused for what was sure to be a fierce battle. The ground foretold many horsemen.

Petra and the boys flung themselves down as well, the boys wriggling about to draw their knives.

Jenna could see between two of the fallen stones, as if through the narrow line of an arrow slit. At first all she could make out were the trees across the road; then a gray cloud of dust from the horses' hooves rising up against the background, obscuring the trees. Slowly, the front line of the oncoming riders resolved itself and Jenna could see that one of the lead horses was gray.

"A gray!" she called over to Catrona, not sure if her voice could be heard in the building thunder. "A company of king's horse."

Catrona nodded.

Jenna could feel a shiver run across the back of her shoulders, as if something cold had snaked its way over her neck. Then she shook her head and whatever it was she had felt was gone. Looking aside at the others, she nodded. The boys nodded back but Petra's eyes were wide and unseeing. Jenna guessed she was praying.

A prayer would not be amiss, she thought, trying to remember one. But the pounding of the hooves and the rising dust and the sun on her head and the fear that her friends might die because of her pushed all prayer from her mind except the one word: *now . . . now . . . now.*

Then Catrona leaped up, sword raised, and Jenna followed, screaming what was left of her fear into the faces of the galloping troop. She could feel heat in her face and the remains of the rosy wine threatening to leave her stomach and a throbbing of a vein over her right eye.

And then suddenly the first of the horses, a black gelding, was pulled to a rearing stop by its rider. Behind it, the gray and then the others fanned out. There were more than twenty-one. Many more.

Jenna's sword hand began to shake. She reached over with her left hand and grasped her right wrist to hold it steady. She heard a strange braying coming from Catrona's direction and could not make it out. She dared a quick glance.

Catrona was laughing and lowering her sword. *Laughing!*

The man on the black horse was laughing as well. When the noise had settled, he spoke. "Well, well, well, Catkin. Like an old copper, ye turn op in the oddest of hands." He grinned, showing a mouth gapped with uneven teeth. His beard was luxuriantly black and white; his eyes narrow and the piercing blue of a cold spring sky; his tongue strange to Jenna's ears.

Catrona sheathed her sword. "As often as not I turn up in *your* hands, Piet."

The man Piet dismounted. He was a big man, his solid flesh starting to run to fat, but he moved with a feline grace. "Ye've not been in *my* hands for so lang a time, girl."

"How long a time?" Catrona asked, almost casually.

Jenna held her breath.

Piet narrowed his eyes even more and grinned. Her caution had not fooled him. "Looking for compliments at yourn age, my catkin? Or somewhat more, eh?" He laughed. Jenna had been expecting a cold sound, and calculating, but it was full and warm. "And where is that dark, daring sister of yourn?"

"She is around," Catrona said. She held out her hand to him and he took it. Instead of shaking it, he simply held it, his massive fingers wrapping hers. Jenna was surprised that Catrona let her hand be prisoned that way.

"I've missed ye, girl. No doubt of it. Nane to drink me doon like ye can, after a good fight. And nane like ye ever for a blanket companion, eh?"

Catrona laughed lightly, gaily, a sound Jenna had never heard her make before.

Clearing her throat, Jenna moved towards Catrona. Petra came over to stand by her side. The three boys, knives still tightly in their hands, clustered together.

"The kittens are restless," Piet said, dropping her hand at last. "Introduce us to this litter of yourn."

Catrona turned and signaled them to her and they came like bidden children, though Jenna was not happy at the thought.

"The boys are from Callatown. Sandor and Marek are, as you can see, brothers. And the small one is Jareth."

Piet put out his hand to them each in turn, nodding and saying their names aloud. Sandor and Marek gave him greeting but Jareth's silence troubled the big man.

"He is mute," Catrona explained.

"From birth?" asked Piet. "Can he sign his wishes?"

"God touched," Petra said, stepping forward. "And it is new."

"Ah, the collar," said Piet, as if he understood. "And ye child, what name is yourn?"

"I am no child, but priestess-trained. My name is Petra." She lifted her head and stared into his eyes.

"Ye be a child still to me, for all ye speak daily with gods. But well come, Petra. I like children—and I like priestesses. They all speak in riddles. It makes a big man like me feel small." He grinned at her. She could not help but grin back.

"And this beauty," he said, turning toward Jenna.

"Watch your tongue," Catrona said, "or she will have it. She is the best of us. She is the reason we are here."

At her tone, his grin faded at once. "And what do ye mean, me girl."

"She is Jo-an-enna. She is the White One. The Anna."

For a long moment Piet stared at Jenna, measuring her by some internal reckoning. Then he shook his head and laughed out loud, a wilder braying than Catrona's. When the bold laughter had run its course, he stared at her again. "The *White One?* Have ye taken leave . . . Catrona? Ye've never owned such nonsense afore. *The White One!* She's nowt but a girl."

"Nonetheless . . ." Catrona began.

Just then the man on the gray dismounted and walked over to them, limping badly, his right leg swinging stiffly from an unbending knee. "Jo-an-enna, you say. Could you be called else? A pet name? Or a family name?" His face was clearly thinned down with old pain, but Jenna thought there was something terribly familiar about his cheeks and the long lashes and the hair.

"Jenna," she whispered, staring at him. "I am called Jenna by my friends." The limping man was and was not like Carum. *But how many years had it been?* He was taller and darker and she felt nothing when she looked at him but a vague tug of reminiscence. *Nothing at all.* How could that possibly be?

"Are you Carum's White Jenna, then?" he asked. Something narrowed in his face so that he had a fox's look, sly, calculating, cautious, and feral. Carum had never looked like that.

Jenna breathed out slowly. She hadn't realized she'd been holding her breath till it sighed out of her. "You are *not* Carum," she said, but it was almost a question.

He grinned, looking more wolflike than fox. "I—Carum? What a thing I shall have to tell him when I see him next. Five years goes by and the girl he loves mistakes his older brother for . . ."

"His older brother!" It was an explosion of sound and relief. "No wonder you look like him. You must be . . ." She reached back in memory and pulled out a name. "You must be Pike."

"Pike . . . I have not been called that in years."

Piet interrupted smoothly, "He is Gorum. King Gorum. Majesty-in-exile now. Best remember."

"Five years in exile then? We have much to talk about, Piet," said Catrona.

"And plenty of time afore dark to speak of it," Piet said. "And after dark—well, plenty of time for that, too, eh?"

Catrona patted his hand.

"But why do ye call *this* girl the White One?" asked Piet. "What signs brought ye to it? Ye, Catrona, of all folk?"

The forty or so men dismounted, gathering around noisily.

Looking them all over, Catrona snorted. "I will tell it once the horses are pastured and we have split a bottle and some bread." She smiled at Piet. "You do have bread? And bottles?"

"What army goes without?" asked Piet.

"Is this an army?" Catrona countered. "Ragtag, and scarcely one shield amongst three? No helms. No pikes—begging your pardon, Majesty." She made a quick almost mocking obeisance.

"It is but part of one," Piet admitted.

"And the rest?"

"On a rade. With *his* brother."

"His brother?" Jenna could feel a strange ache suddenly start up in her belly.

"Him that's called Longbow," Piet answered.

"Longbow? Carum? On a rade? It cannot possibly be. He is a scholar, not a fighter," Jenna said.

"Perhaps back then when there weren't no war, 'twas a scholar, gel. Perhaps he bain reading up on bow shooting in his books. He is a good shot now, though he doesna like swords yet," Piet said. He gave Jenna another searching look, then spoke to Catrona. "Come into the Hame, gel. It's nowt but shambles, but the kitchen still stands. We have bottles well hidden. And bread. And a couple of deer hanging."

"Well, well, well," Catrona mused. "When you are not on a rade, you are in a well-stocked kitchen." She patted Piet's belly. "This is not just five years' growth."

Laughing, Piet put his hand over hers. "This belly's been longer than five years growing, gel, as well ye know. And I've been slimming these last months. But ye be no great beauty yersel. There's gray in yer hair now."

"At least I have it all."

"I have enough," he said, laughing.

Jenna's mouth drew down into a thin line, her eyes narrowing. "Should there be guards?"

"We own the road," the king said, a bit petulantly.

"Not good enough," Petra whispered. "You missed *our* coming."

"What makes ye think ye were missed?" Piet asked.

"You were just not accounted a problem," said the king.

"Not good enough," Jenna seconded, "for the sisters who dwelt here first."

"That is an old, old story," Piet said, his hand still over Catrona's. "And not a pretty one. This is a new."

"Tell us," Jenna demanded. "Tell us the story. *Now!*"

"How is it ye know it not?" came a voice out of the crowd. "If ye be the Anna?"

"And where have *ye* been all these years?" asked another, a man with a scar lacing his right eye like a mask. "Under the hill or somewhat?"

Jareth's hand went suddenly to his collar, and Sandor made a small, sharp sound, like a startled daw.

"Yes," Catrona said slowly, drawing the word out as she drew her hand away from Piet's. She turned toward the questioner. "That is exactly where we have been. Under the hill."

Piet barked a laugh. "Ye have never been a good teller, my girl. And until this moment, I would have called ye the hard-headest warrior I have ever known. But now . . ." He shook his head. "Five years ye've been gone. I went seeking ye, at that Hame of yourn. Looking for fighters, we were. And nane seen the hide of ye. And now ye appear with a child's tale and asking us to believe it."

Sandor murmured, as much to the ground as the men near him: "*She* be saying you would not believe."

"And she is right," the king said. "Under the hill. Which of us can believe such a story."

"Believe it." Jenna spoke the words angrily. "Believe it. Though we still scarcely can credit it ourselves." She would say no more.

When the horses were unsaddled and hobbled to graze outside the walls, they gathered in the open kitchen, where an unbroken chimney thrust up against the sky. There they started a fire in the hearth and set stew pots to boil. It was then that Pike, the king-in-exile as the men called him, began the tale.

THE HISTORY

The so-called Gender Wars took place over a period of no less than five years and no more than twenty, if the Book of Battles *is to be believed. The disparity in numbers is due to the fact that the G'runs counted by the years in a king's reign than by a running tally. As they did not count in the years when the usurper K'las was on the throne, it is unclear exactly how long the battles continued. The reign of the king-in-exile (or the king in the Hills, as*

*Doyle translated it) may be counted sequentially with K'las reign or simulta-
neously. We have few notes from the Continent that refer even obliquely to
the doings in the Dales at that time. It was as if a great cloak of mist had
been wrapped around the island kingdom. If K'las himself ever penned any
histories, they were likely burned by his enemies. History is always written by
the victors.*

*Magon, of course, makes much of the difference in counts, citing legend
and folk stories of the strange passage of time "under the hill" in Faeryland.
But as such passages are common coin in the world's folklore (cf Magon's
own "Telling Time in Faerie" Journal of International Folklore, Vol.
365, #7) such maunderings do little to add to our working knowledge of the
awful, devastating Dale wars*

*That these were wars of succession rather than a war of men against
women, no matter the appellation that has carried down to modern times, is
quite certain. In the Book of Battles we see lists of both sexes fighting side by
side. This was not one great war but a series of small skirmishes over a
number of years in which first one and then another king was placed on the
precarious throne.*

*The seeds of this particular anarchy had been sown when the G'runs, a
patriarchal society from the Continent, had conquered the learning-centered
matriarchy of Alta worshippers. But over the four hundred years of conquest,
the bloodlines thinned for the G'runs married only within narrow clans,
hardly ever mixing with the lower, conquered classes. The once-united clans
began to vie for power after a G'runian king made the mistake of taking a
Dalian for his second wife, naming their son a legitimate heir. One chief of a
powerful northern clan, a crafty warrior named K'las, managed to orchestrate
a bloodless coup. As he was hereditary head of the clan armies (the
Kingsmen) as well as a provincial governor, he had a strong power base. He
ruled, as such army-backed leaders often do, with an iron fist. Or, as it says in
the Book of Battles "never his hand came out in friendship but in anger." Of
course, the book was penned by a member of the opposing party and so we
must read carefully between the lines, as first Doyle and then Cowan have
done. (See especially Cowan's intriguing "The Kallas Controversy," Journal
of the Isles, History IV, 7.)*

*There is a popular legend known as "The King Under the Hill," found in
some thirty-three variants in both the Upper and Lower Dales, in which the
king is killed upon his throne and his three sons flee the province. One is
slaughtered from the back, one is badly wounded, and the third, called majesty-in-exile, lives under the hill with the Greenfolk until his troops rally and
call him forth into the light of day. Magon has taken great pains in trying to*

justify the legend with the history as we have been able to reconstruct it. But much of his verification rests heavily on his own mush-disputed thesis about an historical figure he calls the White One or the Anna or the White Goddess who fights side by side with the king. Magon mixes folklore and history liberally in a soup that ends up lacking both the meat of verifiable research or the good hearty flavoring of the folk. Cowan, on the other hand, lays down a solid substrata of history, reminding us that there is only mention of one son in the Continental books of the period, not three, and he most probably the bastard of the Dale woman, the G'run king's second wife. Also, it would be well for us to remember, three is a potent number popular in folklore.

According to Cowan, the battles for the throne involved not only the overthrown G'runians but a good many of the Dalites as well. After four hundred years of unquestioned subservience to the invaders, the indigenous populations (the Upper Dalite sheep farmers and fisher-folk and the Lower Dalite artisans and city dwellers) had had enough. Young men called Jennisaries (named after one of the martyred leaders, Cowan hypothesizes brilliantly) roamed the countryside destroying the towns and Hames they considered of G'run manufacture. The ruins of one such incursion can still be seen today in the Wilhelm Valley. According to Cowan—and I can only agree wholeheartedly with her—it was not torn down and sown over with sturdy grass as others of its kind because it had become a shrine. The legend goes that it was here that the martyred Jen was murdered and the king crowned.

That the eager young Jennisaries pledged themselves to the new G'run king in exchange for a vow that he would marry one of theirs is something both Cowan and Magon agree upon, though they agree on little else, because it clearly states in the Book of Battles *that "So it is pledged that the dark king and the light queen shall wed, bringing day and night into the circle, that the people themselves might rule."*

However, much else in the Book of Battles *remains unclear. For example, there is little that can be said about the final evocation:*

> *See where the queen has gone,*
> *Where her footsteps flower,*
> *For they lead into the hill,*
> *They lead under the hill,*
> *Where she waits for her call,*
> *Where she waits for her king,*
> *Where she waits for her bright companions.*

Neither Doyle nor Cowan can offer any easy solution to the puzzle of that final piece. And we must utterly reject Magon's ridiculous proposal that the poetry means exactly what it says—that some queen (presumably the one of Dale extraction) remains neither living nor dead under the hill waiting to be recalled to a battle which has yet to be fought.

THE STORY

"My father," the king-in-exile said, "was a good man and a kind man. But he was also a blunt man, given to speak his mind. That good breeding in a farmer but not in a king. He had little talent for the sly exercise of politics and he did not understand compromise. He went where his heart led." Pike's face softened with the memory.

"His wife . . ." promised the man with the scarred eye.

Someone poked up the fire in the broken hearth.

"His first wife, my mother, died giving me birth. She had had trouble birthing my older brother, Jorum, and the doctors warned her that she dare have no more. Jorum was so big he had torn her all up inside. But kingdoms need heirs. One is not a safe number. So I was sown in that ruined terrain. And killed her leaving it." He spoke dryly. It was obviously a story well rehearsed, and the emotion had been leeched from it by so many tellings.

Jenna said in a low voice, "I killed my own mother in just that way." Hesitating, he added, "My first mother."

The men nearest her murmured, turning that bit of information over and over, and one repeated out loud, "First mother."

Gorum seemed not to hear, but continued staring silently into the fire. Then he shook himself all over and went on. "The midwife was a lovely little Dale woman, small and dark. She sang lullabies with a voice like a slightly demented turtledove. She nursed me through that first cold year when my father could not think about babies because they made him so angry."

Jenna burst out, "My second mother was a midwife. She died carrying me in her arms."

Some of the men nodded, as if acknowledging something as yet unsaid, but Gorum simply stared at Jenna for a long moment, then back to the fire and his tale.

"On the day I walked toward him, taking my first baby steps away from her arms, he forgave me. I called him *Papa*, which she had so carefully rehearsed with me, and he wept and called me his *Good son*. He married her in secret at the year's turning, not so much for love but for gratitude. His real love was buried in my mother's grave. When three years later she gave birth to a healthy babe, and she herself still strong, he announced the marriage and claimed the child an heir."

"That was Carum?" Jenna asked.

Gorum smiled at her, the first generous smile she had won from him. "That was Carum. He was small like his mother so, unlike the rest of us, he learned the art of compromise."

"Here, he's not so small as that," cried out a wiry, short man from the sitting crowd. "He be a head taller than me. That's not short."

"Short may-be," said another, "but he baint called Longbow for nowt." The men chuckled at that. Even Sandor and Marek smiled.

Jenna blushed, though she was not sure why, and Catrona sitting next to her put a hand on hers.

"Do not mind them. You will have to get used to it. Men in a mob are all randy-mouthed. It means nothing," she whispered

"It means *less* than nothing to me," Jenna replied, "since I do not know what they mean."

"Then why have you flushed like some spring maiden at a court dance?" asked Catrona.

Jenna looked down at her hands and twisted the priestess ring around her little finger. "I do not know," she said. "I am not sure. I do not even know what a court dance is!"

The king-in-exile laughed along with his men, then took a deep draught of his wine. "The marriage was the mistake Kalas had hoped for. A mistake he could use directly against the king. It was only an excuse, of course. He would have found another in time.

"He began to spread rumors, and those rumors sparked small rebellions: knives in taverns, rocks at the king's gate. What Kalas promised was the sanctity of the clans against the mixing of blood and seed with the Dales. *Sanctity!* As if we had not been sowing babes throughout the Dales for four hundred years! There was never an uncompromised clan on this island since the first days our forefathers set foot here.

"I have bred horses, boy and man, and this I know—the lines without a wild strain thin out. Bones break, blood runs rose. The people of the Dales make the clans stronger, not weaker. My uncle, Lord Kalas, will find this out in the end."

"To the king!" two of the men shouted spontaneously, raising their cups.

"To the kingdom," countered Gorum, raising his.

"To the Dales!" Jenna said, standing. In the late afternoon sun her white hair seemed haloed in light, electric with the puzzling wind.

The rest of the men leaped to their feet, foremost among them Piet and the king-in-exile.

"To the Dales!" they shouted, the thunder of their voices bounding back oddly from the broken walls and cracked stones. "The Dales."

They raised their cups, draining the last of the wine in the resounding silence. And into that silence there insinuated another sound, a low, insistent pounding.

"Horses!" Catrona cried. She was quick to reach for her sword, but Piet was quicker.

Placing his hand over hers, he said, "Those are our own."

"How can you know?" Jenna asked, coming close to him.

"Our watch would have given warning."

"Your watch!" Jenna laughed. "They gave no warning of us."

"We needed no warning of ye—two warrior girls and a priestess all on our side and three unarmed boys."

"What if the watch were slain. That was done at one of the Hames . . ." She hesitated, remembering the girls slaughtered at Nill's. "Then there would be no warning."

"Ye do not understand horses, girl. A man's eye may be fooled but never a horse's nose." He put his finger alongside his nose. "Their horses have been fed on oats and ours on open graze. A horse can smell the difference. But look!" He pointed to the horses still quietly nibbling on the sparse grass outside the walls. "They seem content."

"Oh!" Jenna could think of no other answer.

Piet smiled and clapped her on the back. "How could ye know horses, girl, stuck away all your life in a Hame. Now, me—I was taught by a hard man, name of Parke. Oft I felt the weight of his hand. But he taught me well. His teachings have kept me alive all these years." He spoke with a blunt jollity, but having finished what he had to say, turned and walked purposely out of the kitchen, his hand never straying far from his sword.

As if his movement were a signal, the rest of the men went quickly to what seemed to be appointed places, seven standing around the king-in-exile.

Jenna spoke hurriedly to the boys. "See how the seven guard the king. Do likewise with Petra."

"I need no such guard," Petra began.

"Do it!" Jenna said.

The boys did as they were bid, Jareth drawing his blade, and Jenna went back to Catrona's side.

"You did not tell me about Piet," Jenna whispered.

"You did not ask," Catrona said.

"I did not know the questions."

"Then you deserved no answer."

Jenna nodded. Catrona had been her teacher, her guardian, her sister, and one of her many mothers at Selden Hame. But, Jenna suddenly realized, she had known little—*she had known nothing*—about Catrona. *And she had never asked.*

"Now, why have you told me nothing about this Longbow who calls you White Jenna and has loved you for five years?" Catrona asked.

"You did not ask," said Jenna. "Besides—there is nothing to tell."

"*Yet!*" Catrona laughed. Then her voice got strangely serious. "Did Amalda ever get a chance to explain to you the way of a woman with a man? Or did Mother Alta as part of her preparation for your mission? Though . . ." She made an explosive sound that was supposed to be a laugh but was much too bitter for one. "Though I would guess *that* one knows *aught* of it, as Piet would say. She loves only herself—and her dark sister. Perhaps I should tell you . . ." She glanced at Jenna.

Jenna colored. "I know what I need to know."

Nodding, Catrona said, "Yes—I judge you do. And the rest you can learn. But remember, sweet Jen, what they say: *Experience is rarely a gentle master.*"

The dust of the approaching rides so filled the air then, Jenna was forced to raise a hand to wipe her tearing eyes. When she could see again, there were fully a hundred dark horses milling outside the walls and occasionally pushing in through the broken gates. The smell of them was overwhelming.

Jenna saw a single gray horse in the crowd. If the king had been riding one, she thought Carum might be on the other. *Carum!* She began shoving her way toward the gray.

Using her shoulder, she pushed first one horse then another aside. As often she was pushed back by a large dark shoulder rump. *I shall be flattened for sure,* she thought. *I shall smell like a horse.* She wondered suddenly about her hair, about the clothes she had slept in for days, about the face that must have changed in the five years—*five years!*—since he had seen her. She thought about turning back, but the horses held her hostage to her first impulse.

And then the gray loomed before her. Putting a hand on its neck, she found that her hand was shaking. All around her men were dismounting and cursing pleasantly at one another. Suddenly, she did not dare look.

Only the man on the gray remained in his saddle. At last she raised her face to stare up at him. He was enormous, towering over her on the gray. Heavily bearded, with long black hair bound up in seven braids, he stared back. Each of the braids was tied off with a piece of crimson thread. A red and gold headband, smudged with dirt and blood, was pulled so tight around his forehead, the skin was taut below it. There was a deep gash over his right eye. As he looked at Jenna, his mouth twisted into a strange smile. It was then she noticed his hands were tied behind him

Starting to turn away, Jenna heard his harsh laugh.

"So," he said, "some of Alta's fighting sluts still live."

She paused, her hands growing icy, the palms wet. Drawing in three careful *lanti* breaths, she forced herself to move away from him without speaking. She would not draw sword against him. Whoever he was, he was injured. And bound. But her eyes were as wet as her palms. *With anger,* she reminded herself, *not sorrow or fear.* Blinded with the tears, she bumped into one of the men.

"I am sorry," she whispered.

"I am not."

The voice was deep, deeper than she remembered, as if time or pain had sanded it. He wore a vest without a shirt and his arms were tanned and well muscled. Around his neck, on a leather thong, was a ring with a crest. His head was helmless and his light brown hair, now almost shoulder length, was tangled from the ride. The lashes were as long as she remembered, so beautiful on the boy, even more compelling on the grown man. There was a faint scar running from his left eye that lent him a slightly wanton look. His eyes were as blue as speedwells. He was exactly as tall as she.

"Carum," she whispered, wondering that her heart had not stuttered in her breast.

"I said we would see one another again, my White Jenna."

"You said . . . a lot of things," Jenna reminded him. "Not all of them true."

"*I* have been true," he replied, "though I heard reports that you had died. Still I did not—*could not*—credit them."

"And *I* heard that you are not called Longbow for nothing." She bit her lip wishing she could recall the words.

For a moment he looked startled, then he grinned. "I shoot well, Jenna. That's all. *Stories feed the mind when the belly is not full.*"

She forgave neither of them for the exchange.

Carum reached out and touched a piece of hair that had stayed across her brow. "Do we meet to quarrel? We parted with a kiss."

"Much has happened since then," Jenna said. "I left you in safety to return to a Hame full of dead sisters."

"I know. I couldn't rest there having heard what news Pike had of the other Hames. I feared desperately for you yet I couldn't leave Pike with his wounds. But I told the others all about you. How you were the White One of prophecy, the Anna. How Ox and Hound had bowed before you. They were ready to love you for what you had become."

"And you?"

"I already loved you. For what you were."

"You knew nothing of what I was. Of what I am."

"I know everything I need to know, Jenna." He smiled shyly and she saw the boy behind the face of the man, yet she could not seem to stop picking quarrels.

"How can you know?"

"My heart knows. It knew from the first moment I saw you and cried you *merci*. I cry it again. Here. Now."

Jenna shook her head. "You have grown a fine tongue. Is that what a prince who shoots well says."

"Carum! You are safely returned." It was the king. He threw his arms around his brother. "I always worry, you know." He smiled at Jenna. "I do not forget he is my *baby* brother."

"Not only returned safely, Gorum, but having surprised and killed a company of the usurper's horse and captured the man on the gray." He turned to his own mount and untied something from the saddlebag. It was a helm. He held it out to his brother.

Jenna felt herself turn cold. She had seen a helm like that before, had held one in her hands, had thrown it into an open grave. She stared at the thing in Carum's hands. It was dark, covered wit a hairy hide. There were two ears standing stiff at the top and a snout and mouth with bloody fangs.

"The Bear!" Jenna whispered.

"By Alta's Hairs!" Gorum cried. "You have captured the bloody Bear. Well done, brother." He took the helm from Carum's hands and held it above his head. "*The Bear!*" he cried. "We have the Bear!"

The name echoed around the encampment, and the men who had been waiting joined the returning riders cheering the capture.

THE BALLAD

King Kalas and His Sons

King Kalas had four sons
And four sons had he,
And they rambled around
In the northern countrie.
And they rambled around
Without ever a care,
The Hound and the Bull
And the Cat and the Bear.

The Hound was a hunter,
The Hound was a spy,
The Hound could shoot down,
Any bird on the fly.
The Hound was out hunting
When brought down was he
Alone as he rambled
The northern countrie.

King Kalas had three sons,
And three sons had he,
And they rambled around
In the northern countrie.
And they rambled around
Without ever a care.
And they were the Bull
And the Cat and the Bear.

The Bull was a gorer
The Bull was knight,
And never a man who would

Run from a fight.
The Bull was out fighting
When brought down was he
Alone as he rambled
The northern countrie.

Kings Kalas had two sons,
And two sons had he,
And they rambled around
 In the northern countrie.
And they rambled around
Without ever a care.
And the names they were called
Were the Cat and the Bear.

The Cat was a shadow,
The Cat was a snare,
Sometimes you knew not
When the Cat was right there.
The Cat was out hiding
When brought down was he
Alone as he rambled
The northern countrie.

Kings Kalas had one son,
And one son had he,
And he rambled around
In the northern countrie.
And he rambled around
Without ever a care,
And the name he went under
Was Kalas' Bear.

The Bear was a bully,
The Bear was a brag,
His mouth was brimmed over
With bluster and swag.
The Bear was out boasting
When brought down was he

Alone as he rambled
The northern countrie.

King Kalas had no sons,
And no sons had he
To ramble around
In the northern countrie.
Though late in the evening
The ghosts are seen there
Of the Hound and the Bull
And the Cat and the Bear.

THE STORY

After the horses were unsaddled, brushed, and set out to graze, the men gathered for food in the Hame's roofless kitchen. Jenna heard bits and pieces of the story of the battle as she stood, tongue-tied, by Carum's side. He was so at ease with the men, trading banter and small slanders without hesitation, she wondered what had happened to the shy, scholarly boy she had known so briefly. *War had happened to him,* she thought suddenly. *And something more.* That the *something more* might be the passage of five years was a traitorous thought she pushed far away.

They had come upon the company of horse near a small town. "Karenton," Jenna had heard one man say. "Karen's Town," another. Surprise and numbers had been in their favor. The usurper's bloody men had never had a chance. Some of them had even begged to surrender, but no quarter had been given. Except for the Bear. Longbow had insisted that *he* would be delivered in chains to the feet of the king-in-exile.

When they spoke of the Bear, the men's mouths had been soiled with his name and deeds. They called him "Slaughterer of a Thousand Women," and "Butcher of Bertram's Rest," and yet even as they spoke of the horrors, Jenna could not help thinking that there was admiration as well in their voices. The details of his merciless killings seemed more like tales to frighten young children. She had walked deliberately over to the tree where he had been bound to see whether the sign of his bloodlust was imprinted upon his face.

One of his braids had unraveled into three kinked strands, but otherwise he looked as he had on his horse: big, hairy, leering, but no more a beast than others of the men milling around.

There were two guards standing by him, swords drawn.

"Best not get close," said one, wiping his nose with his sleeve.

"He's a tricker," said the other, the man with the scarred eye.

"He's bound," Jenna pointed out. "And what can he do to me with his hands and legs so prisoned?"

The Bear's head went back at that and he laughed a loud, roaring laugh. Then he turned to the first guard. "She wants to know what I can do without hands or legs? Do you want to tell her—or shall I?"

The guard slapped him hard with the back of his hand, so hard his lower lip split open and his mouth filled with blood.

"Do not speak to the White One that way," he said.

"The White One?"

"The Anna. Who made your brothers the Hound and the Bull bow low."

The Bear sucked on his lower lip until the bleeding stopped, then he stared at Jenna, grinning. His teeth were stained. "So, you are that girl, the one who lost her dolly at the Hound's grave. The one who lopped off the Bull's hand so he died a long, horrible death when the green took him. *That* girl. I will have something special for you, later."

This time the scarred-eye man slapped him. The Bear laughed again.

"I took no pleasure in the killings," said Jenna.

"Well—I do. And pleasure in other things as well."

If Jenna had hoped for forgiveness or understanding, she got none. Not from the Bear nor from the guards, who stared at her puzzled.

"Killing them two was a blessing," the man with the scarred eye pronounced.

"Death is an odd sort of blessing," Jenna said. "The old wisdom is right: *Kill once, mourn ever.*" She walked away.

The Bear's voice boomed after her. "We add, *Kill twice, mourn never!* I will have something *special* for you. Later. And you'll remember *it* ever, you will!"

She thought she heard the sound of yet another slap. And his laughter following. But she did not turn around.

Carum was standing with his brother, Piet, and Catrona, away from the knots of men recounting battles and bawdy tales. As Jenna headed toward them, Carum detached himself from his companions and met her halfway. She stopped and he stopped. Though inches apart, they did not touch.

"Jenna . . ." he began, hesitated, looked down.

"You said to me once that there are some people, I forget their names, who believe that love is the first word God memorized," Jenna whispered, conscious of the men all around them.

"The Carolians," he whispered back, still not looking at her.

"I thought about that. I tried to understand it. I *think* I understood it when you said it but I do not know what it means now."

Carum nodded and looked up. "So much time between us," he said.

"So much blood," she added.

"Is it gone?" His voice, while still strong, held a wisp of agony.

She reached out and touched a piece of hair that had strayed across his forehead, remembering his earlier touch. "You have lived the past five years, Carum Longbow. But I have not."

"What do you mean?"

"If I tell you, you will not believe me."

"Tell me. I will believe."

She spoke of the Grenna, the cave, the grove. She described Alta in her green and gold dress. She told him of the collar, the wristlet, and crown. All the while he shook his head, as if unable to credit it.

"I said you would not believe."

Reaching out, Carum took her hands in his. He twisted the priestess ring slowly around her little finger, then twined his fingers in hers. "We have a saying in my clan that *If you have no meat, eat bread.* Jenna, what you say is unbelievable. But I have no better explanation. You would not lie to me. You have been gone these five years, not a word of you but rumors and tales. You say you lived under the hill along with the Greenfolk and Alta. You say the five years were but a day and a night. Meat or bread. You offer me bread. What can I do but take it from your fingers." He held her hands against his chest and she could feel his heart beating under the leather vest.

"You are seventeen plus five years old. You have lived each year. I am thirteen plus five years, yet I feel thirteen still."

He leaned over and kissed her forehead. "*You* . . . you were never thirteen, Jenna. *You* are ageless. But I have the patience of a tree. I will wait."

"How long?"

"How long does a larch wait? How long does an oak?" He dropped her hands, but she could still feel the touch, as if his skin had fitted exactly over hers.

Side by side, they walked back to where the king, Piet, and Catrona waited.

The sun was low on the horizon, staining the sky with red. A small, cool wind puzzled around the broken walls of the compound, lifting dust and swirling it up and over their boots. From across the road, birds cried out their evening songs, decorating the deeper rumble of the men's voices.

Seeing Jenna, the boys and Petra came forward. They followed her, then stood in a circle, shoulder to shoulder while the king spoke to them in low, urgent tones.

"We have been waiting long for you—or something like you, Jenna. The men have fought hard, but we have been so alone."

"This is all there be to our army," Piet interrupted. "Good men. Brave. Loyal. None better. But they be all."

Catrona nodded her head, as if counting.

Jenna nodded, too, adding, "But what can we do? We are but six bodies more. Yet we are ready to help, if it means helping the sisters."

Piet cleared his throat as if preparing to speak, but it was the king who did the talking. "Already the men are speaking about you. The White One. The Anna. Who made the Bull and Hound bow low. They have recalled the old stories all afternoon."

"Good men they be," Piet added, "but not cautious in their beliefs."

"*You* do not believe I am the Anna," Jenna said, both relieved and a bit annoyed.

"*Belief is an old dog in a new collar,*" Piet said.

"There are the signs," Carum said, putting his hand up and counting them out on his fingers. "The three mothers, the white hair, the Bull and the Hound, the . . ."

"You do not need to convince *me*, little brother," the king said. "I know how much we need her. As does Piet. Our belief is not necessary here. But for the men . . ."

"If we had the Anna," Piet added, "think how many others would join us just to march by her side."

"But I am the ending before I am the beginning," Jenna pointed out. "Remember, that is in the story, too."

"We have already had enough endings," the king said, slapping his bad leg. "My father is dead. Murdered. My stepmother, too. My older brother killed foully in his bath, his blood mixing with the soapy water. So I am king now in truth. But that toad, Kalas, sits upon the throne, poisoning the very air he breathes with his piji breath, while we are forced to live in these ruins and make due with a rock for a throne." His voice roughened as he spoke, his eyes narrowing until they were smudges on his face.

Jenna thought once again that he looked like a wolf, or a dog let run too long in the woods.

"You have had a lot of endings, too," Carum reminded Jenna gently.

Remembering the women, their tunics and aprons stiff with blood, laid side by side in the ruined Hames, Jenna shuddered.

Gorum added, as an afterthought, "Yes, the senseless slaughter of the women in ten Hames. The rape of their daughters." He spoke the words slowly, articulating them with care, but his voice growing raspy again at the finish. "Is that ending enough for you, Anna?"

"Ten?" It was Catrona. "*Ten* Hames?" Her eyes stared unseeing.

"I do not know," Jenna whispered. "I do not know what is enough." She reached out and touched Catrona's shoulder.

Gorum smiled his wolfish smile. "It will be enough for these men. Enough so that they will gladly follow their king. And their queen. For that is in the story as well."

"No!" Carum cried, understanding before anyone else.

"There must be *some* sign," the king said slowly, as if talking to children, "some sign for the men here and now. What better sign—than a wedding. My father married a woman of the Dales. And so can I."

"Never!" Carum cried again. "You cannot think it."

"I *think* what is necessary, brother," Gorum said. "I think what is best for the kingdom. That is what a king does. That is what a king has to do. That is why you would make a terrible king and it is lucky for the Dales that I am still alive."

"Nevertheless, you shall not force her," Carum said.

"I shall do what must be done." Gorum was no longer smiling. "And so shall you. And so shall she."

For a moment they were all silent, so silent the bird-song seemed like a battle cry. Then Jenna spoke.

"Never! There is nothing here for you." She struck herself on the breast with a closed fist.

Gorum leaned toward her. "My dear child," he said softly, "the first lesson in kingship my father taught me was that *In the council of kings the heart has little to say.* There is nothing in here"—he struck himself on the chest—"for you either. I love you only through my little brother's eyes. But the people will love you, for your white hair and your history. Kingship is all symbols and signs."

"No!" Jenna said. "You cannot make me. If you do, you would be no better than the toad on the throne, for all your breath is sweeter. What good is kingship if the heart cannot speak aloud?"

"She is right," Catrona said. "And while you talked much to me this past hour, you said nothing about any marriage."

"The weddings of kings do not concern you, woman of the Hames," Gorum said, turning sharply toward her.

Before Catrona could answer, Petra had moved into the center of the circle, her voice pitched in the strange priestess tone. "As long as men speak to women thus, the ending is not yet reached, whether one Hame is gone. Or ten. Or all."

"Right!" Marek shouted.

"This is our fight as well as yours, Majesty," Catrona said. "Indeed, it was our fight first."

"First before Kalas stole the throne? Never!" exclaimed the king.

"First when Garuns be stealing our land," Sandor said, as surprised as any of them at his outburst.

Hand to his throat, Jareth strained to speak, but what warning he had to give remained unsaid.

"First or last," Carum said, his hand lightly resting on Jenna's shoulder, "our kingship will not be bought back with such a coin."

"*My* kingdom, brother. Not yours. Do not forget it. My kingdom until I die. And my heirs thereafter."

"I will not be the king's bride," Jenna said. "Nor give him heirs. No matter what the prophecy."

Petra intruded with the same strange oracular voice. "On the slant," she intoned. "Prophecy must always be read on the slant. We read it through slotted eyes or we read it wrong."

"Still, there must be a sign," the king said, trying to snatch back the momentum along with the power. "And this sign . . ."

"I know what sign the men be taking," Piet said suddenly. "It is not weddings that claim them." He wheeled from their circle and called out to the restless men. "Come. Come witness the White One's return."

They gathered uneasily, a great crowded circle around the smaller one.

Piet went over to one man, whispering hurriedly in his ear. The man nodded once and, unsmiling, pushed through the circle.

"Tell them," Piet said softly to the king. "Tell them who she is. They'll know her soon enow."

The king held up his hand and there was an immediate silence. Jenna thought it a miracle that so many men could keep so still.

"You have heard of Her," the king began. "And spoken of Her."

Without thinking, Jenna stood straighter, shoulders back, head high.

"She is the White One."

Petra broke in, her soft voice pitched loud enough so that all could hear her: "*And the prophet says a white babe with black eyes shall be born unto a virgin in the winter of the year. The ox in the field, the hound at the hearth, the bear in the cave, the cat in the tree, all, all shall bow before her, singing . . ."*

The men who were Garunian joined her, in the same singsong manner. *". . . Holy, holy, holiest of sisters, who is both black and white, both dark and light, your coming is the beginning and it is the end."*

Petra completed the speaking of the prophecy alone. *"Three times shall her mother die and three times shall she be orphaned and she shall be set apart that all shall know her."*

"She *is* white and dark," cried out a man from the crowd.

"And I heard her talk of three mothers," another shouted.

"And . . ." the king said, "it was her sword that slew the Hound, dropping him into a lonely grave, to rescue Prince Carum."

There was a moment of silence; then suddenly the men shouted as one, "The Hound!"

"And *her* sword cut off the hand of the Bull, Kalas' great pet ox, who later died wasting of the green illness," the king continued.

This time there was no silence. "The Bull!" they shouted back at him.

Just then the man Piet had sent away pushed through the crowd leading the lumbering, bound captive by the front of his shirt.

Piet whispered hurriedly in the king's ear and the king smiled slowly. Jenna did not like that smile.

"The prophecy says the ox and the hound, the bear and the cat, shall bow before her, singing . . ." The king held his hand high.

"Down. Down. Down," the men began to chant as Piet pushed the bound Bear to his knees before the king, pulling his shirt open so that the mat of black chest hair showed.

"Sing, you bastard," shouted the king. "Sing."

The Bear looked up and spit on the king's right hand, silencing the men. Piet drew his sword. The Bear grinned at him. Piet nodded twice, then turned and handed the sword to Jenna.

"Kill him. Kill him now, girl. Then they will follow ye for e'er and ye can marry who ye will!"

Jenna hefted the sword in both hands. It was twice as heavy as her own. She walked over to the kneeling man and stared at him.

"What do you say?" she whispered into his upturned face.

"I say you are Alta's bitch," he answered. "And no better than the dogs who follow when you are in heat. Strike now for you will not have the chance again."

She raised the sword above her head, drew in three *latani* breaths and began to count the hundred-chant to steady herself. Before ten were done, she felt again the strange lightening and she pulled out of her body to stare down at the scene below. There was the kneeling prisoner, laughing up into her face, with Piet, Carum and the king at his back, and the larger crowd of the king's ragtag army and her friends before him. Beyond, smelling the rising excitement, the hobbled horses stirred restlessly.

Jenna felt herself drawn toward the three men at the Bear's back, away from the heat of the crowd. Her translucent fingers reached down to touch them one at a time on the very center of the skull. Piet was a solid white flame, the colors unchanging. The king was a cylinder of blue-white ice that burned to the touch. And Carum . . .

She hesitated before touching Carum. She remembered how he had felt the other time she had let herself be pulled into him at Nill's Hame; how she had been drawn past pockets that were restful and pockets filled with a wild, alien heat. She had fled back into the air again, grateful to be unconsumed by his passions.

But she was stronger now. She reached out, touched him, and let herself fall.

He seemed deeper than before, with more pockets. There were the restful ones, the fretful ones, and ones filled with strange, engaging objects for which she had no name. The alien heat was there still, but somehow it did not frighten her now. Down and down, as if there was no end to him, as if she could explore forever.

Forever. She did not have forever. Her arms ached. She suddenly recalled the sword she was holding. Leaping into her body again, she stared down into the Bear's leering face.

"Kill him . . . kill him . . . kill him . . ." The chant was unrelenting. Jenna felt her arms shaking. Slowly she lowered the sword. When its point rested lightly on the Bear's chest, over the heart, she frowned.

The men were suddenly silent. The Bear's eyes were wide, preparing to look directly at his death. The entire clearing hushed, as if drawing a single breath, waiting.

"I . . . I cannot kill him this way," Jenna whispered. She took a step back and let the sword point drift slowly toward the ground.

The Bear's head went back. He roared and the roar turned into a laugh. Then he stared at Jenna. "*I* would not be so foolish, little bitch. What will your hunting pack do to you now?"

"They will do what they will," Jenna said to him quietly. "But if I am no better than you, then the ending is indeed at hand. With no beginning after." She dropped the sword and walked away.

Carum followed, the men parting to let them through. Only Jareth was smiling.

They walked silently past the broken walls, across the road, and into the trees. Jenna sagged against the thick trunk of an oak and bit her lower lip. Still she said nothing. When Carum reached out to touch her shoulder, she shrugged away his touch.

"No," she whispered.

"I understand."

"How can you understand when I do not understand myself."

"Jenna, you're thirteen going on forever. How could you possibly kill an unarmed man?"

"He is no man. He is a monster."

"He is a murderer. He is a slayer of women. He is a slaughterer of children. He is beyond saving." Carum's voice was steady. "But he is a man."

"And I am but a woman?"

"No—you are the Anna. You're better than he is. Than Gorum is. Than we all are."

"No, I am just me. Jenna. Jo-an-enna. A woman of the Hames. A woman of the Dales. Do not make me more than I am. My Mother Alta once called me a tree shading the little flowers—but I am *not* such a tree."

Carum smiled slowly at her. It was the face of the boy she remembered. "To me you are no tree, no flower, no goddess. You are Jenna. I kissed you once and I know. But for all of them you are *The Anna.* And when you put on Her mantle, you are more than *just* Jenna."

"Jenna could not kill a bound man whatever the Anna might do."

"Jen, the Anna is the best you are. And better. She wouldn't have slain him that way, either."

She leaned over and kissed him quickly on the mouth. "Thank you, Carum. Your brother is wrong: you *should* be king." Then, before he could make more than a slight sound, she turned and walked back across the road.

He had to run to catch up.

The large circle of men had broken into many smaller, knotted groups, arguing loudly. The bound prisoner was nowhere to be seen. Jenna found Catrona in the middle of one of the loudest circles, her hands moving rapidly as if they were a second and third argument.

"Catrona!" Jenna called.

The men in the circle turned and, seeing her, seemed to shrink away, leaving her face-to-face with Catrona.

"One thrust, Jenna," Catrona said. "One thrust and we would have had them. I taught you that stroke with this hand." She held up her right hand. "And now all that training for naught."

"You also taught me that in the *Book of Light* it is written that: *To kill is not to cure.* Surely that means killing a bound man."

"Do not quote the *Book* to me like some petty priestess," Catrona said. "The *Book* also says: *A stroke may save a limb.* Like any maunderings of holy writ, the *Book* can say whatever you want it to say." She was shaking with anger. "Jenna, you must think. *Think.* We need these men. We need this army. We need this king. I would not have you marry him to get his followers. But Piet was right. There was another, a better, way. And the Bear will be killed eventually—by this angry crowd, as like as not. If you had done it then, coldly and with great flourish, it would have fed the tale."

"*I* am no story," Jenna cried. "*I* am no tale. I am real. I feel. I hurt. I bleed. I cannot just kill without conscience."

"A warrior has no conscience until after the war is done," Catrona said.

Jenna put her face in her hands and wept.

Catrona turned away.

The moon rose, pale and thin, over the ruined Hame, climbing until it crowned the kitchen chimney. Jenna stood alone while throughout the encampment the arguments raged.

"You were right," came a voice from behind her.

Turning slowly, she saw Skada.

"And you were wrong," Skada said.

"How can I be both?"

"You *should* not have killed him, but you *could* have done it with words that would have still made them believe."

"What words?" Jenna asked.

"You might have said: *The Bull has bowed down, he need not die by my hand.*"

Jenna nodded. "And I could have said the moon is black, but I did not."

Nodding back, Skada laughed. "No, you did not. And now, my dear Anna, who is both dark"—she pointed to herself—"and light"—she pointed to Jenna—"you are in a fix."

"*We* are in a fix," Jenna amended.

"So now it is *we!* At last you are including me, sharing the burden, parceling out the guilt." Skada's mouth twisted with amusement.

"How can you laugh at such a time?"

"Jenna, there is always time to laugh. And part of you is laughing already, which is why I can. I am not other than you. I *am* you."

"Well, *I* do not feel like laughing," Jenna said miserably.

"Well, *I* do," said Skada. She put back her head and let out a delighted roar of laughter.

Unable to help herself, Jenna did the same.

"There," Skada said, "feel better?"

"Not really."

"Not at all?" Skada grinned.

"You are impossible," Jenna said, shaking her head.

Imitating her, Skada shook her own head. "No, I am not impossible. I am hungry. Let us find something to eat."

Arm in arm, they walked toward the kitchen.

Jareth stopped them halfway. He tried to talk with his hands, painstakingly spelling out his concerns. His frantic fingers wove complicated messages, but all Jenna could read was a warning.

"The cat . . ." Jenna said.

"The bull . . ." Skada added.

Jareth's eyes pleaded with them, his throat straining with the effort to speak.

"We will be careful," Jenna promised. "Do not worry. You have warned us well." When they were away from him, Jenna whispered, "I would cut that collar from his neck and let him speak."

"Whatever the consequences?" Skada asked.

"Whatever the consequences." Jenna's face was tight with anger. "How can Alta's magic be good when it punishes Her followers and Her enemies equally? Ten Hames gone. Jareth silenced. We are made murderers and monsters in Her name."

"And heroes," Skada said.

Jenna turned suddenly to face Skada. "Look around, sister. Look with care. Do you see any heroes here?"

They looked together. By the kitchen's chimney stood the king, a cup in his hand. He was staring sullenly into it as if he read some unhappy future there. By his side towered two guards in dirt brown tunics and torn trews. One was polishing his blade with his sleeve. Around the fires that blossomed throughout the compound were groups of men drinking and telling stories. Near the gate, a small fire illuminated the smudged faces of Petra and the boys. She was describing something with her hands. In a far corner, where the ruins of a staircase still ascended five steps into the air, sat Piet. On one side of him was Catrona, on the other Katri. They were both whispering into his ears. Smiling, he stretched his arms out and enfolded them both in his embrace. They stood together and walked off down the road in the moonlight.

"What does a hero look like?" Skada asked quietly. "Polished helm, fresh tunic, clean hair, and a mouth full of white teeth?"

"Not . . . not like this anyway," Jenna answered.

Skada shook her head. It was as if a breeze blew across Jenna's face. "You are wrong, sister. We are all heroes here."

THE TALE

There was once a tyrant of whom it was prophesied that he would be overthrown only when a hero who was not born of womankind, who neither rode nor walked, who bore neither pike nor sword, could conquer him.

Long reigned the tyrant and many were the men, women, and children who were swept away by the bloody winds of his wrath.

One day, in a small village, a child was born, ripped from her dead mother's womb by the midwife's knife, lifted out through the stomach, though not from the canal. She was put to suck at the teat of a she goat, raised with the goat's own kids.

As the child grew, so did the kids, one male and one female. And they played together as if they were all in the same family. They played butt-head and climb-hill and leap-o'er-me and other games beside. And the girl grew tall and beautiful despite her poor beginnings.

The years went by, and still the tyrant reigned. But he grew old and sour. He even longed for death. But the prophecy held true and there was no hero, not even the greatest swordsman, who could kill him—though many tried.

One day, the girl and her goats came into the capital city. As was her wont, she rode atop first one, then the other, her feet dragging along the ground.

The tyrant was out walking and saw the girl who, though astride, was not riding, for her feet were on the ground. He stopped her and asked, "Child, how was it you were born?"

"I was not born but taken from my dead mother."

"Ah," said the tyrant. "And how is it you ride?"

"I do not ride, for this is my brother. And this is my sister. It is but a game we play."

"Ah," said the tyrant. "You must marry me, for you are my destiny."

So they were wed and he died, smiling, on his wedding night, conquered by love. So the prophecy was true. And the sages say surely a hero is not easily known for who could tell that a girl astride two goats could be a hero when many men with swords were not.

THE STORY

"Jenna!" Carum found them as they stood.

Jenna turned and Skada, in perfect unison, turned with her.

Carum stared, first at one, then the other. "It is true, then. Not twins, but sister light and sister dark. I never dared credit it."

"It is true," they said together.

"All the time?"

"You spoke to me before alone," Jenna said.

"The moon," Skada added. "Or a good fire. And then I will appear."

Carum's face looked troubled, but he did not speak.

"Or a candle by the bed." Skada laughed. "Do not make your forehead like a pool rippled by a stone, Carum. Blow out the candle, and I am gone."

"I would not have you gone, sister," Jenna said, reaching out for Skada's hand.

"There are times when you will," Skada said in a low voice. "And times when you will not." She spoke softly to Carum. "I know her mind and I know her heart, for they are mine as well. Walk into the trees, young prince, where the branches overlace the forest floor. No moon can pierce that canopy nor can a dark sister appear by her light sister's side there."

"But you will still know . . ."

She shrugged. "Jenna is what she is. You loved her before. *And* kissed her knowing."

"I did not know."

"I am what I am," Jenna said. "And you did, too, know."

He shook his head unhappily, but at last admitted, "I knew. And I did not know."

And knowing? Skada left the question unasked but he heard it anyway.

"Come into the woods, Jenna," he whispered. "That we may talk. Alone."

Jenna looked at Skada who nodded. Jenna nodded back, slowly. Then the three walked across the road, the moonlight bright overhead. When they reached the tree-line, Skada began to tremble like a leaf in a breeze though the night was warm. There was a steady *peep-peep* of frogs from a nearby pond. Skada smiled tremulously as they walked into the woods and flickered like a shadow for a moment more, then was gone.

"Skada . . ." Jenna said, turning.

Carum's hand was on her forearm. "Don't go back," he begged. "Don't bring her back. Not right now."

They moved deeper into the dark, just the two of them. But they did not touch again.

Jenna had never talked so long and so intensely with anyone before. They rehearsed their entire lives to one another. Jenna told Carum about growing up in a Hame, and he in turn spoke movingly about life in the Garunian court. She remembered stories and songs which she shared with him; he parceled out tales from the Continent which had been reshaped by four hundred years in the Dales. They spoke about everything except the future. It was as if the past had to be dealt with thoroughly, first; and all the time they had *not* known each other accounted for. In the beginning they spoke hesitantly, offering each piece of the past as a gift that might be refused. But soon the words came tumbling too quickly; they interrupted each other over and over as one past overlapped the other.

"That happened to me, too," Jenna said as a memory of Carum's triggered her own.

"It was that way with me," Carum said, prodded by one of Jenna's tales.

It was as if their lives were suddenly braided together, there in the darkling woods so far from home.

In the middle of one of the Carum's stories about his father, a man who had not let kingship intrude upon his own hearth, there was a sudden great, horrible shouting from the ruins of the Hame, and the loud stampede of horses. Jenna and Carum stood as one, though they could make nothing of the words or the cries.

"Something awful . . ." Jenna began.

". . . has happened," Carum concluded, grabbing for her hand and yanking her to her feet. They ran quickly toward the sound.

Once they were on the road, the moon, almost down beyond the line of trees beyond the Hame, lent them Skada's faint presence.

"What is it?" Jenna called to her dark sister as they ran.

"I know no more than you," Skada answered, her voice a shadow.

Racing through the broken gates, they headed toward the angry boil of men centered by the hearth. Carum plowed a path through them, with Jenna and Skada in his wake.

"Is it the king?" Carum cried.

There were a number of answers, none of them clear.

"The Bear!" someone called.

"Got loose," said another.

"The bastard. He done 'er."

"Gone. Gone to tell." It was the first man.

"No, Henk's got 'em."

"B'aint true. Got his horse. Got the king, too."

"Nah."

"The king!" Carum grabbed the man's shoulder who had mentioned his brother. "Did he hurt him? Did he hurt Pike? Did he hurt the king?"

"Not he," the man said, shaking his head so fiercely long black hair covered his right eye. "Look!" He pointed.

The men moved apart and Jenna could see that the king and Petra were bending over something, but in the shadowy dark she could not tell what held them so. Then she saw it was Piet, sitting on the ground by the broken stair, cradling a body in his arms. When Jenna went over and spoke his name, he looked up. His mouth, with its uneven teeth, opened and closed like a fish; his sky-colored eyes were clouded over.

Jenna knelt on one side, Carum the other. In the darkened corner, Skada was gone. Putting her hand out to touch the body Piet held, Jenna was unable to say the name.

It was Carum who whispered it. "Catrona."

Catrona opened her eyes and tried to smile up at Jenna. There was blood on her tunic and blood trickling down her right arm. "We were so busy . . . we did not hear . . . did not see . . . I missed the thread, Jenna."

"What does she mean—*missed the thread?*" Carum asked.

"She taught me the Eye-Mind Game," Jenna whispered, remembering. "A game to train the senses. There was a thread. I saw it. She did not. It was all so long ago."

"Jenna . . . the thread . . ." Catrona struggled.

"Hush, girl, hush," Piet whispered. "Talking takes yer breath."

Jenna picked up Catrona's right hand and it lay in hers boneless and still.

She remembered when Catrona had first shown her how to thrust, with a sword that was much too heavy for her because Jenna had been too stubborn to set it down. *Your hand is your strength,* Catrona had said, *but it is the heart that strikes the blow.*

"What happened," Jenna whispered.

The king explained. "The Bear—*who should have been dead by your hand*—worked himself loose. He strangled the guards. Took their swords. When he went for a horse, he came upon Piet and his blanket companion, away from the rest. He thrust Catrona from behind, nearly skewering Piet as well. Then he was gone. Others have gone after him. I doubt they'll find him in the dark." He recited the facts as if reading them, little emotion in his voice.

Jenna stared at the ground. *Should have been dead by your hand.* He was right and there was no apology strong enough. She shook her head.

"What good are you to me, White Jenna? You have caused the death of three good fighters. No one will follow you now." His voice was low so that only those bending over could hear.

Catrona struggled to sit up, away from Piet's arms. "No, she *is* the one. On the slant. Listen to the priestess. On . . . the . . . slant." She fell back, exhausted by the effort.

"Oh, Catrona, my catkin, don't ye be going," Piet cried. He began to weep soundlessly.

"I will not let her die," Jenna said.

Piet stared up at her, fighting to control his sobs. "Ye is too late, girl. She are dead already."

"Do not sew the shroud before there is a corpse," Catrona said suddenly. "Do they not say that in the Dales?" She coughed and bright red blood frothed from her mouth.

"I will take her to Alta's grove. She will not die there," Jenna said. "Alta said I could bring one back. It will be Catrona." She slipped her arms under Catrona's body, trying to wrest her from Piet's grasp.

The movement caused Catrona to gasp and another frothing of blood bubbled out of her mouth. She swallowed it down. "Let me die here, Jenna, in Piet's arms. There are no shadows in Alta's grove. No shadows. I would not live forever without Katri. That is no life." She smiled and looked up into Piet's face. "You are alright, my Piet. For a man."

"I've always loved ye alone, girl. Ever since that first time. Your first. And mine. We were children then. I thought to find ye when the king was on the throne. To grow old with ye, my girl. To grow old . . ." He bent his back and whispered into her ear. She smiled again and closed her eyes. For a

moment Piet did not move, just sat with his mouth against Catrona's ear.
Then he put his cheek against hers. No one else moved.

At last he sat back up. "That's it, then. That's the end of it." His eyes
were dry but there was a dark furrow across his brow.

Petra bent over Catrona's body, putting her palm on Catrona's forehead.
She recited in a calm, low voice:

> *"In the name of Alta's cave,*
> *The dark and lonely grave*
> *And all who swing twixt*
> *Light and light,*
> *Great Alta*
> *Take this woman,*
> *Take this warrior,*
> *Take this sister*
> *Into your sight.*
> *Wrap her in your hair*
> *And cradled there*
> *Let her be a babe again."*

The men were silent until she finished the prayer, and then a low murmur of voices began: angry, passionate sounds. A few cursed Jenna out loud,
calling her a "bloodless bitch" and "Kalas' helpmeet."

Petra turned slowly from Catrona's body and stared around at them. She
raised her hands for silence and they were, unaccountably, still. "Fools," she
cried. "You are all fools. Do you not see what this means. Catrona herself
said it. You must read this death on the slant."

An anonymous voice called out, "What do you mean?"

"Who has died here? Catrona. A warrior of the Hames. Also known as
Cat. *Cat!* So the Cat *has* been slain, and all because the Anna chose not to
slay the Bear first."

"But it be the wrong Cat!" the man with the scarred eye said, pushing
his way to the front of the pack of men.

"And how do you know which Cat Alta meant?" Petra asked. "Or which
Cat the Garuns' own prophecy named?"

"But I thought . . ." he began.

"You must not *think* on prophecy. When it comes, you just know."
Petra's face was alive with her feelings. She raised her voice. "Catrona . . .

Cat herself reminded us before she died. She said: *She is the one*. The one who made the Hound and the Bull and now the Cat bow low."

"No!" Jenna cried, slamming her fist on the ground. "Catrona's death was not written." But her protest was swallowed up in the rising swell of the men's shouts.

"The Anna! The Anna! The Anna!" The chorus was loud and Petra, hands above her head, fists clenched, was leading it. "THE ANNA! THE ANNA! THE ANNA!"

No! Jenna thought. *Not for this. Do not accept me for this.* But the shouts went on.

"Men in mobs—so unpredictable. So easily swayed," whispered the king. He grinned and put his hands under Jenna's elbows and pulled her up to stand by his side. "One minute you are a villain, the next a saint. You need not be a king's bride, now, child. You *are* the Anna. *They* have said so. The Anna for now."

The Anna for this turning. Will-less, she stood beside him as the chants continued.

"ANNA! ANNA! ANNA!"

The horizon behind them was stained with first light. The birds, unable to compete with the cries of men, had taken flight and the sky was peppered with them. Even Carum joined the shouting chorus that echoed back and forth across the ruined walls. Only Jareth, who could make no sound, and Piet, who was still holding Catrona's body against his chest, were still.

THE BALLAD

Death of the Cat

The trees were growing high
And the wind was in the west
When a hunter aimed his arrow
Into the Cat's broad chest.
And she died, she died
Against her lover's breast
And we laid her in the earth
So long and narrow.

It was early, so early
In the graying of the morn,
When we sang of the days
Before the Cat was born.
And how from her mother
She was so swiftly torn,
As we laid her in the earth
So long and narrow.

So, come all ye young fighting men
And listen unto me,
Do not place your affections
Upon a girl so free
For she'll take the mortal wound
Another meant for thee,
And you'll lay her in the earth
So long and narrow.

THE STORY

They buried the two guards by the broken gates, but Jenna and Petra insisted that Catrona's body had to lie in state between two great fires until they could find the Hame's burial cave. Piet agreed. When the second fire was lit, Katri's body appeared by Catrona's side and Marek, who had not wept before, suddenly broke into loud, embarrassing sobs which even his brother could not stop.

By evening the boys had found the cave, and they accompanied Jenna and Petra and Carum who carried Catrona's body up on a wooden bier. The king and Piet stayed behind, drinking toasts to the dead warriors with the rest of the men.

"Toasts to Lord Cres, the God of Fine Battles," Carum explained as they trudged up the hill with their bitter burden.

Remembering what he had once told her about those toasts, Jenna added, "May you drink his strong wines and eat his meat forever."

"And throw the bones over your shoulder for the Dogs of War," Carum ended.

Petra shivered. "What a horrible prayer."

"Is it any wonder I prefer none," Carum said.

They placed the bier before the entrance to the cave, and Jenna went ahead to light torches in the wall. The cave was cool and dry and there were many shrouded bodies lying about. She had to be careful where she stepped. When she lit the great torches, the bodies of the dark sisters in their careful wrappings appeared, crowding the cave further.

Leaving the cavern, she took a deep breath. The shrouded bones of the dead sisters had not frightened her. She had been to burials in her own Hame and she knew that the bodies were just the cast-off homes of the women who now lived, suckled against Alta's breast. But those were just bones and what lay at her feet in its bier, wrapped tightly in a torn shirt and blanket, was Catrona: her sister, her teacher, her friend. And the victim of Jenna's conscience.

Kneeling, Jenna put her hand on the corpse's breast. "I swear to you, Cat, the Bear will know my vengeance. I swear to you, another Cat shall die as well. That may or may not be written in any prophecy, but it is written clearly on my heart."

She stood. "Petra and I alone will take her into the cave. It is a holy place and a holy time."

"We understand," Carum said.

The other boys nodded.

Jenna picked up Catrona's body and, with Petra following, went in.

When they left again, it was dark. There was no moon.

They rode out of the ruined Hame at first light, a silent army. Petra rode Catrona's horse, which left only Marek and Sandor doubled up, though they did not seem to mind.

The king, Carum, and Piet rode at the head of the troop, but Jenna refused a place at the front. Shaking her head, she guided Duty to the middle of the pack. The men smiled when she rode among them, thinking she did it for love, never guessing she did it in order to push away the memory of Catrona's lifeless hand in hers.

One thrust, Jenna. She heard Catrona's voice at every turning. *One thrust . . . and now all that training for naught.* Her face was grim with the memory. She took Catrona's death as the death of her own innocence. What did it matter that she had already killed one man, maimed another in the heat of battle? What did it matter that she had buried a hundred dead sisters? It was *this* death that gnawed and fretted her. She felt herself growing old, the years like a cold river rushing past, and she unable to stop the flow.

Jenna spoke to no one as they rode relentlessly down the road, but her mind rehearsed what had been. *One thrust . . . one thrust*, dead Catrona continued to rebuke. *One thrust.*

As they galloped, Jenna flexed her right hand as if feeling the sword again, pommel tight against her palm. Her fingers retained the weight of Piet's heavy blade. She longed to take the moment back, thrusting surely, finally, into the Bear's burly chest. What satisfaction it would bring her now, the slipping of the sharp edges through his flesh, past bone, to strike at last the bloody, pulsing heart. *One thrust.* She could feel his heart's blood spurt up the sword to her wrist, run along the blue branchings of her veins, race past the crook of elbow, across the muscles of her forearm, and snake under her right breast to lodge in her own ready heart.

Lifting her arm at the thought, she watched, fascinated, as if she could actually see the Bear's blood traveling along the route of her arm, as if she felt the jolt of it entering her heart.

She dropped her arm to her side. *One thrust.* Yet it was not in her. She was not such a killer. Even to bring Catrona back she would not kill a bound man. She *could* not. The Anna *could* not. And she *was* the Anna. There was no question of that now. It was not prophecy that told her. Nor Carum's impassioned belief. Nor Alta's soft persuasions in the Grenna's grove. Nor the king's wily importunings. Nor all the shoutings of the men. It was simply this: the blood running from hand to heart rejected the wild hatred of the Bear and his brothers. She *was* the Anna. For *this* time and *this* turning and *this* now.

Jenna urged Duty forward. The other horsemen parted to let her through and she galloped to the lead of the riders, taking her place between the king and Carum, only slightly ahead.

THE MYTH

Then Great Alta drew up the dead warriors with the ladders of her hair, dark warrior by the golden hair, light warrior by the black. She set them to her breast, saying, "You are my own dear babes, you are my own sweet flesh, you are now my own bright companions."

BOOK FOUR

Gender Wars

THE MYTH

Then Great Alta struck the light sister on both cheeks, first one and then the other, for the deaths she had caused. Then she struck her on the back for the deaths she had not caused. Then she faced her toward the sun saying, "Now you must ride long and ride hard and ride well till you start again what has been ended here." She set the light sister upon a great gray horse and blew a wind at the light sister's back that she might have speed on her journey and no memory of sorrow.

THE LEGEND

It was in Altenland, in a village called The High Crossing, that this story was found. It was told to Jenny Bardling by an old cook woman known only as Mother Comfort.

"My great aunt, that would be my mother's mother's sister, was a fighter. Fought in the army as blanket companion to the last of the great mountain warrior women, the one that was called Sister Light. She was almost six feet tall, my great aunt said, with long white braids—not gray, mind—and she wore them tied up on the top of her head. Her crown like. She kept an extra dirk there and, when quiet was needed, would strangle her foe with them braids. She fought like a Fog Demon, all silence and whirling.

" 'Twas known no one could best her in battle for she carried a great leathern pack on her back and in it was Sister Dark, a shadow who looked just like her but twice as big. Whenever Sister Light was losing—not often, mind—she would reach into that pack on her back and set the shadow fighter free. Sister Dark could move faster than the eye could see and quiet as grass growing. They used to say of her:

> *Deep as a spell*
> *Cold as a well*

> *Hard as a hate*
> *Brutal as fate.*

That was Sister Dark.

"Of course she only used that shadow when she was desperate because using it ate away at her, from the inside out. Like all such magicks. From the inside out. My great aunt never saw it proper, mind you. No one did. But everyone knew of Sister Dark. They did.

"Well, Sister Light died at last, in a big fight, a month long it was and the sun refusing to shine all that time. And where is a shadow without the sun, mind. It could only creep out of that pack with the sun bright overhead. Did I forget to tell you that?

"After the month was gone, someone found that pack, resting on the bleached bones that had been Sister Light. Long-boned she was, too, my great aunt said. That someone opened the pack, searching for treasure to be sure, and out crept the shadow. She looked around, eyes dark and nothing to be read there but hate. The land was blasted; what had been green was dust. And Sister Light nowt but bones, mind. She put back her head and howled, a sound they say still heard on that desolate plain.

"My great aunt told me—afore she died—that Sister Dark can still be seen, sometimes, when the sun beats down full over the land. Looking for her mate, maybe. Looking for someone else to carry her. Someone she can fight for, someone she can eat away at.

"You have to be careful, up there on the high moors. Especially in the mid of the day. That's where the saying Never mate a shadow comes. They'll eat away at you if they can."

THE STORY

The first day of long riding tired them all except for Jenna who rode with Catrona's restless voice in her ear. The road passed through small woods of birch and alder alternating with large stands of old oak, across the tops of gently rolling grassy hills, and over two streams. The fords had deeper pools on either side that hinted at trout stoking their fins behind dark granite boulders, but the king did not let them stop. As there was no wind to whisk away the dust of their riding, behind them, for a long way, their passage could be read as a gray sentence up against the blue of the sky. When they stopped at last for the sake of the weary horses and to cook a quick meal over small fires, the king sent three scouts on ahead.

"Catrona would have rested earlier," Jenna murmured to Petra and the boys.

"And be sending scouts afore time," Marek added, shaking his head. Clearly he thought little of the king's woodsense, his own so newly developed.

But an hour later, the three men sent out returned with little to warn against. The road ahead, they said, was clear of Kalas' men, the small farm holdings undisturbed by soldiers or rumor of war. In fact, one shepherd, newly returned from the great market town of New Steading—a good day's ride to the north—reported to them that even the usual company of king's troop had departed before he had left there. If the Bear had gotten back to his master, he surely had not ridden this way, or else he had not mustered them out with his story.

The king thanked them with a drink from his own leathern flask and an embrace that Jenna noticed came strictly from his arms. His eyes and mouth were not smiling. Returning to the smaller circle that consisted of Jenna, Carum, Piet, Petra, and the boys, the king pursed his lips.

"I expect Kalas will wait, choosing the Vale of Cres for a final battle," he said. "It's the gateway to the castle and there his numbers could overwhelm us on the field." He stood with his hands clasped behind him, a line furrowing his brow. "He will wait knowing that if we are to win anything, we must go to him. He will not expend himself over the whole of the Dales."

Piet nodded. He was squatting before a small cook-fire, staring into the flames. He had not eaten, but simply looked into the fire as if discovering some wisdom there.

"He would be a fool to wait so long for us," Carum said, running his fingers through his hair. "And a fool to give us time to gather strength. We might be years coming to meet him."

"I agree," Jenna said. "Surely he will strike at us when he knows he has superior numbers. He has nothing to gain by letting us find more women and men for the fight. He is no fool."

"I agree he is no fool," said the king. "Still, he believes that a troop of his horse can beat any numbers of my men. My untrained Dales men."

"But you just beat the Bear with that untrained force . . ." Petra began.

"And *that*, my dear, is why we are racing so fast, stopping only to keep the men and horses from revolting—or dying. To gather as much brute strength and numbers as we can while we have our lure still fresh and enticing," said the king.

"The lure?" Sandor asked.

"The Anna, my young friend," said the king, gesturing casually at her. "The Anna!"

"Me!" Jenna said at the same time, her right fist over her heart.

"And then we be marching onto the Vale?" asked Marek, eager for the fight now.

"No!" Piet said. For the first time he stood and looked at them all.

"Piet is right," the king said smoothly. "We will go in a great circle around the Vale, recruiting more and more to the Anna's banner. And when we are large enough and strong enough, we will march on Kalas from all sides, a great bloody circle of us, like a noose, tightening around his ugly neck." He closed his fingers slowly into a fist.

"And while we bide our time, Kalas kills more women and fires the rest of the Hames." Jenna's voice was as bitter as if Catrona spoke from her mouth. "We cannot wait. We must not wait."

"By saving a few, we would lose the many," the king warned. "You are too young to understand it."

"I am near as old as you," Jenna retorted.

"Not by ten years—or a hundred," the king replied. "War means that some must die that others might live. A king is no certain age, for he is made up of all those hard judgments. The king—and not his wife or his brother or his war chief or his friend. The decision is mine alone. We ride north to New Steading to start our recruitment."

Jareth grabbed Gorum's arm, spinning him halfway around and Jenna had to hold onto Piet's arm to keep him from striking the boy. Strangled sounds came from Jareth's throat, more animallike than man. When it was clear no one understood, he tried to beat that same message on the king's sleeve with angry fingers.

"He knows something," Jenna whispered to Piet. "We must listen to him."

"He says nothing," Piet said, shrugging away from her grasp.

The king brushed Jareth away from him. "He knows nothing and says less."

"He knows we cannot let more die just for the sake of an argument." Carum's voice was deep with passion.

Smiling the sly smile Jenna had come to fear, Gorum said, "My brother, there is no argument. There is only the king's decision. You have studied too many old texts. I have studied men's hearts. We will go from town to town gathering a great army to us and word of it will reach Kalas. He will try and warn us off by his killings. They will become even more brutal. He will be sure to let us know of them. But with every ugly act, he will win us more men to the Anna's side. And when we can match him man for man . . ."

Carum stared at his brother. "Then you do not care how many more die or how horribly?"

"I welcome it. Does that shock you, brother?" Now the king looked grim. "They say in the Dales, Longbow, that *You cannot cross the river without getting your feet wet.*"

"You are no better than Kalas," Petra said. She turned away and stared at the little groups of men chatting quietly together all down the road.

"I am much better than Kalas, because I do what I do for the right. He is only for himself. I am for my people." The king's voice was very quiet. "*My* people, not his."

Carum cleared his throat. "Gorum, in those texts you so despise, there are many stories in which a small force beats a large one by cunning and guile. Do not forget cunning and guile and rely only on the gathering of brute strength. Do not forget the tale of the mouse and the cat my mother told us the day that bully Barnoo bloodied your nose."

The king smiled again. "Barnoo is dead."

"And Jenna killed him."

"And *I* am alive. *I* am the one with cunning and guile, dear brother, not you. Do not forget it. Such stories of the little overcoming the great are only wishes devised by a conquered people. Your mother was of the Dales. You are half her blood. I am wholly Garun."

"You are . . ." Carum began angrily.

"No, brother, *you* are . . . an open book. I have made *those* books my chiefest study. When I am returned to the throne, you can be my court philosopher, my teller of tales, my fool, dispensing scholarly wisdom. Then you can remind me of the stories your Dalian mother told us and the stories in your pretty books, all interlined with pictures of pussies and mice. But *now* we are soldiers. The stories we want to hear are of our great victories." He patted Carum on the shoulder as one would a scolded pet or a small child. Then he turned and called out to his men: "Mount up. Mount up. We ride to New Steading where we shall show them the Anna." He waved his right hand.

"THE ANNA! THE ANNA!" The call came back to him, continuing under the orchestration of his uplifted arm until he was satisfied. Then he

nodded at them, turned and winked at Carum as if to underline his posses-
sion of the men, and dropped his arm down with a decisive chop. The men
all mounted.

The last one up was Carum, his rage barely checked. Jenna pulled her
horse's head around and urged it toward him with her knees.

"He is right about one thing, you know," she whispered. "Your face is a
clean slate upon which all your thoughts are writ large."

"I am useless to him," Carum whispered back miserably. "And he lets
everyone know it. Even you."

"No, you are right and he is turning now, even as we watch, into as much
of a callous monster as the toad on the throne. But you must tell me of that
story."

"What story?"

She reached out and touched his horse's neck, the skin silken under her
fingers. "The one about the mouse and the cat. If a small force can indeed
overcome a great one, it would comfort me to know how before I try."

He smiled at her slowly. "Before *we* try."

Stroking the horse's neck, she waited.

Carum told her the tale in a few short sentences and when she nodded in
understanding, he sent his horse forward to the front of the line with a
swift, silent, energetic kick.

The next day, close to evening, they rode into New Steading from the
south. It was market day and the stalls were still open, fruits and breads and
silks displayed one next to the other without any discernible order. The
cobbled streets, crowded with buyers, were abuzz with the chants and cries
of traders. Even above the sound of the horses, Jenna could hear the strange
babble of bargains: *Fresh haddock, fresh . . . bread HOT from the . . .
blood root newly dug . . . buy my weave, buy my bright weavings . . .*

Never having been in such a crowd before, she turned uneasily to stare
back at her friends. Petra's eyes were wide with amazement. Beside her
Marek and Sandor were openly gawking and pointing. Only Jareth seemed
contained, as if his own silence cocooned him.

They rode in a disciplined line through the main street. Though a few
glanced sideways down the twisting narrow ways where tiers of narrow
houses leaned familiarly across the alleys, not a one dared straggle. The king
was pleased: pleased with the crowds, pleased with his men, pleased with
the ease of his entry. His face showed it.

At the front of the line of riders, Duty suddenly began a high prancing
which Jenna could not control. It was as if the horse, faced with an appre-

ciative audience, remembered some previous training. Jenna nearly lost her seat at the first sideward motion. She grabbed the reins, jerking hard. This pulled Duty's head in and the horse arched her neck until her chin actually touched against her burly chest. Jenna pressed inward with knees and thighs, thinking that any harder and they would go straight through the horse's sides. Instead, it turned out to be a special signal. In response, Duty raised her own knees in an even higher strut.

Jenna felt a fool, rolling from side to side on the horse's broad back before the delighted crowd. But the market-goers cheered the horse's tricks and the king grinned broadly. No one seemed to think it foolish or dangerous, except for Jenna who clung grimly to the reins, keeping her thighs so hard against Duty, they trembled with the effort.

All the way along the main street Duty danced with Jenna fighting to keep both her seat and her dignity. Behind her, the riders began their chant of her name: "THE ANNA! THE ANNA! THE ANNA!" the sound of it bouncing crazily off the stone facades of the houses. Jenna could hardly believe so much sound could come from a simple echo until she realized there were people leaning out of the windows of the houses, waving their hands and calling back to the riders.

"THE ANNA! THE ANNA! THE ANNA!"

It was not clear that they knew what they were shouting, or if indeed they were shouting any distinguishable name. But the sound of it was deafening and some of the horses were made nervous by it, shying away or houghing uneasily through their noses. Their riders sawed at the reins and one or two actually used their whips, which further agitated the mounts. Only Duty seemed to enjoy the scene, actually playing up to the crowds.

The main street ended at wide stone steps that led up to a palatial building. Duty set her front feet on the first step, stopping suddenly, nearly flinging Jenna over her head. Jenna answered by giving a last, hard, angry pull on the reins, wrenching Duty's head up. The horse whinnied loudly, reared, and kicked her front legs in the air. Jenna hung on. An admiring cheer rose from the children who had scattered along the steps to watch.

When Duty settled down again, Jenna dismounted, shaken, and handed the reins to one eager child. Her legs ached and, for a moment, she was afraid she might not be able to stand. Then she bit her lip, almost drawing blood, and forced herself to face the gathering crowd.

The king dismounted as well, and when he did there were one or two who recognized him immediately despite the worn and tattered clothes.

"It's the old king's son," someone cried out.

"The new king, then," an enormous woman said.

"Gorum!" The name was spoken first by a black-haired young man, taken up quickly two and three times by his friends.

"The king's Pike," one added.

Word of him paced the arrival of more New Steadingers, and soon the square was packed tight with townsfolk, most of whom now swore they had known the king at once.

Gorum let the tension build and build, and Jenna had to admire how he acknowledged it, nodding slowly and turning slowly so that all could get a glimpse of him. As the crowd grew, he moved up one step at a time, always careful to keep Jenna on his right hand, Carum on his left, Piet to guard the back; until at last they commanded the very top stairs before the palace, with his men ranging down the sides like an inverted letter V, the king and Jenna at the point. Jenna wondered if Gorum and his men had long planned such a maneuver, for they moved with such precision, or if kings were just born knowing how to do such things. She glanced across at Carum who just shook his head twice but said nothing.

The king raised his hands and everyone quieted; not all at once but in a kind of ripple, from the point of the V downward. When total silence had been achieved, he began to speak, with a grand enunciation, so different from his regular speech.

"You know me, my good people."

They filled the sudden silence with his title: "THE KING! THE KING!"

He let the echo fade, then smiled. "Not King Kalas. Not that usurping, murdering, piji-eating toad. Not he."

They laughed and applauded each phrase.

"I am the true-born king, Gorum, son of Ordrum and the lady Jo-el-ean." He waited for their approving murmur before continuing. "The king thrust off a throne made vacant by the untimely deaths of my poor murdered father and his wife, your sister of the Dales."

As if this were the very first time they had heard of the murders, the people groaned. Gorum let the groan swell up, then die away, a falling drift of sound. Just before the last of it was gone, he added, "And the cowardly killing of my brother, the saintly Jorum, who was next in line to be king."

They moaned again on cue. Jenna noticed Carum shaking his head slightly, though whether it was at the king's crafty manipulations or the naming of his older brother as a saint, she could not guess.

"But I am here for you, good folk. And as you can see, I am not alone." This time when he waited there was no vocal reaction at all, but the silence was filled with anticipation. Jenna thought he looked pleased. She was not sure why.

"You see Her," he said suddenly. "You know Her. You have already named Her." He held out his right hand to Jenna.

The child holding Duty's reins cried out in a high, piercing voice that carried around the crowded square: "The White One."

Caught up in the mummery of the moment, Jenna suddenly put her hand into the king's, moving closer to him than she had done before. His palm was ice-cold, his fingers iron-strong. Realizing what she had just done, she tried to pull her hand away, but he prisoned it in his. She could not get loose without making an ugly scene, so she stood still, her face a mask.

"Yes," the king continued smoothly as if Jenna's hand in his were easily held, "She is the White One, good folk. The one we have awaited. She was born of three mothers and all of them dead. She killed the Hound to save my brother Carum." He pointed with his left hand at Carum, but Carum neither moved nor nodded and Jenna felt grateful for that show of quiet dignity.

"And she slew the Bull to save her own sister. We have his ring as proof." He opened his left hand as if waiting for Carum to drop the ring in. When Carum did not move, the king hesitated for only a second, then dropped Jenna's hand with a flourish and strode over to his brother. He reached for Carum's neck, fishing up the leather thong around it. At the thong's end was a heavy crested ring. Jenna suddenly recalled the severed hand that had last worn it. Dangling the ring before the crowd, the king smiled. The watching people began to cheer.

Dropping the ring against Carum's chest, the king turned. He let the cheering continue for a long moment and then, with a savage slicing motion of his hand, cut them off.

"And because of the White One, a woman named Cat was killed just two days past." He waited for the challenge he knew would come.

" 'Tis the wrong Cat," the enormous woman called out. "The Cat that was meant still lives. And drinks his milk from Kalas' hand."

Slowly the king turned toward her, his manner courteous but firm. "And do *you,* my good woman, know how to read prophecy? Are you a Garunian priest? Or a priestess of Alta's Hames?"

She looked back at him, discomforted. "I know what I know," she mumbled.

"Then know this as well, woman, prophecy cannot be read straight on. It must be read *on the slant!*" He roared the last so that all could hear. Then he walked down three steps, leaving Jenna and Carum behind him, passing grim-faced Piet, so that he was in the very middle of the V, the center of all eyes.

"The prophecy says but *Cat.* Not *this* Cat nor *that* Cat. But *CAT!* And Cat was killed. That makes three." He held up his hand, counting slowly on his fingers. "One, the Hound. Two, the Bull. Three, the Cat. All killed by the White One, as is writ in prophecy, the Anna for whom we have so long waited. And we have but one more, the Bear, to go and the prophecy will be fulfilled. For She is the one who signals the end of the false reign, the beginning of the new. The Anna." He flung his right hand back and pointed up at Jenna.

"What you call new was once old," the enormous woman whispered, but it was clear any argument she had had already met defeat. Trying one last time, speaking loudly enough so that her nearest neighbors could hear, she added, "Besides girls dressing like men, playing at war . . . taint . . . taint natural. We've all said it." But her voice was drowned out by the cheers, first of the children, then the grown men and women. And mixed in with those cheers were the names of the king, the Anna, and Carum all intertwined.

THE SONG

The Heart and the Crown

They rode into town
On the thirteenth of Spring.
She gave him her hand
And he gave her his ring.
She gave him her heart
And he gave her his crown,
But they never, no never
Went down derry down derry down.

Her horse was pure white
And his horse was a gray.
She wanted to go

But he asked her to stay.
She gave him her heart
And he gave her his crown,
But they never, no never
Went down derry down derry down.

Her eyes were pure black
And his eyes were so blue.
She wanted him strong
And he wanted her true.
She gave him her heart
And he gave her his crown
But they never, no never
Went down derry down derry down.

Come all ye fair maidens,
And listen to me,
If you want your young man
To be strong and free,
Just give him your heart
And he'll give you his crown
Just as long as you never
Go down derry down derry down.

THE STORY

They had supper in the open atrium of the great town hall with the members of the New Steading council. It was a tremendous banquet, more impressive, Jenna thought, because it had been put together so quickly by the townfolk.

Though she was apprehensive, Jenna discovered that no one really expected her to speak. In fact, her presence at the dinner made most of the New Steadingers uncomfortable and few sought her out. However, most tracked her movements around the tables with cautious, fascinated eyes. It was as if they planned to commit every detail of her dinner to memory, making it into ballads and stories after.

Jenna commented wryly to Petra, "And will they sing about *The Day the Anna Ate Apples* or rather *How the White One Washed Her Fingers?*" Laughing, Petra made up an instant rhyme.

> *"When Jenna ate apples,*
> *Her teeth crunched the pips,*
> *She stuck bits of bread*
> *Into melted cheese dips,*
> *She ate stalks of celery,*
> *Drank cups of tea*
> *And after went looking*
> *For somewhere to . . ."*

"Enough," Jenna whispered. "Enough." She put her hand over her mouth to keep from laughing aloud. But when she sat down at the head of the table, beside the king, she found she had no appetite. The near-unseating by Duty's clever prancing, the lingering feel of Gorum's cold hand, the memory of Catrona's burial, the staring of the New Steading strangers, all conspired to kill what hunger she had had. Even though they put a plate before her, she ate nothing, simply pushing the bits of vegetable and browned meats around with her knife.

The watching councillors saw that she did not eat and a few even wondered aloud at it.

The king said, as if under his breath but loud enough for those closest to hear, "The gods rarely eat of our food."

His words passed from breath to breath around the table, as he knew they would. Some even believed them.

Petra heard, but did not pass on the king's message. She could hardly keep from laughing and mouthed at Jenna: *"and after went looking . . ."*

Jenna lowered her eyes to the table and did not notice Petra tucking a piece of chicken breast, a large slice of cornmeal bread, and a spring leek into her napkin. But Jareth sitting beside her did, and he added several white mushrooms and a twist of brown bread to Petra's hoard.

After the dinner, the king spoke again, urging the councillors to conscript men for his army. "To fight the toad," he said.

They needed little urging, especially sitting as they did under the eye of the Anna and with seven or eight hearty toasts of the dark red wine behind them. They even signed a paper promising him two hundred young men and their weapons. He kissed them each on the right cheek for such largesse and promised that they and New Steading would be remembered.

Jenna waited until the writing was done. But during the congratulations, she stood. The moment she was up, all other movement ceased. Even the serving girls, weighted down with platters, stopped in mid-stride. Jenna wondered what she might say to them. The king had such ease with words, and she had none. She suddenly envied him. Opening her mouth to give at least some thanks, she found she had nothing to say, so she closed her mouth abruptly so she might not sound stupid in the attempt.

At the other end of the long table, Carum leaped to his feet. "We have had a long riding," he said. "And another to come in the morning. Even an avatar of the Goddess must rest. Human flesh, though it be just the clothing of a great spirit, tires." He walked to Jenna's end of the table and took her hand in his. Slowly he raised it to his mouth and set his lips formally on her knuckles. *His* hand and mouth were warm.

Jenna smiled. Then slowly, gracefully, she withdrew her hand. He let it slip easily through his fingers.

"Thank you," she said simply to the New Steadingers. "For everything." Then she nodded at the king, at Piet, and Petra with the boys, and turned. Carum followed her to the door.

"Don't worry," he whispered. "I'm right behind you."

They fumbled the first turn in the dark hall and had to backtrack.

"This is worse than the Hame," Carum grumbled.

Remembering which Hame and what she had found there on her return, Jenna said nothing. None of the doors off the hall looked familiar. *Any one of them would do,* she thought. All she wanted was to be away from the oppression of so many staring eyes.

"That one!" she said, suddenly pointing.

They went through the door and found themselves in a large room. A little light filtered in through corbeled windows that looked out onto the great stone stairs. Jenna realized they were in some sort of council room for there was a wooden table set about by heavy wooden chairs. Along the sides of the room were more chairs and several couches. She sat down on the nearest couch, drew in a deep breath, and sighed.

"What would I do without you, Carum?"

"I hope you never have to," he answered quickly.

"Do not play at word games with me. I am not one of your Garunian followers nor a peddler from New Steading."

"I don't play games with you, Jenna."

"All you Garunians play games. Your brother worst of all."

"And you don't?" His usually gentle voice was sharp.

"No. Never."

"Then can you tell me what game it was you were *not* playing when you went to my brother this evening?"

She looked up. He was only a dark shadow in the room looming over her. She could not see his face. "I did not go to him," she protested, feeling again that cold hand under hers, the iron grip of his fingers.

"I saw you."

"He pulled me. He would not let me go."

"You slipped your hand out of mine easily enough just now in the dining room."

"*You* let me go. *You* did not force me."

"I would *never* force you."

"Then what are we arguing about?" She was truly puzzled. Recalling something he had said the weeks, the months—the years—ago when they had met, she suddenly understood. "You are jealous. That is what it is. Jealous." She expected him to deny it.

He sat down beside her on the couch. "I am. I admit it. Horribly jealous." His voice was once again soft.

"And what about that oak?" She laughed. "What about that larch? Are waiting trees jealous?"

He laughed back. "Of every passing wind. Of every flying bird. Of every squirrel on a branch and every fox in its bole. Of anything capable of moving toward you."

She put her hand out blindly in the dark and found his face. She could feel, even without seeing it, that his brow was ridged; he was wearing that furrowed look he got when he was thinking. She smoothed the furrows with two fingers.

"What are you thinking of?" she asked.

"Of how I love you despite the deaths that lie between us."

"Hush," she whispered. "Do not soil your mouth with those deaths. Do not think of the Hound. Do not think of the Bull. Do not remember Catrona or the women of the Hames. We must not let their blood come between us." She realized that she had said nothing of the other word, *love*, and wondered if he realized it, too.

"I saw more of those deaths than even you have, Jo-an-enna. I cannot help think of them. I cannot help think of my part in them." But then he did hush, giving himself over to her ministrations.

For a long moment, her fingers on his forehead were the only contact between them. Then he put his hands up and found her waiting face in the dark. Slowly he ran his fingers down her braids, and began to unplait them. She did not move until he had shaken her hair free of its bindings, tumbling it over her shoulders, where it lay smelling of wind and riding.

She had all she could do to remember to breathe and then, somehow, she was right next to him and his mouth was on hers. They were lying on the sofa, covered in the canopy of her hair. She felt she had to give him something, some great gift, but she could not speak the word *love*.

"My true name," she whispered at last, "is Annuanna. Annuanna. No one knows it now but my Mother Alta, my dark sister, and you."

"Annuanna," he whispered into her mouth, his breath sweet with it.

Then mouth on mouth, tongue to tongue, without ever saying the word *love*, they learned more than she had ever been told or he had ever discovered in his books about it, and they learned it together, far, far into the night.

THE HISTORY

The sexual taboos of the ancient Garunians and Dalites differed so greatly that one would be hard put to find any commonalities. The Garunians had a sophisticated society and had borrowed eagerly from their Continental neighbors for both their hetero- and their homosexual tastes. By the time they had conquered the island kingdom of the Dales, they had been through many baroque periods of alternating orgiastic and celibate marriage modes. We have much evidence of this from Continental sources. (See Doyle's earliest work, her doctoral thesis: "Amatory Practices, Obligatory Vows" which was later turned into the popular book I Do, We Do: Or What the Garunians Did.)*

But of the Garunians after the conquest of the Dales we know little, and must make do with educated guesses. Doyle, sensibly, assumes they carried the group marriage concept, then so popular on the Continent, across the Bay of All Souls with them. Again, with eminent sensibleness, she hypothesizes that polygamy allowed the Garunian nobles to marry within the Garun hierarchy and the Dalian upper classes; a king might have wives from both without violating the strict Dale code of sexual ethics.

As the Dalites were matriarchal at that time (see Cowan's brilliant

"Mother and Son: How Titles Passed Though the Dalian Line," Demo-
graphics Annual, *Pasden University Press, #58) all monies, land, and titles
passed maternally so the conquest by the patriarchal Garuns must have
meant quite a change. There is even evidence that the Dalites did not understand the man's role in the creation of children, believing in some odd form
of female cloning, the "mirror twins" which Magon is so fond of exploring.
(Diana Burrows Jones uncovers this attitude in her chapter "The Papa Per-
plex" in* Encyclopedia of the Dales.*) However difficult the change may have
been on the Dale psyches, things evidently went relatively smoothly for four
hundred years. The Garun kings took wives from the Dales, staying carefully
abstinent with them but nonetheless binding the Dale tribes to them in this
way. The Dale wives were given the title of priestess and made honorary
mothers, or Mother Altas according to Sigel and Salmon, though their evidence is still rather fragmentary.*

*Magon, of course, in his typical inane leaps, tries to prove that many of the
later kings (especially Oran, father of Langbrow, and Langbrow himself)
actually bedded their Dale wives, producing offspring. He cites as evidence a
few old and rather coarse rhymes, including the infamous*

> *When Langbrow put his awl in*
> *To carve a wooden babe*
> *That of a larch and of an oak*
> *Was so securely made . . .*

*as well as the tender dedicatory note writ in hand (and by whose hand we do
not know) on the one extant copy we have of Langbrow's* Book of Battles:
*This littl booke is for thee Annuanna, my luv, my lighte. Leaving aside the
fact that Langbrow's Garunian wife was named Jo-el-ean (the infamous Jo-
el-ean who refused to sit by her husband's side and thus brought down his
reign in ruin and infamy) the name Annuanna, despite its feminine ending
has long been considered a man's name, being the shortened form of Annuannatan. If in fact the dedication is in Langbrow's hand, it makes more
sense that he would sign the* Book of Battles *to a male friend; Annuannatan
can only be his homosexual lover, his blanket companion from the army. If
Dr. Magon had done this kind of root work, he would not now be making a
fool of himself in scholarly circles.*

THE STORY

It was two days before they left New Steading, for it took that long to round up and equip two hundred young men. In fact, there were two hundred and thirty-seven by actual count, including the mayor's oldest son. And there was new clothing for the men already following the king, as well as dozens of pikes and swords loaned by the town fathers. Carum looked splendid in a wine-colored jerkin and trews and a showy white shirt pipped with gold. The king was all in gold weave. Even Piet looked resplendent, though he had chosen green and brown "to blend in with the woods," he had muttered, adding, "Gold is fine for ceremony, my lord, but war is another matter altogether."

Gorum had laughed at that. "Wherever a king is, there *is* ceremony."

"Wherever a king is, there *is* war," Carum had put in, but they ignored him.

Jenna had refused her new clothes since all they offered her were women's skirts and bodices dressed with fancy beading. She knew the skirts would make riding difficult, guessed the beads would catch in any brush and leave an easy trail to follow. Instead she brushed out her old skins, borrowing a needle and thread to mend the few tears. She did not need to be fancy. In war one needed the *proper* equipment. And as Catrona had reminded her in training: *In a fight anything is a sword.*

She did accept their offer of a bath, however, and spent over an hour soaking. Her only regret, as she sank into the warm water, was that the smell of Carum's flesh on hers disappeared in the first soaping, though when she closed her eyes, she could recall its deep, tangy odor. She thought she would know him anywhere, just from that smell. Still, as the water enveloped her, she gave herself over to its ministry. Such long ridings offered only cold country streams and though she was used to the chilly lavings, having had long practice out in the woods, and washed herself dutifully every day they found so much as a catchpool, she had, after all, been brought up in a Hame with a famous deep-heated bath. It was the only bit of civilization she really missed.

When had she taken her last hot bath? It felt like forever since she and

Petra had soaked in the Hame together. But in the Dales they said: *Forever is no distance at all.*

Jenna knew that the distance was there. Something had certainly changed Petra—or changed Jenna. She and Carum had emerged from the council room holding hands but once they found the main door, had moved apart swiftly, walking down into the town square so removed from one another, they could not have touched even by stretching.

They had found Petra leaning against a wall, nibbling on a piece of chicken, eyes closed.

"Petra!" Jenna whispered.

Petra's eyes opened slowly, almost reluctantly.

"And where did you two get to?"

Carum turned and left abruptly, without even trying to offer an excuse. Jenna refused to watch him go.

"I saw you did not eat," Petra continued, as if Carum had never been there at all, had not been included in her initial accusation. "So I saved a whole napkin full of food for you for later. Such theft does not come easily to me. I am trained to be a Mother Alta. And then you were nowhere to be found."

"I was . . ." Jenna began, then realized that she could say nothing to Petra. *Nothing.* Petra was still a girl, after all, and Jenna was a girl no longer. Change *had* happened, slowly, yet suddenly. And Petra had not shared it. Jenna wondered that the change did not show easily—on her cheeks, in her eyes, on her mouth, still soft from all those kisses. Reaching out, she picked off a bit of the chicken in Petra's hand.

"Thanks," she said. "I *am* starved."

"No wonder," Petra said. "If the gods do not eat of our food, they are bound to get hungry."

"*Rarely* eat," Jenna corrected her. "He said *rarely!*"

Petra handed her the leek bulb, but Jenna shook her head, so Petra chewed it herself.

"They want me to stay here," Petra said.

"Who does?"

"Everyone. The mayor . . ." She hesitated.

"Perhaps you should," Jenna said slowly, horrified at the thought.

"They said women should not be at war. That we are not strong as men. The townsfolk said that."

"And what about me? What about the Anna?"

"You are a goddess. That is different."

"Alta's women should be where they will. We are trained to war as well as to peace."

"I *knew* you would say that." Petra grinned. "And that is what I told them. That and that Alta's priestess must ride at the Anna's side. After all, many women have already died that you might ride on and I ride with you."

"That is not why they died."

"You know what I mean."

"Stick to your rhyme. You are clearer that way." Jenna bit her lip. *How could she have said such a cruel thing?*

But Petra laughed, missing the cruelty entirely, or dismissing it. "You are right, of course. If I am to be your priestess, I had better be very clear—or very obscure. But correct either way!" She gave Jenna a hug.

"Whew!" Jenna said. "If you insist on eating spring leeks, your breath will be as strong as *five* men's even if your arm is not."

They both laughed then, friends again, and walked into the town hall.

The ride out of New Steading toward the east had been accompanied by the cheering of the townsfolk. Jenna kept Duty from prancing, having been instructed by one of the men in how to keep the horse under control. She rode next to Carum, but that was as close as they had gotten since he had walked away from Petra's questions. After that they had both been too busy, always surrounded by men.

Over the thudding of the horse's hooves, the fading shouts behind them, Jenna called, "Do you . . . still . . ." She hesitated. How could she scream *that* word where others might hear it?

His mouth twisted wryly, the scar under his left eye crinkling up, as if winking wantonly at her. "Of course I still *remember,* if that is the word you want. I remember every move. Every . . . thing." He gave her a big grin. "An oak remembers. And you?"

She smiled back. "Jo-an-enna means lover of white birches."

"What?" The hoofbeats had obscured her answer.

She repeated it, calling: "If you are a tree, I am a tree."

"I am a man," he said. "Not a tree."

"I know," she whispered. "That I *truly* know."

Then their horses, forced by the ones following, broke into a canter which stopped all talk as they galloped on down the winding road.

They paused at two smaller towns on the way, adding a dozen men to their force, the king showing off Jenna as if she were some sort of exotic animal imported from the Continent. Carum grumbled about it loudly, but even he had to admit the show seemed to be working.

Piet was not so pleased. "Twelve men when we need twelve hundred," he said. "When twelve thousand would not be amiss."

"Then what about women?" Jenna asked. They were stopped at the next rest, the new boys being well introduced while the horses made quick work of the grass by the roadside. "Surely we are near some Hame." She paused, adding quietly, "There must be *some* Hame still unharmed close by. You said ten gone, but there were . . ." her voice cracked, "seventeen."

Piet grunted; what answer he meant to give was unclear. But the king shook his head. "These are not regular army men used to blanket companions. These are boys right off the farms or right out of their fathers' shops. The girls they know cook and sew. If we are to keep their minds on their new swords . . ."

"The women of the Hame know how to wield their swords. And they have a reason to . . ."

"There is *one* Hame nearby," Carum interrupted suddenly. He reached into his saddlebag and drew out a map. Spreading it across his horse's flank, he ran a finger along a wavering black line. "We are somewhere here . . ."

"Here!" Piet said, jabbing at the map with his forefinger.

Carum nodded. "And there—" His finger pointed to a strange hatching of marks. "That is M'dorah Hame."

"M'dorah?" Jenna thought back to the list that Catrona had reeled off when their fateful journey had started. *Selden, Calla's Ford, Wilma's Crossing, Josstown, Calamarie, Carpenter's, Krisston, West Dale, Annsville, Crimerci, Lara's Well, Sammiton, East James, John-o-the-Mill's, Carter's Tracing, North Brook, Nill's* . . . remembering Nill's she set her jaw. *But there had been no mention of a M'dorah.* Aloud, she said, "I have never heard of it."

Looking up, Carum said, almost absently, "It's an odd place, Jenna. Not exactly a regular Hame, at least that's what the books say. They broke away from the first Alta and built their Hame atop an inaccessible cliff. The only way up is by rope ladder. They will have nothing to do with men. They have never sent fighters to the army. And they have never sent . . ."

"M'dorah," Petra mused. "They never send missioners out. My Mother Alta always threatened that if we did not behave, she would send us to M'dorah on our mission: *High-towered Hame where eagles dare not nest.* I thought it but a story."

"Perhaps that's all it is," Carum said. "But it is supposed to be nearby."

"Let us go," Jenna said suddenly. "If it exists at all, we will bring back many women fighters to swell your ranks. And they will be women who want nothing to do with your men, so the boys will not be troubled by them."

The king laughed. "Then you do not understand boys! They can make a woman out of flowers, out of trees, out of dreams. Their bodies smell of springtide all year long."

Jenna blushed furiously.

"There is nothing there. No one," Piet growled. "It means taking time out for a mere tale."

"Perhaps not," Carum put in. "Stories have to start somewhere."

"This one started as a joke after too much wine," Piet groused. "And too few women."

"From the map," Jenna said, "it looks to be less than a day's ride from here. *And* you did say you needed more fighters. And you wanted to buy yourself time. Let me go. I will persuade them."

"Persuade *eagles!*" Piet said.

"You are too precious to let go." The king's face was thoughtful.

"I will go with her," Carum said. "We will return."

Looking at the map carefully, the king traced the road from the hatched site of M'dorah. Finally he turned to Jenna. "We will camp there for the night," he said, pointing to the place where the road to M'dorah turned off. "You will have until morning. No sleep, but then as they say on the Continent: *Surely a dream is worth a little sleep!*" He laughed silently. "Piet will go with you. Carum, you will remain here."

He knows, Jenna thought. *He knows about Carum and me.* The thought embarrassed her, then made her mad, as if Gorum had sullied them by knowing.

Carum began to protest, but Jenna nodded abruptly, cutting off his argument. "Piet," she agreed. "And Petra. I will need my priestess with me if I am to convince them to join us."

"Piet for protection and the girl for conviction. An unlikely pair." He smiled.

"I am my own protection," Jenna said. "And Piet is for *your* convictions."

Gorum nodded solemnly. He put his hand out. "Your hand on your return."

"You have my word on it," she said. "Besides, you have here those I most care for in the world." She gestured to Jareth, Marek, Sandor. That her circling hand did not include Carum was proof to herself that she was not being entirely truthful to the king. After all, she had not mentioned Pynt or

A-ma or the other women of Selden Hame either. Surely *they* were the ones she *most* cared for.

If the king noticed her omission, he did not mention it, holding his hand steadily toward her. She was forced to take it, feeling again its lack of warmth as palm to palm they made their pledge.

The road to M'dorah was hardly a road at all, just an overgrown path where the trees suddenly widened. It was Piet who recognized it as a roadway, though when challenged afterward by Marek, he could not explain how he had known.

The king called a halt and the large company encircled the meadow, setting up camp. Scouts were sent to locate water and to track ahead down the main road. But Piet, Petra, and Jenna turned along the scant path.

Jenna looked back only once, hoping to see Carum watching. But he was nowhere in sight. She entered the trees thinking about the perfidy of men; how love, like memory, *could* be false; and conscious of Duty's broad back beneath her.

The trees were tall and full, a busy forest of much variety. Jenna identified beech, oak, whitethorn, and larch with ease, but there were many trees she had never seen before, some with spotty barks, some with needle leaves, and some with roots that twisted over and around one another above the earth like a badly plaited braid of hair. Ahead of them bright birds piped warnings from the branches, then flew away in noisy confusion. If there was sign of larger animals, Jenna did not notice for Piet kept up a quick pace, threading them through the trees on the ever-ascending path as if he knew where he was going.

After a couple of hours, the path suddenly narrowed and they had to dismount, leading the horses for another hundred yards until the path disappeared entirely. They were forced to leave the horses tied loosely, and set off on foot. The way Piet chose wound upward at an even steeper angle and soon they were all three breathing hard. Jenna felt a small pain under her breastbone but she would not admit it out loud.

It was clear Piet understood the deep woods. He knew how to check before stepping. But Petra, in the full skirts she had been given by the New Steadingers, was having a great deal of trouble in the pathless ascent. Her clothes caught frequently on the thorny bushes and they lost precious time freeing her. Jenna clicked her tongue against the roof of her mouth in annoyance, glad that she, at least, had kept her skins for the trip.

At last the ascending woods thinned out and they could see a clear space ahead. When they reached it, they found themselves at the start of a high, treeless plain. The plain was covered with what seemed to be a forest of gigantic, towering rocks, some slim needle points, others wider sword blades, still others enormous leaning towers of stone, all hundreds of feet high. They had to crane their necks to see to the tops.

"It is true, then," Petra said when she had caught her breath.

"The cliffs at least are true," Piet said. "As to the Hame . . ."

"Look!" Jenna pointed. Atop one of the broadest of the stones, far across the plain toward the north, was some kind of building. As they moved closer, over the rock-strewn plain, they could make it out. It had wooden galleries scaffolded into space and a roof like a series of giant mushrooms. Jenna could see no continuous path cut into the rock's side. "There *must* be steps on the other side," she whispered to herself, but the others heard.

"We'll look," Piet said.

It took them another two hours, into the fading light of evening, to circle the stone, but they found nothing.

"Then how does anyone get up?" Petra asked.

"Perhaps they fly like eagles," Piet suggested.

"Perhaps they burrow like moles," Jenna added.

They were still offering suggestions, when not twenty feet from them first a sound and then a cascading of something down the stone face brought them to the spot. It was a hinged ladder of rope and wood.

"Someone is up there," Petra said, staring beyond the ladder, her hand shading her eyes.

"Someone who knows we are down here," Piet said. He began to draw his sword.

Jenna put her hand on his arm. "Hold," she said. "It is a woman. A sister."

Piet looked up. Someone *was* descending the rope ladder. He slipped the sword back in its sheath, but his hand did not stray from the hilt.

In the swiftly darkening night, it was hard to make out the figure climbing down. The shadow was stocky, heavier on top than on the bottom, somehow badly misshapen. Jenna wondered if only disfigured women—or the deranged—would remove themselves to such a place. Then she remembered Mother Alta of Nill's Hame: blind, twisted, with six fingers on each hand. She had not needed a sanctuary apart from the others. *We women take care of our own,* she thought. *There is another reason for this forbidding Hame.*

The shadow unwound itself from the ladder and stood before them. It was a woman, of that there was no doubt by the closeweave bodice she wore. But her strange humped back was . . .

"A babe!" Petra said.

At that very moment, the child bound to the woman's back gave a cry of delight, waving its one free hand.

"I be Iluna. Who be ye?" the woman asked abruptly.

"I am Piet, first lieutenant to . . ."

Pointedly ignoring him, Iluna stepped up to Petra and Jenna, putting her back to Piet's face. The babe, seeing his heavy beard, stopped laughing and pulled in her little arm tight against her chest.

"Who be ye?" Iluna asked again.

"I be . . . I am Petra," Petra began, "of the ruined Nill's Hame, in training to be priestess to my own."

"And ye?"

"I am Jo-an-enna of . . ."

"She is the White One, the Anna, the anointed of the Great Alta," Petra said. "She is the one of whom prophecy sings."

"Nonsense!" Iluna shifted the baby slightly.

"What?" Clearly Petra was startled, but Jenna decided in that instant that she liked Iluna.

"I said *nonsense*. She is a woman. Like you. Like me. Even in the shadows I can see that. But she is a woman with a message."

"You know . . ." Petra began.

"Else she would not be here. Nor ye. No one comes to M'dorah, lest they be terribly lost, without a message or a quest." She turned back to the stone and put her hand upon the ladder. "Come. After I am half up, put thy hand to steady the rung, then mount. The bearded one stays here."

"I go with them," Piet protested.

Iluna turned, her face unreadable in the almost-dark. "If ye mount the ladder, it will be cut when ye near the top and ye shall fall the hundred feet and we will leave thy bones below. No man enters M'dorah and lives. Be ye starving at the foot of our tower, we will throw down food. Be ye wounded, we will send a healer to ye. But mount the ladder, and we will cast ye down without another thought. Believe it."

"We believe it," Petra said quickly.

"I will return, Piet. On Catrona's grave, I swear it. I will go back with you," Jenna promised.

When Iluna was halfway up, Petra began to climb, holding onto the shaking ladder with sweaty hands. By Jenna's turn, it was pitch-black, the sky overhead sprinkled with stars that gave no light. She grasped the ladder and found rung after rung by feel alone. A slight breeze brushed loose hair over her eyes. Drawing in the spider breaths meant for difficult climbs, she felt her arms and legs begin to move fluidly, the rock face a blankness before her eyes. One slow breath after another, she drew herself up the ladder. When the ladder stopped its strange tremblings, she guessed that Petra had reached the top. Twenty more rungs, and she heard voices above her, calling encouragement. The last rungs held steady as they were wood set right into the stone itself with iron bands.

"Welcome, sister," a woman called.

Jenna looked up into a lantern the woman held. It illuminated the ladder with a strong light.

"Or should I say welcome, sisters!"

"Thank you," a voice said suddenly by Jenna's side, "though in the dark I made little of the climb."

"Skada!" Jenna turned slightly, surprised to see her dark sister clinging to a shadow ladder on the rock face next to her.

"Well, Jen, and what have you been up to these past few days, eh?" In the lantern's glow, her mocking smile was unmistakable.

Unaccountably, Jenna blushed.

"You need not get red-faced on *my* account, sister," Skada whispered. "He *does* smell sweet."

"Sssssskada!" Jenna hissed. Then she laughed uneasily. Of course Skada would know everything.

As if reading her mind, Skada laughed back, "Not *everything*, sister. After all, it was very dark in that room and you lit no candles. I have only your memories . . ."

"I will light no candles. Ever! Carum would not allow it!"

"Hmmmmm," Skada said, "and have you asked him?" But then she was forced to laugh at Jenna's discomfort and Jenna, in turn, laughed with her.

"Come, sisters," the woman called down to them, "ladders are no easy places for conversation. Join us at our meal. It is a simple feast, but there is enough for three more."

"Feast?" Skada said. "And I starving!"

They scrambled up the last few rungs and the woman led them toward the building. Hung now with soft lights that bobbed in each twist of wind, the Hame was of both wood and stone, built to accommodate the various surfaces of the rock tower. Yet unlike a dirt foundation that might be smoothed for the easy placement of a house, the stone had resisted the makers who had to erect according to the cuts and crevices nature offered them. It made for a strange building, Jenna thought, with rooms on many levels and odd risers within a single room.

The dining room was on three different levels, all dictated by the rock. A great table sat on the highest level with over twenty chairs around it. On the next level there were a half dozen smaller tables with between four and eight chairs. The lowest level held serving tables, loaded down with food. When they got close, Jenna saw that the tables and chairs were not of solid make but pieced together.

The meal held many familiar foods: eggs boiled in the shell, forest greens, mushrooms, crisped and browned hare, roasted birds. But there were also strange berries Jenna did not know, and several pies whose fruits were a strange color. There was no wine, only water and a bluish watery milk.

"What of Piet below?" Jenna asked.

"Men can graze like cattle," a woman answered.

"If he were starving, we would throw food down," said another. "But Iluna says he does not have the look of a starving man." She put her hand out before her belly in gross imitation, and laughed.

The others laughed, too, as they brought their heaping plates up to the great table. Jenna, Skada, and Petra were ushered before them. When they were all seated, they introduced themselves one after another, the names coming so quickly, even Jenna could not sort them out.

"And ye three," asked Fellina, the woman who had held the lantern, and one of the few names Jenna had caught. "What message do ye bear?"

Petra began, "I am . . ." but Jenna and Skada stopped her with a hand on her forearm.

"We are sisters from different Hames but with the same message," Jenna said. "And it is a message of war." She slipped the ring from her little finger. "This was given me by the Mother of Nill's Hame."

"*My* Hame," Petra said in a quiet voice.

"Before she and all the women there were cruelly slaughtered," Skada added. "By men."

"Kalas' men," Jenna amended. The women were so quiet, she went on. "Mother Alta said that I must go from Hame to Hame to warn them that: *The time of endings is at hand.* She said the Hame Mothers would know what to do. But you are . . ." Her voice cracked, and she looked down at her plate, suddenly overwhelmed by her memories.

"We are what . . . go on, child," Fellina said gently.

Oddly comforted by being called a child again, Jenna looked up at the women around the table. The faces were different, yet they were somehow as familiar as those at Selden Hame in their concern. She drew in a deep *latani* breath and counted silently to ten. At last she spoke. "Yours is the only Hame I have found so far beside my own that has not been destroyed."

"How many have you actually been to?"

"Two. But . . ."

"But we have had reports of ten destroyed utterly," Petra said.

"Ten of how many?"

"Of seventeen," Jenna answered.

"Eighteen, if you count M'dorah," Skada added.

"No one ever counts M'dorah," Iluna said, unstrapping the baby from her back with the help of her dark sister. She began rocking the child slowly in her arms.

"I had never even heard of M'dorah till yesterday," Jenna admitted.

"I had—but I thought it only a tale," Petra added.

"Ten. Gone utterly. Ten." The number seemed to make its way around the table, drifting down even to the women sitting on the lower level. Slowly they mounted the four steps to stand by their sisters.

Jenna and Skada looked around, waiting until everyone was silent. Then Jenna spoke, articulating the way the king had on the great steps at New Steading, consciously letting her voice carry. These were *her* people. She *had* to speak now.

"I have been called the White One, the Anna, though I have not really claimed it. Whether or not you believe that is who I am, believe this: I come with a message. There is war. Men against women; men against men where women still suffer greatly. Something is ending, so prophecy warns. I do not know if it is the world that is ending, but surely the world of the Hames is being destroyed."

"Destroyed utterly," Petra muttered. "Go on, Jenna."

"We cannot let that world go without fighting to retain something of what it means. Something must remain of Great Alta's teachings. Some of us must be sure there is a place in the new for sisters side by side."

"Side by side," Iluna echoed, spinning the phrase around the table.

"What would ye have us do?" the woman next to Iluna asked.

"Come down from this hidden Hame, from this secret safety and join us. Fight with me, side by side as the old rhymes say. Do not let only men fight for us. For when men fight alone, the victory is also theirs alone."

"Ye would have us leave this *secret safety* to die among strangers? Among men?" Several voices called out, then answered themselves, "No!"

"No!"

"No!" The word spun crazily around the table.

Jenna could not tell which of them had spoken.

"Speak for us, Maltia," someone cried.

A woman and her dark sister stood at the opposite end of the table from

Jenna. They were both tall, with jet-black hair ending in graying braids, as if the crown of their heads were younger than the ends. They stared down the long table at Jenna.

"I be True Speaker of this Hame," one of them said at last. "And this be my sister Tessia."

Jenna nodded her acknowledgment, as did Skada.

"We have no Mother Alta as ye have," Maltia continued. "We have no one ruler. I be the True Speaker but I do not otherwise lead. In this way we broke long ago from the false Alta's teachings, coming to this place of eagles and bright air, worshipping only the true Alta. She who waits in the green hall where it be said *Every end is a beginning* and it is also said *No one stands highest when all stand together.*"

"Jenna," Petra whispered to her, "that is what the Grenna teach."

Jenna pursed her lips and stood herself, Skada by her side. She addressed Maltia directly. "We understand more than you think, True Speaker. We have *been* in Alta's grove with the Greenfolk. We have stood in their circle. We have seen both cradle and hall."

"Ahhhh!" The sound came from all around the table.

"But . . ." Jenna said, hesitating for effect, "we were not women alone there. We were women and men. Petra and I and . . ." This time it was not for effect.

"And thy dark sister?" asked Tessia, her face full of a cunning Maltia's did not hold.

"There are no shadows in the grove," Jenna said quietly, "though you would have me stumble on my memories and say it was so."

"Ahhhh!"

"What men be there with ye?" Iluna asked suddenly.

"*Iluna!*" Tessia's voice was sharp. "*Ye be not True Speaker.*"

Iluna seemed to draw back into herself, holding the baby against her breast as if it were a shield.

"Who *be* those men?" Maltia asked as if there had been no interruption. "Was the bearded one with the belly below one of them?"

For a moment Jenna considered lying, considered saying that Piet had been with them, for such an admission might help him, help their cause. But then she set aside the idea as unworthy—unworthy of the audience and unworthy of Piet himself. She was, after all, talking to their True Speaker. She must be a true speaker herself. To do otherwise, was to be like the king.

"No," she said, still looking straight at Maltia, "they were not three grown men at all, but boys. One Alta gifted with a crown, one with a wristlet, and one with . . ." She put her hand to her throat, for a moment unable to speak.

"And one She gave the collar?" asked Maltia.

"Yes!" Jenna croaked. "And because of it he cannot speak."

"Ye would not have him speak his terrible truths," Tessia said. "They would bring doom on all. True Speaking be as much truth as any human can bear to hear, though it be but a shadow of the Herald's words."

"You know . . ." Skada began.

"They be The Three," said Maltia. "The Young Heralds. The Harbingers. We know. But how any followers of the false Alta could know of this, be too much of a puzzle for me. It be writ nowhere but in the *Second Book of Light.*"

"The *second* Book?" interrupted Petra. "There *is* no second Book."

"It be the Book of M'dorah," said Maltia, "written by the true Alta herself when She left the grove and came to this place of high rocks to build a sanctuary, an aerie where even eagles dare not rest."

"Where even eagles dare not rest . . ." Petra whispered, "Jenna, Alta said others had come to the grove."

Maltia and Tessia sat down heavily in their chairs. "We must think on this."

"You have no time to think!" Skada roared, pounding her fist on the table. "You only have time to act. We must be back down and to our army before the sun's light."

"Skada!" Jenna cautioned, though Skada had spoken only what she, herself, had been afraid to say.

But Maltia and Tessia were lost to them, hands over eyes, deep into *latani* breathing and thought.

Standing suddenly, the baby still clutched against her and her own dark sister by her side, Iluna cried, "I will go, though no one else goes with me."

"And I!" Two long-faced young women stood.

"And I!" A middle-aged woman with deep carved lines from nose to mouth rose slowly. By her side rose another woman, the lines on her face more shadow than real.

Maltia looked up. "Wait!" she cried. "We may not be part of *this* ending, nor part of this beginning either. Do not rush into it. Remember: *If ye rise too early, the dew will soak thy skin.* Do not drown M'dorah in this."

"What of the other signs?" Tessia added. "We have but one, and that may be compounded of our own longing."

"Ye have spoken truly," the middle-aged woman said. "As befits the dark sister of the True Speaker. But the White One knows of the Three Heralds. Surely that be sign enough."

"*One is not a multitude.* It says clearly in the Book." Maltia's voice was low.

"What other signs?" Skada asked. "Tell them to us."

Tessia laughed. "If ye need ask, ye know them not."

"What signs, True Speaker?" Petra was standing. "We have seen many, but how are we to know which are yours without a hint. We will give you all, but you must give us some." Her voice was stronger than Jenna had ever heard, stronger even than when she had spoken at Selden Hame.

"Who anointed her to the task?" Maltia whispered.

Tessia roared out the same question. "Who anointed the White One to the task?"

Petra closed her eyes for a moment and Jenna could almost see memories crowding across her brow. Then she opened her eyes and stared past Maltia, to the window beyond. "My Mother anointed her. My Mother who had six fingers on each hand. Who saw without eyes. Who stood without . . ."

". . . without feet." Maltia's voice trembled. "Who spoke without voice. Who . . ."

"*Who spoke without voice?*" Jenna whispered to Skada. "What by the Great Goddess does that mean?"

"*On the slant,* Jenna," Skada whispered back. "Hush. We have them."

All the women were on their feet now, reciting along with Maltia their litany of the impossible. As their voices rose to the finish, Jenna could feel the excitement. The air was electric with it.

". . . born without a father. She shall anoint the One." Maltia held out her hand toward Jenna. Tessia did the same. "Ye be the One. Forgive us that we did not know ye."

Jenna nodded. If there was more relief than forgiveness in that nod, she did not let them see it.

"We be ready," Maltia said. "M'dorah ends this night, as the *Book* prophesied. And what begins, we will all write together."

It took the rest of the short night for them to pack what they would need: swords, wooden shields, knives, packets of food. There were but three babes, harvested they said from farms as far away as Market, wherever that was, and these were bound to their mothers' backs.

"What place be this army?" asked Maltia as she packed a woven basket.

"At the place where the road to M'dorah and the road from New Steading meet," Jenna said. When no one seemed to understand, she knelt and sketched a map on the floor with her finger.

"Ah, New Steading," said Iluna. "That be what we call Market." She looked up. "Only the youngest of us go there, to get those things we cannot ourselves supply."

"What can you supply, here on this aerie?" Petra asked.

"We hunt. We raise birds. We have gardens," Maltia said.

"Where? We saw none," Jenna asked.

"They be well hid from prying eyes." Tessia smiled.

"And New Steading—Market—is where you take the babes?" Petra asked.

"We take only the ones left out, the ones neglected, the ones ill-treated, the ones thrown away," Iluna said.

Like me, mused Jenna to herself.

"Like my Scillia," said Iluna. "Who has but one arm."

I was whole, Jenna thought, *and still I was given away.*

"They know we will take what they do not want," Tessia said. "So next to the babes, they leave money or gifts of seed. If they leave wine, we do not take it. The *Book* says plainly: *The grape brings slow death.*"

"And they never speak of M'dorah," explained Maltia. "For we take away their shame. They say we do not exist. M'dorah be but a story to them. Women alone are not natural."

"They deny us but still they leave us the gleanings of their poor crops," Tessia added.

Skada laughed. "So it is with the other Hames. What is so different, sisters, that you shut yourselves away up here?"

"Our Alta denied us all men until the coming of the Three. Your Alta went among men and had commerce with them. Our Alta sat in the circle. Your Alta sits on a throne. Our Alta . . ." Maltia said.

"Alta has many faces," Petra interrupted smoothly, "yet in the end we are all babes again at her breast. Is that not so?"

"In the end, and in the beginning, yes," said Maltia. "And by thy coming, we know it be the end. That is why we go from M'dorah, this high and holy place." Her face was bereft of all happiness.

Jenna looked around. All the women, intent on their final duties, wore the same mask of sorrow. *They are in mourning,* she thought, *not for any one death but for the death of M'dorah.*

They set fire to the Hame, each with a torch so that everyone shared equally in the ending. It was accompanied by a plainsong chant:

Came we out of fire
Came we out of grove
Came we from desire
To the rocks above.
Now return to fire
Now remake the grove
Now the heart's desire
Goes to ground with love.

Then, driven by the fierce heat of the conflagration, they dropped a dozen ladders over the side of the rock and began their descent.

Once over the edge, with the fire unable to cast shadows, Skada and the other dark sisters disappeared, cutting the numbers of women in half. Jenna felt more alone than she had in days.

At the bottom of the ropes Piet was waiting, arms crossed. He looked as though he had been waiting in that position all night long.

"What is the fire?" he asked when Jenna reached the ground. "It set the sky ablaze. When I saw it, I would have climbed up to get girl. But there were no ladders and no footholds that I could find."

"It is the end of M'dorah," Jenna explained. "More I will not say. Now we have a hundred warriors to add to Pike's army."

"I count but half that," Piet said.

"When the moon rises . . ." Jenna began.

"It is days until the moon."

"Then the force will double."

He nodded. "But now?"

"Now we have all that move by day. There is no one left in that eagle's nest."

He nodded again and started to turn toward them. Jenna put a hand on his arm.

"Hold, Piet. They will take no direction but my own."

"The king be not pleased at that," Piet murmured.

"The king will have to live with it," Jenna answered. She turned and waved her hand and the women followed her, threading carefully down the pathless hillside. They were more silent than any army Piet had ever heard. Even the three babes, swaddled and strapped against their mothers' backs, were absolutely still.

* * *

When they got to the place where the horses were tied, Piet mounted up but Jenna and Petra remained on foot.

"Ride on, Piet, and tell King Gorum we come with a dozen dozen women behind."

"I was not to leave ye," Piet said.

"If you do not leave now, he will not know in time." Piet nodded.

"And faithful Piet," Jenna said, moving by him and putting her hand on his leg. "I have a special message for you alone, not the king."

Piet bent over, steadying the horse with the reins in his right hand.

Jenna whispered, "These women came not because they believe in me but because of some strange holding of theirs about three heralds, three messengers of their own Alta. Those messengers carry crown, wristlet, and collar."

"The boys . . ." He stopped himself, nodded again.

"Tell them. Tell the boys. Warn them."

"They will be warned."

"And something else." She hesitated. "Tell Carum I . . ."

"He knows, girl," said Piet.

"Knows?"

"And I know. We all know. We have eyes. Cat knew even afore thee."

"No one knew before me."

Piet grinned. "The first, that's the hardest. And the dearest. And the best." There was some sort of forgiveness in his eyes. As quickly, it was gone. He nodded again, sat up straight, jerked the horse's head with the reins, and plunged them both into the undergrowth.

She could hear the sound of his passage for a long time after.

With that many women, it took them several more hours to reach the deep woods. Jenna could read Piet's passage before them and hoped that he was already with the king for the sun was peeking through the interlacing of the trees. When she turned to look at the women behind her, she saw what a great swath they had left.

"An army cannot move easily in the woods," she murmured to Petra.

Petra agreed. "We do not leave a trail but a highway."

"What does it matter what we leave behind?" Iluna asked. "It is what lies ahead that matters." Her eyes were bright with excitement.

"What lies ahead," Jenna pointed out, "is war. And that means some of us will die." Without thinking, she flexed the fingers of her sword hand, suddenly remembering the feel of the sword sliding through a man's flesh. She shuddered. "Many of us will die."

Petra put her hand around Jenna's, folding her fingers tightly under. "But some of us will live, Jenna. You must remember that after the ending is the beginning. So it is prophesied."

"On the slant, Petra. We must read prophecy *on the slant,* or so I have been told often enough," Jenna said.

They walked on.

They were nearly halfway through the woods, following Piet's easy trail, when Jenna held up her hand. The women stopped at once as she strained to listen.

"Do you hear that?" she asked at last.

Petra shook her head. "Hear what?" I hear some birds. The wind through the trees. And"—she smiled—"and a baby chuckling."

Iluna put her finger over her shoulder and the baby took it into her mouth.

"No more baby," Petra said. "And the birds have quieted as well."

"No. Another sound. Deeper. Unnatural."

"I hear something." Iluna moved closer to Jenna. "But it is not one sound. It is several. Some are high, some low. Not the sound of the woods, though. I have been here often on the hunt and that I know."

Maltia and several other women moved closer to Jenna, silently over the fallen leaves and low branches. Only one twig was snapped, and it shockingly loud in the stillness. They formed a tight circle around Jenna, Petra, Iluna, and the horses, and stood in an attitude of listening.

After a long moment, Jenna said, "There. Do you hear it?"

"We hear," Maltia said. The others nodded.

Jenna drew in a deep breath. "Do you know what it means? I *fear* I do. It is the sound of sword on sword and the cries of men. I have heard that sound in my dreams. There is a battle raging—and I am not with them. I must ride." She put her hand on Duty's back.

"I will go with you, Jenna," Petra said.

"No, Petra, you have no skill with a sword, and these women need you."

"Not to show them the way, Jenna. They know these woods better than I."

"You know the world, Petra. That is the way you must show them. Come as soon as you can. And take this." She stripped the priestess ring from her finger, placing it gently in Petra's hand. "You have the map of the Hames and now the ring. If anything happens, you must carry on the warning and the women of M'dorah with you."

"Nothing will happen," Petra whispered. "You are the Anna."

"I am Jo-an-enna first and anything can happen to *her.*" She mounted her horse.

"You cannot go alone into battle," Petra said.

"I will not be alone. The men are already fighting and you will come right after. Besides we have only two horses and who but you can ride." She gathered Duty's reins.

"I can!" Iluna cried. "At least I have been on a horse before. *Once* before." She turned to Petra. "Give me the lines."

"The lines?"

"She means the reins," Jenna said. She pulled back on her own reins and Duty reared suddenly, nearly throwing her. "And take the child from her back."

"I will not be parted from my Scillia. Is it not so with the sisters of thy Hame?"

Jenna nodded her head and quieted Duty while Iluna was hoisted onto the horse by Maltia and Petra and two other women. Mounting was not something Iluna had acquired in her brief riding lesson. But once atop the horse, she sat with the kind of stillness necessary, though whether from fear or from skill, Jenna could not have said. She pulled roughly on the reins once again and, as Duty spun to the right, called out to them all:

"Follow as swiftly as you can. Your swords will surely be welcome. The king thought to pit force against force, but he has too small an army yet. This battle is an unwelcome surprise. His brother and I had hoped to convince him to use cunning, the mouse's wits against the cat's claw. Let us hope that there are some mice left."

Maltia put her hand on Duty's neck. "But if they all be men, how will we know which to draw against?"

The simple question stunned Jenna. What answer indeed? To these women *all* men were the enemy. In battle how could one be distinguished from the other?

Petra smiled. "If a man draws against you, True Speaker, he is your foe. Our men will be the ones who welcome your help."

Jenna nodded, though some part of her still resisted that easy answer, hearing again in her mind the woman at New Steading protesting: *Girls dressing like men, playing at war, taint natural. We've all said it.* Aloud, she spoke only soothing words. "Petra is right. The men who welcome you are the men you should aid." Then she kicked Duty hard with her heels and the horse took off down the faint path.

Behind her Iluna's horse began to trot, with Iluna hanging on grimly to the reins. Jouncing merrily, the baby at her back waved her hand at the women who followed.

It did not take them long to bull their way through the rest of the forest, the sounds of the battle drawing them on. Jenna cursed herself for the meal at M'dorah, the necessary arguments, the slow walk through the woods, all conspiring to keep her from the start of the battle. She knew that she was but one more sword, but if that sword could keep Jareth or Marek or Sandor alive . . . She did not let herself think about Carum. In her mind she called him Longbow, just another warrior in the king's troops. She urged Duty ahead with a hard kick of her heels.

Then they burst out of the woods and the battle sounds exploded around them. Jenna pulled up short when she saw the once-pleasant field. Beside her Iluna, too, reined in her horse.

To the left across the meadow, under a stand of overhanging trees, three men were setting upon one. He was hewing with his great sword, keeping them at bay. Ahead a knot of nearly thirty men were tangled together, their swords gone, wrestling and kicking, and hitting with their fists and knees. Over to the right, where a few horses grazed disconsolately, was a ring of a dozen men, swords drawn, standing shoulder to shoulder. Their swords pointed outward, and inside the circle lay several fallen comrades. One, half upraised on his elbow, was being tended by a great bear of a man. The rest of the field was littered with bodies, some in uniform, some in fine cloth. Jenna scanned nervously for one in wine-colored weave. She thought there were several, but she was too far away to be sure.

Dropping Duty's reins, she whispered, "Too late. Again too late. Just as the Grenna said." Her hands fell helpless to her sides and she was overcome by a sudden strange lethargy.

But Iluna, raising her sword, dug her heels into her horse and headed toward the stand of trees where the one man fought against the three. She screamed "M'dorah!" as she rode.

The three men scattered before her charge. Dropping the reins, she slid off the horse's back and turned to say something to the big man she had just rescued. As Jenna watched from afar, the man lifted his sword and struck Iluna in the middle of the breast with his blade. She fell, twisting at the last onto her side in order to save the child at her back. The man straddled her body and threw his head back, roaring. Jenna could hear it all the way across the field.

Suddenly the warmth of the lethargy gave way to a surge of ice-cold power. Screaming Iluna's name like a battle cry, Jenna dug her heels again and again in Duty's side and they galloped toward the stand of trees.

The man waited for her, grinning. She knew who it was even before she was halfway to him. What had been icy cold running through her body turned into a red heat in her head. She recalled Alta's words in the grove: *Remembering is what you must do most of all.* She remembered the fire on top of the towering stone, and it became a river of fire in her veins. She could feel the sweat on her forehead and under her arms.

Just before reaching the trees, she leaped from Duty's back. The horse veered right, Jenna rolled to the left, then stood, sword upraised. She wondered the man was not seared by her heat.

"So, little Alta's bitch, do you think you have the blood to do now what you could not do before? And with my hands free this time?" He lifted the sword over his head with both hands, swinging it around. It cut the air, making a horrible whirring. The sword was much heavier than hers, its blade still slick with Iluna's blood, but if its weight tired him, Jenna could not tell. She had no hope blade against blade to defeat him. She would have to cool her fire and use cunning, the cunning of the mouse.

Something sounded in the broken grass behind her but she knew better than to turn. It had to be the three who had scattered before Iluna's horse. Whoever they were, if they had been fighting the Bear, they were on her side.

"Name yourselves," she cried out to them, her eyes on the Bear.

"Anna, it be Marek."

"And Sandor."

The strangled sound coming from the third proclaimed it as Jareth. Alive —all three!

"Blessed be," she whispered, then said aloud, "Good boys!"

"Boys they be right enough," the Bear said. "Pups! And even three full-grown hounds are not strong enough to pull me down. Not even three grown hounds *and* their bitch mother." He laughed.

Jenna heard one of the boys gasp and start forward.

"No!" she cried. "Let him waste his breath in boasts. Do not crowd him. His sword has a long reach."

"A very long reach," the Bear agreed. "And after I dispose of the pups, I will teach the bitch a lesson. A lesson you will long remember. At least as long as you live." He laughed again. "Which will not be that long after all."

"Anna . . ." It was Sandor.

"No. After this is over I will tell you a story that Ca—that Longbow told

me. About a cat and a mouse. For now, I would have you remember the
Grenna and how they rule."

"What be your meaning—oh!" Someone had obviously elbowed Sandor
in the side. Probably Jareth. Jareth would have understood first.

The boys fanned out in a wide circle, none higher or lower, none nearer
or farther, under Jareth's silent tutelage. Just like the Grenna's circle.

Then another sound reached Jenna, though she never took her eyes from
the Bear. She suspected from the sound and the slight widening of his eyes
that the tangle of men in the center of the field had at last unknotted itself.
Or the circle of swords had dispatched several warriors. She could tell that
the number of men around the Bear had doubled and guessed that none of
them had arrows left, or he would have been dead by now.

"Follow Jareth's lead," she cautioned to them. "Do not get within the
Bear's sword range."

"Come, little puppies; come, little snuffling hounds," the Bear taunted.
"One of you must make the first move. One of you must be brave enough
to show the others how to die." He kept turning, keeping them off guard,
bringing his sword from left to right. "Which shall it be? You, with the
pretty green band round your throat? Or you, with the long stalks for legs?
Or shall it be Alta's slut, whose white braid I shall cut off and hang upon
my helm?" He continued turning, addressing them all, but Jenna's warning
kept them far enough away so that even when he thrust forward, they were
out of his reach.

"Let him tire," Jenna said. "Do not let his sword take more of us."

"I do not tire," he said. "I will outlast you all."

If she hoped to tempt him into making a false move, he was too smart an
old warrior for that. He continued circling Iluna's body, never losing his
footing, never stumbling over her corpse, occasionally kicking at it as if to
underscore his ability to kill them all, one at a time.

Jenna began to feel his rhythm. Catrona had taught her that: how to
watch for an animal's particular rhythm in the woods. *What the pace?*
Catrona had cautioned them. *What the pattern?* It had been a constant
lesson in the woods, the only way to be sure a hunt would end successfully.
And this was just another hunt, Jenna thought. *Hunting the Bear.*

What was the Bear's pattern then? He moved feint, feint, feint, thrust;
feint, feint, thrust. But always, right before the thrust, there was the slight-
est of movements, a hitching of his right arm that signaled the forward cut
of the sword. She watched another few minutes to be sure, all the while
cautioning the men to wait. The waiting was clearly wearing on them, but it
would wear on the Bear as well.

When his back was momentarily turned to her, she bent swiftly and removed the knife from her boot. Across the circle, several men watched her. One man's eyebrows went up. It signaled the Bear, but he did not quite know what it meant. As he turned toward Jenna, more alert than he had been before, he saw the knife and smiled, guessing what she meant to do. He hitched his shoulder. But fooling him, she flung her sword point first, as they used to do in the game of wands at the Hame.

The Bear startled for a moment and beat the sword away with his hand and was back at attention in seconds. But at the same moment, Jareth, alert to Jenna's every move, flung his sword as well. He had never played at wands and did not understand the balance of a sword, how to compensate for the heavy braided hilt. Instead of going point first, the sword flipped and struck the Bear in the chest with the grip. He grabbed it with his left hand, laughing.

But at the same moment Jenna flung herself through the air. Before he could bring either sword up, she was on top of him, sinking the knife point between his eyes. He fell backward with Jenna on top. When she twisted the knife a half turn to the right, she felt the grinding against the bone. His right hand still clenching the sword came up behind her, as much a reflex as a stroke. One of the boys at her back gasped loudly and she hoped he had not been caught on the blade.

Then she stared down into the Bear's face, watching as the eyes below her glazed over. There was something horribly, hauntingly familiar about the feel of the knife in the bone and the man's dying eyes staring up at her. She could not recall where she had seen such a thing before.

"For Catrona!" she whispered into his slackening mouth. "For Iluna. For all the women you have killed." She could feel his body under hers tremble slightly, stiffen, then relax. He made no answer except to exhale a sour sigh through his rigid lips.

Jenna stood slowly, her hands bloody. Even more slowly she wiped them on her vest. When she turned away, she was shaking uncontrollably, as if she had caught a sudden fever. Jareth put his arms around her, trying to hold her still, but she could not stop shivering.

And then she heard a strange, thin cry that built up to a high, unrelenting pitch.

"Scillia!" Jenna whispered, turning back, all her trembling ended by the demands of that cry. "You poor little babe. You are mine, now."

She unstrapped the child from Iluna's back and held her tightly, but the babe would not be comforted. Her cranky crying—that strange, tearless sobbing—continued.

"Let her cry," Jenna said. "She has lost both mother and home in one short day. If she cannot cry for that, she will cry for nothing all the rest of her life."

"She be just hungry," Sandor said sensibly.

"Or wet," someone else commented.

Jenna ignored them, bouncing the swaddled infant in her left arm and leading them all across the field, past the dying and the dead.

As she walked, she made careful note of their faces. It was the New Steading boys, mostly, who had died upon that lea in their bright clothes and with their untried swords, still sheathed. There were few familiar faces among the dead. But somehow that made her all the sadder, that these boys had died strangers to her, without a word of comfort. She had promised herself not to cry for death, but she could not help it, though she wept silently that no one should hear, tears streaming from her eyes. Seeing Jenna's tears, the baby stopped her own crying and, fascinated, reached out her hand to touch a tear and trace its path. Jenna kissed that tiny hand.

None of the dead men on the field was Carum. Jenna made quite sure of that before heading toward the ring of swordsmen, now relaxed and waiting. As she approached, one came out to speak with her. She recognized him at once, Gileas with the scarred eye.

He put a hand to his forehead, a sketchy kind of salute.

"Anna, you must come quickly. It is the king. He's dying."

"And his brother?" she asked quietly, suddenly aware of the other bodies within the circle of men. "Carum Longbow. What of him?"

"Took!" Gileas answered. "Took like a good many of 'em. They blew a victory on their bloody horns, took what they could, and were fast away, leaving whatever of their men was dead and whichever was still fighting behind. Took!"

Took! Her mind could not quite hold it. She repeated it to herself over and over and still did not grasp it. *Took!*

He guided her to Gorum who lay against Piet's knees. There was a smudge of old blood around his mouth. He was not smiling. How Jenna longed to see that wolfish smile now.

"Pike," she whispered, realizing how easy forgiveness could come. She knelt by his side. The babe in her arms cooed and reached for the king.

Still unsmiling, Gorum lifted his hand and touched the child's out-stretched fingers.

"Jenna," he said, his voice a shadow. "You must find him. Find Carum. Bring him to me. I must tell him. He will soon be king."

Jenna looked up, startled. "No one has told him?"

Piet shook his head.

"Told me what?" The old fire returned to his voice, then trailed off.

"That Carum . . ."

Piet put a finger to his lips.

"That Carum . . . is still fighting. Bravely. Well. Not just with the bow, but the sword, too."

"I was wrong, then. He will make a fine king." He closed his eyes for a moment, then opened them again.

"You are the king," Jenna whispered, "as long as you are alive. And you are not dead yet. You will live long. I know."

"You are a prophecy, girl, not a prophet. I am dead already. A king . . ." He coughed and fresh blood frothed at his mouth. He swallowed it down painfully. "A king knows even more than a girl. That is why I am the king." This time he managed to smile. "You will make a fine queen, Jenna. I was right about that though wrong about the other."

"Wrong?"

"Hush, dinna waste breath," Piet cautioned.

"It doesn't matter, and don't you go being a silly nursemaid now," the king said. "I need to tell her." He tried to sit a little straighter, slumped back into Piet's arms. "I was wrong. We had not the might to go against Kalas. Not yet. Not ever. Remember the story of the mouse and the cat that mother . . . did he tell you? I don't think I have the breath for it now."

"He told me."

His voice was barely audible "Remember . . ."

"I will remember."

"You really are the end," he whispered. "At least, you are mine." His eyes closed.

"I killed the Bear," Jenna whispered, sure she was talking to a dead man.

"Of course," the king said, eyes still closed. "It was written." He did not move again.

They sat for many minutes, Piet cradling the king in his arms. No one spoke, though every now and then a cough shattered the stillness. The baby slept with a bubbling stillness and Jenna carefully set the sleeping child by Gorum's side.

Piet looked up. "Gone," he admitted at last.

Gone. The word reverberated in Jenna's head. *The king was gone. Carum was gone. One dead, the other missing. Both gone.* She was about to speak when Sandor shouted.

"Hold! An army. Through the trees."

"Hold, indeed," Jenna said. "Those are women. The sisters of M'dorah. Do you not see Petra in the lead?"

"Women, bah!" a boy's voice called out. Others echoed him.

"Shut that silly trap of yourn," Piet said. "Have ye never seen a girl fight? I have. Side by side, I have. And they are the best of us. Certainly better than thee, boy. And the Anna here, is the best of all. Hasn't she just done the Bear? What has thee to squawk about now?"

"Nowt." The boy looked down. The ones who cheered him originally were silent.

"Welcome them, then," Piet said. "Raise yer bloody voices and call them in. Girls like that."

They set up a cry, compounded of grief and welcome, and waved their arms, a strange ululating that brought the sisters of M'dorah across the blood-soaked field to their midst.

They buried their own men in one common grave, the men of Kalas' army in another. The king and Iluna had separate graves. Above the king's they set a marker with his name and a crown carved by Sandor, who had some skill. He carved a marker for Iluna's as well, the goddess sign copied from the ring Petra was wearing.

The sisters of M'dorah were good nurses, binding up the wounds of those for whom binding would make a difference, the men who could still ride. The others that Piet determined could stand to travel, he insisted be sent back to New Steading. He had the men build makeshift sleds from the tree limbs, cushioned by blanket strips. These the horses could pull. Three of the older women, who were not warriors anyway, volunteered to guide the horses down the road and report on what had happened.

"The babes go, too," Jenna said. "If this is indeed an ending, then one of the things that ends here is our bringing children into any fray."

"But it has always been done," Maltia protested.

All around her the women nodded vigorously. "Always," they murmured.

"It says in the *Book* that: *A foolish loyalty can be the greater danger.* This I was reminded of by the one who anointed me. Surely you would not disagree?"

There were many looks passed between the women and not all of them, Jenna was sure, signaled an easy agreement.

"One can be as foolishly loyal to past customs as to people," Petra said.

"Yes." Jenna's voice was firm. "And this custom ends here. Today. We will, I am sure, sing of it in the future." She handed little Scillia to the True

Speaker. The child whimpered as she went from hand to hand. "But I shall return and take this child for my own."

"She belongs to us, Anna," Maltia said. "She belongs to M'dorah."

"M'dorah is no more," Jenna reminded her gently. "When I took her from Iluna's care, my hands were still red from the blood of Iluna's killer. She is mine, little Scillia. I will love her well."

"I will keep her until ye return," Maltia said. "And then ye can tell me, without the wind of battle in thy mouth, how well it is ye love her."

Jenna nodded.

The other two babies were handed to the sisters, with many whispers of farewell. Then the women embraced, not once but many times. Strapping the children onto their backs, Maltia and the other two women took up the horses' reins and started to guide the line of roped horses and their sleds down the road to New Steading.

"Mount up!" Piet called when they were nearly out of sight.

"We do not know how to ride," a woman cried out.

"You will learn on the way," Jenna promised cheerily, "even as I did."

"Horses!" a rosy-cheeked young woman said, and spat. "They be an abomination."

"But a necessary and quick one," Petra said. "If the Anna can learn to ride, anyone can." She smiled.

After several missteps and one disastrous hard fall suffered by an older woman with a chunky face and a determined mouth, the sisters were finally mounted.

"Which way now?" Jenna asked Piet.

"Farther north. They rode off that way and, I suspect, to Kalas' holdings. With prisoners—especially the young prince—they will not be staying in the old king's palace. Too many of his supporters live there yet. Besides, Kalas always had the biggest dungeons."

Jenna digested that information, then asked, "And they will not return here to end what they so foully began?"

Piet smiled sourly. "They believe it already ended. And so it seemed to me, girl. The Bear slew the king. They carried off Prince Longbow and another double dozen of our fighters. They trust the Bear to finish the rest and that he will follow."

"Do you truly believe that?" Jenna asked.

"I bet my life upon it," said Piet.

"You just have," Jenna answered. "And mine as well." She turned and signaled them all to follow and they rode, three abreast, toward the north.

THE TALE

*There was once a nest of seven mice who lived behind the kitchen wall.
They had been warned by their Mam before she disappeared that when they
were old enough to go out of the nest, they had to go with great care and all
together, not one at a time.*

*"For if you go one after one," she said, "the great cat who lives by the stove
will eat you up. It will catch you if it can."*

*Now the little mice listened to her, but that was all she said. And so how
could they be afraid of an It they had never seen? One by one, when they
were old enough they crept out of the hole. And one by one they disappeared
into It's mouth. Until at last there was only the smallest mouse left, named
Little Bit.*

*Little Bit's turn came on a bright spring day. But he had heard the sound
of It's teeth and claws outside the hole. And though Little Bit was small, he
was cunning. He peeked out of the hole and sure enough there was the
monstrous It, snoring by the stove, with one eye open.*

*"This needs a plan," he told himself. So he searched throughout the hole
and all along the inside of the boards, until he came up with enough materi-
als to complete his plan. He worked for many days, well into the evening, for
plans take patience and time. But at last he was done. He looked at his
handiwork: an army of twenty mice made from sticks and gray cotton, with
raisins for eyes and string for tails. He tied them one to another and the last
he tied to his own tail with a special knot.*

*"All home free!" he cried as loud as he could, to alert the cat. "Come on,
boys!" Then he ran out of the hole hauling those toy mice behind him,
lumpity, bumpity, over the floor.*

*Well, It was up in a single jump, certain of the fine meal ahead. And It
picked off the mice from the back end first: one, two, three . . . but they
were all stuck together. Their tails tangled in It's claws. It howled in anger
and stuffed two in It's mouth. Phew! Phwat! Psssaw!*

*Little Bit ran free, as the knot slipped loose from his tail. When he got to
the kitchen door, he stopped for a moment, singing out:*

> *"I am just a Little Bit,*
> *But I made a fool of It.*

*Greedy guts and greedy paws
Makes a tangle out of claws"*

Then he ran out into the spring meadow to look for his Mam.

THE MYTH

At last Great Alta shook her hair and a gift fell out of it onto the land below. The gift was a Babe in whose right hand was a star of purest silver. Her left hand was hid behind her.

"The star is yours, though you were not born with it. And in your left hand is a star of gold. Whichever you choose shall shine brightest of all. The star will be both your guide and your grief. It will be your light and your loss. It will be your close companion."

The child tossed the silver star into the night sky. It glittered there and shone down on the roads throughout all the land.

At this the child smiled and brought her left hand to the front. She opened it. There was no star there.

Then Great Alta smiled. She braided up her hair, both the dark side and the light, and pinned it on her head as a crown. A golden star gleamed in the center.

"You have chosen and it is so," quoth Great Alta. "Blessed be."

BOOK FIVE

The Dark Tower

THE MYTH

Then Great Alta set a pillar of darkness on the one end of the plain. On the other she set a pillar of fire. In between ran a path as thin as the edge of a knife and as sharp.

"She who can walk the path and she who can capture both towers is the one I shall love best of all," quoth Great Alta. "But woe to the woman whose foot is heavy on the path or whose heart is light at the tower, for she shall fail and her failure will bring doom to the land forever."

THE LEGEND

There is an odd plain not far from Newmarket that grows neither grass nor trees. All that is there are dozens of high rocks, great towers of stone, some hundreds of feet in the air. The tallest of all stand almost two hundred feet high, one on the north side and one on the south.

The rock on the north side of the plain looks as if it had been blasted with fire. The rock on the south has the mark of the sea.

Atop the Fire Rock are strange remains: wood ash and bone buttons and the carved handle of a knife with a circle and a half cross incised in it. Atop the Sea Rock there is nothing at all.

The folk of Newmarket say that once two sisters lived on those two towers of stone, a black-haired one on Fire Rock, a white-haired one on Sea Rock. They had not spoken in fifty years. Their argument had been lost to memory, but their anger was still fresh.

One day a child came riding across the plain on a great gray horse. The child was beautiful, his hair a dazzling yellow, his face Great Alta's own.

Both sisters looked down from their rocks and desired the child. They climbed down and each tried to cozen him.

"I will give you gold," said the dark sister.

"I will give you jewels," said the light.
"I will give you a crown," said the one.
"I will give you a collar," said the other.
The child shook his head sadly. "If you had offered love," he said, "gladly would I have stayed though you gave me naught but stone to eat and naught but rock for a pillow."
The anger that the sisters had so honed for one another bubbled hot once again, and the desire that each had conceived for the child added to it. The dark sister took the child by the right hand, the light sister by the left. They pulled first one way and then the other until the child was pulled entirely in two. Then they scrambled up each to her own lonely rock, cradling the half child in her arms, singing lullabies to the dead babe, until they died of grief themselves.
Their tears and the child's blood watered the top of the tower of rocks causing a lovely flower to grow. Partling, the Newmarket folk call the flower, and Blood-o-babe. It brings ease to the pain of childbirth when boiled in a tisane.

THE STORY

Kalas' army, having no need to disguise its trail, was easy to follow.

"North and north and north again," Jenna pointed out.

"To the castle," Piet added.

"And the dungeon," Jenna whispered grimly. "Surely it is not as bad as you say."

"Worse, girl. It is called Kalas' Hole and them that calls it so, mean no mere hole in the ground."

Piet made sure their approach was little noted by the few villages along the way. This was accomplished by breaking the riders into smaller groups, though the women of M'dorah refused to ride alongside any men. Marek, Sandor, and Gileas rode carefully ahead, reporting back every few hours. Though Jenna was frustrated by their slow progress, she agreed fully with Piet when he remarked, "Speed brings notice."

They supplied themselves in the woods without any great trouble, even with so large a group. The women of M'dorah were wily hunters and it being late into the spring, there were ferns, mushrooms, and good berries aplenty. For half the trip a small river paralleled the road and their skin bags were kept topped off with fresh water. Even when the stream turned and meandered on a more easterly route, they were never far from some small pond or stream. Fish were plentiful.

One man became sick from a purple berry, and seven of the remaining New Steading boys deserted one night. Two of the M'dorans developed horrible sores on their inner thighs from riding. The man recovered, though for a day he wished he might die. The boys were gone for good, but no others joined them. The two women could ride no longer and were left at a lonely farmhouse in the care of an old woman who welcomed them rather stiffly but nevertheless promised to treat them well.

That left barely one hundred riders, though they were well supplied with swords and knives, bows and shields.

Jenna had never been so far north and was amazed at the change in the woods. Used to the fellowship of larch, elm, and oak, she recognized fewer and fewer trees but the hardy pine which left scattered beds of sweet-smelling ground cover. When they camped the first time, Jenna remarked to Petra, "If there were not such need to go on, I could almost enjoy this."

"You do enjoy this," Petra said, leaning on one elbow. "You enjoy it for all that you know blood waits at the trail's end."

Jenna thought about Petra's words as they rode the next day. She wondered if Petra was right, and if so, what that meant about her own nature. How could she enjoy a journey whose ending would undoubtedly be blood-soaked? How could she admire a countryside that was the burial ground for so many good women and men? How could she let the scented pine needles rain through her fingers when the man she loved above all others lay in a foul-smelling dungeon? How could she even notice the difference in meadow and wood when they were potential battlefields? Her mind boiled like a soup pot with the questions. But the road held no answers for her and Duty's steady rolling stride only brought her closer to the bloody ending of which Petra warned.

The journey would take seven days.

"Four," Piet explained, "if care were not needed."

"Three," Jenna added, "if you and I went alone. And did not sleep."

"It would be good, girl, to cut that time. But then we'd be cutting our chances as well. Kalas' castle is nigh impregnable. All rock and stone with but one big gate and three portcullises, inner iron gates. Well guarded, too. They built it right into the cliffside so the back cannot be attacked. Then they made another cliff for the front."

"There is one thing good," Jenna said.

"And that be?"

"The M'dorans are rock climbers."

"I am thinking that, too." There was approval in his voice for the first time.

"They could be the other mice pulled along behind me . . ." Jenna mused aloud.

"For the cat to snatch up first." Piet chuckled. When Jenna looked surprised, he said, "That is an old family tale of mine. My mam told it to my little sister and me and she told it to her sons."

"Her sons . . ." He had thrown in the revelation so casually, Jenna could scarcely credit it. Finally she blurted out, "Are you . . . the king's uncle?"

He laughed. "The king's uncle? What be . . . oh, no, girl. They be Garuns and I be wholly of the Dales. No mixed blood in me at all. But my little sister and Carum's Mam, were childhood friends." He rubbed his finger roughly against his beard. "Met those boys when Carum was five years old. Prettiest little child ye ever did see. The darling of the court. And smart as a . . ."

"Not Carum's uncle then." She felt, somehow, disappointed.

"I was just back from the Continent. Horrid place. Full of foreigners," Piet said, throwing his head back in a laugh.

"So you knew them all?" Jenna asked. "Even saintly Jorum?"

"Jor—saintly? Who gave ye that idea? He was as sly as they come. Always in trouble. Always running up stairs to put the blame on someone else. And Carum always willing to take it. If there be a saint in that family . . . but not their uncle, no. For all they were good kings, they dinna think much of the folk of the Dales. Garuns first—and the Dales to make the sacrifice. That were the way. Though they were good to me and mine. And Carum, being half Dale, he was good altogether."

"Would . . ." Jenna suddenly interrupted. "Would it be wrong to pull the others along behind, to sacrifice them that I might get to the castle and get Carum out?"

"That is no sacrifice, girl. That is a ruse." He stroked his beard again and looked at her strangely. "Young Carum is king now. We must all do our part to set him free and some will likely die. That is the bloody way of war."

They rode on.

The days were as warm as ever, but as they rode north the evenings turned chilly, and the nights were positively cold. Northern weather made no obeisance to spring. The men were forced to share blankets with other men, the women with women.

The first time Jenna and Petra lay side by side, Jenna's blanket on the ground beneath them, Petra's on top, Jenna could not sleep. She stared at the sky for a long time counting the stars and Petra's smooth, even breaths. She got to a thousand before making up her mind.

At last she peeled back her side of the blanket and slipped out, careful not to disturb Petra. Signaling the men on watch, she walked to the edge of the woods, some fifty feet from the sleepers. Someone was there before her; she recognized one of the M'dorans, a young woman whose name she had never actually heard or, if heard, did not recall.

"You could not sleep either?"

The young woman grunted her response, then as if the question released something, began to talk in a whispery voice, alternately braiding and unbraiding one of a dozen thin plaits in her hair.

"Sleep? How could I sleep? I grieve. Iluna was my friend. My *closest* friend, closer even than my dark sister. And now she is gone. Gone. Gone where I cannot follow."

Jenna nodded, having neither an answer nor an easy sentiment to offer. She knew that sometimes simply talking out a grief made it easier to bear.

"I do not understand," the girl continued. "One minute we were all so . . . so . . ." She hesitated, looking for the right word, her hands still busy with yet another braid. "Happy—unhappy. Those words had no meaning on our rock. We were . . ." She gave a sharp tug on the braid as she found the word she was looking for. "*Content.* We were content. And then ye came, a prophecy most of us had never heard of and some of us could not believe in. Word become flesh." She turned slightly, her face all in shadow. It was as if a mask spoke.

"I thought . . ." Jenna began. "I thought you all recited the prophecy together and that was what convinced you."

"Words!" the girl said, voice shaking. "That is all it was: words. But Iluna was real. She was flesh and blood. Flesh of my flesh, blood of my blood. We swore to love one another always. We even cut our fingers and mixed our lives in blood when we were children. See." She turned and held out her hand to Jenna.

Jenna took her hand and held it up, as if she could read the girl's history there, but it was only a hand. Like her own. Nothing more.

"Words are for the old women. Iluna and I, we planned to leave M'dorah together. To see what else the world held. And when we were satisfied it held nothing, then we planned to return. But together. Together. And now she is . . . she is . . ." She began to snuffle, running the hand she had held up to Jenna across her mouth and nose, as if to stifle the sound.

Jenna nodded. "I understand. You will want the child after."

"The child?"

"Scillia."

"Oh no. I had told Iluna the child was not to come. It was our one argument, the only one we had ever had. No, White One, ye can keep the babe. I only want"—the snuffling began again—"Iluna." The name was a sob in her mouth.

Jenna put her arms around the girl, letting her cry. But she could not still her own thoughts. What if Carum said the same thing when she told him of the child. Would he cry out, "I want only you"? Would she still take the little one-armed babe if he denied it? She bit her lip hard to remind herself that her entire rehearsal of that conversation depended upon finding Carum alive. Taking the girl by the shoulders, she shook her.

"Enough! Iluna would not have you cry for her. She would have you remember with courage."

Pulling away from Jenna's grip, the girl nodded. She scrunged her shirt-tail over her face, drying her eyes and blowing her nose loudly. Then she walked away as if embarrassed that Jenna had comforted her at all.

For a moment Jenna considered following her. Then she shrugged and turned back to the encampment. Jareth, who happened to be on watch, stared at her, his hand covering his throat.

"Just battle jitters I expect," Jenna said, brushing a stray hair back from her face. She sighed. "Oh, Jareth, I am so tired of this. I want to be home. I want . . ." She looked at him. "I want to be able to talk to you. You were such a comfort before."

He stared at her for another moment, then took his hand from his neck. It was bare.

"Jareth—the collar—where?"

He mimed a sword cut, an upward blow. She suddenly remembered the sound of a gasp behind her when she had buried the knife between the Bear's eyes.

"Then you can talk now? You have been able to talk these past days?"

He shook his head vigorously, pointing strangely at his mouth.

"Gone?" she whispered. "The collar off and your voice still gone? Was it all a lie, then? Like the cradle and the hall? Is Catrona dead, Carum captured, and all those buried back there in the field for a lie?" She reached out to touch his arm, heard a noise behind her, and turned. Marek and Sandor stood close together.

"He can talk but he *will not,* Anna," Sandor said carefully, using her own dialect. "He *dare* not talk else he shatter the fellowship."

"What fellowship," Jenna asked, her voice heavy with sarcasm. "Women who will not speak to men and men who laugh at women. A Dale warrior who rightly blames me for the death of his beloved, and three boys who believe a scared, incompetent girl is some sort of goddess?"

"You be leaving out Petra," Sandor said softly, slipping back into his own speech.

"A rhyming priestess," Jenna said, "who surely could not kill without getting sick on it."

"We be all that," admitted Marek. "Do you be feeling better saying it?"

"No," Jenna said miserably.

"Well, we be a fellowship nonetheless," Sandor said.

"That we be," Marek added, smiling.

"But what if it is lies," Jenna whispered. "If it is *all* lies?"

"He still be not talking, Anna, because he *believes,*" Marek said.

"And I," added Sandor. "Not until the king be crowned and the king's right hand be winning the war."

"You be his right hand," Marek said.

"And Carum king. I be glad of that," Sandor finished.

"Oh, you brave, loyal boys," Jenna whispered, suddenly remembering Alta's fire that went ever before. "So much braver and so much more loyal than I."

They put their arms about her then, all four thinking about what had already been and what must surely come. Jenna, Sandor, and Marek whispered memories back and forth as if telling themselves a wonderful tale, but they did it quietly, so as not to disturb the sleepers around them. And when at last they pulled away from one another, their faces hot and tight with unshed tears, they were each silhouetted against the night sky. To Jenna the three boys looked as though they had been crowned with stars.

She went back to the blanket which Petra had now firmly wrapped around herself. Unwilling to wake her for a share, Jenna lay down on the cold ground beside her and willed herself into a dreamless sleep.

THE SONG

Well Before the Battle, Sister

Well before the battle, sister,
When the sky is crowned with stars,
And the world is clean of wounded,
And the ground is free of scars.

Well before the battle, sister,
When content with what we know,
We will sing the lovely ballads
From the long and long ago.

THE STORY

By the time they reached the outskirts of Kalas' Northern Holdings, on a path which Piet insisted was marked by blood, though there was nothing to show it—not bones nor broken armor nor mounds of buried dead—the moon was coming into full again. That doubled the number of women at night, making even Piet uncomfortable. The men came up with both feeble and outrageous suggestions as to where the women had come from.

"Out of the woods," Gileas said to the New Steading boys. "They be trailing us all along."

"Mayhap they live here around," one boy said.

The others thought that a foolish idea, and told him so loudly.

"Nay," Piet said. "They be friends of our girls. Cousins, most like. See how much they resemble one another." It was the explanation they settled on in the end.

But it meant that at night, at least, the enlarged band was hard to disguise. Since Piet knew the land well, having served one year in the North, he kept them in the forest as deep as could be managed with horses.

Under the heavy cover of trees, their numbers were once again halved. If the men wondered about it, they did so silently.

They left the horses crowded together in a small dell and went by foot the last mile towards Kalas' castle, single file and without talking. At the woods' edge, Piet signaled them to halt and they fanned out along the edge, being careful to each stay behind a tree.

Under the eye of a leperous moon, Kalas' castle was a great black vulture throwing a vast predatory shadow over the plain. It had two stone wings, the crenellated walls like feathers of rock. A single tower stretched up, the bird's naked neck. And in the single window, like a staring eye, a light gleamed. It was the only visible light in the place.

"There," Piet said, pointing. "The girls will climb straight up that rock face while I take the men to the gate there." His hand moved slightly. "We will make a great clamour and a rattling of swords. If they lower the gate to get at us, some will go through it. If it stays up, we will climb up it ourselves."

Jenna nodded.

"Two lines of mice are better than one against *this* great cat," Piet added.

"And the dungeon?"

"There is no way but from inside. That is why you go up the tower." His pointing finger shifted two palms worth to the left, where the rock seemed to grow right out of the ground forming an impenetrable wall.

"Kalas' tower!" Jenna whispered.

"How will you get up that, Jenna?" Petra asked.

Where the rock ended, the tall brick cylinder rose straight up into the air. Not a vulture's neck, Jenna thought, but a spear jabbing at the sky.

"Slowly," Jenna said. "And with a great deal of difficulty. But I will get up it all the same."

"If anyone can, you can," Petra said in her ear. "The prophecy knows it. Alta will see to it."

Jenna looked steadily at the tower. It was at least a hundred feet high. Privately, she prayed that Alta had a very long arm. "When I get to Kalas' room," she said steadily, "I will put my knife to his throat and make him take me personally to the dungeon to set the king free. If there is blood this night, it will be Kalas'." She spoke with the firm enunciation she had learned from listening to Gorum, but her heart beat erratically as she spoke. She was not nearly as certain as she appeared.

"We will have the surprise this time," Piet said grimly. "They think us all dead."

"We be having the right on our side as well," Marek added.

"Ah, lad, on the Continent they say: *The mice may have the right but the cat has the claws.* Whenever did right guarantee a victory but in a tale?" He stared ahead at the castle. "Do not be counting on the right. King Gorum did, and we buried him. I dinna want to bury you, too."

"Nor we you, Piet," said Jenna.

They waited until a shred of cloud covered the moon, then the women raced forward to the near wall, the men veering off toward the only gate.

Jenna set off on her own, avoiding Petra's attempt to catch her eye. If she thought about Petra or about all those who might be killed in the attempt on Kalas' castle, she knew she would become paralyzed, unable to climb. She forced herself to think only of the rocks ahead.

When she got to the precipitous stone, its sheer size overwhelmed her. At its base, she could see nothing above and nothing to either side but more and more stone, an endless wall of it. In the dark she could discern no handholds at all. Then suddenly the moon came out of its covering of cloud, and Skada was beside her pointing out the route.

"There!" she said. "And there."

"An odd sort of greeting," Jenna complained, tucking her braid down the back of her shirt.

"We have no time for pleasantries," Skada said, fixing her own hair. "And you are already breathing hard even before the climb."

"If I could appear and disappear under the light as you do," Jenna said testily, "I would not need to breathe at all." But nonetheless it was a good reminder that she had forgotten the first rule Mother Alta had taught her so long ago, that of proper breathing. She forced herself to think about the careful spider breaths for climbing. As she did so, she heard Skada's breathing synchronizing with her own.

Slow hand by slow hand, feet slotted into the shallow ridges, they began to climb. Every few moments they waited together, breathed together, gathered strength, then moved on up. The soft leather of their boots was scraped, their skin leggings had a hole in the right knee. Still they climbed.

The moon suddenly disappeared behind another cloud and Skada was gone, but Jenna, so intent on the rock under her hand, foot, and face, never noticed.

A minute later the moon came out again and Skada reappeared, clinging as Jenna did to the stone.

"You breathe hard, sister," Skada said.

"In my ear, sister," Jenna replied. "You are doing this to annoy. I wish to

Alta you would stop." But she slowed her breathing down again and found the climbing easier.

The wall, shadow-scarred and crumbling, fooled both hand and eye. What seemed a chink was often solid. What appeared solid, a handful of dust. The mistakes cost them precious minutes, took them equally by surprise. Jenna wondered whether the others had reached their goals, the women scaling the far side of the castle, the men at the gate. But when she thought about them, her right hand slipped and she found herself desperately grabbing for rocks that kept falling to pieces beneath her. One shard cut deeply into her palm. She cursed, and heard an answering curse from Skada. With great concentration, she found another handhold and Skada's sigh was a welcome sound.

Above them—way above—was the lighted window. Jenna knew that they had to be there before dawn because she needed Skada, both for the sword she could wield and the comfort she might give. She said so aloud.

"Thank you for the thought," Skada whispered, "but keep on climbing."

For a moment, Jenna stopped, put her right palm to her mouth, and licked the small, bloody shred. Skada did the same, almost seeming to mock her. Neither of them smiled. Then Jenna set her hand back on the rock and began the climb once more.

Inches were gained at the cost of minutes. The wall did not so much fight them as resist them; their own bodies became their worst enemies. There is only so much stretch in the ligaments, so much give to muscles, so much strength in even the strongest arm and thigh. But at last Jenna's hand felt along the top of the stone wall.

"Tower base," she whispered. But the moon was once again behind a cloud and there was no longer anyone to whisper to.

"Alta's Hairs!" Jenna muttered, using a curse she rarely allowed herself. She pulled with both arms, heaving herself over the top. Even the skins were little protection against the wall. She could feel the roughness of the stone through the hides.

Rolling to her knees, she found herself staring at a large pair of boots.

"Look up slowly," came a voice. "I would like to see the surprise on your face before I strike you down. Look up, dead man."

From her knees, Jenna looked up slowly, never stopping her prayer for a sliver of moonlight. When she finally stared at the guard, his face was suddenly lit by a full and shining moon.

Jenna smiled at him.

"By Cres, you are no man," he said, relaxing for a fraction of a second and starting to smile back.

Jenna looked down coyly, a maneuver she had seen on the face of one of the serving girls in New Steading, and held out her hand.

Automatically the soldier reached down.

"Now!" Jenna cried.

Startled, he stepped back. But he was even more startled when, from behind him and below his knees, he was struck by another kneeling form. He tumbled over and was dead before the blade came sliding out of his heart.

Jenna hoisted the man's body on her shoulder and heaved it over the wall. She did not wait to hear it land. When she turned to speak to Skada, Skada looked stunned.

"What is it?" Jenna asked.

"I . . . I have never actually killed a man before," Skada whispered. "The knife went in and out and he was dead."

"But we killed the Hound," Jenna pointed out. "And the Bear. And cut off the Bull's hand which led to his death."

"No, Jenna, *you* did that."

"You are my dark sister. You feel what I feel. You know what I know."

"It . . . is . . . not . . . the . . . same," Skada said, pulling each word across her tongue with great difficulty.

"No," Jenna said at last. "You are right. I do not feel about this unnamed guard what I felt about the others. My hand does not remember his death in quite the same way."

They touched hands for a moment. "We had better resume the climb up that tower. This is just the first stop. If there are other guards . . ."

Skada nodded.

"And once daylight comes, you are of no practical use. If I die . . ."

Skada smiled grimly. "You do not have to remind me. Every dark sister knows the rules of living and of light. I live as you live, die as you die. Only get up that wall. I cannot start without you."

Jenna stared up at the tower wall. The bricks were newer than the stone along the great wall they had just climbed, but the ravages of the northern winds had pulped part of the facade. Bits of the brick would crumble underhand.

As they began the new ascent, whispers volleyed between them, though nothing so loud they would awaken any guards. Occasionally, they cursed. The curses served as a cup of borrowed courage might, strengthening their resolve and reminding them that anger would serve when purpose faltered.

Jenna reached the tower window first, but only fractionally. Below one torn fingernail blood seeped. The cut on her palm ached. Her legs were beginning to tremble with the effort of climbing. There was a spot between her shoulders that was knotted with pain. She ignored them all, concentrating all her effort on the windowsill and the light filtering over it. Under her tunic, muscles bunched as, with a final pull, she hoisted herself up to the sill onto her stomach. The sill was broad and her legs kicked Skada's head. All she felt was relief to be off of the wall and irritation with Skada.

"Out of the way."

"It is your legs that are at fault," Skada answered huffily. "My head only moves in a limited direction."

Pushing herself up, Jenna tumbled them both off the sill. She caught hold of a lantern to stop the fall and dashed them both against the floor. The lantern landed first and went out; the fall seemed to take forever.

Voices scrabbled around Jenna in the dark.

"I have him," someone cried and Jenna felt her arms seized. She was pushed to her knees, the sword belt slashed from her waist. Struggling did no good; it only forced her arms up higher behind her till she was sure they would break. She relaxed into the hold, waiting.

"Light the torches, fools," came a command. The voice was soft, but no less powerful for its softness.

A torch was lit, stuttering to life. It was held over Jenna's head. An odd scrambling sound from the corner made the voice from the darkness add: "There's a second one, double fools. And idiots, all. Bring the torch over there."

Two men, one with the torch and one with a drawn sword, ran over to the corner but the strong light dispelled all shadows. Only along the far wall, where no one but Jenna looked, were a bent leg, a quick turn of head.

"There is no one, Lord Kalas."

"Just a trick of light," Jenna said smoothly. "Would I have been captured so easily if I had had a companion? I come alone. I am always alone. It is . . ." She hesitated thinking of the right word to cozen him. "It is my one conceit."

The men brought the torch back and held it close to Jenna's face.

"It is the White One, my lord Kalas," the man with the torch said. "If we have her as well as the prince, the rebellion is all but over. They say . . ."

"They say . . . they say altogether too much," Kalas said. "Let me look at her. Why, she is scarcely out of childhood." He laughed. "I had thought her a grown woman. She is but a long-legged, white-haired colt."

Meanwhile Jenna looked at him, past the glare of the torchlight. She had heard many things about him from Carum and Piet, and none of them good. But could this faded coxcomb, with the dyed red hair and the dyed red beard that only emphasized the pouching under his eyes, be the infamous Lord Kalas of the Northern Holdings? How could he be that wily toad they all so hated and feared?

"I'm not interested in what the others say, but you may be fascinated by what that late, lamented, sniveling princeling Carum—who calls himself Longbow for no discernible reason—says about you."

Jenna controlled her tongue, thinking quickly that Kalas had put Carum's name in both the past and the present. But the guard had not. Was Carum dead? It was not possible. She would have *known*, she would have felt something if he had died. *Late. Lamented.* Perhaps Kalas was referring to the title of prince and not the man himself. Garunians liked to play with words. She allowed herself to smile up at her captor, showing him nothing of what she felt.

"And shall I tell *you* what the very late and not at all lamented Bear had to say about you, you dyed rooster?"

"Ah," Kalas whispered, "not a child then. A woman with a woman's wiles. I should have known you even had you changed *your* hair color. Longbow's White Goddess. He said your mouth opened as quickly as your legs, like most women of the Dales."

"Carum would never . . ." She closed her mouth, feeling like a child, indeed, to have fallen for a such a trick.

"A man on a rack says many things, my dear."

"Few of them true," Jenna added.

Kalas leaned over and put his hand lightly on her head, as if to stroke her. Instead he pulled the braid out of her shirt and yanked.

"Girls playing at women have a certain kind of charm. Women playing at girls another. But women playing at warriors bore me." He pulled a smile over his discolored teeth, yellowed with piji. "And you, for such a pretty girl, do it badly. Your prince is in the dungeon, not my chamber, so all your climbing has been for naught . . ." He tapped her right knee with the flat of his blade. "Except to strengthen those comely legs."

"By Alta's Hair . . ." Jenna began, hoping that by swearing she might better disguise her feelings.

"Alta's Hairs are gray and much too short to keep her warm," the smooth, mocking voice replied. "And that is what we have you by—Alta's short hairs!" He laughed at his own crudity. "But if you insist on playing a man's game, we will treat you like a man, and instead of warming my bed— which you would doubtless do with little grace though youth does have certain advantages, even Dalian youth—you will freeze with the others in my dungeon."

Jenna bit her lip, trying to appear frightened, when actually the dungeon was the very place she wanted to be. Though she wanted to be there with both her sword and her dagger.

"Ah, I see you have heard of it. What is it they call it?" He yanked her braid again, this time wrapping it three times around his fist and bringing his face close to hers. For a moment she was afraid he was going to kiss her. His breath was sickly sweet with the odor of piji. The thought of that mouth on hers made her ill.

"They call it . . . Kalas' Hole," she whispered.

"Enjoy it," he said, pulling his face away. "Others have." He turned from her so quickly, his lizard-skin cape sang like a whip around his ankles. Then he was gone.

The guards pushed Jenna down the stairs, descending it quickly. *Much more quickly,* she mused, *than the laborious climb up that wall.*

Her hands were so tightly bound behind her, she had lost the feeling in her fingers by the second level. The one consolation was that the man with the torch went ahead, and so the shadows of their moving bodies were ranged behind them. If he had been at the end of the line, there would have been a second bound woman on the stairs, with a dark braid down her back, leggings with a hole in the knee, and a head that ached.

Jenna promised herself that she would do nothing to make any of the guards look back to where Skada was following; neither by a remark nor by a movement would she betray her.

The stairs twisted round and round through the tower. When they began a straight descent, Jenna knew the tower had ended and the main part of the castle had begun. At each level, the air grew cooler and mustier. There were great wooden doors on either side, with a single barred window. As they passed, she could see pale patches at the windows, but it was only after the third that she realized they were faces. After that she lifted her head, turning toward the doors, so that whosoever was inside might see and recognize her. She would not be buried in secret.

At the stairs' end was a final heavy wooden door barring the way. It took three keys to unbolt the door and when it was finally opened, Jenna was pushed in without further ceremony and the door locked behind. Not a word had been spoken the entire trip down the stairs.

The dungeon certainly deserved its name. Lord Kalas' Hole was dark, dank, wet, and smelled like the hind end of a diarrhetic ox. Even without ever having been behind one, Jenna knew the smell.

To keep herself from gagging, Jenna turned back and shouted at the departing guards, "May you be hanged in Alta's hair. May She thread your guts through Her braids and use your skull . . ."

"I have never heard you curse before," came a voice made almost unfamiliar with fatigue. "But you could at least try something original."

"Carum!" Jenna whispered, spinning around and trying to find him in the dark. "That we were put in the same cell."

"Oh, this is the special one, lady," came another voice from the dark. "The worst."

It was not wholly black. Some faint light trailed in through the barred window in the door. After a bit she could distinguish some shadows, though she was not sure which was Carum and which the other captives. Of Skada there was no sign, but with just that splinter of light, Jenna hardly expected to see her. And she did not wish her dark sister the pain in her wrists.

She felt fingers touch her shoulder, move down to her bound hands, and begin to work at her bonds.

"Actually," Carum whispered in her ear, "I think you have it wrong. I looked it up once. The curse is really: *May you be hanged by Alta's heirs*, meaning the sons and daughters she bore. Not the long braids you copy. It was in a book at Bertram's Rest. Still, I love your hair. You must never cut it. I mean to shake it free again in the light."

He was having trouble with the ropes around her wrist and she stood absolutely still to let him work on them, though her legs suddenly trembled. He smelled nothing like the Carum she knew, but she doubted she smelled very good either.

Finally he got the knots undone and silently rubbed her aching wrists. "There. What good is my right hand tied?"

"What good am I at all," Jenna asked wearily, "if I am caught? At least I know you are alive. I had hoped to stick my knife in Kalas' mouth and pick his piji teeth."

"Did you see him?" Carum's voice was suddenly cautious.

"See him? The toad caught me. As easily as a child catches an eft."

"Did he . . ." He stopped, drew in a breath, and let it out saying ". . . touch you?" His arms encircled her protectively.

Very gently she turned in his arms. "He said since I was playing a man's game, he would treat me like a man."

"Bless your Alta for that," Carum said.

"Could his bed be worse than this dungeon?" Jenna asked lightly.

Carum did not answer, but someone in the dark did.

"Far worse, lady, for the girls of the Dales. He worships the Garunian women. They, alone, are exempt from his foul attentions."

She whistled a long, low sound through dry lips.

Carum whispered again, this time so softly no one but Jenna could hear. "Are you by yourself?"

"I am here in the dark," she answered as softly.

"I don't mean Skada. I know she is gone without the light. But the others? They aren't all . . ."

"Dead? Gone? No. Though your brother . . oh, Carum, you are the king now. I am sorry." She turned so that the light in her face just a little that he might see that she was truly sorry.

"It's as I expected," he whispered. "As Kalas hinted. And Jenna, I'm sorry, but it's as prophecy wrote. You are to be the king's bride, and I would let no one else wed you. I'm not surprised."

"You will not be king if we are in a dungeon. And by my sword, which I have unfortunately lost and my dirk which . . ." She felt in her boot knowing it was gone, too. "And by my temper, which is fast going, *I can't think in the dark.*"

"You can't think with your hands tied," Carum said, raising his voice to match hers. "But you do very well in the dark."

For a moment she was furious with him, turning their lovemaking into a joke. But when she heard the slight rattle of laughter around them, like cold water over bone-dry stones, she realized it was the first laugh these men had had in days. It stumbled inexpertly out of their mouths, but it *was* a laugh. She knew instinctively that men in dangerous situations needed laughter to combat that feeling of helplessness that would, in the end, conspire to defeat them. She put her pride behind her and added a line to his. "Longbow, you do fairly well yourself in the dark." Then she spoke rapidly, more thinking out loud than a question to him, "But why so black? Why is there no light at all?"

A slight shift of sound and a shadow moved. One of the men stood up. "Lord Kalas' jest, Anna. He is a true Garun. He says one's enemies are best kept in the dark."

Her wrists still hurt where the ropes had cut into them, and she rotated them to work out the ache. "When do they feed us? And do they do that in the dark as well?"

"Once a day," Carum said. "In the morning, I think, though day and night have little meaning here."

"I came in the night," Jenna said, adding as casually as she could, "and there was a fine moon."

Nodding, Carum whispered, "Skada?"

She did not answer him directly. "But do they bring light then?"

"They bring a single torch, Anna," came a voice by her shoulder.

Another added, "They set it in the wall, over there, by the door."

"For all the good it does. It shows us how degraded we have become in three short days." Carum laughed a short angry bark. "Or two days. Or ten. Is it not ironic what a little bit of dirt and dark and dank and a delicate diet can do to beggar a man?"

"Carum, this does not sound like you," Jenna whispered, furious.

"This doesn't look like me either, Jenna," he answered. "Oh Jen . . ." His voice caught suddenly. "I've made a royal hash of it." He laughed shortly at his own bad joke. "And I wouldn't have you see me this way."

"I have seen you many ways, Carum Longbow," Jenna said. "And not all of them handsome. Do you remember the boy running from the Ox, scared and curious at the same time? Or the boy dressed in girl's skirts and scarf at the Hame? Or the drowned ratling in the River Halle?"

"As I recall it, *you* were the ratling and I the rescuer," Carum said, his voice almost back to normal. Then it dropped again. "How could I have let Gorum talk me into . . ."

One of the other men put his hand on Jenna's arm. "They put something in the food, Anna. A sprinkling of some witch's berry. It takes a man's will away. Yet we must eat. Each of us has his moments of such despair. Do not tax him with his answers. We are all like that—high with expectation one moment, low and despairing the next. You will feel the corrosion of it soon enough. We are our own worst torturers."

Jenna turned back and placed her hand against Carum's cheek. "It will be better by and by. I promise."

"Women's promises . . ." he began before his voice bled away, like an old wound reopened.

"What do you mean?"

"It be an old bit of wit from the Continent, lady," a new voice said. "Best leave it."

"No—tell me," Jenna said.

"No, Anna."

"Carum, what do you mean?"

His old voice was suddenly returned. "It is something Kalas is fond of saying: *Women's promises are water over stone—wet, willing, and soon gone.*"

"Water over stone . . ." Jenna mused. "I had that advice once, long ago. Be water over stone. It meant something quite different."

"Don't tax me with it, Jen," Carum pleaded.

"I keep *my* promises, Carum, and well you know it. All I need is that light."

Carum was about to speak when one of the other men broke in. "It will do you no good, Anna. It does none of us any good. They hold the light up to the hole in the door and then they make us lie down on the floor, one atop another."

"One atop another?" Jenna asked.

"It is a cruel and humbling act," Carum said. "They do it in the dungeons of the Continent. An invention of Castle Michel Rouge, where most of the instruments of torture come from as well. Kalas has cousins there." He hesitated, finally admitting, "As do I."

"They count us aloud, lady, afore they open the door. After each lock they count us."

"Better and better," Jenna said mysteriously.

"If you have a plan, tell me." Carum's voice was strong and full again.

"Tell us," a dozen men's voices agreed.

Jenna smiled into the dark, but with her back to the single sliver of light in the door, none of them could see. "Just be sure," she said to them, "that I lie on top of the pile."

The men gave forced, muttered laughs, but Carum added—as if he understood—"It would not do to have the Anna, the White Goddess, lie beneath."

Jenna laughed with them, extending the joke. "Though there have been times when I have fancied *that* place as well . . ." She was glad they could not see her face, hot with furious blushes. If Carum continued *this* jest, she swore to herself she would kill him before Kalas ever got the chance. But sensing her desperate embarrassment, he let it go. The men were as buoyant as they were likely to be. Jenna walked over to the door. Holding up her hand into the splinter of light, she watched as Skada's hand appeared faintly against the far wall. Jenna waved and was delighted to see Skada's hand return it.

"Will you be ready?" she called to the wall.

Thinking she was addressing them, the men cried out, "We will, Anna."

"For whatever you require," Carum added.

But Jenna had eyes only for the hand on the wall. It made a circle between thumb and finger, the goddess' own sign. For the first time Jenna felt reason to hope.

* * *

Forcing herself to sleep on the cold stones, Jenna gave her body time to recover from the long climb. She curled next to Carum, breathing slowly, matching her breath to his. When she slept at last, her dreams were full of wells, caves, and other dark, wet holes.

The clanging of a sword against the iron bars of the window woke them all.

"Light count," came the call. "Roll up and over."

The prisoners dragged themselves to the wall and attempted a rough pyramid, not daring to complain. Last to sit up, Jenna watched as the sturdiest six, including Carum, lay down on the floor. The next heaviest climbed on top, and then the next until a final skeletal two—obviously long interred for other crimes against Kalas—scaled up to the perch, distributing their weight as carefully as possible. It was easier to see all this because of the additional light from the torch shining through the window in the door.

The sound of the guard's voice counting began. "One, two, three . . ."

"Wait!" It was a new voice, well in command. Not Kalas' voice. Jenna was disappointed but not surprised. After all, why should Kalas himself oversee a dungeon full of prisoners?

The voice had a soft purr to it. "You misbegotten miscalculators," came its smooth mockery. "Don't deny us the best. His highness, King Kalas, spoke movingly of the lady. Is there not room on top for her?"

"There is room," Jenna said, her voice soft so that the speaker had to come closer to the door to hear her. She could only see a shadow, a smallish shadow, almost boy-sized.

"Always room," came the purring voice, "because a pyramid is altogether a pleasing figure."

Jenna guessed. "The Cat!"

He laughed. "Smart women are annoying. But I understand I have nothing to fear from you. You have already killed one cat. And I have lives to spare, is that not so?"

His men chuckled.

"Climb up, my lady. Ascend your throne."

"Why should I?"

"Ask the men upon whose backs you will make your climb," the Cat said in his purring voice.

"We tried denying him his pleasure in the pyramid," Carum said, "and they simply refused to feed us at all until we lay one atop another."

Jenna nodded and kicked off her boots. Then she set her right foot carefully on someone's buttocks and began the climb. When she reached the top, she lay down gingerly, trying to distribute her weight evenly.

"Will they bring the light now?" Jenna whispered to one of the men under her.

"Yes," he whispered back. "Look, here it comes."

Two men—one with a torch—entered the room. The Cat, disdaining to draw his own weapon, entered after them. He was a small, wiry man who looked pleased with himself, like a puss over a saucer of cream.

The light-bearer stood at the head of the pile of bodies counting them aloud once again. The second went to a corner, sheathed his sword, and dropped a bag that had been draped over his shoulders onto the floor. He emptied its contents on the stone. Jenna made out a pile of hard breads and wrinkled her nose. Then she looked up at the wall nearest the door where shadows thrown by the flickering torch moved about.

"Now!" she shouted, flinging herself from the pile.

She calculated her roll to take her into the shoulder of the guard at the pyramid's peak. His torch flew into the air, illuminating another hurtling body that seemed to spring right out of the far wall. Skada rammed into the Cat, just as he unsheathed his sword.

Jenna reached for the guard's weapon as Skada grabbed for the Cat's, then completed identical rolls in a single fluid motion and stood up.

At the moment of their impact, Carum and the other captives collapsed the pyramid. The strongest leaped to their feet, surrounding the guard near the bread and stripping him of his sword and a knife in his boot. Holding the torch aloft, Carum laughed.

"At least one of those lives ends here, my Cat."

"Perhaps," the Cat said, smiling. "But indulge me for a moment and let me ask the lady why at yesterday's count, there were twenty prisoners in this cell. Yet today, though there should have been twenty-one, a perfect pyramid, there was one extra. Where did the extra come from?"

Skada laughed behind him. "From a darker hole than you will ever know, Cat."

Jenna hissed through her teeth and Skada was immediately silent. But the Cat smiled.

"Could it be . . ." he said, his eyes crinkling, "could it be that the stories about you witches raising black demons out of mirrors is true? Mages lie, but images . . ."

Skada made a mocking bow. "Truth has many eyes. You must believe what you yourself see."

Jenna bowed as well. When she stood straight again, the Cat had a finger to his lips, obviously thinking.

"I see sisters who may have had the same mother but who had different fathers." He took the finger away. "It is well known that the mountain women take pleasure with many men."

"Some," Skada said, "take no pleasure with any men."

The Cat laughed, and at the same moment leaned forward dashing the torch from Carum's hand. It fell to the stone floor, started to gutter, and almost went out. Without the light, Skada was gone and the Cat's sword which had been in her hand clattered to the floor. He bent quickly and picked it up.

"Like my Lord Kalas," he said into the dark, "I chew piji. It stains the teeth but gives one wonderful night sight." His sword rang against Jenna's.

"Dark or light," cried Jenna, "I will fight you. Stand back, Carum. Keep the others out of the way. And *do not move!*"

The Cat was not as strong as the Bear, being a small man, and so he could not overcome Jenna with sheer strength. But he was a clever swordsman, quick on his feet, and cunning. Twice his sword stroked open a small wound, once on her right cheek, once on her left arm. But he counted too much on his night sight, thinking it an advantage. What he did not know was that Jenna, like the other Hame warriors, had learned swordplay and wandplay in both dark and lightened rooms. Though she could not see as well as he in the blackness, she had been taught to trust her ears as well as her eyes. She could distinguish the movement of a thrust that was signaled by the change in the air; she could read every hesitation of breath. She could smell the Cat's slight scent of fear under the piji, the change in the odor of his sweat when he realized that he did not have the upperhand after all.

She slowed her own breathing to give her the steady strength she needed and with one last twist of her wrist managed to catch up his blade on hers and send it clattering away into the corner.

"Light!" Jenna called.

Carum picked up the torch and held it overhead. Once off the cold stone it managed to flutter back into smoky life.

The Cat stood with both hands held out, almost playful in his surrender, though no one was fooled by his stance. Jenna's blade remained in his belly. Behind him, Skada had her sword at his back.

"If you move," Skada whispered to him, "I will spit you like a sheep over a roasting pit. And I will turn that spit very, very slowly."

He shrugged, but with exaggerated care.

"You have rightly guessed that Jenna and I are sisters," Skada continued. "And that we are not at all alike. I do not yet have your blood on my blade, though it is she who has sworn your death."

Jenna turned to Carum. "Keep the torch high, my king. And stand at the head of the line as we go. Skada and I will take the rear."

They left the Cat and his two men locked in the dungeon without any light at all, and made their way up the stairs. Carum held the torch in his left hand, one of the guard's swords in his right. After him came his men. At the rear was Jenna, the wound on her cheek and arm wiped clean of the fresh blood and already starting to close, though both still stung. And, when the light was right, Skada trotted along behind.

At each new door they fumbled the locks open with keys they had taken from the Cat's belt. Carum greeted each released prisoner in turn, both those who had ridden with him and those who had been in Kalas' Hole for other crimes.

All in all, they opened eight dungeon doors and gathered almost a hundred men, most still in fighting condition, though they had only three swords and nine torches for weapons. There was not even a chair or a table that might be broken into cudgels.

"My lord, Carum," a thin voice cried.

Jenna strained to make out the speaker in the flickering torchlight. Carum spotted him first and, handing the torch to someone, gave his hand to the speaker. The man was as thin as his voice, and knobby; his hands were too big for their wrists, his nose oversized on a bony face.

"What is it?" Carum asked.

"I know this castle well, sir. I have served here all my life, first as serving lad, then as cook's boy, now as cook."

Someone laughed. "Don't they say: *Measure a cook by his belly?* This one is all bones."

The man shook his head. "I have been in the dungeon four or five weeks now. It thins a man."

"Maybe less," someone cried. "If he cannot remember."

"He's a spy," another called.

Carum held up his hand for silence. "Let him speak."

"If I do not remember rightly," the cook said, "it is because time has no dominion here. Day is night. Night is day."

"That be true enough," a man with a blond beard said.

"To your point," Carum urged.

"I know every passage in this castle, every hall and every stair."

Coming forward, and heedless of Skada following her, Jenna put her hand on the cook's arm. It trembled slightly beneath her touch. Skada took his other arm. His trembling increased.

"Then tell us where this passage leads to."

"Out of the Hole, lady."

"He is a spy," came a voice.

"He must give us more," came another.

"And what does the door open into," Jenna persisted. She suspected he was the kind of man who could not say anything straightaway but must have it pulled from him.

"An arras, lady."

"What does *that* mean?" asked someone.

"A curtain, he means. An arras is a curtain," explained Carum.

"He *is* a spy. Spit him!"

Jenna tightened her hold on the cook's arm. "These men are getting restless and Longbow and I will not be able to control them if you do not speak plainly."

"No, listen to me," the cook said hastily. "This passage leads to an open door in the wall of Kalas' Great Hall and it is hung over, covered over, by an arras."

The muttering men hushed.

"That is better," Jenna said, relaxing her grip.

"Much better," Skada said from the other side.

But the cook, once started, seemed unable to stop. "It is a heavy arras," he said. "One of the finest in the castle. A tapestry dedicated to Lord Cres. He is feasting with his heroes and they are . . ."

"Throwing bones over their shoulders to the dogs of war," Skada whispered to Jenna.

The cook did not hear and continued in his thin voice, ". . . hangs over the door. But often King Kalas . . ."

The men began to mutter again at that, an angry sound, like bees. Carum silenced them with a cut of his hand.

". . . I mean, Lord Kalas when he dines has the arras pulled back to listen to the cries from the Hole. He calls it *seasoning* for his meals."

Carum's lips closed tight together but he made no comment other than a nod.

"Lord Kalas had been away much lately, but he returned precipitously a few days ago. After a message from one of his chiefs."

"The Bear!" one man said, turning to stare at Jenna.

"Na, how could *he* know all that?" asked another.

"They tell it to me, the guards," the cook said quickly. "To crow over it. My pain their pleasure; their gossip my only meat."

"I don't like it, sir. 'Tis too easy," one of the men cautioned Carum. Several others agreed.

"But it makes good sense," Jenna mused.

"Who guards this arras, this tapestry?" Carum asked in a harsh whisper. "How many? What arms?"

"It is an *open* door, my lord. Kalas' boast is *No one escapes from the Hole whole.* Sometimes he shows the gaping door to the ladies, just to frighten them a little bit."

"What ladies?" Jenna asked, hardly breathing.

"The ones he captures. The ones he beds. Young ladies, some of them. Scarce more than girls."

Jenna shivered, thinking of Alna and Selinda, thinking of Jareth's Mai, thinking of the children from Nill's Hame.

"Do you mean *no one* guards it?"

"I mean it opens directly into the Great Hall which is always full of an army of men, especially when Kalas is home."

The men mumbled their opinions, volleying them back and forth. Crowding tightly together, they discussed their options.

"It's no good then."

"We're doomed."

"Better dead at once than dying slowly down there."

"Wait," Skada said. Now that the torches were close together, she held her shape. "Listen. There is something you do not know."

Jenna nodded. "There are one hundred armed women on the walls outside who may have already made it to the top."

"And fifty armed men battling through the gate."

The cook laughed mirthlessly. "There are three portcullises between the gate and the keep. They will not get in."

"Whether they get in or not," Skada said, "they will be a distraction."

"They are the mice," Jenna cried to Carum.

"And we already have the Cat!" he rejoined.

"Listen," Skada said, "we have few weapons but the torches."

"Do you mean to burn him out?" asked someone.

"Trust me," Skada said. "Set all you can on fire. If it is day and the women have gotten in, they fight—better—near a fire."

"Better a hot woman than a cold dinner," someone called.

Laughing, they started up the stairs again, but became quiet at the next turning for it was clear the exit out of the Hole lay just ahead.

Jenna and Skada signaled them on, and they crept silently up the rest of the cold stone steps, amazingly quiet, Jenna thought, for so many men. Since only Carum, Jenna, and one other man were armed with stolen swords, they went ahead. Skada, with her shadow weapon, followed close behind. When they reached the last step, Carum poked the sword slowly at the heavy curtain, looking for a way out. Finally Jenna knelt down; she tried to lift the arras. It was a heavy weave and weighted along the bottom. She gestured with her head for help. Two of the unarmed men stepped forward to lift the curtain up, and Jenna and Skada crawled through, sliding their swords before them.

It was bright daylight on the other side of the tapestry and Jenna blinked frantically, trying to adjust her eyes to the sudden light. She turned to speak to Skada but Skada was gone. Jenna felt a terribly loneness, as if she had been forsaken, though she knew it was but a trick of the sun. Skada would be back again in the evening. If they were still alive by evening.

Then she realized that the room was unnaturally quiet for the central room of a castle. Slowly she looked around. No one was there.

"Empty," she whispered at last to the slightly raised tapestry.

The curtain inched its way higher until there was a doorway held between hands. The rest of the prisoners boiled through, blinking awkwardly in the light and staring about in confusion. If they had expected anything, it was not this. The Great Hall was totally deserted.

"I don't understand . . ." Carum began.

"I do," Jenna said. "Listen!"

They all heard it then, the faint tumble of voices coming from outside where an uneven battle was being waged.

"We must help them," someone cried.

"First set fire to this hall," Jenna said. "You—the curtains there. And you —the arras on the other wall."

"And break up those chairs. At least we will have clubs to fight with," Carum called.

The tapestries smoldered slowly at first, refusing to take up the flame, till at last one section flared suddenly, and within minutes that Cres and his heroes were completely consumed by the fire. The men armed themselves with chair legs and the table bracings and several caught up cushions from the chairs to use as shields. The rest of the furniture they piled in the middle of the hall and set on fire. As the central flames rose higher, Skada danced next to Jenna for a second.

"I will follow whenever I can," she said.

"I know," Jenna whispered, then waved to the empty air as she followed Carum and the men out of the door and down a wide hallway.

Racing along the door-lined hall, they followed the cook's shouted directions, heedless now of any noise. They came upon two guards who turned to face them but were quickly and efficiently disarmed and bound by Carum and three of the men wielding clubs. The guards' swords were taken up by two of the men, and a dagger in a boot was found as well.

"I will take that," said the cook, pointing at the dagger. "And I'll dice the next one into small, bite-sized pieces." He giggled.

"Just get us outside," Carum cried, "and you can carve up who you will."

The cook led them to a wide stone stairs flanked by a pair of magnificent banisters polished to a high gleam. At the bottom of the staircase, ranged across it to block them, were some twenty castle guards armed with swords and fully shielded.

"What now?" Jenna asked. "We have but five swords and a knife."

"Let them come up to us," Carum said. "They'll have a harder time of it, unbalanced on the stairs, though what I would give for a bow now. Still, we have more men. And clubs."

As if guessing Carum's strategy, the guards remained below, unmoving. Long minutes went by.

At last Jenna said, "We cannot just wait."

"If we go down there one at a time, they'll take us one by one. If we try and rush them with the weapons we have, it will be a slaughter."

"Then we must fool them with a line of false mice."

"Too late. They've seen us and counted our weapons. Time is on their side," Carum said.

"Cook," Jenna said suddenly, turning. "What of those doors we passed in the hallway. Any escape there?"

"They are closets, lady. With extra dishes and linens and . . ."

"Ha!" Jenna said, turning back to Carum. "We will have our mice! You" —she touched one of the men on the shoulder—"take my sword. And you —take Carum's." When they hesitated, she shoved her sword at one, took Carum's and handed it to another man. "And you three"—she pointed to some of the weaker-looking men—"come with us."

Carum chose a raw-boned, blond-bearded man to be in charge while he was gone, then ran to catch up with Jenna. "Where are we going?"

"To make us a line of mice."

Kicking open the first door, she stripped the shelves of priceless wool and linen weavings, of banners and toweling.

"Take it all," she told them.

The second closet yielded goblets and platters and, best of all, carving knives.

A third closet would not open even to their frantic kicking, and they left it, hurrying back to the stairs with their treasures. The guards were still waiting below with the studied calm of hunting cats, but the men at the top of the stairs had not been as patient. A few were several steps down and pacing. One had already tried to get through the line by himself, his bloody body testimony to the foolishness of such an act.

"He was not one of us, my lord, but a prisoner of Kalas' from before. He had not our training," the blond-bearded man said.

"Still we must count him as ours," Carum said softly. "He died on Kalas' blades."

"Here is what I would have us do," Jenna said, showing them how to tie together the line of banners and linen, threading into place the cups and platters and bowls.

"A woman's wiles," complained one man.

"A mouse's," Carum said, smiling grimly. "Listen to her."

Below the soldiers were curious at first, but at a shouted command from their captain, stilled again, waiting with swords raised.

It took precious minutes to complete the *little mice*, as Jenna called the strange assortment of cobbled-together tableware. She traded the men carving knives for cudgels, adding the pieces of wood to her strange tapestry. Then she gave the final orders in a whisper, telling the men of their places.

"The signal," she explained, "is *For Longbow!*"

She stationed herself at the top of one banister, one end of the tied banners slipknotted around her waist. Carum stood at the other. He had a similar line bound around. They each held a sword. Behind them, not yet taut across, was the quick weave and behind it, the waiting men, knives, torches, and three swords at the ready.

"For Longbow!" Jenna shouted suddenly, and at the signal she and Carum both leaped onto the banisters as if onto horses. They pulled the line taut between them, a strange curtain of heavy implements, and slid straight down. Screaming their defiance, the men came trampling down the stairs right after. The bemused guards watched their advance.

The mouse-line hit the guards neck high, tangling them long enough for Jenna and Carum to slip the knots from their waists. By the time the guards had gotten free of the weaving, Carum's men were on them, too close for the swords. The carving knives, sharp enough for tough venison, found little resistance in the soft meat of a man's neck. It was over in minutes, and only one of Carum's crew had been injured from tripping in the lines himself and cutting his shin on a piece of broken glass.

Quickly they stripped the guards of their weapons and shields and then hurried, under the cook's nervous direction, toward the main doors. A heavy piece of wood deadbolted the door, but they managed to push it aside. When they flung open the doors, the scene outside in the courtyard was bedlam.

Outmanned but fighting steadily and well were the women of M'dorah, light sisters only, battling under the glaring eye of the afternoon sun. There was no sign of Piet and his men.

"They are still behind the gates," Jenna cried.

"Or caught in the trap between the portcullises," Carum added. "We must raise those gates."

"I will, my lord," cried the blond-bearded man. "I'll take several with me." He hurried out, careful to sidestep a number of the fighting guards. Jenna watched as he made his way across the courtyard and knew they could count on his success, for he was single-minded in his march, and the men around him saved him from many a blow.

"And where is Kalas?" Carum cried. "Where is that toad? I do not see him."

Jenna realized that she had not seen him, either.

"He is where toads always are, my lord, hiding in a hole," the cook said. He smiled and Jenna saw that his teeth were as yellow as Kalas' had been. As yellow as the Cat's. She wondered that a cook could afford such an addiction.

"In his dungeon?" Carum asked.

"In his bolt-hole," the cook said. "He will wait there till he is sure of his victory."

"Are *you* sure?" Jenna asked, staring in fascination at the man's teeth.

He nodded and, mistaking her attention, picked at his teeth with the knife.

"And you know where that hole is?" Carum asked.

"I do, sir, I do. Surely I do. And haven't I many times taken him his meals there?"

"The tower!" Jenna said suddenly.

The cook nodded his bony head. "The tower."

"Take me," Carum said. "I have a score to settle with him."

"Take us both," said Jenna. "We have lost more than one family each."

* * *

They trailed after him back up the stairs, along the hallway, and into the Great Hall again. The fires they had started there had sputtered out, and one wall of the tapestry was but partially burned. There was still heavy smoke in the air, as if the floor had been draped with gray bunting. Putting their arms across their faces to shield themselves from the smoke, Jenna and Carum followed the cook to a door in the wall next to the gaping opening down to the dungeon.

"Here," the cook said, pulling open the door and pointing up the twisting stairs.

"You go before," Carum said. "I trust you more in front of me than behind."

"He has done nothing wrong, Carum," Jenna said, though she was uneasy as well.

"Like my men, I feel things have been too easy so far," Carum said. "And as they said at Nill's Hame: *The day on which one starts is not . . .*"

"*. . . the day to begin one's preparations.* You are right," Jenna said. "*Better to be safe than buried,* we said at our Hame. He will go in front."

The cook mounted the stairs before them. The passage wound up and up, unrelieved by any landings or windows, and was the darker since they had just come from the light. They went up by feel alone, putting their feet where the stone was worn smooth by many treadings.

"If we had a torch now," Carum whispered.

"Skada would appreciate that," Jenna whispered back. "And we could certainly use the extra sword."

As they rounded the final twist, a sliver of light announced an open door. Jenna pushed aside the cook and put her eye to the crack. She could see nothing but a wedge of light on a polished wood floor, but she could hear Kalas' voice speaking in an oily, cozening fashion. Having heard it only for a few minutes the night before, she could still not forget it. It was at once powerful and weak, full of dark promises and hinting at even darker secrets.

"Come, my dear," Kalas was saying, "it will not be so bad as all that. Once done and it need never be done again. At least with me."

Jenna breathed slowly. So he was alone—with only a girl as company.

There was a silence, and then a young woman's voice, wheezy and achingly familiar.

"Leave me be," she said, catching her breath. *"Please."*

"Alna!" Jenna's mouth shaped the name though she did not speak it aloud. Surely that was her Hame mate's voice. Alna, who had been on her mission year to Calla's Ford, had been stolen away. But it had been weeks— no, years in actual time—since she had heard Alna. She could not be sure without seeing her. Still, she could feel heat rising to her cheeks, could feel her stomach roil, as if her body already believed what her mind hesitated to accept. Turning to Carum, she whispered, "Kalas is alone in there with a girl. I can handle this. Best you see to the others."

"No. I will not leave you."

"The sword is my weapon, not yours. This is my fight. That is my Hame mate in there."

"It is my fight, too. Kalas murdered my family."

"I will not match blood with you. But if you stay and your men below go marching off to Lord Cres because you did not lead them . . ."

He kissed her cheek, turned, and left, so light on his feet she did not hear his footsteps go. When she turned back it was to see the cook tapping lightly on the door.

"No!" the woman inside screamed, then coughed violently.

Jenna pushed the cook hard on the small of the back, and he fell against the door, springing it open.

"It is a trap!" the woman cried, but she was too late.

Jenna was already inside. Before her was Alna, hands bound behind her, lying on a great canopied bed. To her right Kalas squatted toadlike on a carved chair. Ranged before him were seven large men. *Very large men,* Jenna thought. Seven to her one, with little room to maneuver as the door swung shut behind her. The stranger's sword in her hand was lighter than she was used to, the pommel sitting awkwardly in her hand.

She knew she had to stall. Stall—and silence the cook who had betrayed them. She took a half step to the side and kicked the fallen man in the head, hard enough to quiet him for an hour or two, not hard enough to kill him. But her eyes never left Kalas and his men.

"Jenna!" Alna managed to get out, "it *is* you. I could not be sure it was not another lie."

"Alna!" She could not spare her old friend another glance, not even out of the corner of her eye, though she had known her at once. Alna was older and thinner than when they had parted on the first day of their mission year. And that, Jenna thought wryly, was the day she had believed that her life was at its worst, when she had been separated from her best friends and sent off to a strangers' Hame alone.

"Alone again, White Jenna," Kalas said slowly, as if he had been able to read her mind. "What an odd habit you are developing. Always arriving uninvited into my little tower room."

"Perhaps not entirely uninvited," Jenna said. "I think you sent the invitation by way of this skinny bit of . . ." She kicked again at the cook, this time deliberately bruising his ribs. He did not stir.

"Ah, you have uncovered my little deception," Kalas said, smiling. "But not—alas—soon enough."

"Tell me," Jenna said, "was he at least a good cook?"

"A terrible cook, but he had his *other* uses."

"What I do not really understand," Jenna said, "is why you let us get away, why you did not just kill us in the Hole."

"Such an uninteresting death, don't you think?" Kalas asked. "And I have made such a study of death, it would not do to just kill people outright. Besides"—and he laughed, showing again his horribly yellow teeth and running his fingers through his thinning red hair, which exposed darker roots—"I did not believe that even you, Prince Longbow's White Goddess, would really dare the castle on her own. I needed you as bait for the redoubtable King Pike, who is even now at my door."

Jenna's eyes opened wide, but she let nothing else betray the fact that she was startled. So Kalas did not know that Carum was king; did not know that Gorum was dead. She would keep that little piece of information to herself.

He smiled again, reminding Jenna of her Mother Alta when she had a particularly devastating bit of news to impart. "I did *not* expect you to escape, not with my Cat watching carefully at the Hole. What a fascinating little mouse you are. But I have clipped the Cat's claws for him. He will not make that mistake again."

Jenna nodded. *Keep him talking,* she reminded herself. "But how did you know we had gotten out?"

"Oh, little girl, I know everything. This castle is mined with passages and set about with traps. You cannot go from one level to another without my knowing. *Everything.*"

"Then we could not have gotten out without you letting us go?"

"Not in a hundred years," Kalas said. "Not in a hundred hundred years."

She had her back to the tower's one window, could feel the sun warming her. She could always leap out as a last resort, but she knew—having climbed it so painfully the night before—that it would be a long and fatal fall to the wall below. And that would leave Alna to the mercy of Kalas still, and the rest without their Anna.

There would be no help from Skada either. The sun was only half down the sky, so Kalas had no torches lit. Carum was gone below, sent away by her, past recalling. And Jenna knew she was out of polite conversation.

"Get her!" Kalas said to his guards, no change in the pitch of his voice.

They moved in a well-trained wedge toward her and she stepped quickly to the other side of the bed, putting it between the men and herself. When they split and three came after her, she leaped onto the bed, straddling Alna, and beating them back with some quick, though awkward sword work. Then with a quick slash of her weapon, she severed the hanging curtains from the canopy's crossbar, tangling the men below in its heavy brocaded folds.

As they fought to free themselves, their companions came to their aid, giving Jenna just a moment. It was all she needed. She flung the sword point first into the breast of one of the guards. He did not have the Bear's quick hands and the sword pierced him straight through, skewering the arm of a man beneath him who cried out in agony.

Jenna bounced once on the bed and grabbed the cross bracing of the canopy, swinging herself feetfirst nearly out of the door.

"After her!" Kalas cried.

But before the remaining guards could untangle themselves, Carum and two of the M'dorans burst through the open door, swords in hand. Behind them came a fourth woman, carrying both a sword and a torch. She flung the torch onto the bed.

The linens caught fire at once and Alna, moving faster than Jenna would have guessed, rolled off the bed on the window side, scrambling over the guards, where she cowered against the far wall.

As the cloth flared to life, Jenna moved around the bed to stand between Kalas and the flames. She was weaponless while he still had a thin rapier in his one hand. The other hand rested on a heavy tapestry behind his chair.

"My sword, Jenna!" cried Carum, ready to fling it to her.

She shook her head, smiling. There was nothing sweet in that smile. "I need no sword, *my king.*" She spoke the final two words with deliberateness, to be sure Kalas understood, then added, "Do you not remember that tribe in the East you told me about so long ago."

With one sharp movement, Kalas drew back the tapestry disclosing an open door. But Jenna put her hand in back of her neck, pulling her white braid forward, stretching it between her hands, like a rope. Behind her was the blazing bed sending crazed shadows against the wall. One of those shadows, framed in the doorway behind Kalas, was a womanshape holding a black braid stretched taut between her clenched hands.

Jenna reached up, exposing her breast to Kalas' blade, and leaned forward. He smiled triumphantly until he felt the braid from behind slip over his head and catch him, suddenly, around the neck. He dropped the blade and tried to rip the noose from his throat but Skada and Jenna had, simultaneously, pulled their braids tight, twisting and twisting it.

Kalas' face turned a strange, dark color as he struggled against the garroting plait. At the end his hands dropped to his sides and his feet beat a final tattoo against the wooden floor.

"Alaisters!" Carum said suddenly. "Alaisters was the name of the tribe. They were . . ."

". . . never weaponless because of their hair," Skada said, unknotting the noose from Kalas' neck.

"Promise me you will never cut your braid," Carum said.

They both nodded, but neither one of them smiled.

THE BALLAD

The Ballad of Langbrow

When Langbrow first was made the king,
Proclaimed by all his men,
He took to him a goodly wife
Whose name was Winsome Jen.
He took to him a goodly wife,
Her name it was Sweet Ann,
And light her hair, and long her limb,
And Langbrow was her man,
And Langbrow was her man.

When Langbrow first was made the king,
Proclaimed by all his peers,
He opened up the prison gates
That had been closed for years.
He opened up the prison gates
With just one little key
And all the men condemned within
Straightways were all set free,
Straightways were all set free.

When Langbrow first was made the king,
He killed the callous crew
That tortured many a fine woman
And slaughtered not a few.
That tortured many a fine woman
And brought them many a shame
Till Langbrow came to rescue them
Returning their good name,
Returning their good name.

When Langbrow first was made the king,
The country did rejoice
And sang the praises of the king
With cup and wine and voice.
We sang the praises of the king
And of his winsome Jen
And of the men who followed him,
And also the wo-men,
And also the wo-men!

THE STORY

Carum carried Kalas' body down the stairs and into the courtyard where he threw it onto the stones. Jenna stood by his right side, her hands clasped together, watching.

As soon as Kalas' body hit the ground, a strange hush fell upon the crowd. The soldiers, most of whom had been hired from the Continent, flung down their weapons. Those who were Garunian bred knelt, offering up their swords.

Carum ignored their fealty, speaking instead as if it had always been his, saying, "I am the one and true king, for my brother Gorum is dead. And here"—he pointed to the corpse at his feet—"here is the one who would have severed us. Even Lord Cres will not have him, for only heroes feast at the dark lord's side."

The kneeling men stood, sheathing their weapons. Behind them, rising slowly over the crenellated castle walls, came the moon. Jenna saw it and smiled.

Carum took the leather thong from around his neck, holding up the crested ring that they all might see. "Here is the sign of the Bull and it belongs where I vowed it belonged—on the body of its dead master."

The ring bounced on Kalas' chest and tumbled onto the ground beside him. Watching silently, the crowd waited for Carum's next words.

Instead, Carum took up Jenna's left hand and set his mouth solemnly on her palm. Then he looked up again at the waiting men and women before speaking. As if weighing his words carefully, he said at last, "By my side is the one who was promised us, the White One of prophecy. Born of three mothers, born to lead us out of the ending of one era and into the beginning of the other, she is both light and . . ."

At that very moment, as though he had timed his speech exactly, the great full moon cleared the walls entirely, moving above the crenellations. Shimmering like water and starlight, Skada came into being next to Jenna, her black hair and dark eyes marking Carum's text.

There was a sharp intake of breath from the watching men who did not even notice that the same was happening to all the women by their sides. Only Carum, staring down at them, and Piet, who stood near his king, saw that for every M'doran woman there were now two.

Carum held his hand up again and there was a complete hush.

"She is both light and dark, and shall rule by my side. She has made the hound, the bull, the cat, and the bear bow low. She has herself killed Kalas, and with that brought to an end his hideous reign." For a moment after, the courtyard seemed to echo with his words.

Then Petra mounted two steps to stand in front of Carum and Jenna. She bowed her head to him briefly, solemnly, before turning more toward Jenna and raising her hands above her head, fingers extended, palms flat.

"Holy, holy, holiest of sisters," she intoned.

The men chorused back, "Holy, holy, holiest of sisters."

Petra turned and signed to Sandor and Marek to stand by her, and they climbed to her side.

"And Alta said this one shall crown the king," Petra cried.

"The first Herald!" shouted one of the women.

Reaching into his shirt, Marek took out the circlet of sweetbriar which was, by some miracle, uncrushed, and placed it carefully on Carum's head.

A great cheer went up from the crowd.

Petra raised her hand for quiet, and there was complete silence again.

"And Alta said this one shall guide the king's right hand."

Sandor slipped the wristlet of wild rose off his own arm and slid it onto Jenna's. It hung loosely around her wrist.

An even wilder cheer, this one led by Piet, rose from the men and women.

Petra spoke into the noise and they quieted at once. "And Alta said that one shall be True Speaker for all, yet say nothing until the king be crowned, lest he sever the fellowship. Can you speak the truth to us now, True Speaker?"

Jareth pushed forward from the crowd, holding up the piece of green rag that had been his collar, calling in a strange croaking voice: "The king shall live long and longer yet the queen. They shall be for us whenever there is need."

"Long live the king!" Piet shouted.

The crowd gave back its answer: "Long live the king!"

"And his queen, Jenna," a woman with a wheezy voice cried.

"Long live the queen!" the crowd answered.

Petra turned her head slightly and winked at Skada who winked back. Then, as if singing an ancient chant, to the tune of the most sacred Altan prophecy's plainsong, Petra let her voice ring out over the crowd:

> *"Then Longbow shall be king,*
> *And Jenna shall be queen,*
> *So long as moons they reign,*
> *So long as groves be green.*
> *Holy. Holy. Holy."*

"And what will *that* one turn into?" Jenna whispered.

"Some ballad sung in taverns and accompanied by a plecta and nose flute," Skada answered. "Called *When Langbrow was Made the King* or *How the Warrior Jenna Broke Heads* or some such."

"But," Carum added, grinning, "it will be lovingly sung."

THE HISTORY

To the Directors, Dalian Historical Society
Sirs:

   Although I have been a member in good standing for twenty-seven years, a past president, and two-term general secretary, I find it impossible to remain a member any longer now that the Society has seen fit to give its highest award to that charlatan Dr. "Magic" Magon.

   By so honoring Dr. Magon, you have given credence to his theories about the dark and light sisters, and his left-wing ravings about the circle of the Grenna as well as the cultural superiority of the indigenous populations of the Dales.

   History must needs be even-handed and there is nothing surer than that legend, myth, balladry, and folktale are cultural lies that tell us the truth only on an incredible slant. To believe them without adjusting the glass, as Dr. Magon does, makes for warped history and a warped historian.

   That this Society is now crediting such history and honoring such a historian forces me to tender my resignation until such a time as history itself shall prove me the prophet and Magon the liar.

                                        Yours,

THE AFTERWARD

   Carum Longbow ruled the Dales for a full fifty years, till his hair was as white as Jenna's and age had bent him.

   Jenna was not always by his side, for she called the throne "a troubling seat" and she was ever uneasy with ceremony. Often she took long journeys into the countryside, accompanied by her one-armed daughter Scillia or one of her two sons.

   At these times she sometimes traveled back to the southern parts of the

Dales, passing by the Old Hanging Man and Alta's Breast, to visit with old friends. Selden Hame, where the last of the remaining women of Alta lived, was always a home to her.

At Selden there were no priestesses anymore; the last—Jenna's original Mother Alta—had died twenty years earlier. The M'dorans who had settled at Selden Hame had chosen a singleton without a dark sister as their True Speaker. Her name was Marget, still known to Jenna as Pynt, and she helped all the women in the Hame learn new ways, though that is another story altogether.

When Jenna was at court, her closest friends were Petra and Jareth, who married after a long mourning period for Jareth's Mai. Petra proved a gentle stepmother for Jareth's five girls, the eldest of whom was called Jen.

But Jenna did not stay at either court or Hame very long. She always found herself searching the woods and fields, the small vales and great valleys, for something. She could not have named it, though Skada—if asked—would have said she was searching for another great adventure. And perhaps Skada, who knew her best of all, was right.

However, her daughter swore that Jenna was looking for a simpler time, her sons, Jem and Corrie, for a finer one. Carum made no guesses at all, but welcomed her back from each trip with open arms and no questions asked except one: *Are the people happy and well?*

And they were happy and well. Carum made certain that all his people— Dale and Garum alike—were well fed, well housed, and safe from marauding strangers. With Piet as the head of the army, the Dale shores were patrolled and the peace kept. Marek stayed on to become one of Carum's advisors, but Sandor returned home, taking over his father's ferry and writing the story of his youthful adventures in a small spidery script for his own sons.

It was fifty years and a week since the coronation that Jenna came back from one of her sojourns in the hills. She had been uneasy the whole time, though she could not have said why. The journey had been undertaken alone, with nothing in her pack but a skin of spring wine and a loaf of bread. The hunting had been plentiful; she had not wanted for food. It was midway through the moon time, and Skada had not appeared, except for one evening when Jenna had put her blanket right next to the fire. They had quarreled briefly, for no reason, Skada as uneasy as Jenna, so that Jenna had not been cast down when the fire burned out and Skada was gone.

Jenna cut the journey short, heading back to the castle, for it was in her mind that perhaps Carum had need of her. Often they knew one another's thoughts before a word was said, even as she did with Skada, though with Carum it came from living with him so many untroubled years.

She rode up the long, winding road on her white horse, one of Duty's great granddaughters, with the smoothest canter and the sweetest mouth of any horse she had owned. As she went forward, the great gates opened and a rider came galloping toward her. She knew immediately it was Scillia by the missing arm.

They greeted one another from afar, Scillia calling, "Quickly, mother, it is father. He is sick and the doctors fear for his life. I was coming to trail you."

Jenna nodded, her uneasiness gone. She knew now the author of her unhappiness. They raced back into the castle together.

Carum was propped up in bed surrounded by both sons, the doctors, and even Petra, as gray-faced as Jenna felt. Jenna sent them all away. She sat on the bed by Carum's side and did not speak until his eyelids had fluttered open.

"You have come back in time," he whispered.

"I am always in time."

"Ich crie thee merci."

"I will give it, my love." She held his hands in hers. "I will take you to the grove. Alta said I might bring one back. And we will live there, young again, until the end of time."

"I cannot leave the kingdom," Carum said.

"Nonsense. Our sons and our daughter have been helping you run it these past twenty years. You have trained them well in castle ways."

"And you in the forest."

"So . . ."

He smiled, that old slow smile. The scar beneath the one eye, caught up in the wrinkles of laugh lines, disappeared. "So . . . I never *quite* believed in the grove."

"Believe it," she whispered. She kissed his hands and then leaned over and kissed his brow as well, before standing. "It will be a short journey, Longbow, and you will go in comfort."

A carriage with a bed carted Carum to the King's Way where the forest still lay unbroken on either side.

"We are almost there, my love," Jenna whispered to him when they had stopped. "Now we come to the difficult part. You must leave your comfortable bed and ride on the sledge."

"As long as you are near, my Jen," he said, his voice hardly audible with the wild caroling of birds around them.

She dismissed the men and women who had accompanied them, then turned to Scillia.

"You must make sure that they all return to the castle. No one"—she stopped, then repeated—"*no one* must remain behind."

"Do you know what you are doing, Mother?" Scillia asked.

Jenna reached out and smoothed a lock of Scillia's hair that had come unbound in the ride. "Oh, I do. And so do you and Jem and Corrie. You belong to now and your children to the future. It is another turning."

"Riddles! You know I hate that kind of talk."

"Ah, Scillia, I learned long ago that riddles hold their own truth. And the truth is that your father and I were the beginning, but . . ."

"Will I ever see you again?"

"When you look in the mirror, child. When you speak to your own daughters and sons. Kiss me now. I will be with you when you need me most."

They embraced, and Scillia turned away, before her mother could see her tears, gathering the others to her. Jenna watched until they were out of sight, then tied up her braids atop her head like a crown. Picking up the ends of the sledge on which Carum was bound, she pulled it off the roadway and across the grassy field.

The Grenna met her halfway through the meadow. She could not tell if they were the same ones she had met before. They *looked* the same: ageless, with the translucent green glaze of skin over fine bones. They made a circle with Jenna, Carum, and the sledge in the center, but they did not offer to help pull. Carum watched them fascinated, often half sitting up until the motion exhausted him.

Three times the circle stopped that Jenna might make Carum more comfortable and give him a drink of water. For a while he tried to get them to talk, but they were silent. When the odd procession got to the woods, where even the shadows were green, one of the Grenna said, "Here." That was the entire conversation. At the Grenna's voice, Carum slipped into a kind of fitful sleep.

A new moon rose overhead, but Jenna had only intermittent glimpses of it through the lacings of the trees, and it was not until they came to the clearing that ended on the cliffside that Skada appeared. The moment she was visible, the Grenna faded back into the trees. But Skada only smiled wryly, and bent to take one pole of the sledge. It moved more easily then and they brought it quickly to the front of the black cave entrance framed by oaken doors.

Jenna touched one of the carvings, Skada another.

"Apple," Jenna whispered. "Bird."

"Stone, flower, tree," Skada countered. "Jenna, you must choose."

"I know," Jenna said. "I have thought of nothing else since this journey began."

"Alta said you can bring *one* other into the grove, Jenna. One."

"And there are no shadows within." Jenna paused. "I do not know how this will end."

Carum moaned, then opened his eyes. "Are the Grenna gone, Jen? Are we there?"

"Almost there," Skada answered him.

"Good, you are here, too, Skada. For we are all three, or we are none," Carum whispered.

"Candle by the bed or not, I know you loved me well, my king," Skada said.

"I loved you best for your true tongue," Carum answered.

"You have been listening!" Jenna's voice was suddenly accusing.

"A king's privilege." He tried to shift a bit on the sledge, and moaned again. "The trip was long. But I would not have missed it. Jenna, you do not have to choose between us. I am dead already. Let the stories tell what they will. Our children will rule wisely and well." He closed his eyes again. "And whatever we do here matters not. It's the stories told about it that will last."

Jenna smiled. "I know that, my love. But still we must do what the heart reminds us. Sister? Are you ready?" She held out her arms.

Skada smiled, her arms out as well. "Ready, sister."

THE LEGEND

There are two tales told about White Jenna and how she returned to Alta's cave. One is told by women and one is told by men.

The men's story speaks of a sledge on the cliffside, where, years ago when the Wilhelm Valley was mined for gold, it was discovered before an entrance to a cave. The sledge held the long bones of a man bound to it with bindings of leather and gold. Still, the men say, on moonlit nights two women can be seen running naked through the glades, women compounded of starlight and water. They run through the glades, past the rocky cliff, step over the long bones, and disappear into the cave just at dawn.

But the women tell a different tale. They say that White Jenna carried her lover, King Longbow, in her arms through the cave to the grove where Alta greeted them. And there they were made young again, and hale. They wait there, with their bright companions, feasting and drinking, until the world shall need them again.

THE MYTH

Then Great Alta took down her hair, both the golden side and the black, and lifted the dark and light sisters out of the abyss of the world, saying, "You have come at last to the end of this turning. Whether you go forward or whether you go back, whether you go left or you go right, whether you go up or you go down, the end is the beginning. For each story is a circle, and each life a story. The end is the beginning and only I am the true end and only I can begin the circle again."

Here Ends Book 2:
White Jenna

THE WISDOMS OF THE DALES

The heart is not a knee that can bend.
Telling a tale is better than living it.
Fish are not the best authority on water.
When a dead tree falls, it carries with it a live one.
Wood may remain twenty years in the water but it is still not a fish.
If your mouth turns into a knife, it will cut off your lips.
Miracles come to the unsuspecting.
Spilled water is better than a broken jar.
There is no medicine to cure hatred.
Does the rabbit keep up with the cat?
Words are merely interrupted breath.
The sun moves slowly but it crosses the land.
You must set the trap before the rat passes, not after.
Better the cat under your heel than at your throat.
No tracks, no trouble.
Three are better than one where trouble is concerned.
Spring berries are for dye and dying.
Downy head and thorny spine/On the roots you safely dine.
Hunger is the best seasoning.
A foolish loyalty can be the greater danger.
Wicked tongues make wicked wives.
Laugh longer, live longer.
Sleep is the great unraveler of knots.

Not to know is bad, but not to wish to know is worse.
The day on which one starts out is surely not the time to begin one's
  preparations.
Do not measure a shroud before there is a corpse.
In the wrong, in the Rest.
Better in the Rest than in the battle.
They stumble who run ahead of their wits.
Sisters can be blind.
Sleep is death's younger sister.
The heart can be a cruel master.
A cat who boasts once is a cat who boasts once too often.
No blame, no shame.
It is a fool who longs for endings, a wise woman who longs for
  beginnings.
It is best to eat when the food is before you than go hungry when the food
  is behind you.
In a flock of black birds, t'would be harder to miss one than find one.
The gift horse is the swifter.
A crow is not a cat nor does it bear kits.
The swordsman dies by the sword, the hangman by the rope, and the king
  by his crown.
An hour can spare a life.
A man's eye is bigger than his belly and smaller than his brain.
In war one takes quickly and saves regrets for the morning.
Stand in the way of a cart and you will have wheelmarks across your face.
If a man calls you master, trust him for a day; if he calls you friend, trust
  him for a year; if he calls you brother, trust him for all ways.
Perfection is the end of growing.
First up, first fed.
First up, finest fed.
Experience is rarely a gentle master.
Stories feed the mind when the belly is not full.
Kill once, mourn ever. (Kill twice, mourn never.)
If you have no meat, eat bread.
Belief is an old dog in a new collar.
In the council of kings, the heart has little to say.
To kill is not to cure.
A stroke may save a limb.
You cannot cross the river without getting your feet wet.
A warrior has no conscience until after the war is done.

In a fight, anything is a sword.
Forever is no distance at all.
A dream is worth a little sleep.
Every end is a beginning.
No one stands highest when all stand together.
If you rise too early, the dew will soak your skin.
One is not a multitude.
The grape brings slow death.
The mice may have the right but the cat has the claws.
Women's promises are water over stone—wet, willing, and soon gone.
Measure a cook by his belly.
Better to be safe than buried.

THE MUSIC OF THE DALES

The Ballad of Langbrow

With a lilt

When Lang-brow first was made the king, Pro-claimed by all his

men,_ He took to him_ a good-ly wife Whose name was Whit-som

Jen._ He took to him_ a good-ly wife, Her name it was Sweet

Ann,_ And_ light her hair, and long her limb, And

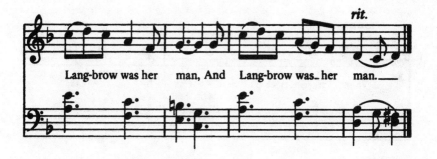

Lang-brow was her   man, And   Lang-brow was her   man.

2. When Langbrow first was made the king,
   Proclaimed by all his peers,
   He opened up the prison gates
   That had been closed for years.
   He opened up the prison gates
   With just one little key
   And all the men condemned within
   Straightways were all set free,
   Straightways were all set free.

3. When Langbrow first was made the king,
   He killed the callous crew
   That tortured many a fine woman
   And slaughtered not a few.
   That tortured many a fine woman
   And brought them many a shame
   Till Langbrow came to rescue them
   Returning their good name,
   Returning their good name.

4. When Langbrow first was made the king,
   The country did rejoice
   And sang the praises of the king
   With cup and wine and voice.
   We sang the praises of the king
   And of his Whitsom Jen
   And of the men who followed him,
   And also the wom-en,
   And also the wom-en!

Ballad of the Twelve Sisters

2. A handsome sailor one did wed,
   Rosemary, bayberry, thistle and thorn,
The other sisters wished her dead
   On the day the child was born.

3. "Oh, sister, give me your right hand,"
   Rosemary, bayberry, thistle and thorn,
Eleven to the one demand
   On the day the child was born.

4. They laid her down upon the hill,
   Rosemary, bayberry, thistle and thorn,
And took her babe against her will
   On the day the child was born.

5. They left her on the cold hillside,
   Rosemary, bayberry, thistle and thorn,
Convinced that her new babe had died
   On the day the child was born.

6. She wept red tears, and she wept gray,
   Rosemary, bayberry, thistle and thorn,
Till she had wept her life away,
   On the day her child was born.

7. The sailor's heart it broke in two,
   Rosemary, bayberry, thistle and thorn,
The sisters all their act did rue
   From the day the child was born.

8. And from their graves grew rose and briar,
   Rosemary, bayberry, thistle and thorn,
Twined till they could grow no higher,
   From the day the child was born.

Anna at the Turning

With emotion

Gray in the moon-light, and green in the sun,

Dark in the ev-e-ning, bright in the dawn, Ev-er the mead-ow goes

end-less-ly on, And An-na at each turn-ing.

2. Sweet in the springtide, sour in fall,
   Winter casts snow, a white velvet caul.
   Passage in summer is swiftest of all
      And Anna at each turning.

3. Look to the meadows and look to the hills,
   Look to the rocks where the swift river spills,
   Look to the farmland the farmer still tills
      for Anna is returning.

The Long Riding

With a rocking motion

1. In-to the val-ley, come rid-ing, come rid-ing, In-to the mead - ow and
2. In-to the vil-lage, come rid-ing, come rid-ing, In-to the hames where the

in - to the dell, In-to the moon-light where shad-ows are glid - ing,)
sweet wom-en dwell, In-to the rests where the men are a - bid - ing,)

In-to the for-est where en - e - mies hid - ing, Rid - ing, rid - ing,

Three come a - rid - ing In - to the mouth of hell.___

The Trees in the Forest

Sister's Lullay

King Kalas and his Sons

Boisterously

King Ka-las had four sons, And four sons had he,

And they ram-bled a-round In the north-ern coun-trie.

And they ram-bled a-round With-out ev-er a care.

The Hound and the Bull And the Cat and the Bear.

2. The Hound was a hunter,
   The Hound was a spy,
   The Hound could shoot down
   Any bird on the fly.
   The Hound was out hunting
   When brought down was he
   Alone as he rambled
   The northern countrie.

3. King Kalas had three sons,
   And three sons had he,
   And they rambled around
   In the northern countrie.
   And they rambled around
   Without ever a care.
   And they were the Bull
   And the Cat and the Bear.

4. The Bull was a gorer,
   The Bull was a knight,
   And never a man who would
   Run from a fight.
   The Bull was out fighting
   When brought down was he
   Alone as he rambled
   The northern countrie.

5. King Kalas had two sons,
   And two sons had he,
   And they rambled around
   In the northern countrie.
   And they rambled around
   Without ever a care.
   And the names they were called
   Were the Cat and the Bear.

6. The Cat was a shadow,
   The Cat was a snare,
   Sometimes you knew not
   When the Cat was right there.
   The Cat was out hiding
   When brought down was he
   Alone as he rambled
   The northern countrie.

7. King Kalas had one son,
   And one son had he,
   And he rambled around
   In the northern countrie.
   And he rambled around
   Without ever a care,
   And the name he went under
   Was Kalas' Bear.

8. The Bear was a bully,
   The Bear was a brag,
   His mouth was brimmed over
   With bluster and swag.
   The Bear was out boasting
   When brought down was he
   Alone as he rambled
   The northern countrie.

9. King Kalas had no sons,
   And no sons had he,
   To ramble around
   In the northern countrie.
   Though late in the evening
   The ghosts are seen there
   Of the Hound and the Bull
   And the Cat and the Bear.

Death of the Cat

With great emotion

The_ trees were grow-ing high_ And the wind was in the west

When a hun-ter aimed his ar-row_ In - to the Cat's broad chest.

And she di - ed, she di - ed A - gainst her lov-er's breast

And we laid her in the earth So long and nar-row._____

2. It was early, so early
   In the graying of the morn,
   When we sang of the days
   Before the Cat was born.
   And how from her mother
   She was so swiftly torn,
   As we laid her in the earth
   So long and narrow.

3. Come all ye young fighting men
   And listen unto me.
   Do not place your affections
   Upon a girl so free.
   For she'll take the mortal wound
   Another meant for thee,
   And you'll lay her in the earth
   So long and narrow.

The Heart and the Crown

2. Her horse was pure white
   And his horse was gray.
   She wanted to go
   But he asked her to stay.
   She gave him her heart
   And he gave her his crown,
   But they never, no never
   Went down derry down derry down.

3. Her eyes were pure black
   And his eyes were so blue.
   She wanted him strong
   And he wanted her true.
   She gave him her heart
   And he gave her his crown
   But they never, no never
   Went down derry down derry down.

4. Come all ye fair maidens,
   And listen to me,
   If you want your young man
   To be strong and free
   Just give him your heart
   And he'll give you his crown
   Just as long as you never
   Go down derry down derry down.

Well Before the Battle, Sister